ATTACK!

OF THE
B-MOVIE MONSTERS
Night of the Gigantis

Edited by

Harrison Graves

A
Grinning Skull Press
Publication

ATTACK! of the B-Movie Monsters: Night of the Gigantis
Compilation Copyright © 2013 Grinning Skull Press

"Anticipating Disaster" copyright ©2013 Gary Mielo
"Night of the Nanobeasts" copyright ©2013 D. Alexander Ward
"The Taterific Tale of Coral Beach" copyright ©2013 Lachlan David
"Day of the Prairie Dogs" copyright ©2013 John Grey
"Trouble in the Sewers" copyright ©2013 Ben McElroy
"Waste Not, Die Not" copyright ©2013 Randy Lindsay
"Claws" copyright ©2013 Eryk Pruitt
"Stone Cold Horror From the Stars" copyright ©2013 Brent Abell
"BFF" copyright ©2013 Kerry G.S. Lipp
"Gams" copyright ©2013 Tracy DeVore
"Bezillgo vs. The Allerton Theatre" copyright ©2013 Gary Wosk
"Catgut" copyright ©2013 Terry Alexander
"Nathan's Folly" copyright ©2013 J.M. Scott
"GRONK!" copyright ©2013 Doug Blakeslee
"The Shapeless Things to Come" copyright ©2013 Christofer Nigro
"Going to Work" copyright ©2013 Colin McMahon
"I Was a Fifty Foot Househusband" copyright ©2013 Nicole Massengill
"Giant Mutant Tiger Slugs vs. Salty Angel Gimp Warriors in Leather" copyright ©2013
    Jay Wilburn
"Vermin" copyright ©2013 Kevin Bampton
"Siege of the Silurids" copyright ©2013 Gerry Griffiths
"The Worm People Want Your Limbs" copyright ©2013 Jonah Buck

The Skull logo with stylized lettering was created for Grinning Skull Press by Dan Moran, http://dan-moran-art.com/.

ISBN: 0989026922 (paperback)
ISBN-13: 978-0-9890269-2-5 (paperback)
ISBN: 978-0-9890269-3-2 (e-book)

DEDICATION

To the memory of special-effects legend Ray Harryhausen (1920–2013), whose creations ignited a life-long love for the monstrous in so many people.

TABLE OF CONTENTS

ACKNOWLEDGMENTS

I would like to take this opportunity to thank Michael J. Evans and Michael R. Danaitis, Jr. The late night hours were made all the more bearable thanks to you two. I would also like to thank the authors who submitted to our second anthology. This one was a long time coming, so I thank you for your patience. I hope you are all as happy with the final product as I am.

A WORD FROM THE EDITOR

I didn't go to the movies much when I was a kid. Being the youngest of five, a family outing to the movies proved to be quite costly, even back then. As a result, I had to rely on whatever was showing on the television. Movie programs like WPIX's *Chiller Theatre*, WOR's *The Million Dollar Movie*, and ABC's *The 4:30 Movie* became staples for me. It was through shows like these that I had my first exposure to what, in my opinion, are some of the best horror movies I have ever seen, and it was through these same programs that I developed a love for a certain type of movie: Giant Creatures. I never missed an opportunity to watch *THEM!*, *Tarantula*, *It Came from Beneath the Sea*, and the host of other movies that featured giant monsters terrorizing towns and cities. No matter how my tastes have changed throughout the years, my love for these movies has never grown old. In the 1970s and 80s, I couldn't wait to see films like *Night of the Lepus*, *The Food of the Gods*, *Empire of the Ants*, and *Alligator*, and more recently, although not nearly as well made as the films that I grew up watching, I never miss SyFy's attempt to revive the Giant Creature genre with their "all-star" vehicles like *Mega Snake*, *Snakehead Terror*, *Supergator*, and the destined-to-become-a-classic *Mega Python vs. Gatoroid*. I mean, who could forget rival teen-idol pop stars Tiffany and Debbi Gibson's food fight, or the two stars standing in the swamp at night trading quips lifted word-for-word from the songs that had made them popular.

When it came time to decide what our next anthology should be, I thought it would be fun to pay homage to these movies. I wanted the authors to have fun with it and challenged them to use their creativity. I

1

wanted to see giant creatures; what I didn't want to see was a rehash of what had been done before. They didn't disappoint.

The authors weren't restricted to creatures spawned by the aftermath of nuclear testing, either, although that was certainly an option; they were free to come up with their own reasons why these giant mutations came into being, and while a majority of the stories do deal with creatures born from scientific experiments gone wrong, some of the authors embraced the challenge and ventured out on their own. Eryk Pruitt was one of these authors, and his story, *Claws*, is supernatural in origin. Brent Abell and Kerry G.S. Lipp offer up otherworldly terror, and J.M. Scott's creation might be a survivor of prehistoric times.

As you read through the stories, you might find one that stands out as not being like the others, and you might find yourself wondering why it was included in this collection. As you read Gary Wosk's *Bezillgo vs. The Allerton Theatre*, keep in mind the original intent of this collection, an homage to the films of the 50s, and what better way to pay tribute than with a story about a child's love for these types of films. It strikes close to home, as it stirred up quite a few memories of my own childhood.

The collection opens with Gary Mielo's essay, *Anticipating Disaster*, where he sets the stage for the stories you are about to read. In it he discusses the popularity of the atomic-age films of the 50s against the backdrop of the very real threat of The Bomb. It is the perfect lead in to D. Alexander Ward's *Night of the Nanobeasts!*, a chilling tale of a scientific experiment gone wrong.

So without further ado, grab yourself a bowl of popcorn, find a comfy chair, dim the lights a little, and prepare yourself for *ATTACK! of the B-Movie Monsters: Night of the Gigantis!*

Harrison Graves
Editor

ANTICIPATING DISASTER

Gary Mielo

Nearly seven decades ago, the Atom Bomb had a big birthday. It was created in 1945 on July 16th in Alamogordo, New Mexico. Its christening occurred a few weeks later on August 6th in Hiroshima.

For many a baby boomer, the terror it unleashed was both real and reel. Unintentionally, The Bomb spawned a completely new form of entertainment: the atomic cataclysm.

It was high-quality nightmares that youngsters of the 1950s craved. After all, feelings of impending doom permeated the decade. Stock footage of atomic bomb blasts were relentlessly shown on television, in movie newsreels, and during school assemblies. Innumerable times, we saw the same palm trees sway back and forth and then suddenly burst into flames. This was invariably followed by the same house that quivered, shuddered, and finally fell in on itself. These stark, grainy, black and white images were highly effective at striking terror into the hearts and minds of even the toughest of bullies.

The threat of The Bomb was an unnerving, yet routine, part of growing up. It was a time when schools inflicted irreparable paranoiac damage by practicing pointless civil defense drills that involved huddling in pretend apprehension under the imagined protection of wooden desks. It was a time when yellow air-raid shelter signs, hanging on the walls of virtually all candy stores, ice cream parlors, and other public buildings, reported the way to alleged underground safety, but we weren't fooled. The Bomb was a weapon for which there was absolutely no defense. We all knew that there wasn't a school desk made that could withstand the blast from one of those weapons.

The merchants of pop culture reinforced the dread of doom for us. Candy store best sellers such as Nevil Shute's anti-war apocalyptic fantasy *On the Beach* and Reay Tannahill's *The World, the Flesh and the Devil* were displayed alongside sizzlers like *Peyton Place* and the recently unbanned *Lady Chatterley's Lover.*

Radio broadcasts, particularly *Dimension X* and its reincarnation *X-Minus One*, and television shows like *Tales of Tomorrow* and *The Twilight Zone*, regularly dramatized end-of-the-world scenarios. Science-fiction pulp novels were particularly explicit in their lavishly illustrated, lurid cover stories that often dealt with doomsday bombs and their resultant weird offspring.

However, of all the media, the movies succeeded in creating a most plausible, highly personal, thoroughly horrific mythology for catastrophic consequences of The Bomb. We kids wanted more explicit films, ones that could rival those images of flaming palm trees and imploding houses.

Throughout the 1950s, but particularly during the middle of the decade, the entertainment industry's roster for twitching, hormonal, overcharged kids was a spate of science-fiction films featuring radiation-spawned people, places, and things. It was especially the things that captured and captivated the imaginations of most ten year olds.

After the theater lights dimmed and a momentary stillness swept across the audience of wriggling kids, the ominous opening music to one of these films usually was strong enough to foreshadow fantastic, apocalyptic images. These notes heralded stories that promised grand-scale destruction and unimaginable horrors.

The best films personified The Bomb by adroitly combining horror with science fiction, mixing hope and apprehension into an entertaining concoction. The ride up to the summit of a Coney Island-style roller-coaster brought scientist Paul Christian and marksman Lee Van Cleef to a face-to-face confrontation with *The Beast from 20,000 Fathoms*, a 1953 prehistoric creature thawed by atomic bomb tests.

Similarly, the 1954 descent into the storm drains to find and destroy the radiation-enlarged queen ants' nest brought policeman James Whitmore and FBI Agent James Arness into direct contact with *Them!* Raymond Burr, reporting the Hiroshima-like demolition of Japan, was hospitalized after a close encounter with *Godzilla, King of the Monsters* in the 1954 American release of the film. The trip to Metaluna and the subsequent flight back home in *This Island Earth* (1955) became a vehicle for Rex Reason to save Faith Domergue and the world from Metalunan scientists who needed "uranium in gigantic quantities" to continue an interplanetary war.

A cozy glow of safety enveloped us as we smugly witnessed monstrous destruction and retribution while chewing through large bags of buttered popcorn. These showdowns exemplified the idea that individuals were capable not only of challenging, but also of defeating seemingly unstoppable, radioactive adversaries. It was reassuring to know that humans could take on a giant, a behemoth, a monster several stories high and, like David against Goliath, prevail.

Once the threat to life and limb was averted, our bodies struggled to return to normalcy. Slowly, the adrenaline subsided, our pulse rates slipped back to even levels, and our sticky palms dried.

As the house lights brightened and the ordinary world was brought back into focus, the streets seemed safe. Even so, every now and then, we would quicken our pace as we walked past shadowy alleyways. We could almost hear the muffled roar of a yet-to-be-unleashed mutant.

NIGHT OF THE NANOBEASTS!

D. Alexander Ward

1

Scientists have been creating technological wonders of immense power for some time and have been striving to make these creations ever smaller. The future is bound to a destiny where mankind will operate machines on a molecular level, or so they say. And it was these same scientists who jeered and laughed at Dr. Henry Breach for his peculiar quest. For in this world bent on miniaturizing everything, Henry Breach sought to make the smallest organism quite a bit larger.

The nanobe, a creature that, according to some, did not even exist as a living thing, had long held Dr. Breach in its sway. His admiration of and longing for a greater understanding of this thing was consuming and—as many of his colleagues were heard to declare—left poor Henry a little unhinged.

But they would all soon know that Henry's madness was not merely the stuff of clichéd midnight movies. On this night, the scientist was on the cusp of a breakthrough.

He stood before his whiteboard and studied the mathematical formulas scrawled across it in his deplorable chicken scratch that was indecipherable to anyone but himself and his lab assistant, Jane Coffer.

Check and re-check. That was the key. The slightest inaccuracy in his formula would mean yet another in a long line of failures. Dr. Breach chuckled to himself. Science was, at its heart, not a science, but rather an art. Processes and logic could get a man only so far toward the brass ring of greatness, but to grasp it required the unrefined human quality of instinct.

"Ms. Coffer," he called out to his assistant and turned to find her leaning over the veculizer's service panel with a precision screwdriver, making some final adjustments. Her pressed white lab coat greedily hugged her curves, and she unknowingly made the faintest of gyrating motions as she turned the tropian dial on the machine.

Speaking of instinct.

"Yes, Doctor Breach?" she replied, standing straight in her blue polka dot pencil dress, her bosom barely contained beneath the modest plunge of the neckline.

Not for the first time, Henry found himself a little flummoxed as he regarded her.

"Doctor?" she asked again after he gave no reply.

"Yes," he said, stammering a little. "Sorry, I was just thinking about the formulae. Is the veculizer prepped?"

"I had some trouble getting it into the slot," she said, fingering the shaft of the screwdriver, "but I did manage to get it turned to the low setting like you asked."

"Excellent!" he replied.

He removed a handkerchief from his pocket and dabbed at the perspiration on his forehead as he looked over the lab, taking inventory of what still needed to be done. It seemed, however, that the preparations for the experiment were complete.

"The preparations for the experiment are complete, Doctor," Jane declared, slipping the long, slender driver into the pocket of her lab coat.

"So it would seem, Ms. Coffer. Very well then. Begin charging the veculizer and I shall fetch the specimens."

"Right away, Doctor."

Henry stole across the lab to the walk-in cold storage unit. On the shelves there were sealed jars with DNA specimens, as well as other packets that held slides. Over the course of several weeks, Henry and Jane had painstakingly applied extracted nanobes to these slides. It was a new approach and one that Henry hoped would yield better results than placing the nanobes into the veculizer unmoored.

What they were endeavoring to do was deceptively simple, really. The veculizer, a machine conceived of and built by Dr. Breach himself, was a DNA fuser and rapid growth accelerator. The lynchpin of his hypothesis about the nanobe was that it was not merely a crystalline mineral structure, but a living thing, and therefore comprised of DNA. The nanobes, however, were too small to be properly studied.

Therefore, Henry needed to make them larger.

For the pairing of the nanobes, Henry had chosen DNA from the Japanese spider crab. He theorized that the exoskeletal nature of the animal would provide a welcome component with which the nanobes could bond, and the long lifespan of the spider crab—easily a hundred years or more—would allow for the nanobes to exist in their larger state long enough to be documented and studied before breaking down. After an hour in the growth chamber, they would swell to the size of a quarter. He expected to have no more than a few minutes.

Henry plucked the specimens from the shelf and returned to the lab to find Jane dutifully waiting beside the veculizer. The control panel indicated that the charge had reached over ninety percent.

"I see we're nearly ready, Ms. Coffer," he remarked as he set the specimens down on the steel table next to the machine.

"Ninety-seven percent, Doctor."

They both stood and watched the indicator illuminate from left to right. They spoke not a word, the anticipation of this moment pervasive in the room.

The final indicator lit up and the terminal monitor read that the veculizer was ready.

"Open fusion chamber one, Ms. Coffer."

She reached up and pressed the button that opened the metal door to the first chamber. As it silently rose, Henry unscrewed the cap on the specimen bottle. Inside, a blob of gelatinous material that held the raw DNA of the spider crab shimmied. He slipped his hand into the chamber and turned the bottle over. The blob tumbled out and came to rest on the collection plate.

"Secure chamber one, please."

Her delicate fingers sought out the button again, and this time the door closed with a hiss as all the air was sucked out of the chamber.

"Now for chamber two, Ms. Coffer."

She pressed another button and a second door opened on the machine. Handling the packet gingerly, Henry pulled the seal back and used a pair of tongs to remove the nanobe slide. He hardly even breathed as he lifted it to the open chamber and then set it down with a light chink on the collection plate.

"Secure chamber two."

With the press of a button, the chamber was sealed. The terminal indicated that the machine was initializing internal sensors, and after a moment, the screen announced that the material had been received and the chambers stabilized.

Jane looked over at the scientist, who stared at the machine's doors as if he could see through the half inch of steel.

"It's the deep breath before the plunge, Ms. Coffer," he said and then drew in a long, slow breath that raised his shoulders.

"I'm just thrilled to be plunging with you, sir."

He gave her a smile and nodded at the machine.

"Engage the machine for fusion and growth."

In the center of the machine there was a red switch housed beneath a clear, protective cover. She flipped the cover open and grasped the switch with her fingers, then applied some force. But the switch would not budge.

"Problem, Ms. Coffer?"

"The… uh… switch seems to be stuck, Doctor Breach. I can't get it up."

"It's the cool air in this lab, that's all. Let me help you."

Without thinking, Henry reached up and placed his hand over hers, his fingers atop hers. In this way, they both lingered for a moment longer than they should have. Then, with the combined effort, the switch was flipped up and the machine engaged. A low hum emanated from the veculizer and the terminal displayed row after row of data being gathered by the sensors as the fusion process began.

Jane leaned against the table and watched as Henry carefully analyzed the data stream.

"Perfect," he whispered.

The fusion process was relatively short, and they would know in a moment if it had been successful because the green indicator light would flicker on and the terminal would announce that stage one had been completed. At least that was how it *should* work. Since they had never successfully fused the materials, they did not know for sure.

"Come on, girl," Henry said, his eyes scanning the screen. "That's it. Come on…"

Abruptly, the humming ceased and the lab went dead quiet. The sudden silence alarmed them both and Jane leaned in next to Henry. Just as she did, the green indicator light went on and the screen went blank. After a moment, the terminal beeped and a single line of text was visible in brilliant white letters: *Stage 1 COMPLETE. Stage 2 ENGAGED.*

Henry went around to the sensor panel and flicked on the monitor. He fiddled with the controls for a moment, adjusting the optic scope in the machine to the target area on the delivery tray inside the growth chamber. Once there, he zoomed in and adjusted for clarity.

"Phenomenal," he remarked, then looked over at Jane. "Successful fusion of specimens complete and viable growth already beginning. We've done it, Ms. Coffer!"

Her heart leapt with joy at this news and she bounced on her toes, hardly able to contain her exuberance. She rushed toward the scientist and grappled him in a congratulatory hug. As they pulled away from each other, though, something unexpected happened. Their hands met again, and for a moment they were suspended above the earth, staring into each other's eyes. Jane didn't know what it was—maybe the streaks of gray in his wild, unkempt hair, maybe the crow's feet flanking his cold eyes from too many nights spent in the lab, maybe the slightly pervy mustache that sat atop his lip like a shorn, black caterpillar, or maybe the musk of pure genius and brilliance that radiated from him in that moment—but whatever it was, the feelings it brought out in her would not be denied, and she drew his face down to hers and kissed him.

And there they stayed for a long moment.

When they parted, Henry had a stunned look on his face as he struggled to find words.

"I... I'm... I'm sorry, Ms. Coffer. I shouldn't have—"

"Oh, Henry," she sighed and pulled him to her again.

"Oh, Jane."

Then their lips were sealed together once more and their bodies were pressing against one another. Roaming hands sought eager flesh through the layers of their clothing.

"Ravish me, Henry," she pleaded with him, her loins afire. "Do what you will with me."

He looked around the lab. "Not here, though," he said. "It's a clean room. And there's nothing clean about what I'd like to do with you."

"Doctor Breach!" she squealed as he pulled her across the room toward the door that opened to the hallways of the university's science department.

With victory and lust in his eyes, Henry Breach rushed down the hall, his comely assistant in tow, toward his office and a seldom-used leather fainting couch. There they would adjourn as the growth process in the veculizer ran through to completion.

Once in his office, they made rough, desperate love to each other, falling all over the room from the door to the desk to his chair to, finally, the couch. The radio was on and Billie Holiday crooned "Body and Soul" to the lovers as they gave in to months of unspoken longings and tension, conducting a fusion experiment of a very different kind.

Their moans and sighs were unbridled, for they knew there was no one to hear. Henry and Jane frequently worked late into the night in the science department, and the building was always deserted. Tonight, they would make the most of that isolation.

Outside the science building, dark clouds had gathered. Rain began to fall, lightning created jagged fractures in the night, and the thunder pealed. The new lovers were oblivious to all of it.

2

For all her technical competence and her value as a lab assistant to Henry Breach, Jane had made one critical mistake that evening as she calibrated the tropian dial on the growth accelerator. Counterintuitive to most all other things, the lowest setting was all the way to the right and maximum growth on the left. In what had been a simple and innocent mistake, she had turned it to the left. During previous experiments, it would have been no trouble at all; simply another failed result. But tonight, the brilliantly mad Doctor Breach's decision to place the nanobes on a slide had made all the difference. They were succeeding.

But along with the successful fusion, there were some unexpected results occurring within the unattended veculizer. The resulting creature did not render in the manner that Henry had anticipated, and where there was meant to be only one, there were many. It was reproducing, and the legion of creatures was growing at a frightfully accelerated rate.

* * *

Fox Blacker hated his job.

And why not? Who would actually like being the midnight janitor at some creepy New England college? His calling was to be an actor, he just knew it. To head out west and make it in Hollywood. After all, movies were his life, so it only made sense. Not to mention he had seen the lauded academy award-winning films that were rife with pedestrian acting and poor writing. Not like the director, Roger Corman's body of work. Now *that's* what cinematic gold looked like!

Sure, he was just a mop jockey at the university now. But when his ship came in, he was going to take Hollywood by storm. He'd turn his own life into an inspired biopic that would endear and terrify and draw both laughter and tears. Yes indeed, then Fox Blacker would show them some real movie magic.

He was halfway down the north hallway, mopping, wringing, and mopping as he went when he heard a ruckus in one of the labs. The painful

11

screech of metal being pried open, glass breaking, and tables and furniture being overturned.

"What the—" he said and leaned the mop against the wall.

He walked down the hall, checking each lab until he was able to determine from which one the sounds were coming. The name placard outside of the door to Lab #21A read BREACH. The only thing he could figure was that some of the college students had broken in and decided it would be a fun Friday night activity to trash the place. Probably all hopped up on grass, too.

He tried the handle, but the door was locked.

"You little punks better knock it off in there!" he hollered at the door as he located the proper key on his ring and slipped it into the lock. "You'll answer to Dean Armitage for this! Right after I put my foot up your—"

Fox pushed the door open and stepped inside, but what he saw there in the lab stopped him cold. He couldn't run, didn't even have the chance to scream before one of the things skittered across the floor toward him, a large crystalline spear of an appendage raised. Like a deer in the headlights of an oncoming car, he watched as that spear descended, following the arc as it plunged through his abdomen.

The door shut behind him and began to thud repeatedly as the pack of creatures began to feast upon him, arterial blood ejecting from his torn throat in great bursts that covered the door and painted the portal window in a lowering curtain of red.

This is how my movie ends, Fox thought as he lost consciousness. *That's a wrap*.

3

Henry lay on the couch with Jane atop him, having collapsed where she was when they finished for the second time. Sweat covered their bare bodies, and Henry clicked the remote to activate the ceiling fan as they lay entwined on the leather couch, smoking cigarettes from a pack of Lucky Strikes that he kept in his office.

"Do you know how long I have waited for this night?" she asked him, running her fingers through his thick chest hair.

"I know," Henry replied, smoke rolling out from between his lips as he spoke. "It's extraordinary to think that in only a few more minutes we'll have the opportunity to document the existence of the smallest organism known to man."

She raised an eyebrow. "I was speaking of you and me, Henry."

"Oh, *that*. Yes. Well, that was also extraordinary."

"It certainly was," she said, a twinkle creeping into her eye, her hand wandering down below his waist. "And there were no small organisms involved, either."

She was tempting him again; he wanted to yield to her and begin a third round of sweaty, wanton copulation, but the hour was nearly at an end and they needed to get back to the lab.

Jane noticed him checking his watch and knew their interlude was finished. She rolled off of him and they both began to dress. After a moment, a loud noise echoed from beyond the door to Henry's office. They looked at each other in bewilderment.

"What could that be?" she asked as she reached over her shoulder to zip up her dress.

"I've no idea," Henry said. He was still buttoning up his shirt when he rose and went to the door. He opened it and leaned into the hallway for a look, but there was nothing to see. Jane joined him, leaning in close. That was when something rounded the corner at the end of the hall and came into full view.

Jane gasped and her hand went instantly to cover her mouth as she and Henry stared wide-eyed at the monstrosity.

Standing six feet tall with legs as long as a nightmare, the enormous creature bore a strong resemblance to the Japanese spider crab. But unlike the normal species, it was far greater in size and its exoskeleton appeared comprised of hard, quartz-like mineral.

As they took in every detail of the creature, they were all too aware that it was studying them, too.

Worse, as they ducked back inside and the thing began clicking down the hallway toward them, they saw other long, gigantic crystal legs coming around the corner directly behind the first. There were more of them.

When the door closed behind them and Henry slid the lock into place, Jane brought her hands to her face and let go a mind-rending scream. She then began to babble, clearly delirious.

Henry moved toward her, grabbed her by the shoulders. "Get a hold of yourself, Ms. Coffer!" he exclaimed, then pulled his arm back to give her a sobering slap across the face.

Instead, he doubled over as her knee connected with his groin.

"Oh, Henry," she said, "I'm so sorry. My mother was a rabid feminist who made me take all sorts of terrible self-defense courses. It was just a reflex!"

He groaned and stood. "That's alright, my darling."

They needed to get out of that office. There were horrors the likes of which they had never seen coming for them.

"Oh, Henry, it was a horror the likes of which I've never seen!"

"I know," he replied. "And they're coming for us. We have to get out of here."

"But, Henry," she blubbered, "what are they?"

"My experiment gone awry, Ms. Coffer. That's what they are. An awful, bastardized combination of the specimens." He looked at the door to the hallway, pale with fear. "Like some kind of... *nano-beast!*"

4

The academic offices were all connected, like a honeycomb of small spaces at the center of the Tillinghast Science Hall, and Henry and Jane slipped out of his office into the next just as an enormous claw of one of the nanobeast ripped the door from its hinges and tossed it into the hallway like a soda can.

As it saw its prey disappear behind the other door, it let loose with an awful inhuman howl. The other members of its brood answered in kind, their combined cries of rage shaking the very foundation of the building.

They continued to run from office to office, Jane following closely behind the scientist as he unlocked door after door and they drove deeper and deeper into the maze of academic offices, though to what end she did not know.

"Where are we going, Henry?"

"There's no time to explain!" he replied, reaching back to make sure she was close on his heels.

Behind them, doors and walls were being ripped apart by the nanobeasts as they closed in on the pair. Glancing back, Henry could plainly see that—astoundingly enough—the creatures were still growing. Like the phenomenon of centrifugal force, the accelerated growth process that had begun in the veculizer had been assimilated by the growing creatures, like some kind of rapid evolutionary adaptation, and now the momentum simply continued. When it would stop... *if it would stop*... was anyone's guess.

The things had to be destroyed.

Henry and Jane had managed to get two or three doors ahead of the pursuing nanobeasts, and as they entered Doctor Pembrooke's office, they heard a roar of thunder from the storm outside and the crack of lightning striking somewhere close by. The lights in the office flickered, and then all went dark.

Behind them, the rending of brick and steel and wood ceased, and as Henry listened to the creatures clacking about behind them haphazardly, he knew that for whatever strange reason, the darkness confounded them, confused them.

"Doctor," Jane whispered, clinging tight to his arm, "it sounds like the darkness has confused them."

"Yes, I know."

Henry didn't think it would last long, though. The accelerated mutations set off by the veculizer would soon cause them to adapt to it, to master it, and then there would be one less weakness to exploit.

"We must move quietly," he said, taking her hand and moving through the darkness to the door on the opposite wall of Pembrooke's office, which opened to the hall on the south side of the building. They crept out into the hallway and flattened against the wall outside of the office.

With the power outage, the backup generators had kicked in; only critical systems and emergency lighting had power, though these small, dim lights low on the walls did not provide much in the way of visibility, and for this they were thankful.

Across the way, taking up nearly the entire length of the south side of the building, were the chemistry labs. If they could lure the creatures there, it might be their only chance to be rid of them.

"Not much farther now," he whispered, giving her hand a reassuring squeeze. "Come, Ms. Coffer."

They stepped cautiously across the hallway, and when they reached the door, Henry turned the knob slowly. Opening the door just a crack, they slipped in and closed it silently behind them.

"What are we doing here?" Jane pleaded. "We need to get out of the building."

"I'm afraid, Ms. Coffer," he replied, pulling a penlight from his breast pocket, "that what we must do is prevent those things from leaving the building."

She clung to him. "But, Henry, how are we going to do that?"

He shone the beam of his light over the counters in the middle of the room. At each end there sat a star-shaped configuration of metal; natural gas valves used to power Bunsen burners for experiments.

"Those valves are on every counter in every lab on this side of the building," he explained. "We must open them up and fill these rooms with hydrocarbon gas."

"Then what?"

"We set the trap," he said. "And when the moment is right, we destroy this building, and the nanobeasts along with it."

"But," she whimpered, the dark realization spreading over her face, "what about us, Henry?"

"I'm afraid our survival is not paramount, Jane," he replied.

A heavy silence fell between them.

5

They moved stealthily from lab to lab, opening all the valves before moving on to the next room to do the same. They were more than halfway down the length of the building when the effects of the gas began to take hold of both of them.

"I don't feel well, Henry," Jane said as she leaned, woozy, against the counter and struggled to turn on the valves. Her vision was blurring and her hand could find no purchase on the handles.

Henry, whose head was light and aching, was still managing. He opened the valves on his end of the counter and then clicked his penlight on and pointed it across the room onto the array of valves to help Jane see what she was doing.

Then Henry drew back in horror.

"Jane," he hissed, "don't move."

But it was too late, and Henry knew it the moment the beam from his penlight illuminated the hulking shadow of one of the nanobeasts. It had been there, lying in wait to ambush them. As he beheld it and the creature acknowledged that it had been discovered, its mandibles chattered together, dripping some clear, viscous fluid to the floor, and its crystalline armor began to radiate an eerie green glow.

This is its adaptation to the darkness, he thought. *Like the sea creatures of the deep, it has become a light unto itself.*

Its round, black eyes were devoid of any emotion and glittered in the muted light.

"Run!" he cried out to her.

She turned and began to shamble awkwardly toward Henry when a length of glowing appendage shot forth and grasped Jane in its enormous claw.

She was screaming. Henry was screaming. The nanobeast was chattering so happily that the noise had to be what passed for laughter among its brood. Then Jane was ripped in half and torrents of blood and gut-matter sprayed Henry, standing there and wielding his ineffectual penlight like a sabre.

Jane's upper body fell away as the creature brought her still-kicking legs to its maw and began to eat. Henry dove forward and grasped her hand, turned, and went stumbling wildly out of the lab into the next, dragging her torso behind him all the way. Nearly slipping several times, he made it through two more labs before his gassed, fading mind gave out and he collapsed in a fog.

Henry pulled Jane's torso up next to him where he was propped with his back against the counter. Above him, the open valves hissed. Lightning tore across the sky outside again and again, illuminating the lab with shocks of white electrical light. In the hallway beyond, Henry could hear the *click-clack* of the other nanobeasts closing in on him.

"Henry," he heard Jane say, her voice drowning as her lungs and trachea bubbled with her own blood and fluids.

"Yes, Ms. Coffer?"

"I'm all for you," she said, recalling the words of the Billie Holiday song playing on the radio as the pair had made love in his office earlier that evening. "Body and soul."

She gasped her last breath and then fell forever silent.

Looking at her shorn pencil dress covered in gore and the missing half of her below the waist, Henry supposed that the sentiment was at least partly true.

He fished a hand into the pocket of his trousers and found the pack of Lucky Strikes there, as well as the book of matches. Resting his head on the shoulder of Jane's corpse, he waited until he could hear the things ripping apart the doors and bursting through the walls. These monstrosities that he had created would be his end. Regrettably, though, it wouldn't be the first time an experiment-gone-wrong had run amok in the halls of the legend-haunted university, and tomorrow they would clean up the mess just as they always did. His death would amount to little more than another incident report in the Dean's file drawer.

And Henry Breach would still be a laughing stock to his New England colleagues. A sad and ironic footnote in the history of genetic science. A Shelley-esque cliché after all.

They were drawing near, his creations.

"Come and get it, boys," Henry croaked, striking the match and flaming up the end of his cigarette.

He even managed one good pull from it as the spidery, crystal behemoths came toward him and the match still sizzled in his fingertips. Then the ignition took place and the south side of the Tillinghast Science Building roared open in a plume of orange and black conflagration that blew out the windows of other nearby university buildings. Half of the roof collapsed into the pit of hellfire that was unleashed, and had anyone been present to witness it, they might have seen strange, gargantuan creatures with long, spindly legs climbing out of the rubble, covered in flames, and roaring into the night.

THE TATERIFIC TALE OF CORAL BEACH

Lachlan David

Protesters were out in full force that morning. Several powerful environmentalist groups, some with the backing of Washington, had rallied together every health nut and worried mother in the seaside town of Coral Beach. They came with their picket signs and chanted hateful slogans at the employees of the Agricultural Research Center as they entered and exited the building. In their eyes, everyone was an evil Frankenstein who dangled the fate of mankind over the open lid of Pandora's box. "GE FOODS—Tested On Your Children!" "GE—Death Knell To Mother Nature!" "What's On *Your* Table??" These signs were meant to strike fear into the hearts of families who only wanted what was best for their loved ones, but they grated on the nerves of genetic scientists like Nolan Proffer, whose only goal was to create better, more durable food to feed the world's ever-growing population.

He pushed his way through the crowd as they shouted epithets and accusations of crimes against humanity at him. He wondered how long it would be before he finally gave in to his urge to grab one by the face and push him to the ground. But he made it to the door without incident and opened it with a swipe of his badge. Once inside, he headed straight through the lobby to his lab, where he was greeted with an urgent message from his lead assistant.

"Doctor Proffer, we have confirmation of our research results. Everything checks out." He fanned the stack of papers in front of Nolan's face.

"Were there any chemical differences between our potatoes and the natural ones?" Nolan asked.

"None."

"And the mice, how did they compare?"

"No difference," his assistant said. "They've been eating these potatoes for months, now, and they're every bit as healthy as the control group. Doctor Proffer, I think this is it. We've finally discovered the key to growing superfoods like we've never seen before. Now that we've isolated the growth gene in these giant squid and successfully spliced it into a potato, we should be able to do the same for all types of fruits and vegetables."

"That really is something," Nolan said as he thumbed through the reports. "And to think, all this time the answer to world hunger has been sitting there right off the coast of Coral Beach. A whole school of giant squid just lying at the bottom of the ocean, and it took some beer-guzzling fishermen in a glorified dingy to find them."

Nolan tucked the reports under his arm. "I'll write this up right away for presentation to the FDA. I think it's time to show them what we have."

On the way to his desk, Nolan stopped by the mouse cages. He watched the control group busily gnawing away at pieces of ordinary russet potatoes. Then he observed the experimental group where another assistant was preparing their morning meal. Sitting in front of her on a metal tray was a single russet potato that was easily as large as a picnic ham. She was cutting small wedges from it and placing them in dishes for the mice.

"She's a beauty," Nolan said while reaching down and picking up a potato wedge.

"That's not even the biggest one," the assistant said. "Have you seen the most recent crop? They just keep getting bigger."

"Yeah, I've seen them," Nolan said with a satisfied grin just before tossing the potato wedge into his mouth.

His assistant watched him chew it with mild apprehension. "So, you think they're completely safe?" she asked.

"The mice seem to like it."

"Yeah, but…"

"There's nothing wrong with this potato. It looks the same, tastes the same, smells the same. I would feed it to my own family."

"It does seem that way," she said as she began placing dishes in the mouse cages. "It's just that the research is so new. It's going to take me a while to get really comfortable with it."

"There's nothing to worry about," he assured her. "In fact, I might even take one home to my wife. We'll cook it up and celebrate."

He left his assistant to her work and headed out the back door of the lab. It opened up to more than an acre of carefully cultivated experimental potato plants. A dozen or so field hands were working in the morning sun, harvesting the enormous potatoes. Instead of just pulling them from the ground, these plants required the use of shovels, and sometimes the effort of two or more men. Then they stored them in large bins with other potatoes ranging in size from a softball all the way to a small child. The filled bins were placed near the lab door for use by the research team.

Nolan reached into a bin and sorted through the potatoes like he was shopping for a Halloween pumpkin. He chose one of the smallest ones and pulled off the sprouts. The rapid growth of the potato sprouts was the only perceptible difference between these genetically engineered potatoes and the natural ones. But this was a minor inconvenience compared to the potential benefits of such an oversized tuber. He brought it inside to take home with him that evening.

* * *

Sharon stared at the obnoxious vegetable that had been sitting on her kitchen counter for two days. Its eyes had already sprouted several inches long and were causing the potato to resemble its tentacled cousin, the squid. The few eyes that hadn't sprouted almost appeared to stare back at her, and it gave her an eerie feeling. Nolan promised her it was no different than an ordinary potato, and he wanted her to serve it for dinner, but Sharon wasn't so sure. Last night, he asked her whether she had used the potato with their meal. She told him she forgot about it, but that excuse would only work once. Now, she had almost no choice but to cook it.

The potato was too large for just the two of them. She considered cutting it into chunks and saving the rest for later, but she wasn't sure if the raw potato would keep well. She decided to cook it up in the microwave first, and then she could store the leftovers for later.

She removed the sprouts and discovered she had to forcibly pluck them out like feathers from a bird. Then she scrubbed the potato clean and pierced its skin with a fork before putting it in the microwave. Within two minutes, the potato began making a high-pitched squeal as though it was steaming. She opened the microwave and poked it with a fork. It still felt raw, so she let it cook a little longer. As the microwave continued counting down, the squealing became louder and higher in pitch. After four minutes, she noticed that small areas of the potato were beginning to pucker.

Sharon opened the microwave and poked it again. The puckered areas were overcooked and too tough to push the fork through while other areas were still raw. It was clear she would need to cut the potato into smaller pieces to cook it right. As she reached into a nearby drawer for a knife, the doorbell rang and a muffled voice call through the door, "Sharon, Sharon, are you there?" It was Claudia, her neighbor.

Sharon set the knife on the counter and answered the door. "Yes, I'm here! I was just cooking dinner," she said.

"Oh, I won't be long," Claudia told her. "I was just wondering if you planned to go to the next HOA meeting. They're supposed to discuss the Robertson's house at this one. I think they're going to make them repaint it."

Sharon and Claudia stood at the door and discussed the Robertson's choice of house paint while the potato sat in the microwave and waited to be cut into pieces. Its overcooked skin began to blister and sweat much like someone who had been burned. It twitched a couple of times, then trembled as several eyes sprouted and grew. The ones that didn't sprout split open to reveal black, glossy pupils that blinked and evaluated their surroundings. Once the sprouts grew long enough to reach outside the microwave, the potato pulled itself out and fell to the floor, where it let out an agonized squeal.

Sharon heard the noise and remembered the potato. "I don't mean to rush off," she told Claudia, "but I left something cooking. Maybe we can talk about this another time."

"Sure! Don't let me keep you," Claudia said. "I'll see you at the meeting, then. We have to put a stop to this, or before you know it, people will be painting their houses any color they like."

Sharon said goodbye then returned to the kitchen, where she picked up her knife to finish cooking the potato. But when she looked inside the microwave, she was surprised to see the potato was gone. She wondered for a moment whether she had taken it out and forgotten. Then she heard something moving at the back of the kitchen. She turned around, knife in hand, and saw the potato. Its sprouts were more than three feet long and swirling menacingly through the air. Sharon hitched her breath and screamed.

The potato screeched, then scurried across the kitchen at Sharon. She ran to the back door and threw it open, but not in time to escape. The potato wrapped its sprouts around her ankles and jerked her to the floor. She stabbed at it with her knife, but the sprouts spiraled around her body and constrained her. Some of them reached her face and snaked their way down her throat so she could no longer scream. Others thrust themselves into her ears and nostrils, entwined themselves around her brain and squeezed. Sharon's eyes rolled back as blood and cerebral fluid poured out of every orifice in her head. Her body jerked like a floundering fish, stiffened, and then collapsed. The potato held onto her long enough to feed on her brain. Then it slowly pulled its bloodied sprouts out of her head and released her body. It moved toward the open back door and escaped.

Claudia had heard Sharon's screams and was banging on the front door demanding to know if she was all right. She had already called the police on her cell phone by the time the potato rolled off the back steps. It reached an opening under the fence while sirens blared down the street toward the Proffers' home. Then it found a storm drain in the alley and lowered itself inside. By the break of dawn, it found its way to the Agricultural Research Center and crawled back into the potato field through the irrigation system. Its sprouts dug deep into the soil, and by the time the first field hands arrived, the potato had already buried itself and died.

* * *

It had been several weeks since Sharon's death, but the Director of Research assured Nolan that if he needed more time away from the lab, he could take it. Even so, Nolan insisted on coming back. After what had happened to his wife and the scene the police found, he had to return to his research if only to convince himself that his hunch wasn't true.

When the police arrived the evening of Sharon's murder, they found the microwave open, as though it had been in use when she was attacked. The back door was open, and they concluded that was how the intruder had entered and escaped. While examining Sharon's wounds, however, they couldn't determine what kind of weapon had been used. The autopsy results only raised more questions for which they didn't have any answers. They took tissue samples and were in the process of analyzing them, but it would be several more weeks before they had any results.

Meanwhile, police dogs had followed a bloody trail from the kitchen to a nearby storm drain. It appeared the intruder had dragged the unusual weapon there to dispose of it, but the police never found it. Nor had they found footprints, fingerprints, hair, or blood from the perpetrator anywhere around the scene. Sharon's fingernail scrapings and the knife she held only showed traces of potato skin and starch. The police concluded she must have been chopping potatoes when the intruder came, although they were unable to find any trace of them except the sprouts. They were baffled as to why she hadn't used the knife to defend herself against her attacker. But Nolan had a theory, a horrible, unthinkable theory that he would never mention to anyone until he knew for sure. The last thing he wanted was to jeopardize his research by coming up with ideas that lent credibility to the protesters. But he had to know the truth.

On his first day back, he requested for the submission of his research to the FDA to be put on hold. He then spent the rest of the day in the lab examining wedges of genetically engineered potato. He cooked several pieces in the microwave that morning and kept returning to them to see if they had changed, but he found no changes. He threw the wedges away and decided he needed a new potato, a fresh one. He went outside into the potato field and found a bin that hadn't yet been filled. Most of the potatoes were huge, but he found one near the bottom that fit nicely into his hand and took it.

The lead field hand was standing nearby as Nolan slipped the smallish potato into his lab coat pocket. "Doctor Proffer," he called to him, "the men noticed a new plant this morning growing over by the irrigation pump."

Nolan turned around. "What kind of new plant?" he asked.

"A potato plant, like these. Here, let me show you."

Nolan followed him to the irrigation pump. "Where did it come from?" he asked.

"I don't know. We didn't plant nothing over here. I think it's too far away to sprout from the old plants."

Nolan kneeled down to have a closer look. Several bees were buzzing around the new blossoms collecting pollen. He gently shooed them away with his hand. "I want you to pull it up," he said. "I don't want it to cross-pollinate with the others. It might contaminate them and ruin our research."

"Yeah, that's what I was thinking," the lead said and pulled it out of the ground.

Nolan returned the lab with the new potato in his pocket and was surprised to see the Director of Research waiting for him at his desk. "Hello, Director. What can I do for you?" he asked.

"What's this I hear about the project not being ready for the FDA? What's the hold up?"

Nolan struggled to come up with an adequate answer. "I wanted to do more research before sending it, that's all."

"What for? I saw the reports. Everything looks good. Is there something you're not telling me?"

"No, of course not."

"Then, what's going on, Doctor Proffer? We have a lot of money riding on this, a *whole lot* of money. There are people depending on us," he slammed his fist into his palm, "powerful people who are ready to see this thing through. Mayor Greene, himself, has fought hard to keep this place running, and he's gone to bat for us countless times against those environmentalist hippies out there at the risk of his own political career. If I have to go back and tell him it's all on hold, he's going to want to know why."

Nolan nodded. "Okay, Sir. I'll tell you what's going on… but not here."

The Director led Nolan to his office, where he sat behind his large mahogany desk and showed Nolan to a smaller chair in front of it. He leaned forward, pressing his palms together in front of his face, and waited for Nolan's explanation.

Nolan stroked his chin for a moment as he considered how to begin. "I was thinking about what happened to my wife," he finally said, "the way they found her."

"Uh-huh?"

"I think it might have been the potato. I took one home to her, and I think that might have been what did it."

"You think she was poisoned?" the Director asked. "I thought there was an intruder, maybe one of those crazy protesters."

"That's what the police think. But they found no trace of another person. None. And here's the other thing. They found no potato. It was gone, like it fled the scene."

The Director drummed his fingertips together. "Let me understand this," he began. "You think one of those potatoes out there attacked your wife?"

"Yes, Sir."

"And not some intruder?"

"I don't think so."

"A potato."

"Yes, a potato. With its sprouts like tentacles. You know, like a squid."

"Squid are pretty docile creatures. You know that, don't you?"

"I'm aware, but I think something might have happened to it. She tried to cook it in the microwave."

"Right." The Director leaned back in his chair slowly. "Doctor Proffer, I know you've been through a lot recently and you want to get back to your normal routine as soon as possible. I understand that. But I have to insist you take a little more time off. I really think you need it."

"Director, Sir, I'm not crazy. All evidence points…"

"Doctor Proffer, take your leave," the Director interrupted. "I'll continue to oversee your project and make sure the FDA gets that paper in the morning. Everything's going to be fine."

"Director, you can't! It's not ready!"

"Go on," he said. "Take some more time off. Get some rest." He stood up and showed Nolan to the door.

"Mister Director, those potatoes might be dangerous. Just give me more time to look into this. If I'm right, the consequences could be horrific!"

"Good day, Doctor Proffer!"

Nolan left the Research Center and was met by angry jeers from protesters whose efforts never waned. But he ignored them all. He had to discover whether these potatoes really were safe before the FDA approved them for consumption.

* * *

It was awkward working with a student's microscope after years of using state-of-the-art equipment at the Research Center, but it was all Nolan had at the house to view slices from the potato he had placed in his pocket. He started by cooking them in the microwave just as he had done at the lab. The results were the same; they appeared no different than any other cooked potato. He cut off a larger chunk to see if size was a factor. After a short time in the microwave, he took it out and shaved off a small specimen of cooked potato to place on a slide. The chunk was still a little raw in the center, so he decided to include some of the partially cooked potato for comparison.

His first look under the microscope showed no change to either specimen. Then, some minute cellular movement in the partially cooked potato caught his eye. Nolan strengthened the magnification and centered the lens over the activity. Cells began dividing, multiplying, and shaping into strands before his very eyes. They were reaching out and connecting to each other until all the raw tissue was used up. Then their growth slowed down and the cells became dormant again.

Excitement and fear raced through Nolan as he realized what he had just witnessed. He placed the rest of the potato in the microwave and turned it on, but only for a minute. The potato steamed and squealed under the radiation until the timer went off. Then he took it out and shaved off another specimen, this time using only the raw portion. He watched it under the microscope until it began moving and growing again. "That's it!" Nolan said. "The radiation! Too much will kill it, but just enough will change this thing into a living creature!" Nolan laughed over the excitement of stumbling upon the key to new life. The implications were huge. But it wasn't until he turned to grab the rest of the potato that he fully realized what he had created.

The sprouts on the potato had grown several inches long since he had removed it from the microwave. Black shining eyes peeked out from between them, blinking and studying the room. The potato used its sprouts to push itself over the edge of the plate and onto the counter. As it rolled over onto its cut side, it let out an anguished squeal.

That squeal jolted Nolan into action. He picked up his knife, and before the potato realized it was in danger, he stabbed at it several times. Shrill cries erupted from the potato as its sprouts reached up and wrapped around Nolan's arm. Their ends poked downward with surprising strength and punctured his skin. He reached out with his other hand, picked the potato up, and pounded it onto the countertop over and over again until the potato broke into pieces. Its sprouts loosened their grip and Nolan was able to shake them off. He rubbed his arm, noticing a few drops of blood where the potato had successfully penetrated his flesh.

He wasted no time getting rid of what was left of the potato. He took the pieces to the sink, where, one by one, he fed them into the garbage disposal. It wasn't until he picked up the last piece that he reconsidered destroying them all. This piece had three sprouts and an eyeball with small vein-like structures winding through its flesh. This was just the proof he needed to convince the Director that these potatoes were dangerous. He placed it in a plastic bag and kept it in the freezer until he could take it back to the lab.

Nolan arrived at the Research Center the next day, and once again pushed his way through the crowd of protesters. But when he reached the door and swiped his badge, it did not open for him. He turned to the security guard and asked, "Why can't I get in? I work here."

The security guard made a call to see if there was a mistake. After hanging up the phone, he said, "I'm sorry, Doctor Proffer. The Director has deactivated your badge until further notice."

"What do you mean? This is insane! Get the Director on that phone.

I need to talk to him. Tell him it's very important. Tell him I have proof!"

"Proof of what, Sir?"

"Just tell him!"

The security guard made another call and relayed Nolan's message. He was placed on hold, then spoke to the Director. "The Director will meet with you in the lobby," he told Nolan, and then opened the door for him.

Nolan went inside and waited in the lobby until the Director arrived. "What is this about, Doctor Proffer?" the Director said.

"I was right!" Nolan said and pulled the plastic bag containing the potato piece from his pocket. "Look, I took a potato home last night and started running some experiments on it with my microwave. I discovered that if you only cook it for a little while, it stimulates the cells into growing and they become this, this... creature!" He shook the bag in front of the Director's face.

The Director took the bag and opened it, wincing at the pungent odor that wafted out. "It just smells like rotten potato," he said.

"But look at it," Nolan said. "It has eyes like a squid, and I would even dare call those sprouts tentacles. Look at what it did to my arm." He rolled up his sleeve. "It attacked me, and it was strong. I have no doubt in my mind it was the potato that killed Sharon. I had to smash this one to bits to get it off of me. And I'm not sure it won't regenerate and come back to life, even now."

The Director dumped the potato piece onto the reception desk and poked it with a pen. The potato had thawed and its flesh was the consistency of raw calamari. "Are you sure this isn't just a piece of squid?" he asked.

"I'm absolutely sure. And I think I can duplicate this for you if you want. Just let me into the lab and I'll show you."

A troubled look came across the Director's face as he realized what this would mean to their FDA approval. He used the pen to push the potato piece back into the bag, sealed it, and held it behind his back. "So, you're taking these experimental potatoes home with you, is that right?"

Nolan suddenly became guarded. "I took a couple."

"Right. You know, you could be placing the public in real danger by allowing this genetically engineered potato outside of a controlled setting. You wouldn't want our environmentalist friends outside to find out about it, would you?"

"No, of course not."

"Then I suggest you keep all of this to yourself," the Director warned. "The moment the public finds out that one of our scientists is taking these tainted potatoes out of the lab without FDA approval, we'll have no choice but to punish you to the fullest extent of the law. Our hands will be tied, and I would hate to see that happen to such a promising scientist as yourself."

"Now, you're just playing dirty, Mister Director!"

"Is that so, Doctor Proffer? I don't think you've seen just how dirty I can play. Do you think our dear mayor is playing PR field goalie for this project just because he likes us?"

Nolan hung his head.

"I think not," the Director said. "Now, for the last time, go home, Doctor Proffer. I'll let you know when, or if, you will be allowed back into your lab."

* * *

It had been a wet, stormy winter at Coral Beach. Seas were choppy, fishing was bad, and the whole seaside community was on high mudslide alert. Had the potato project not been closed already, the staff would have been worried they would lose their entire crop to rot. But they were no longer concerned with potatoes. They were on a new project that involved getting similar results with carrots and zucchini. The intermingling of these vegetables with a giant squid was still in the developmental stage, so the potato field remained unattended until they were ready to plant their new experimental crop. As the rain poured down on the neglected field, new plants sprung up from the potatoes left in the ground. By the end of the season, the plants had grown several feet tall and covered the ground like a miniature jungle canopy. Left unchecked, the newest potato crop grew large, and they waited patiently beneath the ground for harvest.

Late one evening, as a heavy storm beat down from the sky, harvest time had arrived. The rain turned the ground beneath the potato plants to thick, viscid mud. The surface began undulating as small white sprouts poked through, snaked across the ground, and took leverage wherever they could find it. Then the mud roiled, the surface broke open, and hundreds of potatoes of all sizes, some as large as golf carts, pulled themselves from the ground. Their eyes blinked away the dripping rain and mud. Their sprouts continued to grow in size and number until, one by one, the potatoes gained enough strength to push themselves across the field. They moved like a rolling, writhing battalion to the main gate. Several were pushed screaming through bars as if through a crude potato slicer. Their pieces fell to the ground like chips. Eventually, their collective weight broke down the gate and they swarmed into the street toward the sleeping population of Coral Beach.

Their first stop was a quiet residential neighborhood just down the street from the Research Center. Most of the homes were dark by now, but they soon arrived at a house that still had lights on in the living room. Inside, retired insurance salesman Max McGray lay slumped against the arm of his sofa, sound asleep and snoring in front of his television. His wife, Hilary, lay with her head against the opposite end, snoring as loudly as her husband.

The potatoes surrounded the front lawn and waited in the pouring rain as the largest in the group approached the living room window. Its many eyes peered through an opening in the curtains and were mesmerized by the glow of a lamp standing next to the sofa. It didn't notice Max until he stretched and shifted position.

The large potato screeched, and the others joined in. The sound rose above the driving rain and jolted both Max and Hilary awake. They scrambled to get up from the sofa. "What's that noise?" Hilary shouted over deafening potato cries.

"I don't know," he said, then headed toward the front window to look. The window crashed open and the enormous potato sprung at him, knocking him to the floor while others invaded the room after it. Hilary screamed as she was overtaken by them, her voice lost among the potato shrieks. The McGrays fought to break away, but the potatoes twisted their sprouts around them, binding their arms and legs to their bodies and squeezing until the McGrays could no longer scream. The potato sprouts plunged into their faces, coiled around their brains, and fed.

Several neighbors heard the commotion coming from the McGrays' home. Their houses lit up as they jumped out of bed to investigate. This drew the attention of the potatoes that were still outside, and as soon as these neighbors opened their doors, they fell prey to the vindictive spuds. Meanwhile, those who had been more cautious remained hidden in their darkened homes and called the police.

* * *

The phone rang in the middle of the night, hours after the Director had gone to bed. He reached blindly into the dark and picked it up. "What is it?" he asked in a voice heavy with sleep.

"Sir, this is Frida from Vigilant Security. I'm calling to inform you we have received several alarms at the Agricultural Research Center's service entrance. An officer is on his way to investigate. He has asked that you to meet him there to assist."

"Those damn environmentalists," the Director grumbled to himself. Then to the operator he said, "Yeah, tell him I'll be down there in a bit."

The Director arrived to find a police officer in a drenched slicker waiting for him. The officer approached the car as he got out and opened his umbrella. "I'm Officer Dunlavy. Are you the Director?" he asked over the radio chatter at his hip. He reached into his slicker to lower the volume.

"Yes, that's me." The Director showed him his identification badge. "What did you find?"

Dunlavy shined his flashlight toward the service entrance. The gate that once enclosed the potato field had been torn down. "It looks like someone may have taken a bulldozer to that gate," he said. "Did you have any heavy driving equipment back there?"

"We're not using that field right now," the Director said. "There shouldn't be anything back there."

"Are you sure?" Dunlavy waved for the Director to follow him. They walked around the leveled gate and past piles of white, unknown disk-like objects. They reached the potato field, where Dunlavy cast his flashlight over the ground. Something had recently overturned the soil and left uprooted potato plants strewn all over the field. As the Director kicked at one of the outlying plants, a creature about the size of a cat squealed and jumped straight toward Dunlavy's flashlight. The flashlight fell to the ground and the creature scampered away into the darkness.

The men looked at each other. "What was that?" they asked together.

"I think we need to take a look at your security tape," Dunlavy advised.

The Director led him to the surveillance booth, where they watched security footage from earlier that evening. After watching several minutes of rainfall on a lonely, overgrown field, they noticed the ground began to move. Then hundreds of potatoes broke free from the earth, banded together, and stormed the gate.

"Holy Jesus," Dunlavy said as he removed the tape. "Is that what you guys are working on here? Those protesters might be onto something."

The Director's heart began to race as he thought about what Dr. Proffer had told him. The theory that a potato might have murdered his wife seemed ludicrous at the time, but it was quickly becoming more plausible. "That's classified information," he said to Dunlavy with words edged in ice. "Now, if you don't mind, may I please have that tape?"

"Mister Director, we may need this tape if anything happens. I'm keeping it."

"That tape is property of this facility! You can't just come in here and take what you like without some kind of warrant."

"Yes, I can. You invited me into this facility. I can seize whatever I deem necessary."

A tense silence followed. It was broken by Dunlavy's radio.

"All units, we have a disturbance on the nineteen hundred block of West Canterbury. All units in the area, please respond. Over."

"Unit Delta Three One Seven responding. What's the nature of the disturbance? Over."

"Delta Three One Seven, we have received several reports of citizens being attacked by…" the air went silent for a moment, *"… potatoes. Over."*

"I'm going to have to get on this," Dunlavy said while pulling out his radio. "Please come with me, Mister Director."

"What, am I being arrested?" the Director asked incredulously.

"No, but we may need your help in finding out what's going on here. You know more about these potatoes than anyone else."

The Director massaged his forehead while he considered this. Then he clasped his hands together and said, "No, I'm sorry, officer. I will not go with you, not unless you're arresting me. Besides, all the information on this project is here at the Center. I think I would be far more useful to you here."

The officer studied him for a moment before picking up his radio. "This is Unit Bravo Four One Six. I'm responding to this call, as well. I think I may be able to assist in discovering the origin of these potatoes. Over and out." He slipped the video tape under his slicker. "Mister Director, you stand by in case we need you," he said and left.

The Director wasn't sure what to do. He decided to call Nolan to see if he had any ideas. After several rings, a drowsy voice answered.

"This is Nolan."

"Doctor Proffer, it's the Director. We have a real problem. It seems a whole army of your potatoes just broke out of the field."

"What? What do you mean, 'broke out'?"

"They're alive, Doctor Proffer! The potatoes have come to life, and I think they're attacking people. The police are already on it! You have to tell me how to stop them!"

"With all due respect, Mister Director, you'll remember I was trying to find out more about these potatoes when you took me off the project. This problem lands squarely on you. Once they find out you were aware of this possibility and did nothing to stop it, this whole project is toast. They'll probably shut down The Center."

"You would like to see that happen, wouldn't you, Doctor Proffer? Well, I'm not giving you the satisfaction!" The Director hung up the phone and went to his office, where he searched his files for Nolan Proffer's home address. "He's going to tell them everything," he muttered to himself. "He's like that, you see? No loyalty to The Center. No loyalty to progress. No loyalty to *science*. Well, I'll put a stop to this."

He went to his desk and unlocked a secret drawer underneath. There was a small pistol hidden there that was intended to protect him if the protesters ever stormed the Research Center. But tonight, it would protect The Center against a different enemy.

The rain had lightened up by the time the Director exited the building. He looked to see if Officer Dunlavy was still on the premises. The parking lot was empty and dark, save for the porch light above his head. As he descended the steps, he heard something move near the ground. He looked down in time to see a cat-sized potato latch onto his leg with its sprouts. The Director pounded at it. "Get off! Get off!" he shouted, but the sprouts wrapped around his arm and began climbing. The potato scrambled up to his face and into his screaming mouth, where it ripped open his jaw to get inside.

Blood poured from the Director's hanging chin while he clawed at the potato to get it out, but the sprouts were wrapped around his head. He collapsed, and after several convulsions, his body lay still in the drizzling rain. The potato dug its way further into his head and emptied his skull before it rolled away to join the others in town.

* * *

Nolan had been off the potato project for several months and had no idea what the Director had done with his work in that time. As he tried to get to the Research Center to find out, he had to pull over several times while police lights and sirens blazed past him. In the end, he was stopped by a crowd of angry citizens in the streets and protesters parading with their signs in the air. Nolan parked his car and got out just as a news van pulled up alongside of him. The news crew jumped out and started removing their equipment from the back.

"What's going on here?" Nolan asked one of them.

"Man-eating potatoes! They're on a rampage!" one of them said.

Nolan pushed his way through the crowd to see for himself. His way was blocked by a police barricade thrown across the road. From there, he could see a huddle of police vehicles further down the street with their flashers and spotlights shining on a swarm of living potatoes. They were completely surrounded as the potatoes rolled, leapt, and knocked themselves into the vehicles with the clear intention of breaking in.

The sheriff's vehicle was parked just a short distance from Nolan, and he could hear him speaking over the radio. "All officers hold your positions. Whatever you do, do not leave your vehicles. Stand by."

A bald, rotund man in a business suit came out of the crowd and approached him. "What's this I hear about potatoes, Sheriff?" he shouted. "Someone calls me up in the middle of the night and tells me my citizens are being attacked by giant potatoes? How is that possible?"

"Mayor Greene, we have a situation like I've never seen before," the sheriff explained. "One of my officers tells me that your Research Center up there just let loose a bunch of mutant potatoes, and now they're killing innocent people. Right now, my officers are surrounded. They've all but emptied their guns on them, and it hasn't even slowed them down. We may have to get the National Guard on this one."

Mayor Greene's eyes grew wide. "Not the National Guard!" he said. "Not here at Coral Beach. We'll be all over the news!"

"Do you think the media won't find out?" the sheriff asked.

As though to prove his point, the news crew lit up the area with their camera lights while a reporter stood beneath them testing his microphone.

"No!" Mayor Greene shouted. He pointed to the surrounding police officers. "Get those people out of here!"

The sheriff was about to object when they heard someone scream.

Nolan turned to see what happened. The crowd stirred as people dodged and swatted at a flurry of golf ball-sized potatoes headed toward the news crew. They leapt at the bright camera lights, knocking most of them to the ground. As the lights went down, so did the potatoes. They swarmed around like moths on a porch light, bumping and pushing each other out of the way. As each light shattered and went dark, they moved on to another one until they were all swarming around the last surviving light.

"That's it!" Nolan shouted and ran to the sheriff. "Sheriff! Have them turn off the lights! Have everyone turn off the lights!"

"Who are you?" the sheriff asked.

"My name is Doctor Nolan Proffer," he said, and then with some reservation, "I worked at the Agricultural Research Center."

The sheriff narrowed his eyes at Nolan. "Doctor Proffer," he said, "are you the one responsible for making these monsters?"

"They were part of my project," Nolan explained, "but I had no idea they would do this."

"Arrest him!" the mayor shouted. "And find the Director! I want him arrested, too!"

The sheriff nodded his consent and several deputies moved toward Nolan with their cuffs.

"Wait!" Nolan shouted. "I think I know how we can control them."

The sheriff raised his hand and the deputies stepped back. As they did, the final camera light went dark. The potatoes fled from the shattered light and started going after headlights on nearby cars. A few of them jumped on people's legs and were quickly pulled off and stamped out by the crowd. "Well, if you have any ideas, Doctor Proffer, we'd like to hear them," the sheriff demanded.

"They go after the light," Nolan explained. "The potatoes are part squid, and they are attracted to light. If you tell your police officers to turn off their lights, the potatoes will stop attacking them and they can get away. Go tell them, quick!"

The sheriff got on the radio and gave the command for them to turn off their lights. As Nolan predicted, the potatoes abandoned their assault and began to move away from the police vehicles, but it didn't stop them completely.

"Sheriff, this is Unit Bravo Four One Six. We still have a dire situation here. Most of the potatoes ceased their attack on us, but now they're going back into the neighborhood. People are shutting their doors, but some of those potatoes are knocking out windows to get inside. People are being killed, Sheriff!"

"This is the sheriff. Keep your lights off and fire at those monsters with whatever you got left. I'm calling for backup. Over."

"But there's too many of them, Sheriff. We can't just shoot them all down."

"Do what you can! Over and out!"

He turned to Mayor Greene. "Get on the phone, Mayor. We're calling the National Guard."

"There must be something…" the mayor stammered.

"The National Guard! Call them now, or there's blood on your hands!"

Nolan watched the huddle of police as some of them exited their vehicles and started shooting the potatoes trying to break into the houses. He saw that most of the potatoes were gathering around porch lights and illuminated windows while the largest potatoes were breaking into the windows with the brightest lights.

"Don't call the National Guard, Mayor," Nolan said. "Call the power company. Tell them to turn off the power to the city. The whole city."

The mayor, still reluctant to call the National Guard, looked to the sheriff for approval.

"Now, listen here!" the sheriff shouted at Nolan. "You caused all of this. You're lucky you're not sitting in the back of some squad car on your way to prison! Don't go telling people they don't have to follow my orders. You're not in charge here!"

"Yes, I know!" Nolan said. "But you're never going to shoot them all down. Not even the National Guard can do that. Hell, we have a bunch of small potatoes right here among us knocking out headlights. We'll be finding them for ages behind bushes and under cars. If even a few of them grow into new plants, we'll be dealing with this all over again in a few months. Is that what you want?"

"Then what do you suggest?"

"Have the city turn off the power. Make everyone turn off their headlights and any other lights they have. Then when it's dark, have your police cars turn their lights on like a beacon and then head out of the neighborhood. I'll bet you anything those potatoes will follow wherever you want to take them."

"It sounds like an excellent plan," Mayor Greene said to the sheriff. "There has got to be someplace we can take them where they won't come back."

The sheriff considered this option for a moment. Then, over the sound of gunshots in the background, a blood-curdling scream rose from somewhere in the neighborhood. "Not my baby! Not my *baby*!!" a woman's voice cried out.

"Call the power company," the sheriff told Mayor Greene, then got on the radio. "All units, I want you to get back in your vehicles. This city is going to go dark in a while, and when it does, I want you to turn your lights back on and head slowly out of the neighborhood. With any luck, those potatoes will follow you without boxing you in again. You're going to lead them away to a location yet to be determined. Stand by for further orders."

He turned to Nolan. "Now, here's the problem. Where do we take them?"

"I don't know, maybe a football field or somewhere else with bright lights," Nolan suggested. "Then we can turn them on and hold them there indefinitely."

"Or until morning," the sheriff pointed out. "I don't think stadium lighting is going to compete with the sun. They'll just roll away again."

"Then we'll lock the gates on them."

"According to one of my officers, that's not going to work. He has a surveillance video that shows these guys busting out of your field through a security gate. They just pushed it down."

A young man with a notepad approached Nolan and the sheriff. Nolan recognized him as the news reporter who had been standing under the lights before the potatoes attacked them. "Excuse me. I was listening to your conversation," he said, "and if you don't mind me interrupting…"

"Now, who's this?" the sheriff asked Nolan. "Is he one of your scientist buddies?"

"No, I think he's from the news crew," Nolan said.

"Stop him!" Mayor Greene shouted as he ended his call. "Get him away from here! I won't have him dragging my city's reputation through the mud!"

The reporter raised his notepad and pen as though surrendering a weapon. "I was just going to suggest that since we have the whole ocean out there, maybe we should dump the potatoes in there. Do they swim?"

"I don't know," Nolan said. "But I'm guessing the saltwater will make them float."

"Okay, what if we could lure them way out, like, miles away? Whether they swim or float, I would think the salt and the sun would do them in before they could reach land again. If they die in the ocean, they're not going to grow again, right? Not without soil."

The lights in the city were going out in large swatches as the power grid went down. Headlights came on two by two just before the officers pulled out and drove slowly away from the neighborhood.

"We better get this figured out," the sheriff said. "My officers are coming this way, and they're going to need to know where to lead this herd."

"Yeah, yeah. Okay." Nolan thought about it. "That might work. I mean, if we took them out far enough. But I don't know how we'd get them out there."

"If you can just lead them out to the bay where all those fishing boats hang out, the current will carry them away," the sheriff said. "It pains me to admit it, but we've lost some important criminal evidence that way."

"The fishing boats!" the news reporter said. "They fish for squid at night. There's probably some of them out there right now. I bet they'll help. When they turn on their lights, the squid just flock to them. They can use those same lights to lure the potatoes out to deeper water. The current can take care of the rest."

The men looked at each other.

"Let's do it," the sheriff said and got back on the radio to give the orders.

"Yes!" the mayor shouted. "My city is saved!"

After he put down his radio, he got into his vehicle and announced over his loud speaker, *"All citizens, go inside your homes. Close all doors and windows. Do not go outside. All motorists, keep your headlights off and stay inside your vehicles."* He drove down the street ahead of the police procession with nothing but his turret lights on and repeated his orders while leading the way to the bay. Most of the crowd that had gathered around the scene obeyed his orders and either got inside their cars or moved away from the street. A few protesters remained on the sidewalk, chanting and waving their signs. As the police passed by with the swarm of potatoes following behind them, several protesters were attacked. Most of the protesters were able to throw off their attackers and run, but at least two of them fell and met their demise.

Nolan stuck around for none of this. He got back into his own car and took side streets down to the bay. Pulling up to the dock, he noticed several small fishing boats anchored nearby. Just as the news reporter had described, their fishing lights below the water were surrounded by swirling droves of squid. He faced his car out toward the water and started flashing his headlights at one of the boats. When it appeared he had their attention, he stood on the shore waving his arms. "Over here!" he shouted. "Help! Over here!"

The fishermen pulled up their fishing lights and turned the boat around. Soon, they had sidled up to the dock. Nolan ran to meet them. "Thank you! I need your help," he said to the boat captain as he stepped onto the dock.

"Are you hurt?" the captain asked.

"No, but several people in town are. I know this is going to sound nuts, but there are hundreds, or I don't know, maybe thousands of these… potatoes out there. They're from the Agricultural Research Lab, part of our genetic engineering project. They broke away from the field and now they're attacking people."

The captain exchanged a glance with his crew, who had joined him on the dock. None of them were buying it.

"Sir, I don't know who you are," the captain said, "but I'll have you know, you just pulled us back from one of the best squid fishing nights we've had all year. If this is some kind of prank, me and each of my boys is going to take turns whupping your ass."

"No, it's not a prank. I'm Doctor Nolan Proffer from the Research Center. I helped make these monsters. I had no idea how dangerous they were at the time. But now that I know, I have to get rid of them. You see, they're part squid."

The men laughed.

"Yes, I know," Nolan continued. "It sounds crazy, but if you would just hear me out. All you need to do is lead them out to sea with your lights, just like they were squid. Then the ocean current can take them away from here. You can do that, can't you?"

The captain didn't answer, but began pulling his work gloves from his hands. The others followed his lead as they prepared to fight, but then the police procession turned a corner in the distance, their lights pointed toward the bay.

"Here they come!" Nolan shouted.

The fishermen looked up and saw the lights. Within a few minutes the police had arrived, followed in the distance by the swarm of rolling, leaping potatoes.

"You weren't kidding," the captain said, disbelief still lingering in his voice. "Someone get on the radio and tell the others to come ashore. Tonight, were doing some potato fishing."

Nolan got back into his car while the police huddled in the street and waited for the potatoes to catch up. The sheriff turned off his turret lights and pulled alongside Nolan. He rolled his window down and asked, "What are we going to do with them when they get here?"

"Hold the potatoes here until the other fishing boats arrive," Nolan said. "When they get here, have your officers turn their lights off. The fishermen will turn theirs on and the potatoes should follow them."

The potatoes arrived before the boats could reach the shore and once again surrounded the vehicles. But as soon as the fishing boats arrived with their lights on, the police vehicles went dark. The potatoes were momentarily stunned by the switch. Once they recovered, they headed toward the shore. At the water's edge they paused, reaching out with their sprouts to feel the surface, as though unsure if it was safe.

"Don't tell me it's not going to work," Nolan whispered to himself from inside his car.

"Come on, come on…" the sheriff urged as he watched from inside his own car.

The largest potato, about the size of a compact car minus several chunks that had been blown away by gunfire, pushed its way through the smaller potatoes and reached out to the water with its sprouts. It allowed them to wade through the water and splash a bit. Once it was sure the water posed no threat, it scooted its way in. The water reached about half way up before the potato broke loose from the shore and began to float. Its sprouts swirled around and it swam in several directions before it became comfortable with its new environment. It took off toward one of the fishing boats with the other potatoes following right behind. Each of them went afloat. It only took a few moments for them to get their bearings before swimming after the boats. The boats sailed away, maintaining a moderate speed just ahead of the floating herd to keep out of the potatoes' reach as they led them to open water. As they approached the mouth of the bay, the potatoes began to tire and stopped their pursuit. They bobbed in the water and offered no resistance as the current took them out to sea.

All the police and everyone who had followed them stepped out of their vehicles and cheered.

Mayor Greene ran up to Nolan and shook his hand. "You did it, Doctor Proffer! The potatoes are gone and there was no need to call the National Guard!" He glared at the sheriff for the last part.

"It wasn't just me," Nolan said. "Everyone helped out here, from the police to the fishermen to every citizen who turned off their headlights. Coral Beach really pulled together for this one!"

At that moment, an officer approached them, a video tape in hand, and offered it to the sheriff. "I'm Officer Dunlavy, Sir," he said. "I was the one with the surveillance tape. I think you should take a look at it. It might help us understand what happened here tonight." The sheriff took it from him. "Meanwhile, if you don't mind," he continued, "I'm going to go back to the Research Center and see about placing the Director under arrest."

"Thank you, Officer Dunlavy," the sheriff said. "Take care of that for me while we start cleaning up things around here."

* * *

The bay at Coral Beach was a notoriously easy place for fishermen to catch squid, but Rob Baker was looking for something a little more challenging. Rumor had it that further out on the open water there was a large school of giant squid resting at the bottom of the ocean. On a warm summer night, he loaded his fishing boat with lights and nets, then sailed out to see if he could catch some calamari worthy of a photo shoot.

About five miles out, he turned to his crew and said, "Let's stop here. I'm told this is where they found them."

He killed the engine and joined his crew as they peered over the side of the boat into the dark water. "Turn on the lights!" he shouted. "Let's see if there's anything down there."

The lights lit up the surface of the water and several feet beyond, revealing small silvery fish that swam in circles then whipped out of sight as they realized they had been discovered. The men waited to see if anything else would happen. After a short time, their patience was rewarded when a few curious squid drifted gracefully toward the surface.

"Here they come!" Rob said.

Then the true show began. Billowing swarms of squid raced back and forth beneath the surface, a squid catcher's dream dancing before their eyes. Except, none of them were the giant variety Rob had wanted to see.

One of Rob's crewmen noticed the disappointment in his captain's face. "If they're at the bottom, it might take them a while to come up," he suggested.

"Yeah, let's just keep waiting," Rob said.

"What's that?" Another crewman pointed down at the water. The men looked and saw a small, round creature swimming among the swarm of squid. It was brown and covered with long tentacles that propelled it with speed and agility.

"Don't know. I've never seen anything like that before," Rob said. "Look, there's some more."

Several others gathered near the surface and began attacking the surrounding squid. Before long, the squid scattered in fear, leaving only the round, tentacled creatures in their place.

"They look like potatoes," another crewman said, "like maybe one of those ones that attacked Coral Beach last year. I heard they dumped them all in the ocean."

"Those potatoes are long dead," Rob said. "Besides, these aren't potatoes. They've got tentacles. Let's take a look at one." He grabbed a net and dropped it into the water to catch one of the strange creatures.

Suddenly, a large tentacle reached up from under the boat and snatched the net out of his hand. Rob screamed and jumped back. Another giant tentacle reached up and grabbed one of the crew around the neck, pulling him over the side. Other crew members grabbed their captured comrade by his feet, but the creature was too strong. They lost their grip and the man was pulled under the surface of the water.

"Oh, hell no! Those squid are too big for me," Rob said. "We're getting out of here!"

Another tentacle reached over the side of the boat and listed it starboard before he could return to the helm. He fell to the deck and slid toward the edge. The tentacle twisted around his leg and tried to pull him overboard. The crew snatched up any weapons they could find, from hatchets to fillet knives, and used them to free their captain, but as they fought, more tentacles, some as thick as fire hoses, reached out of the water and wrapped themselves around the vessel. They pulled the boat under and dragged it down to its captor, almost a mile below the surface. A brown, potato-like creature, as large as a submarine and larger than any of the giant squid that used to inhabit those waters, rested on the ocean's floor. Its many eyes watched as the vessel, crushed within the coiled tentacles, was pulled closer and shoved into its cavernous maw.

DAY OF THE PRAIRIE DOGS

John Grey

"What happened, Fred?" asked the tow-truck driver.

"I wouldn't have believed it if I hadn't seen it with my own eyes," muttered the stunned Fred Jenkins as he crawled out of the ditch.

His crumpled-up Vanguard utility was wrapped around a tree on the opposite side of the road.

"You been drinking, Fred?" asked Sheriff Matozza.

"Just the one, Sheriff, I swear."

"Luke," said the Sheriff to his deputy, "go smell that man's breath."

Luke reluctantly obeyed. One whiff though, and he staggered away from Fred Jenkins as if he'd been shot in the stomach.

"Thought so," Matozza muttered. "Now where the hell is that ambulance?"

"I'm okay," said Fred. "Nothing broken. I just need someone to drive me into town."

"Why is it every other drunk in Heboygan is content seeing pink elephants and hippos, but our Fred has to imagine giant prairie dogs rollicking down the road like Hannigan's mare got loose?"

"I swear to you, Sheriff, on the Bible, if you have one handy. I did see it. Big as a house it was."

"Amos, when you're done there, can you give Fred a ride into town?"

Amos McGrath nodded. He was in the midst of trying to douse the burning utility vehicle, but the hose on Heboygan's only fire truck wasn't cooperating. Barely a trickle dripped from the nozzle.

* * *

The phone rang in Sheriff Matozza's office.

"Could you answer that, Luke."

Luke was pacing back and forth in the jail's only cell rehearsing his role in the local theater group's production of *Richard III* while Ernie Gold, Fred Jenkins' only rival for town drunk, precariously lifted himself up off his favorite bunk to read the parts of the king's wife, sons, and brothers.

"A horse. A horse. My kingdom for a horse."

"Luke, answer the goddamn phone!"

The aspiring thespian deputy reluctantly interrupted his death scene to obey his superior. The sheriff lay back in his brand new swivel chair, chewing on a cheroot, as Luke lifted the receiver.

"You saw what... and it... well, I'll be a hog's hindquarters... no, sir... are you sure? No, I believe you. We'll be out there in two shakes of Hannigan's mare's tail." He hung up. "Well, I'll be a hunchbacked Plantagenet. That was Bill Haguchi—he has the potato farm outside of Southpoint—he says his entire crop was tore up and eaten overnight by a bunch of giant prairie dogs."

Sheriff Matozza near swallowed his cheroot.

Luke returned to his makeshift stage. The sheriff lay back in his chair almost to the horizontal. The phone rang again.

"Luke, come and answer the phone!" the sheriff shouted.

Once again, Luke forwent his battle scene to follow his superior's orders. It was the Cataracts this time, farmers out by Northpoint.

"Charlie Cataract says a giant prairie dog ate two of his sheep. They didn't even leave him the wool."

"Jesus," said the sheriff. 'They've tasted flesh. None of us is safe now."

"What we gonna do?"

"I was afraid something like this might happen."

"You never mentioned it."

"Didn't want to scare you, boy. Didn't want to start a panic. I got nothing against a panic you understand. I met Missus Matozza during that there *War of the Worlds* business. She was running 'cross her father's turnip field shouting, 'The Martians have landed.' Loveliest thing I ever saw."

Burt Longpants burst into the office.

"I warned you all, but you wouldn't listen. When they was building that facility out by Westpoint... all them big white buildings... and the ten-story wireless tower... and the electric fence and the trucks driving in and out at all times of the day and night. That's the U.S. government, that's what it is, and they've been conducting some kind of weird experiments out there."

"Last week, you kept raving on that they was the Chinese," interrupted the sheriff. "Now you're saying it's the U.S. government. You sure it ain't some of them there rock and rollers like I hear on the radio."

"Oh, it's the U.S. government, sure enough. I recognized the flag. And now look what we got. Giant prairie dogs! And what's going on out there now in them buildings at Westpoint? Nothing. That's what. They make a mess, and then they vamoose quicker than Hannigan's mare with an M-80 up her butt."

"I didn't know they left," said the sheriff.

"They sure did," continued Burt. "The place is shut up tighter than Hannigan's mare when the breeding season's done. Not a soul in the place. I drove by there the other day, and there wasn't even one of them Rottweilers left behind."

"Prairie dogs probably ate 'em," cut in Luke.

"Now, why in hell would the U.S. government be getting into the giant prairie dog business?" asked the sheriff.

"I've seen them movies," blurted Burt. "Saturday afternoon at the Bijou. I never missed a matinee. Experiments go wrong. Radiation leaks. Creatures grow a hundred times their normal size. These Hollywood types don't just make this stuff up. It happens. And it's happening in Heboygan."

"Well, I'll be a hog's pecker," said the sheriff.

"Ditto," dittoed Luke.

* * *

Bart and Amy Rogers had grown cotton just outside Heboygan for as long as anyone could remember. After a hard day in the fields, they loved nothing better than to plop onto their couch, light up Chesterfields, and watch Arthur Godfrey.

"Sounds like thunder," remarked Amy.

"Didn't say nothing about no storms on the weather."

"Maybe they're blasting down at the coal mine."

"Sounds like a herd of elephants."

"Circus ain't due here until late July."

The loud rumble was growing nearer and nearer. The walls of the house began to shake.

"Must be a tornado!" shouted Bart.

He grabbed Amy's arm, ready to drag her down to the cellar when suddenly, with the sound of a mammoth pair of jeans being unzipped, the entire roof was ripped off the house. The couple looked up and froze.

Staring down at them was the enormous head of a creature that was at once familiar and yet unfamiliar.

Amy broke the tension with a loud scream. Bart flew into a panic, first trying to figure where he left his rifle, then bursting into all he could remember of "Onward Christian Soldiers."

The beast began to sniff at the odd life forms its curiosity had exposed. Its nose was the size of the coffee table. Its cheeks could barely fit between the fireplace mantle and the large photograph of Bart's grandfather that hung on the opposite wall. Huge, sharp whiskers prodded the wallpaper, poked through holes in the back of the television console, and knocked a row of Myrtle Beach souvenirs from the mantle. Amy and Bart did their best to dodge these fearsome lance-like hairs.

Then the critter opened its mouth to expose huge, sharp, ominous rodent teeth. The two made a run for the kitchen, but their assailant was too quick, too powerful. With tractor-size paws, it smashed against the walls until they toppled like a busted up house of cards. Amy and Bart were totally at the mercy of this predator.

Wherever they darted, it blocked their way with a whisker, a claw, or just its ample furry body. It appeared to be toying with them. But the action caught the attention of a gathering of others of its kind on a nearby hill. One rumbled down to investigate, followed by another.

The creature had no wish to share its play things with others of its kind. One paw lashed out at Bart, its claws cutting through his chest like a fork in a haystack. The creature shook Bart's body and blood spurted all over the furniture, the ruined walls, and Amy's face and dressing gown. It then popped the cotton grower in its mouth and, with one crunch, he was gone.

Amy screamed for a second time, but this didn't perturb the animal. It passed up the pleasure of skewering the woman. Instead, it merely leaned over her quivering frame, opened its jaw wide, and whisked her down its gullet with a pink Persian carpet-sized tongue.

* * *

"This is bad," the sheriff said to Luke as the patrol car coughed and spluttered its way toward the Cataract farm.

"Needs a tune-up," replied his deputy.

"No, I mean all these farmhouses. Or what's left of them. And the cornfields. Not a stalk left standing. And the lima beans. And the coffee crop. And the poppies. And where's all the cows? And the horses? This

46

ain't natural."

"Wasn't that the Rogers' cotton plantation?" Luke pointed to a bare stretch of ground.

"Yep. No cotton socks for me this Christmas."

"Do you think there really are such things as giant prairie dogs?"

"I'm not saying there is, and I'm not saying there ain't. What I am saying is that this here gives every indication of being a crime scene. And that means criminals."

Luke's face dropped. "Criminals? That's a bit out of our league, ain't it?"

"You could say that. Bit like entering Hannigan's mare in a boat race. We need to take this up with the mayor."

* * *

"This is bad, Sheriff," said Mayor Burgess. "We need to take this up with the governor."

* * *

Mayor Burgess drove Governor Coombes and his personal secretary out to Westpoint, the site of the abandoned research facility.

"All kinds of trucks and fancy equipment came here one night, constructed this here place, didn't consult me, didn't even drop by the house with some of that smelly city cologne for the missus."

"I don't see anything, Mayor Burgess. What are you talking about?"

"Those buildings. That electric fence."

"You sure you haven't been drinking. What about you, Sam? What do you see?"

"If you say there's no government buildings, governor, then there's no government buildings."

"Exactly."

Mayor Burgess was so annoyed with the governor and his secretary that he stormed up to the main gate of the facility, grabbed the iron bars, and shook them fiercely. "Then what in hell am I..."

Ten thousand volts of electricity poured through the mayor's body. He burst into flame and then fizzled down dead.

"Take me straight to the airport, Sam. I have a meeting at three with the Vice Commission."

* * *

"I'm glad you could come, Professor Sherbet." Burt Longpants grabbed hold of his old science teacher to prevent him from falling.

"As soon as I received your telegram, Phil..."

"It's Burt. Burt Longpants. And I called you on the phone."

"You had a brother named Phil."

"No."

Professor Sherbet had been a giant in his field of Macro Botany, but at almost ninety-nine and not getting any younger—older in fact, in human years, than Hannigan's mare—his days of beating back giant spiders with an acetylene torch were far behind him. "I need young blood."

"An assistant?"

"No. A transfusion. Is there a hospital nearby?"

"There's one in Eastpoint. But we don't have time."

"Exactly. Which is why I called for assistance. I'm ninety-nine next birthday. I just hope my suit is back from the cleaners by then."

Assistance arrived in the shape of Brick Craddock, tall, handsome, muscular, with a degree in something or other from a mail-order university and a crew-cut as sharp and short as a bed of nails.

"Glad you could make it, Brock."

"It's Brick. Brock's my brother."

"And not Phil? I've also invited Doctor Heather Shanks."

There was a knock on the door and in strutted Doctor Shanks, twenty-two years of age, curvaceous, and long-legged, with blonde hair all the way to its split ends, and a sweater so tight, her bra cried mercy.

"My God," screamed Brick. "You're a woman."

"With a name like Heather, what did you expect?"

"Oh, I don't know. But not a woman. Maybe a cross-dresser."

"I'll have you know," she sneered, "I'm the world's foremost authority on creatures larger than they have any right to be."

With this team of crack scientists gathered together in his small apartment above Heboygan's Waste Disposal Plant, Burt Longpants explained the situation. And then, with this team of crack scientists gathered together in his small apartment above the Waste Disposal Plant, Burt Longpants explained the situation to Professor Sherbet for a second time.

"It's this ear trumpet," the old man muttered. "It's as useless as Hannigan's mare in a massage parlor."

The three scientists piled into Burt's station wagon, and he drove them out to the Shelby's farm near Centerpoint. The old homestead was nothing but a pile of rubble, and Clara and Midge Shelby were nowhere to be found. Across what used to be tobacco fields, the ground was indented with footprints as large as A-list movie stars' swimming pools, and just as deep.

"Will you look at that," said Brick.

They all looked at that.

"Prairie dogs all right," remarked Heather.

Brick sidled up to the woman voted lustiest undergrad in Princeton three years in a row. "Heather, when this is all over, maybe you and me could… well, you know."

"Brick," she replied, "I try not to mix business with boredom."

Professor Sherbet had a similar speech prepared, but instead of sidling up to Dr. Shanks, he tottered, then stumbled into her. She booted him away from her heaving hour-glass frame with the haughty ease of a giant prairie dog kicking Hannigan's mare through both goalposts of a Texas pre-school football stadium.

"We have to get into that government lab," said the Professor as he lifted himself out of a nearby prairie dog footprint. "If we can find out the formula that made these animals grow to such an enormous size, maybe we can reverse it. But first, I need to contact General Tomasko and have him crash and smash and bash his way into Heboygan with a small battalion of tanks and rocket launchers and armed-to-the-teeth infantry-men to blast away at these gigantic creatures and barely dent a prairie dog's toenail. It may seem like a waste of time and money to you folks, but in the armed forces, they call it Code Name Genus Cynomys."

* * *

After entering the complex through an abandoned prairie dog tunnel, the scientists were soon hard at work.

"I have it," declared Dr. Shanks. "Look at this mouse." She held it up by its tail. "A moment ago, it was a rat. And five minutes before that, a capybara."

"Great work, doctor," said the professor.

"Atta-girl!" Brick shouted.

"If we spray the prairie dogs with this, it will shrink them back to their normal size."

Brick saw this as an opportune moment to sidle up to Heather for a second time.

"Don't sidle too close," she warned.

But it was too late. In his desperate lunge to take her luscious body in his arms, his elbow knocked over the beaker full of Dr. Shank's shrinking formula, and it spilled down the front of his trousers.

"Now look what you've done!" she screamed at him.

Brick stared helplessly at the unexpected and unfortunate curtailing of the Craddock family line.

"Don't worry about it, son," said the professor. "When you get to my age, you'll forget what it's for anyhow."

"Now I'll have to make up some more," snarled an angry Doctor Heather Shanks.

Brick, for the first time since he lost the Sonny Tufts look-a-like contest when he was eighteen years of age, burst into tears.

* * *

"Shit!" exclaimed General Tomasko. "The bullets, the shells, the missiles, bounce right off those bastards. Get me Washington on the phone. We're gonna have to drop the big one."

* * *

"Jesus, Andy! If you don't fix that antenna soon, then I'm going to miss Lucy."

Andy Hempstead was perched atop his farmhouse roof, hands around the item in question, twisting it this way and that. Millicent, like Hannigan's mare, was growing increasingly off her oats. She'd plunked herself down on the parlor couch for a side-splitting half-hour with Lucy, Desi, Fred, and Ethel, but the console screen was a mixture of blurry, fuzzy, ghosted, and rolling images. The crows had knocked the antenna out of whack again, and she'd ordered her husband up to the roof to fix it.

He was doing just that when something in the distance caught his attention. "Well, I'll be a hog's breakfast."

There, in what used to be the Leary's mary-ju-wanna crop, some kind of weird creatures that appeared to be giant prairie dogs were engaged in a pitched battle with the United States Army. Based on the number of soldiers the prairie dogs were downing like candy, the armed forces didn't appear to be winning.

"Millicent!" he cried out. "You don't want to miss this."

"What's going on up there? The show's half over. By the time you fix that thing, it'll be the damn epilogue already."

"But Milly, love. It's our brave boys in action over at the Leary's. Makes you proud to see them in full retreat."

Millicent had had enough. She came storming out of the house. "If you've been ogling Clara Leary through her bedroom window again, I'll…"

She stopped in mid-speech at the sight of the loud, but colorful war between military and mutant rodent. "Well, I'll be grandma's bustier."

"Can't be looking in Clara Leary's bedroom window because Clara Leary ain't got a window. Ain't got a bedroom. Where their place used to be is now nothing but trenches teeming with the best and brightest dead bodies of the United States Army Corp. Wow, look at that prairie dog toss that tank like it's a rag doll. This is better than Tee Vee any day."

"Some of them animals seem to be coming this way."

That was true. With the battle nearing its end, a few of the prairie dogs had become bored with .30 caliber machine gun bullets pinging off their rumps and were off in search of farmhouses to demolish and farmers and their families and livestock to devour.

"Don't worry, they won't harm us," said Andy. "We're civilians."

The prairie dogs showed no mercy. The bounty concealed inside these wooden nests no longer surprised them and certainly didn't intimidate them. Their high-pitched warnings were now warrior calls to arms. The vertical stretch of the body, the toss of the forefeet in the air, the instinctive "jump-yip" had become a victory dance.

Andy was licked and devoured like candy. Millicent's last words as a giant prairie dog chomped her in two were something about her mother being right, and she should never have married a dirt-poor dairy farmer.

* * *

"Let me make this clear to all of you," said the governor, "we have the situation in Heboygan well in hand."

The giant prairie dogs had made short work of the house that had been in Andy's family for generations, but oddly enough they had left the television alone, and now, though there was no one left alive to watch it, the reception was as clear as if the viewer were right there in the Channel 97 studio with the governor and his entourage.

"There have been reports of giant creatures resembling prairie dogs on the rampage in that fine town that, in the last election, voted overwhelmingly for me, but let me tell you up front, as direct, as unequivocal as I can possibly be, these reports are absolutely false. What we have—or should I say had?—in Heboygan, which, by the way, it was seventy-three percent for me, twenty percent for my lying jail-bird opponent back in '53, what we had was an outbreak of Communism—some outside agitators—but it was quickly contained by our brave fighting men. In addition, those rumors of some kind of secret government laboratory in the Heboygan area is, once again, nothing more than propaganda put out by those Reds in the unions and the high schools. There's as much chance of that being true as there is of Hannigan's mare having Husky triplets."

A giant prairie dog came loping down the hill and, with one almighty gulp, silenced the television forever.

* * *

The helicopter whirred above Heboygan. At the controls was Burt Longpants, his chopper learner's permit tucked firmly into his hip pocket. On board were Professor Sherbet, Dr. Shanks, Brick Craddock, and a dozen spray cans filled with the shrinking formula.

Below them, the giant prairie dogs were making short work of the Enriques' sugar-cane plantation.

"Okay," said Brick. "Let's see what this spray of yours can do, girlie."

"Don't call me girlie," Heather snarled.

With one smooth kick of her heels, she bounced Brick out of his seat, through the open helicopter door, and down into the waiting jaws of a giant prairie dog.

But before the creature had time to say "yum yum," Heather shot him in the face with a full blast of her serum. She followed this up with another rodent bulls-eye, and then a third. Before long, the fields of Heboygan were swarming with tiny creatures scurrying here and there in search of the holes in the ground of their faraway youth.

The professor was overjoyed to the point of near-collapse. "You did it, gi… Doctor."

Burt let go of the controls for the moment and turned toward Heather. "Doctor Shanks—Heather—I've been meaning to ask you this ever since I first laid eyes on you. Will you marry me?"

"Of course, darling," she sighed.

Burt wiped his brow. "Phew. Excuse me for saying this, dear, but I've had vague suspicions that you were some kind of lesbian."

"Not in the 1950s, honey."

Burt and Heather embraced. The helicopter spun out of control and smashed into the Heboygan Arts and Crafts Hall just as dress rehearsals for the upcoming production of *Richard III* were coming to a conclusion. Five hundred years after perishing by the sword on Bosworth field, the hunchbacked English king was decapitated by a helicopter blade.

* * *

Hannigan's mare couldn't believe her luck. Half the fence that once surrounded that old secret government laboratory had been knocked down by the giant prairie dogs, and now she had access to all the lush grasses that surrounded the installation. Day after day, she nibbled away to her heart's content. And she grew and grew. Pretty soon, she was licking the rooftops of all those fine white buildings and picking her teeth on the wireless tower.

* * *

"What happened this time, Fred?" asked the tow-truck driver. "Not that I'm complaining, mind you. You're my main source of income."

"I wouldn't have believed it if I hadn't seen it with my own eyes."

Fred was beginning to think the ditch he was crawling out of looked awfully familiar. His re-crumpled-up Vanguard utility was wrapped around a tree on the opposite side of the road.

"You been drinking, Fred?" asked Sheriff Matozza.

"Just the one, Sheriff, I swear."

"Luke," said the sheriff, "go smell that man's breath. Luke. I said, Luke. Sorry, I forgot. He got beheaded doing that Shakespeare thing. Fred, I'll take your word for it. Now, where the hell's that ambulance."

"I'm okay. Nothing broken. I just need someone to drive me into town."

"Why is it that every other drunk in Heboygan is content seeing giant prairie dogs, but our Fred has to imagine a humongous Hannigan's mare rollicking down the road like… like… like I don't know what?"

"I swear to you, Sheriff, on the Bible, if there's one about that ain't been chewed to pieces, I did see it. Big as a house it was."

"Amos, when you're done there, can you give Fred a ride into town?"

Amos McGrath nodded. He couldn't get the fire truck started, so he had bicycled out to the scene of the crash. Luckily, it was starting to rain.

TROUBLE IN THE SEWERS

Ben McElroy

Something large splashed in the cavernous drainpipe behind Alejandro Martinez and Mario Lombardi.

"Let's get a move on," Mario said. "I've heard rumors there're some wicked aggressive, overgrown sea lions living down here. Haven't seen any myself, but why take a chance on meeting up with one?"

The Boston Water and Sewer Commission employee grabbed Al's arm and pulled the mayoral aide toward the distant surface. Never one to handle any of the dirty work himself, Boston Mayor Geoffrey Wright had sent Al down here to check on the progress of the long-term Reserved Channel Sewer Separation Project. It was running behind schedule, and it was his job to find out just how far behind.

They'd been slogging through watery sludge for a few minutes when an organic bellow made its way to the two men. Not wanting to stick around to confront whatever was responsible for that sound, Al quickened his pace. Mario followed suit.

Soon, daylight streamed down through an open manhole. Al paused and glanced over his shoulder. The ferocious roar repeated a second time.

Between heaving breaths, Mario said, "You first, Mister Martinez."

Al acknowledged the offer with a nod and grasped the highest ladder rung that he could. While he pulled himself up, he continued to glance over his shoulder every few seconds.

When he finally emerged onto the street, he found Mario's co-workers standing around in a clump, smoking cigarettes and chuckling. One of them, Murray, peered over at Al.

"Let me help you out of there, Mister Martinez," Murray said, approaching Al with a grin. "Say, where's Mario? Off jerkin' his gherkin?"

The other men laughed; Al ignored the remark. He looked back at the manhole, where Mario had started to lift himself onto the street.

"No comeback this time, Mario?" Murray asked.

Al smiled, for Mario had decided to play a little prank of his own. The BWSC employee made like he was trying to pull his foot free, as if it were caught between rungs.

Seconds later, however, Mario's trick wasn't so funny anymore. His body jittered, then it jerked up and down. Concerned now, Al thought maybe the guy was having a seizure.

Mario dropped out of sight with a scream that echoed against the surrounding buildings. Al ran over to the open manhole. He grabbed Murray's proffered flashlight and directed its beam down into the sewer's dank depths. The meager illumination revealed a whole lot of blood and what appeared to be a massive sea lion's rear end retreating into the shadows.

With trembling fingers, a stunned Al unzipped his coveralls and retrieved his cell phone from his pants pocket. He wasted no time dialing the mayor's direct line.

Answering during the first ring, Wright asked, "What is it now, Alejandro? Can't you go more than an hour without bothering me about some trifling matter?"

Al swallowed the build-up of saliva in his mouth before he said, "We have a public relations nightmare on our hands, Mister Mayor."

"Explain."

"A BWSC employee got killed at the end of my Reserved Channel Project tour."

"Were there any witnesses?"

"The unfortunate man's coworkers saw it all."

"Damn it, Alejandro," the mayor said. "It's an election year."

"Yes, sir. I know that."

"So clean this mess up. I don't care how; just do it. And I better not hear one more word of this foolishness from anyone. That includes you and the media. Understand?"

Fear giving way to anger, Al kept quiet for a moment, did a slow count to ten to calm himself down, and then said, "Of course, Mister Mayor."

Wright ended the call without another word, and Al began the process of covering up things for his boss.

* * *

Alejandro slumped in a hard, wooden chair at his kitchen table, his frayed nerves now soothed by an entire six pack of Sam Adams Boston Lager. He glanced around the studio apartment he moved into after his divorce from Gloria, his wife of fifteen years.

After draining the final brown bottle of its yeasty contents, he belched. The mayor was a prick. As if to emphasize the point, Al chucked the empty bottle at the wall. The glass container shattered. Shards rained down onto the stove and floor.

Sure, there'd been plenty of hush money available, but the devastated expression on the face of Mario Lombardi's widow when he'd shared with her the tragic news of her husband's demise was something no amount of money would ever be able to wipe from his mind.

If Al wasn't so desperate to hold onto his current job, he'd have resigned a while back, but his future in politics—a lifelong ambition—meant making certain decisions and acting in certain ways that made him feel like a major sleaze. He just had to find a way to turn a blind eye to that facet of his career if he wanted to rise to a position of power someday.

* * *

Three weeks later, Mayor Wright sat at a conference table with Alejandro and several other city officials and campaign employees.

Al said, "We have got to do something about the lingering trouble in the sewers, Mister Mayor."

"You haven't forgotten our conversation regarding such fanciful talk, have you, Alejandro?" asked the mayor with a cruel sneer.

"I saw the damn sea lion myself that day."

"Why worry about a handful of mistaken notions regarding sea lions in the sewers?"

Al felt the sudden anger color his face as he asked, "How can you be so flippant under the circumstances, sir?"

"Must I remind you yet again that I expect to hold this office for the next term before moving on to a more elevated leadership role? Speaking of which, how am I doing in the most recent polls, Paul?"

Paul Liu, the mayor's campaign manager, said, "Fine, sir, just fine."

"See, Alejandro? There's absolutely nothing to fret about," Mayor Wright said.

"What about the six BWSC employees who died down in the sewers during the past month?" Al asked. "The families of these victims are demanding answers from you."

"Alleged victims, Alejandro. You know full well the number of sewer work-related deaths that our city endures on a yearly basis," said the mayor, studying his manicured fingernails. "It's a dangerous job. If, and mind you, I said *if* these deaths have been caused by giant, man-eating sea lions, where have they been hiding up until now? It's pure malarkey."

Turning away from Al and toward the only woman in the room, the mayor said, "Anusha, has my suit been dry cleaned yet? I intend to be the best-dressed candidate on stage at the final mayoral debate tomorrow night."

Anusha Patel, the mayor's administrative assistant, said, "Yes, sir. Dry cleaned, pressed, and ready for you."

Mayor Wright smiled. Al fumed at the fact that his legitimate concerns had again been dismissed by his boss.

* * *

Despite his bad day at work, Alejandro was elated after Game Seven of the American League Championship Series at Fenway Park later that same night. The Red Sox had beaten the Yankees twelve to two. Even better, his twelve-year-old son Miguel had caught the ball during Big Papi's fifth-inning home run.

"Don't get too far ahead of us, boys," Al said to his son and the boy's friend. "We don't want to lose you with all these people around."

Miguel and Jeremy ignored Al's warning and were soon in danger of being swept away by the post-ballgame crowds.

Not quite yelling, Jeremy's father, Tom, said, "You should listen to your dad, Miguel. Here in the city, you gotta watch out for the monster sea lions that live in the sewers more than these Yankees fans."

"Monster sea lions?" Miguel asked.

"Never mind, Miguel. It's just a silly urban legend that's been going around for the past couple months," Al said, though he knew there was some truth behind those tales.

"Tell us about it, Dad," Jeremy said.

"Well," Tom said, smirking, "I heard that some whacko environmentalist group rounded up some sea lions when they migrated to Boston Harbor last summer. The tree-huggers fed the animals fish infused with some sort of experimental growth hormone that they stole from one of the biotech labs in Worcester. Then these freaks forced the whole group of sea lions into a runoff pipe and herded them so deep into the sewer system that the animals got lost and still haven't found their way out."

"What happened then?" Miguel asked.

Tom said, "All the pregnant females died giving birth to their litters because the babies were the size of half-grown adults. Within weeks, the babies grew to be gigantic. As big as elephants. Now, some of those monsters are finding their way out and eating people. It's supposed to take about three days for their stomach acid to digest you after swallowing you whole. Or so some people claim."

Tom's serious expression melted into a silly grin. The boys laughed and ran ahead a little bit, tossing Miguel's souvenir baseball back and forth between them. Al and Tom walked faster in order to keep their sons in sight. Soon, they all found themselves passing the mouth of a narrow alley.

Miguel threw his friend a pop fly. Jeremy ran into the alley, weaving back and forth as he waited for the ball to descend from its high arc. Noticing that the ball had changed course, he leapt forward with his arms outstretched to snatch it out of the air. Jeremy grimaced as the ball first landed and then tumbled out of his hands and into the shadows at the far end of the alley.

"That better not get lost in there," Miguel said as he ran over to Jeremy and shoved the other boy to the ground.

"Hey, what'd you do that for?" Jeremy asked.

"You find my ball, or I'll kick *your* balls all the way into Quincy," Miguel said.

"Boys, boys," Al said. "Quit fighting. It's just a baseball."

"But, Dad," Miguel said, "it's not just any baseball. It was my Big Papi home-run ball that I caught all by myself."

"I'll get it," Tom said. He stepped into the alley. Peering into the gloom, he searched for the ball. In order to get a better look, he moved deeper into the shadows and was soon enveloped by the murk. "I can't see anything in here. You still have that tiny flashlight on your key chain, Al?"

Something bellowed in reply. Al backed away toward where the two boys were standing.

When Tom came out of the shadows, he stumbled and fell back, and then his body vibrated as if he'd received a series of electric shocks. His feet were raised high into the air, then the thing that had roared dragged him back into the darkness.

Driven by the need to rescue his friend from a particularly gruesome death, Al hurried toward the mouth of the alley. Tom was barely visible in the shadows, and Al reached to grab Tom's arms to pull him to safety, but the man was stuck. A growl emanated from the darkness. Al renewed his efforts. This time, Tom slid back so easily that Al almost lost his balance.

After planting his feet, he continued to drag Tom out of the alley.

When they emerged onto the sidewalk, the streetlight revealed Tom's fate. Blood saturated the top half of his blue shirt, and below his friend's waist there was... nothing. His thighs were bloody stumps. Al backed away from this grisly sight. He turned to tell the boys to avert their eyes, but they'd already seen too much.

Jeremy screamed as tears flowed down his flushed cheeks. Miguel shivered and pointed.

Al followed his son's finger back to the alley. A six-foot tall sea lion rushed at him from the shadowy depths. Al's heart beat heavy in his chest, as though he'd just run a marathon. He stumbled backward, turned, and grabbed both of the boys by their hands before running for his life.

The Fenway faithful still filled the surrounding streets in all directions. Al screamed at them to flee. Most of the people ignored his antics. The few that gave him any attention at all laughed. Soon, though, screams started to ripple through the throng.

Al glanced over his shoulder. The massive sea lion was in pursuit. It knocked some pedestrians aside; others it crushed beneath its undulating body.

Facing forward again, Al said, "We're going back to Fenway. It should be safe there."

Ten minutes later, they stood outside the Park's gates on Yawkey Way. A trickle of fans exited, but some still lingered inside at the concession stands. Al tugged Miguel and Jeremy through the least-congested gate. A security guard blocked their way shortly after they'd entered.

"Hey, hey! Stop right there," the guard said. "Once you're out, you're out. No re-entry. Can't you read the signs? They're everywhere."

Struggling to catch his breath, Al managed to say, "You have to keep as many people in here as possible. One of the monster sea lions is out there, and it's coming this way."

"Get outta here with that kind of bullshit," the guard said. He moved toward Al with his arms spread out to either side.

"Run," Al said to the boys as he released their hands.

Miguel and Jeremy sprinted by the guard, who spun around to stop them. He was too slow, though. Meanwhile, Al went back to the gate and began to close it.

Just as Al completely shut the gate, the sea lion flopped by him. It paused and turned back, sniffing at the air. When it laid eyes on Al, the animal roared. Al backed away and bumped into someone.

"I'll find those boys later," the guard said, taking Al's upper arm in a bone-crushing grip. "I'll deal with you first."

"Don't you see it, you fool?" Al asked. "It's right outside the gate."

The guard peeked past Al. His hands fell away from Al's arm, and he turned and ran off into the bowels of Fenway, hollering.

"Shit. What now?" Al asked aloud.

A few of the stragglers milled about in confusion, wanting to know why the gate was down. A great clanging reverberated nearby. Al didn't know how long the gate would keep out the sea lion. He reached into his coat pocket to retrieve his cell phone. Once he had it out, he dialed 9-1-1.

And got a busy signal. As soon as he put the phone away, distant sirens added to the overall din. The Boston PD emergency dispatch must've been flooded with calls from people on the outside. Help should be here soon.

"Dad! Dad!" Miguel shouted.

Al ran in the direction of his son's voice. He found him and Jeremy near the entrance to the lower-deck bleachers behind home plate.

"They're getting in everywhere," Miguel said. The boy's body trembled. "I don't think they can make it onto the field. We should be safe there."

Not knowing what else to do, Al followed the two boys onto the recently vacated field. When they reached the Green Monster, they stopped. Al scanned the stands. A few maintenance workers were cleaning the mess left behind by the multitude of spectators, oblivious to what was going on outside the park.

Movement down by the Red Sox dugout caught Al's attention. He expected to see some players or maybe a couple coaches reliving the best moments of the game. Instead, an overgrown sea lion squeezed out of the dugout. Several more of the beasts joined their brethren. The animal in the lead made some sort of moist grunt. Then, as if they had received an order from the lead animal, the pack turned as one and shuffled toward Al and the boys. The beasts varied in size, ranging between six and eight feet in height and were a good twelve feet in length.

"I'm scared, Dad," Miguel said, reaching over to grasp his father's hand.

Jeremy stood there and gaped at the approaching creatures. A gleaming string of saliva slipped from between his slack lips. He didn't seem to realize the danger that was coming their way.

Al grabbed Jeremy's shoulder and shook the boy, who collapsed weakly to his knees. He rocked back and forth mumbling nonsense syllables. Miguel started to bawl as he backed away from his friend.

"Miguel, I'm going to carry Jeremy, so you'll have to run on your own," Al said.

"No. I can't. Carry me. Please?" Miguel said.

"You have to be brave for me, son. You can do that, can't you? For me? For Jeremy?"

After a moment's pause, Miguel nodded. Tears still leaked from his red-rimmed eyes.

The sea lions were already at second base by that point. Al tried to swallow past the dryness in his throat. He leaned over and scooped Jeremy into his arms. Once he got a decent hold on the boy, he turned to his son.

"We'll head to the door that goes behind the scoreboard, okay?" Al asked. "You lead the way."

Miguel nodded, then hurried over the scoreboard door and tugged on it. It didn't budge. He increased his efforts and gave the door a hard yank. Still nothing. He whimpered as his movements became more frantic and, thereby, useless.

"It's locked, Dad," Miguel stammered.

Al placed Jeremy back on the ground. He glanced at the sea lions. They'd reached center field. Ignoring them for now, he met his son at the door and tried to open it himself. Miguel was right; the damn thing was locked. What now?

The unmistakable report of multiple gun shots tore through Fenway Park. Al spun toward the noise. The sea lion bringing up the rear collapsed. It raised its head and issued a mournful cry that echoed through the empty park, then lowered its head back to the ground. The massive bulk shuddered, as though the animal was in the throes of a seizure; then the beast was still. Undeterred by the death of one of their own, the other four animals continued on their mission.

A loud voice sounded over the cacophony. "You three people by the scoreboard. Remain where you are, but get down on the ground while we subdue the sea lions."

Al did as he was instructed, pulling both boys down with him as he tried to become one with the ground. He wished there was something between them and those monsters to deflect any stray bullets, but there wasn't. Once he was sure the boys were safely down, he turned his head so he could watch the assault on the sea lions.

The perimeter of the ball field was suddenly filled with what appeared to be the entire Boston police department. Most held shotguns and high-powered rifles at the ready. The man in charge shouted orders into a bullhorn. A volley of gunfire ensued, deafening Al.

He peeked over at Jeremy; the boy had rolled over to the Green Monster and huddled against it. Then Al gazed at Miguel. His son quaked, but held his position. Al was proud of him.

Returning his attention to the massacre on the field, he saw that only one sea lion remained. Blood oozed from various wounds, some superficial and others grievous. Still, it was determined to reach Al and the boys. He wanted nothing more than to run from the imminent danger, but his fear of being shot outweighed his flight instinct.

At that moment, a lucky bullet burrowed into the back of the sea lion's head. The bullet's exit pulverized the animal's face. It plodded forward for a few more steps, then just stopped. So did the shooting.

Ignoring what common sense dictated as the best course of action, Al got up onto his hands and knees and crawled over to Miguel. He wrapped his son in a tight embrace. Miguel seized Al around the waist and clung to him as if his life depended on it.

Sometime later, someone tapped on Al's shoulder. He looked up into a uniformed woman's face.

"Sir, please come with me. We have a couple questions for you," the police officer said.

"I have to get my son home," Al said.

"This won't take long."

Al stood and went over to Jeremy. He looked like he was sleeping. A couple EMTs hovered over him.

"Sir," the female officer said. "We have to go now. They'll take good care of that young man."

Although the officer had promised the inquisition wouldn't take long, it lasted well into the night.

* * *

After dealing with the police for three hours, Alejandro finally was able to bring Miguel home. Since witnessing the gargantuan sea lion attack at Fenway, the boy had withdrawn into himself, and while it was understandable, Al couldn't help but feel uneasy. What if Miguel never recovered?

Tonight, the situation in the city had crossed the line from Al's professional life into his personal life. He no longer cared about his job. There were others like it out there. Better ones in better places, he figured.

When he pulled up to the brownstone in which Miguel and Gloria lived, Al asked, "Want me to go in with you? You know, to help explain the situation to your mom? She probably got most of it on TV anyway, but I can fill in the gaps."

Miguel looked at his father with bloodshot eyes. He opened his mouth, presumably to answer Al's question. Instead of speaking, however, Miguel offered a weak nod.

Taking a few deep breaths, Al opened his door and got out of the car. Trying to put off the inevitable, he stood staring up at the building. He dreaded the coming confrontation; it was going to be rough, and that was the last thing he wanted to deal with after everything he'd already been through. The divorce hadn't exactly been an amicable one. As a result, he'd maintained minimal contact with Gloria.

Sensing Miguel's growing need to be comforted by his mom, Al rounded the car and let Miguel out of the passenger side of the vehicle. Together, they headed up to the front door.

The entryway light flickered on and the door burst open. Al glanced up at Gloria. Her scowl told him everything he needed to know without her having to say anything.

"Before you say anything," Al said, "Miguel's fine. A bit shaken up, but he's fine."

With obvious sarcasm dripping from every word, Gloria said, "A bit shaken up? Try traumatized. What kind of father—"

Trying to maintain an even tone for Miguel's sake, Al said, "Stop right there. I had nothing to do with what happened tonight. I didn't initiate it, nor did I have any prior knowledge that it might occur."

"Typical political spin. I see our esteemed mayor has you properly trained."

Ignoring Gloria's outburst, Al crouched down to look his son in the eyes as he said, "Please try to get some sleep. We'll talk more about what happened tonight if and when you're feeling up to it. Until then, know that I'll always love you and do whatever I can to keep you from harm."

Struggling to keep his own tears at bay, Al stood up and watched Miguel walk toward his mother. He waited until they were safely in the building before turning back toward the car and heading home.

Mayor Wright could no longer pretend that this very real sea lion problem didn't exist. Not after tonight. A solution had to be devised and implemented before anybody else died. And what really sucked was that due to the mayor's inaction, one of the most recent victims had been Al's best friend.

* * *

Despite the horrific events of the previous evening, the JFK Library held about five hundred mayoral debate spectators, Alejandro among them. Throughout the proceedings, he seethed. He had intended to visit with Miguel in order to further console him after last night's nightmare.

Instead, the mayor had ignored Al's personal needs, and even though he'd worked all day, his boss had forced him to attend this event. And to guarantee that his staff stayed for the entire debate, a mandatory meeting was to follow. He supposed it had something to do with the phone call Wright had received earlier that day from the lead researcher responsible for studying the sea lions that had been killed at the ball park. Although he knew it was wrong, Al had listened in on the call and what he heard struck terror in his heart.

As big as those sea lions were, they weren't the real problem. The real problem had yet to surface. When Wright wanted to know what the man was babbling about, the scientist had confessed that the bodies they were examining were those of pups barely six months old.

Al had nearly dropped the phone. If those were infants, how big were the adults?

As the debate started to wind down and the floor was opened up to questions from those in attendance, Al perked up. In light of last night's events, he was curious as to what kinds of questions would be thrown at the candidates. He didn't have long to wait.

A woman in a well-tailored suit forced her way to the front of the crowd. She voiced her questions, but it was impossible to make out what she was saying over the murmur of the crowd.

Mayor Wright stared at the moderator, WBZ-TV's political analyst Kelly Johnston, and said, "A microphone for the lady, if you please, Ms. Johnston."

Kelly left the podium to deliver the requested piece of equipment to the woman. She then stood aside and let the woman have the floor.

The woman wasted no time putting Wright on the spot. "Mister Mayor, what do you plan to do about the sea lion problem that's been plaguing our city?"

All of the other candidates on stage turned toward the mayor and smirked. This was, of course, the hot topic, as the area around Fenway was still in shambles. Over a dozen people, including Tom, had lost their lives during the sea lion stampede. More than twenty others had sustained injuries of varying degrees. The citizens were, justifiably, in an uproar.

Wright straightened his already meticulous tie before launching into his spiel. "Let me begin by assuring you that last night's incident was an aberration and will be looked into until a viable solution has been ascertained."

The woman cut him off before he could continue spewing his lies. "That's not good enough. My husband, Mario Lombardi, was the first of many victims, sir. I demand to know how you plan to avoid any more sea lion-related deaths here in the city."

After a pause, during which the audience became animated, the mayor said, "Missus Lombardi, please accept my most sincere condolences on your loss. I was hoping I wouldn't have to say anything until we had some solid answers, but since the issue has come up, I feel the need to let you know that the scientific community is hard at work studying the sea lion corpses in order to learn more about their origins, their overgrowth, and most importantly, how to stop them. In fact, just this morning I created a special task force to delve further into this matter from a logistical perspective."

Al's mouth dropped open at the mention of the fictional task force.

"I'm going to call the governor's office if I don't see results very soon," Mrs. Lombardi said. "What do you have to say to that?"

Mayor Wright sputtered. The audience erupted into applause. The other candidates' grins widened. Al silently cheered Mrs. Lombardi for her courage and lambasted the mayor for being such a dickhead.

* * *

A few days later, Alejandro, Mayor Wright, and two members of the now very real task force stood on the street next to an open manhole, the entry point into the sewers and the on-going Reserved Channel Project. Journalists snapped photographs of the group.

From the corner of his mouth, the mayor said to Al, "Whether or not I'm re-elected, consider yourself terminated. Effective immediately upon our return from this excursion."

Al blinked once, but managed to keep quiet. Rather than say anything, he pressed a hand to his breast pocket in which rested a Big Papi trading card that Miguel had given to him this morning as a good luck charm. And even had he wanted to say something, there wasn't time; seconds after, Wright terminated him, the man waved to indicate that the photo session was at an end. He then approached a podium, stepped behind it, and grasped the sides with white-knuckled hands.

"Fellow citizens, it is with the utmost determination that I will lead this task force on its mission to help establish the cause of the tragic happenings in our fine city's sewers and in our streets. And while I'm looking below ground, my team of scientists will continue their work on the dead beasts. We have several days' worth of supplies, and we will not return to the surface until the problem has either been repaired or eradicated.

"Rest assured that I have only your best interests in mind as I begin this journey. I will not fail you. And please remember to vote at next Tuesday's election."

Additional pictures were taken, then the task force entered the sewers amidst half-hearted applause.

* * *

Mayor Wright and his three men rounded a bend in the mazelike drainpipes and entered an open junction where half a dozen tunnels joined. They were huddled together despite the fact that they were in a relatively open area beneath the city.

The mayor said, "We've been down here for more than six hours, and so far we've seen no sign of the giant sea lions' breeding and nesting grounds."

"You'll have to give it some more time, sir," Al said through gritted teeth. "There are miles and miles of tunnels down here. It might be days before we encounter—"

"That's impossible," one of the other task force members said, cutting him off. The man happened to be a high-ranking Massachusetts Water Resources Authority manager. "I've personally inspected nearly every square inch of this sewer system, paying special attention to the areas adjacent to the ongoing Reserve Channel Project, and I've never seen anything like what attacked Fenway last week. My guess is that was all of the animals."

"How can you be so naïve and narrow-minded?" Al asked.

"Don't be a chump, Al," said Murray, the token BWSC employee on the team. "That guy knows what he's talking about."

"This is absurd," Al said. "Why don't the rest of you mindless municipal morons go home and leave the investigation to me?"

"Alejandro, Alejandro," the mayor said. "Calm down. We're not insinuating that the sea lion problem was limited to the attack on Fenway, as you put it. Instead, we're imploring you to consider that we have nothing more to worry about."

They had just entered one of the wider storage tunnels when the

MWRA manager said, "Hey, what's that blockage down there?" He aimed a flashlight beam down the tunnel.

"Never seen anything like it," Murray said with a brief shrug.

The task force approached the pile of unknown material. As they got closer, the heap shifted to one side. A humongous sea lion raised its head and started toward them. There was only about a foot of clearance that separated its dirty hide from the concrete walls of the twenty-three-foot diameter storage tunnel. This monster was bigger than those that had surfaced; it was almost four times the size of a full-grown bull.

"We should call for back-up," Al said. He lifted his two-way radio to do just that, but his boss grabbed the device and hurled it to the floor, where it shattered into useless fragments.

"Fine suggestion, but I'd prefer that the task force sees this matter through without another party's intervention," said Mayor Wright.

A sudden growl from behind the four men disrupted their discussion. They all spun around. Another colossal sea lion filled the tunnel. It wasn't quite as big as the one that was behind them, but it was close.

Face pale and lips trembling, the mayor turned toward Al. Before either man could say anything, Al latched onto Wright's arm. He dragged his struggling boss around the smaller lumbering beast that blocked their way. It swung its head to the side and tried to bite them. It missed by mere inches. Then the sea lion began to contort itself in an attempt to turn and pursue Al and the mayor.

Meanwhile, Murray and the MWRA manager screeched as the larger sea lion charged them. Blood and entrails splattered against the walls.

Once they were away from the massacre, Al released his hold on the mayor, who peered frantically about the tunnel. At one point, the older man screamed. A sea lion so immense that its head almost filled the drainpipe lay in wait up ahead. A mass of scar tissue protruded from the side of its head where an eye used to be. It was so large it couldn't maneuver through the tunnels and had become wedged there. Four squares of light reflected off of the beast's slick head. Al's eyes followed the light upward to its source, a manhole cover.

The ground on which they stood vibrated as the sea lion roared at them. Al froze. The mayor sank to his knees and started to pray.

Fearing they might have stumbled into Ground Zero, Al had a decision to make. He realized his only chance of getting out of this alive meant striking out on his own. The mayor would only slow him down. But could he, in good conscience, abandon the mayor to whatever Fate held in store for the man? He was still trying to come to a decision when the mayor spoke.

"I didn't realize it would get so out of hand."

"What do you mean?" Al asked.

"I did this," Wright said. "I'm to blame."

"The sea lions? You brought them here?"

"No. Well, not directly," the man stammered. "My wife's cousin is a marine biologist with radical environmentalist leanings. Once I outlined my plan to bring the city to its knees and then become its savior, he agreed to take care of the sea lion part of it for me. I figured what better way to be elected governor a few years from now?"

Still kneeling, Mayor Wright grabbed onto Al's leg. The aide looked down at his boss. Everything came flooding back to Al: the poor way he'd been treated by this foolish man, the mayor's total disregard for his aide's needs and obligations outside of work, the fact that he'd fired Al during the task force's press conference before descending into the sewers. And suddenly Al had his answer, for he had not totally discarded his own political ambitions.

"Mister Mayor, save yourself. Once you get to the surface, come up with a way to kill these things. You'll be the hero that you intended to be at the outset of this debacle."

Roars echoed through the tunnels. There was no way to tell how many were in the area, but Al suspected it was more than the three they had seen.

"Leave now, sir," Al said when he caught sight of a flickering shadow on the wall. One of the beasts was approaching. "I'll do my best to distract that sea lion." He suspected the mayor was so terrified he had no idea the massive creature in front of them couldn't move. "Boston's going to need a strong leader during this time of strife. I'm expendable; you're not."

With a last, puzzled look at his aide, the mayor stood and fled toward the growing shadow. As his ex-boss disappeared around the curve in the tunnel, Al darted to the wall-mounted ladder and climbed it to the manhole cover. The metal disc would be heavy, but not impossible to move. Safety was just inches away. As Al began to slide the cover open, the Mayor's screams echoed throughout the cavernous depths of the sewers.

WASTE NOT, DIE NOT

Randy Lindsay

Troy tossed an old coffee filter onto the garbage heap behind the lab. As much as it bothered him to contribute to the unsanitary eyesore, it was a necessary part of the project. At least with the castoff coffee remnants he had added a personal touch to the experiment.

"Enjoy it while you can, chum." He tossed a faux military salute to the pile of garbage. "Your days of plaguing mankind are nearly at an end."

"Doctor Manly." Private Johnson snapped a salute as crisp as his military green uniform, stopping Troy as he re-entered the research facility.

"At ease, Johnson." Troy pulled out his ID badge and showed it to the freckle-faced soldier. "You don't have to salute me; I'm not an officer. I'm not even military."

"Yes, Sir," Johnson called out. The private looked over the badge and gave him a nod. "Have a nice day, Sir."

Troy strolled down the hall, whistling. The problem with the military was that they were all rules and regulations—no inspiration or imagination. Too bad they were in charge of this project.

Inside the central control room, General Stokes stood waiting, rigid as a flagpole, with a woman next to him. She wasn't exactly a beauty, but had that sexy librarian look that a lot of the guys liked. Lose the glasses and put her in a tight skirt, and then she would be more in line with the kind of girls Troy preferred.

"I'm glad you could join us, Troy." Only the general's mouth moved. The rest of his body stayed firmly at attention. No hand waving. No smiles—or frowns. No wasted motion of any sort.

"Who do we have here?" Troy asked.

"This is Helen Thorne," said General Stokes. "She works for the Global News Service out of New York. My superiors have cleared her to do a news story about our work here."

"That's odd," said Troy. "The military is pretty tight-lipped about their research projects. What changed their minds to allow a reporter to snoop around here?"

"I do not snoop," Helen responded coolly. "The White House asked me write about the beneficial research that is being done here for the American public. I was told that everyone here would be *happy* to cooperate with my interviews."

Helen's arched eyebrow said more than her words. It sent an unmistakable message that the two of them could play nicely or they could play rough.

"Of course," said Troy. "That's what I meant."

"Good," said General Stokes. "You can take the lead and explain to Ms. Thorne what we're doing."

Troy stepped up to the raised platform along one side of the room and pointed to a series of poster-sized images on the wall. He used a yard-long wooden pointer with a plastic tip for his presentation. The handheld prop was a nice addition to the white smock and dark-framed glasses that he wore. They combined to form the traditional uniform of the scientific expert, and in Troy's case, he wore them well.

"The United States faces a growing problem." Troy spoke in his best narrative voice, making sure to keep frequent eye contact with Ms. Thorne, a task made all the easier due to the deep emerald hue of her eyes. "Industrial output is at an all-time high. That's great for the country and great for all of us, but there is a downside to it. Many of the manufacturing processes generate a staggering amount of waste that cannot be simply dumped back where it originated. Some of it undergoes expensive treatment to render the toxic properties inert. Much more of it has to be stored until such time as we have the technology to deal with it properly."

Troy rapped the pointer against a picture of a strip mine, making a popping noise with the contact. An ugly pile of slag sat in the forefront of the image. He pulled back to smack the neighboring picture—

"Excuse me, Doctor Manly," Ms. Thorne interrupted. "It sounds as if your project involves cleaning up industrial debris. Is that correct?"

"Not just industrial." Troy hurried to the final image, which depicted their very own trash heap out back; the one they used for testing. "Garbage of any kind can be eliminated through our process. Cannibalistic Locomotive-Enzyme Attack Nodules will benefit everyone from big corporations right down to small families with a rubbish problem."

"Since the beginning of time, men have been leaving messes for women to cleanup." Ms. Thorne smirked. "It looks as if you have finally gotten around to cleaning up after yourselves."

"Not quite." Troy placed the pointer back on the peg where it normally hung, then turned around to face Ms. Thorne. He took off his glasses and stared into her eyes. "The whole idea is to create a refuse bin that takes care of the mess for you."

"In other words," said Helen, "a garbage can that eats garbage."

"Technically speaking, but it isn't the container itself that eliminates the waste products. It's the new strain of enzymes we've developed that does that. The advanced refuse receptacle maintains and regulates the enzymes. Right now we're working on a smaller version of the system, but there's no reason this can't be scaled up to handle the largest of industrial needs."

"That sounds fantastic," said Helen. "I'd love to see a demonstration."

A wave of mumbled protests from Troy's colleagues passed through the room. Heads shook and eyebrows furrowed, but none of them addressed Ms. Thorne directly.

"I'm afraid that won't be possible," said Troy at last. "This is a top secret project and I'm not authorized to show our results to anyone."

Ms. Thorne deflated a bit. Eventually she shrugged and took out a steno pad and a yellow number two pencil and started writing, her lip curled ever so slightly in disappointment.

"However, I am authorized to make that decision," General Stokes spoke out authoritatively. "You, Doctor Manly, will give a demonstration of your work, and we will ask Ms. Thorne to exclude any specifics of the process out of respect to national security."

"That's not a good idea," said Troy.

"Your objection is noted." Stokes tilted his head back in a way that allowed him to look down his nose at Troy.

"I don't think you understand," said Troy. "The enzymes aren't ready for testing. It could be dangerous."

"Dangerous? How?" Ms. Thorne asked.

"We don't know the exact threat involved in prematurely testing the process. Any number of things could go wrong. These are highly corrosive enzymes."

"Doctor Manly, I won't have my orders questioned. Unless you are aware of any specific dangers that might result from the testing, we will continue. If you refuse to conduct a demonstration for Ms. Thorne, I will restrict you to your quarters until you can officially be removed from the project. Then I will have one of your assistants carry out my request. Is that clear?"

Troy gritted his teeth and nodded. He motioned for one of the research team's junior scientists to come over.

Barely out of his teens, Richard was mostly arms and legs with just enough body to connect them. His eyes burned with a bright eagerness. "Did you want me to ready a batch for testing?"

"If you don't mind." Troy paused a moment, putting his hand to his chin. "We have a couple of insecticide sprayers in storage that can be used to disperse the enzymes. Make sure you put on one of the protective suits and double check the seals."

"No problem." Richard flashed a thumbs-up and dashed towards the chemical lab.

"Alright everyone, please follow me to the observation booth."

The booth, or the "scenic overlook" as the team called it, occupied the room directly opposite the garbage heap. A large bullet-proof glass window was positioned in the center of the exterior wall. Clean and spotless, only the thickness of the glass prevented it from looking like a hole cut into the side of the building. A bank of steel-gray instruments ran along the bottom of the window, and even more covered the other three walls, each of them with an assortment of dials, modulating gauges, and blinking lights.

Even though the observation room had a self-contained air system, looking at the pile of refuse—weeks-old grass clippings left in the sun, burnt fried fish left on the counter overnight, rotting vegetables, along with a host of other unidentifiable organic refuse—hinted at unpleasant odors. All of the smells tugged at the nose through the impenetrable glass.

Designed for a small group to occupy at any one time, it filled quickly with the invited collection of scientists, soldiers, and guests. Ms. Thorne pressed in as close to Troy as possible without touching.

"I didn't mean for General Stokes to force a demonstration," said Helen. She stood on her tip-toes and spoke in whispered tones. "Please believe that I wanted to come here and work with you on getting the best possible story for the American public."

A stinging retort died in Troy's throat. The look on Helen's face made it impossible to stay angry with her—or the situation. "You'd have to be some kind of nut not to want to clean up the country. Right?"

"That, too," said Helen coyly. "But mostly I really respect the work that scientists do. I wanted to be one myself when I was a little girl."

"Ready when you are, Doctor Manly." Richard's announcement

through the intercom ignited a buzz of excitement and brought a halt to any further small talk between them.

Troy raised his hands in the air to get everyone's attention. Then he pointed to the stick figure in the yellow, plastic suit outside.

"The sprayer Richard is carrying contains the Cannibalistic Locomotive-Enzymes that are the center of our technology. These lab-engineered brutes are a fusion of the digestive enzymes found in humans and a commercially developed strand used in meat tenderizers. We then modified them for better mobility and instilled a rudimentary intelligence that allows them to remain active and adapt to the task of consuming whatever trash they encounter. The end result is a substance that will live off our waste products and excrete a highly effective fertilizer in the process."

Richard received the signal to start and laid down a fine mist over the pile of garbage. He worked his arm back and forth in short arcs, covering the center of the test area. Then he stepped backwards, nearly tripping over a broken office chair.

The pile of garbage sat there. After a few minutes, some of the softer refuse, like wilted lettuce leaves and rotten tomato slices, gained a yellowish-green hue. At the end of ten minutes, the same items resembled bright green vegetable pudding.

And that was it.

"Doctor Manly," said General Stokes. "Can we speed up the process, please? Have your man apply another coat of the enzymes. Really douse the garbage with it this time."

"We've already sprayed it with ten times the amount of enzymes required for a rubbish heap of that size. Adding more would be unreasonably reckless. Ideally, we should wait until morning and see what happens."

"Nonsense." Stokes leaned forward and signaled Richard to do it again. Richard looked questioningly at Troy, but the General emphatically repeated the motions.

The second batch managed to turn the brown banana peels on top into a gooey brown glop that drizzled between the larger chunks of debris, deeper into the heap. Even that took another half hour.

"Can't you just zap it with some radiation and get it to work?" Stokes held his hands behind his back, a frown now camped out on his face.

Troy chuckled… until he caught the General's expression. "That only works in monster movies. It's Hollywood fake science, not the real thing."

"Very well." Stokes spun around and marched towards the door, people scattering before him. "I will have my assistant prepare a room for Ms. Thorne so she can stay the night. We will assemble here at oh-six-thirty to finish the demonstration."

The General whisked out of the room like a storm front and the soldiers trailed after him like leaves in his jet stream.

"That's it, Richard. Go ahead and clean up. We're done for the day." Troy let his hand drop from the intercom and turned to address Helen. "Do you have plans for dinner?"

"That depends on whether you're going to let me grill you about the project while we eat." Her words meant maybe, but the way her body leaned in towards Troy said yes.

"If you insist," said Troy. "I know a little Italian place in town where we can sit on the terrace and smell the lilacs. It's a bit of a drive, but they serve a lasagna that will knock you dead."

* * *

At oh-six-thirty everyone gathered in the observation room.

Everyone, that is, except Richard.

General Stokes dispatched one of the soldiers, Private Millard, to find the scientist and escort him back for the next part of the demonstration. In the meantime, those who were present looked out on the garbage pile.

The area that had been sprayed the previous day now contained a pool of greenish, slightly phosphorescent goop. A few hardier items remained—the steel legs of the office chair that Richard had nearly tripped over, shards of a broken ceramic plate, and a stainless steel pen. Both the plate shards and the pen appeared relatively untouched.

"That doesn't look right," Troy said, to no one in particular. "There should be more of the processed residue present. None of the mass is destroyed; it's just transformed into an environment-friendly sludge."

Private Millard burst into the room, nearly knocking over the pair of guards that stood just inside. He pushed his way through the crowd until he reached General Stokes at the observation window.

"No sign of Richard, Sir." Millard cast an uneasy glance at the people surrounding the General, especially Ms. Thorne. "I checked the locker room where they keep the hazard suits. One of them is missing. And right below where it should be is a yellow puddle of gunk that smells like someone set fire to a plastic gas can."

Richard. While a bit eccentric at times, the man was never late and never missed a meeting. Troy excused his way through the gathering of scientists and soldiers. Once in the corridor, he sprinted to the locker room, carefully avoiding any contact with the liquefied remains of the hazard suit. The suit should have been immune to any attacks from the enzyme.

Troy hastily donned a fresh suit and stepped outside. He took each step as if he were walking on a carpet of banana peels. The residue should be safe to touch, but if they had been wrong about the hazard suits, then they could be wrong about that as well.

When he reached the center of the remaining trash, he bent over and examined the pen. Richard had a stainless steel pen that he had picked up when he worked for NASA. Although the paint had been eaten away, Troy could still make out the etched portion of the space agency's logo. He had found Richard's pen.

He scanned the slime at his feet. Perhaps he had found Richard as well.

"Is anything wrong?" Helen asked through the intercom.

"We have a problem." Troy's tone was stark. He and Richard had been on the project from the beginning. The two of them had been friends for years, colleagues for even longer.

Then a scream echoed from another section of the building.

A sick feeling dropped into the pit of his gut. The missing portion of the garbage pile, Richard, and the scream all had to be connected, and he didn't like the direction his thoughts were headed.

Troy stood back up and risked a faster exit from the test area than he dared during his entrance. His right foot slipped out from under him, but his momentum carried him into the hall, to land hard on his shoulder.

He scrambled to his feet and shucked off the hazard suit, letting it fall on the floor where he stood. Pulling his feet out of the rubber boots, he raced down the hall.

By some miracle, Troy reached the central corridor before the others. The screaming had stopped.

"What's going on?" Stokes asked when he finally caught up with his soldiers.

"I'm pretty sure that Richard is dead," said Troy, his voice cracking briefly from the loss. "And that scream... that may be our second fatality."

"Get on the radio and have all the guard posts check in," General Stokes ordered one of the soldiers before forming the scientists into two groups of three. "Until we find out exactly what the problem is here, nobody operates alone. Ms. Thorne, you will stay with Doctor Manly and myself."

Helen nodded.

"All posts check in," Private Millard announced over the radio.

"Post One," a voice crackled. "All clear."

"Post Two. All clear."

For nearly a minute, only static broadcast out of the radio.

"Post Four. All clear."

"Post Three is located at the exit next to the kitchen." General Stokes pulled his polished .45 pistol from its holster and motioned for the two soldiers with the group to move out.

Two abreast, the group marched down the hall, their steps tapping out a slow, unsynchronized charge. On the floor, a trail of pearl-green sludge led the way to the mess hall. Their pace increased. The two soldiers burst through the door, with the rest entering seconds later.

The room smelled of trash. A horrid combination of spoiled meat, rancid vinegar, and old, soggy coffee grounds assaulted Troy's nose long before anyone spotted the heap. If possible, the odors of garbage had been intensified, bringing tears to his eyes.

One of the soldiers pointed towards the kitchen door. His mouth opened and closed, but all that came out was, "Garrr, ga, ba ba-ba bage."

Across the room, a pile of garbage slithered towards them. It contained the recognizable elements of their test heap: clumps of crushed egg shells, withered watermelon rinds, congealed gobs of used grease, shards from shattered beakers, mold-spotted bread crusts, empty plastic dissolvent containers, and a filthy throw carpet that had once served duty in the men's bathroom. All of it was connected with an ooze that had once been the softer, more easily broken down, uneaten remnants of their meals.

Among the familiar elements were two new additions. A soldier's helmet sat atop the pile, and the butt of a rifle poked out from the large bulge in the center of the mound.

"It's moving," Helen hollered.

Both of the guards lifted their rifles and shot at the rogue garbage. Their carbines popped in near rapid fire as they put round after round into the heap.

Bullets punctured the goo, occasionally shattering a piece of glass or splintering larger chunks of garbage, but appeared to have no effect on the monster. It slid towards them, the rifle butt and a broken leg from an office chair wagging in the air like mismatched arms.

Firing pins landed on empty chambers. The soldiers had run out of bullets in the magazines of their rifles. Private Millard stepped back and started reloading. The other soldier flipped his rifle around and jumped towards the creature, clubbing it with his weapon.

The portion of the throw rug that remained above the surface of the garbage snaked around the soldier's ankle and pulled the man down, holding him fast until the slow-moving pile slid close enough to strike him with the rifle butt.

Troy and General Stokes lunged forward simultaneously. Each of them grabbed an arm of the fallen soldier and pulled. They dragged the soldier towards the exit. And they dragged the monster along with him.

When the gooey sludge moved past his boots, the soldier started screaming.

General Stokes continued to pull on the soldier's arm with his left hand and emptied a clip from his .45 with his right, shooting wide of the soldier's trapped foot. Only when the monster spit out a blob of brown gelatinous material at the General did he finally let go.

Hands grabbed Troy and General Stokes from behind, pulling them away from the rampaging trash heap.

"Our weapons are useless against it," said Private Millard. "If we stay here, all of us will die. We gotta go."

Looking back, only the soldier's arms stuck out of the monster. They no longer thrashed about.

"Time to regroup." Stokes holstered his pistol and helped push Troy out of the room. "I want everyone in the compound to gather in the armory. Let's see what implements of trash destruction we have in stock."

Less than ten minutes later, all of the research center personnel milled around inside the armory. Really, it was nothing more than a large storage room with an extra security lock on the outside and a several rifle racks inside. The military must have been hoping for better armament funding because it held mostly empty space.

There were fifteen of them in all: six scientists, including Troy; seven soldiers; General Stokes; and Helen. While the civilians had taken positions well away from the door, the soldiers clustered around the weapons. Helen stood next to Troy, furiously scribbling in her notepad.

"Grenades?" asked Private Millard.

"Probably not a good idea," said Troy. "Too high of a chance of it creating several smaller monsters out of the one we have now."

"Bazooka?" asked Private Millard.

"Use your head, boy." General Stokes shook his head. "It has the same problem as the grenades, but with a bigger bang. Besides, you don't want to be firing it in the same area as your target."

"I guess the fifty-cal is just as useless as our rifles," said Millard.

No one responded.

Troy watched Stokes as the man scanned the room and eventually laid eyes on the flamethrower sitting on a test bench. The General grinned.

"Back home," said Stokes, "we put our garbage in a barrel and burned it. I don't see why that wouldn't work here?"

"Doesn't that run the risk of burning down the facility?" asked Helen.

"In order for it to work, we'll need to get that thing outside," said Stokes.

"That should be easy enough," said Troy. "When we encountered it in the mess hall, it was headed for the kitchen. My guess is that it was hungry. I can lay down a trail of food that will lead it wherever we want it to go."

"Use these." General Stokes opened one of several wooden crates that had been stacked in a corner. From out of it he pulled several packages of C-rations. "Millard can give you a hand. In the meanwhile, Jenkins can strap on the flamethrower and we will wait for you out on the tarmac."

Troy split up the pile of packets and gave half to Private Millard.

"Chipped beef?" Millard sneered. "I know it's a monster and all, but... uh... Chipped beef?"

"Get a move on it, Private." Stokes leaned in as Millard passed him. "You look after Doctor Manly while you're out there. First sign of that mobile trash dump, you grab him and high-tail it to us."

"Understood," said Millard, then dashed out the door after Troy.

* * *

A dotted line of government-packaged foodstuffs enticed the monster to leave the motor pool, and eventually the building. Biscuits, coffee powder, and cans of potted meat all maneuvered the creature to where they wanted it—one snack at a time.

The pile of garbage had grown. It had added a human thigh bone and a couple of ribs to the collection of protruding parts. Along with the rifle butt and the chair leg, they waved about like cilia on an amoeba.

"Jenkins and Nash," General Stokes shouted. "The two of you set up with the flamethrower next to the utility shed. As soon as the monster has enough distance for you to torch it without burning down the facility, you do it."

The monster finished the last of the C-rations and slid towards Troy, its faux limbs slowly thrashing the air. Bits of refuse surfaced only to be sucked back into the pungent morass below. The slime that composed the majority of the body formed bulbous modules that grew and eventually imploded.

When it reached a spot about twenty feet from the building, Jenkins unleashed the fire, covering both the creature and the concrete around it with petroleum-induced flames.

Tremendous clouds of oily black smoke billowed in all directions, engulfing the flamethrower team immediately and then spreading out, briefly lashing the rest of the group with thin wisps of the tainted fumes.

Troy gagged. The stench was so strong that it produced a vile taste at the back of his throat. He retreated from the smoke and resisted throwing up.

Helen had shown greater insight and backpedaled as soon as the cloud formed. Out of the civilians, she was the only other one who avoided heaving her breakfast all over the cement.

Dark clouds continued to expand, masking any activity within it. Violent sounds of retching inside the cloud diminished, leaving only the crackling and popping of the fire. Even that eventually faded.

"Jenkins," Stokes hollered. "Nash. Give me a sit-rep."

Neither responded.

"Sir," said Millard. "I can go around to the front entrance and get the gas masks from the armory. Then we can mount a rescue effort for them."

"Snap to it, son. They won't last very long in there—if they're not dead already."

The remaining soldiers lined the fringes of the smoke cloud, searching. A hissing sound drew their attention and they circled closer to the noise.

Then an explosion spewed flames in all directions and set the soldiers on fire. Seconds later, burning chunks of trash rained down on everyone except Helen.

Soldiers screamed as they burned. Phillips, a short stout man, ran about wildly and entered the cloud, only to be silenced moments later. Two others dropped to the ground thrashing. And acne-faced Private Zimm just stood there.

General Stokes limped towards his men, running as fast as his war wound allowed. "The fuel tank for that flamethrower must have been breached."

He tackled the still-standing soldier to the ground, using his jacket to beat out the flames. One after another he attacked the flames that attacked his men. When the jacket caught on fire, he switched to using his bare hands. When his hands sustained too many burns to function, he rolled the men over the ground with his forearms.

The civilians had been standing too far from the explosions to be hit with the petroleum-based fuel. In their case, burning garbage had struck them and clung to their clothing. Troy shed his lab coat and used it to extinguish the flames on the others.

Helen ran in and helped.

The scientists fared better than the soldiers. Charred clothing could be replaced and rattled nerves would eventually calm. Only Breckinridge suffered serious injuries.

"These men need medical attention right away," said Helen.

"We have an infirmary," said Troy. "But it won't hold this many injured people."

"It'll have to." Helen rushed to the nearest soldier and examined his burns.

Private Millard returned with an armful of gas masks. He stopped short, looking at the carnage before him. His mouth hung open.

"Millard," Troy called out. "We have to get these men out of here. Help us carry them to the infirmary."

Immediately, Private Millard dropped the gas masks and dashed over to the General. He dithered about Stokes, hands held out, but hesitant to grab hold of his commanding officer.

"I can walk," Stokes growled. "See if you can hoist Newman over your shoulder and get him to the aid station. Double time!"

Millard picked up the man that Stokes had tackled, glanced over at the General, and then lit out of there, carrying his friend as if he were no heavier than a sack of potatoes.

By this time, Troy had organized the scientists. Helen supported Breckinridge as he hobbled in the direction Millard had headed. The other four doubled up to carry the two remaining soldiers. And General Stokes left last of all, tugged along by Troy, looking back at the cloud of toxic fumes.

The pile of garbage slimed its way out of the dark smog. Blackened chunks of it fell by the wayside and the gooey trail it left still bubbled from the recent heat. It had been reduced in size, but sported a new helmet.

"What about the rescue mission," General Stokes mumbled.

"At this point," said Troy, "we'll be lucky to rescue ourselves."

* * *

"We can't stay here," said Troy. "It's only a matter of time before that monster arrives. Then we're all trapped."

"There's no choice," said Helen. "If we move these men, they'll die."

"Then we give that creature something else to chase." General Stokes had propped himself against the wall. At his own suggestion, he leaned forward and tottered to a standing position. "I'll buy you some time, but you need to find a way to destroy that thing."

"You'll be killed," said Helen.

"Probably." Stokes stood straight and firm. "But I'm not going to let that stinking people-eating garbage get away with murder."

"Let me go, Sir." Millard placed himself in front of the General, barring his way out of the room.

"Private, I need you here to protect these men."

"That's the thing, Sir. If the monster is busy chasing me, everyone else is safe."

"I can't trust a mission as vital as this to a mere Private," said Stokes.

Millard's headed drooped. "Yes, Sir."

"Well, don't just stand there, Sargeant Millard; get busy. And make sure you stay out of that thing's reach."

"Yes, Sir." Millard tossed a quick salute in Stokes' direction and bolted down the hall.

"The rest is up to me," said Troy.

"What do you plan to do?" asked Helen.

"I need to get to the lab. Maybe I can find something in my notes that will help."

"Then I'm going with you," said Helen.

"It'll be safer here," said Troy. "Besides, the men still need medical attention."

Helen laughed. "I'm a reporter—remember—not a nurse. I've given them all the help that I can. From here on out they need professional help. And I don't plan to miss out on the big finale of this story. It could be the biggest break of my career."

"Alright. You're probably as safe with me as anywhere. But if that thing shows up, you have to promise me you'll run as fast as you can out of there."

"Oh, that I can promise."

"Good luck to both of you," said General Stokes as they hurried out of the room.

The halls smelled of burnt garbage. It grew stronger the closer they got to the lab. Troy posted Helen at the door to watch for the creature. If it appeared at either end of the hall, they could simply run the other way. Then he brought out a stack of notebooks and flipped through the pages.

"What do you think went wrong?" asked Helen.

"As easy as it would be to blame General Stokes for pushing us to test it before we were ready, I think it could be anything. Maybe man was just not meant to meddle with the forces of automated-recycling."

"Before you started the test, I noticed that there were some broken beakers in the pile. Is it possible that whatever was in them altered the enzymes?"

"If even a tiny portion of an earlier batch were consumed by the enzyme that could result in the unexplained changes we've seen. The adaptive nature we engineered into it should only allow it to alter the chemicals it uses to match the material it consumes. Instead, it gained advanced mobility and a partial immunity to fire. That last one is the most troublesome."

"Why is that?"

"Normally, heat is used to neutralize harmful enzymes. The General had the right idea about burning garbage. But we saw how that turned out."

"It certainly has quite an appetite." Helen leaned against the doorframe as she scanned the hall. "Too bad it didn't develop a bad case of indigestion."

Troy's head whipped around to face Helen. "What did you say?"

"Nothing." Helen shrugged. "Just kidding about the monster's appetite."

"You said you wanted to give it indigestion."

"Can we do that?" Helen looked puzzled.

"We can do something better." Troy sped across the room and pulled out bottles from the supply cabinet. "Remember when I mentioned earlier that we used a cross between digestive enzymes and meat tenderizers. Anything that works to prevent stomach acid from causing indigestion has a chance of working against this thing."

"So all we need is an enormous Bromo-Seltzer and we can kill the monster?"

"Basically, yes." Troy mixed a solution of magnesium hydroxide and then poured it into one of the unused sprayers. He tested it to make sure it worked; a fine stream of liquid shot across the counter. "Keep your fingers crossed and let's go find Sargeant Millard."

They found the young soldier outside, quick-stepping a path around the building. The monster followed less than a dozen yards behind him. Even though it had taken them nearly an hour, Millard looked as if he could keep going at this pace all day.

"The cavalry has arrived," said Troy.

Millard pulled up next to them, and all three waited for the traveling trash heap to move within range of the improvised weapon.

At twenty feet, Troy held the spraying arm high in the air and shot a stream of it at the monster. It spattered on the concrete, missing the creature, but forming a small pool.

When the creature reached the pool, it stopped. The edges that en-countered the mixture quit bubbling and it lost its fluorescent sheen. It slithered around the pool, leaving a small bit of dead trash behind.

"It works," shouted Troy.

"Give it some more," hollered Millard.

"Thank heavens for indigestion," hooted Helen.

Troy sent another stream at the monster, hitting it squarely in its center.

The heap shuddered. It spastically brandished the protruding chair leg and bones, but the gun butt drooped until it touched the ground. When the monster moved on, it trailed large lumps of trash behind.

Step back. Spray. Step back. Spray.

Troy fell into a rhythm of movement, a dance of death for the monster. It ended when the sprayer went dry and nothing was left of the creature except a strung-out line of rotting garbage.

Helen moved next to Troy and put her arm around him.

"We're safe," said Troy.

"Are we?" asked Helen. "Or is it just the beginning of a war against trash?"

CLAWS

Eryk Pruitt

Vern Herman took a right just past the end of the state highway and headed his pickup south down a bumpy, dirt road, into the swamplands. There stood the sycamore where high school kids were known to gather to smoke weed, drink a beer or two... Never had anyone cause to travel past that. The pickup never so much as flashed a brake light as it sped past it.

"Slow down," said Jordy Wells from the passenger's seat. He held a half-smoked cigarette far from his body as he bounced around the cab like a pinball. Vern let up on the gas a bit, then steered carefully into the woods.

Suddenly, it was pitch dark. Folks in Maupassant grew up hearing stories about that swamp. There it was, three in the afternoon, but beneath that canopy it could have been midnight for all anyone knew. Herman switched on the headlamps and they both leaned forward in the bench seats for a better look through the windshield.

"You sure she lives out here?" asked Jordy.

"My brother used to come out here when he was our age," said Vern. "I'm sure."

There wasn't anything in that swamp that wasn't out to get you. Snakes, thistle weed, gators... Everything hurt to the touch. But nothing scared young folk from town more than talk of Madame Jolene. To some, she was a witch, a conjure woman on the fringe. To others, just a crazy hobo, a throwback to the old Creoles who'd long up and left. To all, she was someone who everybody knew just enough to talk about, but who had only been seen by a scant few.

"Folks say she married five fellas," said Vern, "and she done buried all five of them."

"Is that so?" said the Wells boy.

"I heard she used a black widow spider every time. I heard she keeps it in a jar for her sixth fella."

"I got no use for conjure stories," said Jordy.

"Then what are we doing out here?"

Jordy glared from the darkness. "You know damn well what we're doing out here."

They rode in silence a bit, high beams cutting a swath through the darkness. Inside the cab, the only light came from the cherry ember from Jordy's cigarette. Spanish moss, hanging low from the live oaks, slapped the windshield. They dodged cypress knees. They slowed even further, to a crawl, then stopped.

"What gives?" asked Jordy Wells.

"Shh."

Jordy whispered. "What gives?"

"That's her house," Vern said, pointing, his long finger stretched before him and directing his friend's attention past the windshield.

Jordy followed it to a small hovel just shy of the waterline. Despite the early evening hours, candles lit the inside. He shuddered. Not a bit of the house looked anything less than waterlogged. A small pier extended beyond it, cutting the swamp in two. Vern slipped the truck into park.

"I don't know about all this," said Jordy. He tapped another cigarette from the pack, but never lit it. He kept his eyes on the shack.

"What do you mean this ain't a good idea?"

"Just what I said."

Vern eyed him real careful. "It ain't a good idea to go backing out. You want to win this weekend or not?"

Jordy seethed. He breathed in, then breathed out. He straightened his shoulders. "Yeah, I want to win."

They opened the car doors. Jordy wore boots. They picked up every bit of swamp silt and left plenty of footprints behind. They walked to the front door of Madame Jolene's place. A crow took flight from an eave on the eastern side, bitching the whole way. Jordy stopped short of the front porch.

"You made it this far," said Vern.

Jordy shot him the stink eye. He sank to his knees, then lowered himself until his elbows rested on the rough, splintered surface. He spit the cigarette onto the porch, then puckered his lips and lowered them to the boards. He stopped just shy of the poplar wood, then rose. He looked to

Vern, who he found shaking his head.

"Ain't no way," said Vernon. "You got to kiss it."

"I think the point is to see whether or not I come all the way out to Dorémieux Swamp."

"That's not at all the point," said Vern, "and if you truly believed that, you wouldn't have gotten out of the truck."

Jordy crossed his arms, but didn't get up from his knees.

Vern continued. "So you going to come all this way and risk the entire season because you won't put your lips to it?"

"My lips ain't touching this property. This shit ain't Christian."

"That's the rules," said Vern.

"Then to hell with the rules." Jordy stuck out his lower lip. "I ain't kissing no hoodoo land." He rose from his knees and tapped a cigarette from the pack, stuck it between his lips.

"How long you think you can keep playing football the way you smoke those?" asked Vern.

"Ain't been a problem so far," said Jordy, lighting up.

"Some folks beg to differ." Vern narrowed the distance between them. "Your numbers ain't been shit compared to the first two games of the season."

"We're winning, ain't we?"

"We're winning, sure. But that ain't everything."

"Oh?"

Vern shook his head. "There's a scout coming this Friday. You don't have a game better than them games you've been having and you won't do better than McNeese when it comes time for college. I know you don't want that."

"McNeese ain't so bad." He took another drag from the cigarette and studied the front of the shack.

Vern spun him around and faced him. "Then if you don't care about your own damned self, think of the team. Every one of those boys has their dreams pinned on this crummy game and you're going to piss it away on beer and cigarettes. You're the damned quarterback, Jordy. You're supposed to be a leader."

Jordy bit his lower lip and turned back to the house. Somewhere in the dark, something fell into the water.

"It ain't Christian," he grumbled.

"Neither is letting your team down," said Vern. "And the school. All of Maupassant is counting on you."

Jordy sighed. "And this works? You're sure of it?"

"It always has," said Vern. "You remember ten years ago? When Joe Bob DeBorde ran for two hundred yards against Allansboro? How come ain't nobody ever got that kind of yardage on an Allansboro defense in the history of Louisiana? That's because Coach Defontenay trucked Joe Bob all the way out here—same as me with you today—and made him kiss that there poplar porch."

"P'shaw," smiled the Wells boy. "That's hogwash."

"Ain't just football, neither," said Vern. "How do you think ol' Sylvie Laney gets such good grades and got a perfect score on the SATs? How Mikey Noniados got out of trouble after that girl accused him of rape. Folks even say there ain't been a Louisiana governor since Huey Long who ain't trucked out here and kissed those poplar boards."

Jordy chewed on his lower lip and watched the house. "Still," he said, "it ain't Christian."

"I ain't asking you to take steroids," said Vern. "I'm asking you to kiss the base of that porch. I'm asking you to take all of Maupassant upon your shoulders and have the game of your life. Get into LSU or someplace like that. To follow your destiny." He put his hand on Jordy's shoulder. "Think how Renee will feel after the big game, her boyfriend the town hero. Think about how excited she'll be that night."

Jordy blushed. "Shut up," he smiled.

"Remember, take pictures of it and put it online," Vern said, slapping his back. "Or else it didn't happen."

Jordy needed to hear nothing more. He slapped his hands on his thighs, then returned to the top step of the porch. He dropped to his knees, then again to all fours. This time, when he lowered his face to the poplar boards, he put his lips against them and left them there. Behind them, a pelican or a heron or something pretty damn huge took flight and made a ruckus doing so. Jordy rose from the poplar boards and looked to his friend.

"That's it?" he asked.

"That's it." Vern took in the swamp around him and, for the first time, shuddered. "Now let's get out of here. We have a date with destiny."

Jordy didn't leave just yet. He rose from the porch step and walked to the side of the house. He hitched his pants, then unbuttoned his fly and loosed himself. He quickly set to pissing against the side of the house.

"I got a question," he called.

"What's that?"

"I kiss these boards and now I'm supposed to have the game of my life."

Vern nodded. "That's how the story goes."

Jordy put himself away and buckled his pants. He shook another cigarette from the pack and slipped it into his mouth. He lit it. "I'm supposed to throw for all kinds of yards and win the game and the scout is going to love me, my girlfriend is going to love me, the whole town of Maupassant is going to love me."

"I don't see where the problem is."

"Problem is," he said, "what's to stop somebody from Allansboro from coming over here and kissing them poplar boards?"

"I don't follow."

Jordy dragged from the cigarette and blew smoke to the treetops. Somewhere far off, a hoot owl did its thing and he stared his friend in the eye. "It's really quite simple to figure, actually. We need a big game against Allansboro to make the playoffs. Allansboro needs a big game against us. Any one of those players can truck out here and do the same as we're doing and then what? That is, if all this hoodoo talk about Madame Jolene is true."

"It's true."

Jordy nodded. "If that's the case, then we best make sure nobody else comes out this way to kiss that porch."

"How do you propose we do that?" asked Vern. "We can't sit out there at the state road cutoff every minute of the day, waiting to stop one of them corn-fed Allansboro boys. That would be ridiculous."

"Sure it would," said Jordy. He made his way back to the truck, reached into the back, and hefted out a can of gasoline. "I wouldn't dare stand way out in the darkness of Dorémieux Swamp after kissing the poplar boards of Madame Jolene's house and propose nothing ridiculous."

With the cigarette still between his lips, he splashed gasoline across Madame Jolene's porch. Then, for no other reason than there was plenty gas left, he poured it along the side of the house, at the boards, the base, and even on the fresh silt surrounding it. When all was well and done, he stood a ways back and held the smoking nub of cigarette with thumb and forefinger. He turned his head, as if to allow Vern opportunity to protest, but flicked it against the side of the house.

It caught, and in a *whoosh*, Madame Jolene's house was awash in flame. Jordy hooted and hollered and slapped his ball cap against his thigh. "Boy howdy!" he hollered. "Will you look at that?"

Vern didn't enjoy it near as much. He shook his head and watched his friend dance and strut. He looked around, out of instinct. He knew no one of consequence had seen what they did, and even if someone had, no one would care. Folks would have said it long needed doing. But still, he felt something had gone *wrong*. Something had happened they'd never be able to undo.

"Let's go," he said, then said it again more firm. He climbed into the truck and started the engine. Jordy Wells lit another cigarette, then climbed in as well. "You look about as pleased with yourself as a dog done shit the carpet."

"It weren't Christian," growled Jordy as they drove away. "But it's going to be a good game. A good one indeed."

They raced out of there just as fast as they entered. So fast, they didn't notice the one-eyed woman standing in the thicket, angrily watching from the shadows and pointing a crooked finger after the pickup. Nor were they able to hear the words she said, the tones she chanted. And neither were they able to see the mud atop which their tires raced... and oh, how it bubbled and stewed.

Vern Herman was right. Something was coming, and it was something they would long wish could be undone.

* * *

The fella had fussed and hollered about one thing or another all night, so Tessa Sherdeman paid him no mind while he carried on about being bit. She put her mouth on as much of his lips and neck as possible, hoping to keep him in the mood because, when she itched for something, she tended to get it. And Lord Almighty, was she itching.

"I'm serious," the man said, "something is biting me."

"Mosquitoes," said Tessa. She fiddled with the buttons of his dress shirt. "It's the Louisiana state bird. Nothing some Epsom salts won't fix."

"We really should go back to my hotel," he said. "It's not far from here. At the very least, it's air conditioned. Aren't you sweating?"

"You have no idea," said Tessa. She popped another button and kissed his chest. "Hold still a bit, baby."

The fella had definitely been out of his element all night. Initially, that's why she had been drawn to him. He was nothing like the other folk in Maupassant. For one thing, she'd picked him up in a bookstore. She reckoned this to be the first guy she ever picked up in a bookstore. For another, she got dinner out of the ordeal, but what an ordeal dinner had been. He insisted himself a bit of something called a *gourmand* and that he wanted to eat how the locals ate. Turned out, he really wanted nothing of the sort.

"These aren't at all like lobsters," he'd insisted over dinner. After finally managing the gumption to pick up one of the crawdads, he held it between his thumb and forefinger and stared into its tiny black-beaded eyes like he were Hamlet and it were the clown's skull. It took all Tessa had not to spit her Abita across the table in a fit of laughter. "You say they live in the mud?"

"Just eat the tail and chase it with a bit of that… what did you call it?"

"Sauvignon Blanc," he said dryly. "And I now highly doubt this was the proper selection."

"Highly doubt away," she said, then tried to explain *sucking the head* in the most suggestive manner possible.

But coming down to the bayou for a little loving pushed him to his limit. She hadn't set to tinkering below his belt yet, but got the feeling this would be more work than it would with a local boy. She cursed her desire for culture, for meaning, and for an overall longing to get the hell out of Maupassant, Louisiana.

"Can we at least get back to the car?" he asked, pointing to the rental. "All this wallowing around in the mud is starting to make me feel dirty."

"That's the point," she said. "That motel room you got has a shower, don't it?"

"It's a *hotel,* and yes, it does." He slapped at his ankles again. "Seriously. What the hell is that? That isn't a mosquito."

She sat up. "Can I ask you a question?"

"Sure."

"You like girls?"

He stopped fussing with his ankles. "I beg your pardon?"

"It's okay if you don't," she said. She waited for the cicadas to take a breath. "It's just that I'm doing a lot of work over here and I'm starting to wonder if I'm barking up the wrong tree."

"Of course, I enjoy women," he said. He straightened his shirt, lifted himself out of the dirt with his elbow. He put his other hand on her bicep. Tenderly. "Don't be ridiculous."

"I just mean, with that… what did you call it again? Your drink?"

"Sauvignon Blanc. It's a white wine from Bordeaux. Well, not the one they served back at… what did you call it?"

"Gator Charlie's."

"Yes." He smiled. "I imagine the wine I sampled back at Gator Charlie's to be completely devoid of all original characteristics of a true Sauvignon Blanc. Looking back, in fact, I would find the crayfish we ate to be more in line with the bouquet of a Sauvignon from South Africa. Normally I find the pungency of the grape to overpower cuisine, but in this case—"

"This talk is turning you on, ain't it?" Tessa squealed, delighted. She hopped off his lap like he was a Santa in the mall. "Oh my God, it is!"

"What are you talking about?"

"All that talk about wine and stuff has got you a little action down there! I felt it!"

He sat forward and put his hands in his lap. "Don't be absurd."

Tessa jumped into action. All that work was headed down the bayou and she wasn't having that. The bars would close in a half hour. She'd never make it back in time, and the only thing waiting for her back at the trailer was two channels with bad reception and maybe, if she was lucky, a bottle of Jack with more fruit flies than booze. No, this was her best chance at fun tonight.

"I think it's sexy," she cooed. She got back to work on him. "I like finding out what you like." She started in again with the buttons. "You can tell me more about what you like, if you want." She kissed his chest. "Or you can let me figure it out on my own. Tell me more about Salisbury Blanc. Where else do they have it?"

"They have Sauvignon Blanc in many different... uh, different regions. There's... oh dear, there's some in France... the... oh my, the New Zealand grape is a bit... oh... oh my, there's some in South America, but it's so horribly young and... dear, Tessa... I swear you are something of a delight..."

Tessa let him talk, figured at this point he could do most anything because she had him right where she wanted him. He'd told her where he was from, but she couldn't remember, so she reckoned it to be somewhere up North. She didn't care. She could get used to things up there. No more mosquitoes, no more drunk rednecks, no more trailer parks. From the cut of this guy, she reckoned it was style all the way. Steaks and Sauvignon Blanc. Trips to France and Chicago. She could get along. She focused on that, rather than the task before her, until his kicking and squirming got out of hand.

"Seriously, what the hell is wrong with you?" She sat up.

"What the dickens is that?" he demanded. He kicked at each ankle with the other foot as if fighting off snakes or—

Snakes. Say no more, Tessa was up and headed to the car. She counted that as another reason to favor moving up North. "Let's go," she said. She didn't wait for him. She climbed into the passenger seat and locked the door.

"What is it?" he asked. He twisted his legs this way and that and jerked up his pant leg. He laughed. "Tessa. You've got to see this!"

"Let's go back to your hotel," she said through the windshield. The mere mention of snakes sent her into a tizzy. Now who was childish? "Come on!"

He picked something from his feet. "You'll never believe it. Come see!" He held up something. She leaned forward in the passenger seat and squinted to get a better look. Unsatisfied, she reached over and clicked on the headlights. The fella was awash in light and threw up his other hand to shield his eyes. He was holding up a little crawdaddy, its pinchers clicking this way and that. "It's a crayfish!" he called.

"Do what?"

"A crayfish! Like we had for dinner."

"Crawdad," she corrected.

"Beg pardon?"

She rolled down the window. "Never mind," she called. "Look, let's go. I've changed my mind. Let's head back to your mo— *hotel.*"

He waved the crawdad around, making it dance in the high beams. "This don't make you hungry?" he laughed. "Looking at one of these don't get your stomach rumbling?"

"Are you making fun of me?" she yelped. For the first time after a night of Abita beer, mudpuppies, and sampling that foul wine he'd ordered, she had a bad taste in her mouth.

"No, honey," he said. He couldn't wipe the shit-eating grin from his face if he tried. "I'm just having a bit of fun. Come back out here."

"No way," she said. She rolled up the window. He said more, but she didn't hear it. His mouth kept moving and he kept waving the damned crawdad. She crossed her arms. All the dreams of getting out of Maupassant flushed themselves down the bayou with the rest of the shit. Christ, she couldn't even remember the guy's name. Had she compunction for it, she'd have hated herself. Instead, she chose to hate the grinning idiot playing with the crawdad out by the creek.

Seeing he made no traction and could quite possibly lose the girl, he tossed the crawdad aside and stood. He took good measure to dust the bottoms of his trousers and straighten his shirt, as if cleanliness was any longer a virtue. She watched him do so with revulsion, wondering if this was the manner of all Northern men or had she merely picked the runt of the litter. Once satisfied with his efforts, he looked up and smiled into the headlights.

Behind him, creek waters roiled and splashed and made such a to-do that she found herself surprised all of Maupassant didn't come running. She pointed and hollered, jumped up and down in the passenger seat, but all for nothing. He couldn't hear shit with the windows rolled up and didn't mind the carrying on behind him. By the time he noticed, it was half-past way too late and it was already up on him. He cried out and tried to make a run for it.

He wouldn't make it.

* * *

"A giant crawfish?" Deputy George Yates thought he'd heard it all. He leaned back in his chair and put his muddy, duct-taped boots up on the desk. Flecks of swamp dirt, mess, and cow pie scattered across his paperwork. He hated paperwork. The only thing he reckoned he needed to read was the one side of the paper that said "dollar" and the other side with "in God we trust." But he'd read considerably more and knew plenty of the reputation standing before Miss Tessa Sherdeman. "Missie, do I look like a clawfoot tub full of water run cold?"

"Do what?" Tessa looked around the police station and wished the Sheriff or anyone else save George Yates was around. No luck.

"I said, do I look like a clawfoot tub full of water run cold?"

She shook her head. "No, George, you don't."

"Then why you trying to yank my chain?" He turned the tin badge on his chest so it caught the fluorescents overhead. She squinted as if to see him better. "Because when you want to drain the water in a clawfoot, you pull the stopper with a chain. So the water drains. To empty the tub..."

She shook it off. "Listen, George, I ain't pulling your chain or whatever. Me and this—"

"Deputy Yates," he corrected. "We ain't in high school no more, Tessa."

"Fine," she said, exasperated as all get out. "Listen, *Deputy George*, you have to listen to me. Me and this tourist fella went out to the bayou after dinner and he got attacked by the biggest crawdad I've ever seen. One minute he was sitting there by the creek, and the next minute, one of its claws pulled him off into the water."

"And you ran off in his shiny rental car?"

"I wasn't waiting for that thing to get me, if that's what you're asking."

He chuckled to himself.

"That is what you're thinking, ain't it, Geo— *Deputy*." Tessa balled her fists. "Look, where's Sheriff Woodrell? Is he around?"

"He's out on a call," said Yates. "Somebody done killed all the hogs out on Old Man Keyhoe's place, and he had to see to it. Left me to deal with the rest of you crackpots."

"Maybe I should wait for him to get back," said Tessa.

"Maybe," said Yates. "But I have another option. Why don't you tell me how you really come to be in possession of that dude's rental car."

"I told you, George." She slammed a fist to the desk, rattling his cup of pencils. "What is your problem?"

He pulled his feet off the desk, his boots leaving an angry trail of muck across the top, and stood to face her. She was a head shorter, but that didn't keep him from putting a finger to her face, much like her daddy should have long ago. "Listen here, Tessa Sherdeman, this ain't the first time you've headed out to the woods with a fella and come back alone."

"That's not—"

"How many cars you ended up with the past two years?" Yates yanked open a file cabinet at the bottom of his desk and rummaged through the folders. "How many times have we picked you up with credit cards didn't belong to you? And each time, weren't nobody calling in to complain about it. You just come across these things."

"Geo— Deputy Yates, you have got to believe me." She was on the verge of tears, but Yates could care less. He reckoned without the Tessa Sherdemans of the world, he'd be without a job. He allowed for a touch of humor when dealing with the lot that slithered from the trailer communities out on the edge of Maupassant, but sometimes enough was enough. This was hardly the type of town to attract outsiders with a mess like this going on.

"I ain't got nothing to do except toss you in that cell and forget about you until Sheriff Woodrell gets back," said Yates. "And that's what I aim to do."

She had no time to react other than to back up and throw a hand to her mouth, which is all she managed before Yates was up and upon her, spinning her around and slapping the first handcuff around her wrist. He was just north of gentle and pulled her body against his, his own heart jumping through his chest and onto her back as he brought her other hand around. His breath reeked from stale coffee, his mouth stopped just shy of her left ear.

"Ain't this like old times," he chuckled.

She closed her eyes and was transported to long, long ago when she was still just a girl and Deputy Yates was George, the drunkard's kid. Him in tears over this, that, or the other and her the only person who'd be seen with him. Them both young and curious and with plenty of time to kill, which is how folks in towns the size of Maupassant got to know one another. But that was then and this is now, and in no time, she found herself whisked back to the police department, where Yates had her other hand back and cuffed and was escorting her to the cell.

"George," she said, suddenly feeling so heavy.

"I heard enough lies from you to fill seven lifetimes," he said. He took her to the cell and led her inside. She turned to say something, but iron on iron shut her up, and, with the door closed, he returned to his desk. "Giant crawfish. That's rich, even for you, Tessa. I expected something more along the lines of—"

But it was his turn to be interrupted, for the radio went nuts with the Sheriff hollering on the other end for someone, anyone, for the love of God, to please help him.

"What the hell is happening, Sheriff?" screamed Yates into the walkie. The radio squelched static in staccato bursts. Some bits of voice broke through. "Sheriff… You're breaking up…"

Tessa pitched a fit in her cell. She paced up and down the floor and shook the iron bars like a caged gorilla. "Let me out of this cell, George."

"Shut up," he hissed. He turned back to the radio. "Sheriff, please repeat. What is happening?"

Outside and down the street, an explosion rocked the building. Yates fell to the floor. Tessa held tight to the bars.

"Yates," said the Sheriff through the walkie. Bits of static popped and cracked and little was heard, just a word here and there with increasing immediacy. By the end of the transmission, the sheriff was shouting— *pleading* almost—and Tessa hung her head. For she knew what she only imagined Yates was due to discover. Yates rose with the walkie, strained to hear better, but couldn't make out anything the sheriff was saying. Nothing, that is, except for one word:

Crawdads.

And then the transmission fell silent.

Yates held the walkie and stared into it as if he half expected it to start singing. Tessa sidled up to the bars and stuck her hand through them as far as she could, but wasn't able to get any closer to the deputy.

"George," she said softly, "you need to open this cell. Listen to me, a lot of bad things are happening out there and—"

"Hush, Tessa," said Yates. "I need to think…" He slowly set down the walkie to the desk and put a hand to his own chin. He seemed to be mulling things over when from outside came the sound of screeching tires and a resounding crash, then the long, sustained car horn. He shook his head, checked his gun at the belt, and ran to the station door.

"George, don't leave me in here!"

"I'll be right back!" he shouted, and was out the door.

* * *

Once upon a time, Maupassant had been a quaint fishing village, a small community where folks carved out a living by crabbing, shrimping, and fetching anything that swam or crawled from the brackish bayou waters that bordered the town. The oil spills in the Gulf scattered industry to the wind and things dried up; it took some time to recover. After a small renaissance downtown, new shops opened and attracted a new class of tourist traveling between New Orleans and the rest of the free world.

But that being then and this being now, all the hard work done by civic boosters and city fathers had gone up in flames... literally. A speeding pickup had crashed into the side of Bordage's Filling Station, and the explosion damn near took out the entire street. There wasn't a window intact for three blocks. Power lines hung limp and lifeless, but more dangerous than ever. The donut shop was now in a shambles.

All of this was the least of anyone's concerns. Those chucked to the forefront were the three giant crawfish, looming large over the tallest buildings in Maupassant. Some eight to ten stories high they stood, claws clicking and legs waving this way and that. And for reasons anyone had yet to decipher, they were mad.

There was one crawdad up near the corner of Fremion and Broad Street, its tail dragging and plowing a wake of crumbled asphalt and destroyed vehicles. In its enormous left claw it held Brent Sozeby's prized '65 Mustang, and in its right was Crooked Tom, the short-order cook from the diner. Two blocks down stood a second crawdad, its antennae afluster and front legs trembling and whirring.

Deputy George Yates took cover in the alley behind Les Petites Curiosités, hunkered down behind a dumpster. With him were about half a dozen townsfolk, most of whom were armed to the teeth. Some had shotguns, others with rifles, and all sought revenge for what was being done to their town, all except the high school teacher gripping the ground as if it would soon be pulled from under him. Judging from the events of the evening, who knew—it just might.

Tessa Sherdeman rushed up the alley and joined them, standing just behind the two varsity players who took turns firing potshots at the crawfish up Broad Street. Yates stopped shooting long enough to thumb more shells into the chamber of his service revolver. Upon seeing Tessa, he could have breathed fire.

"I thought I left you in the jail cell," he seethed.

"You did," she answered. "I'll be sure to thank you for that at a more appropriate time."

"How the devil did you get out?"

She took a moment to catch her breath before saying, "Through the hole in the wall."

"Hole in the wall?" Yates' anger did not abate. "There ain't any holes in the wall."

"There are now."

"What in the hell put a hole in the jail?"

Tessa shrugged. "The tail, I think. Maybe it was the claw."

They were interrupted by another hail of gunfire, a series of pops and blasts, each resulting in a high-pitched, horrible wail from the monsters towering above them. Nothing seemed to work. Each bullet merely bounced off their rough exoskeletons, ricocheting back down to earth so that, after each barrage, it seemed to rain artillery from the heavens.

"What is going on here?" demanded Yates. He reached down and grabbed Mr. Hubert from the alley floor and brought him to his face. "Where did these things come from?"

"How the hell am I supposed to know?" screamed Mr. Hubert in reply.

"You're a scientist, aren't you?" Yates had reached his limit. "Aren't you people supposed to have an explanation for this?"

"I'm a high school biology teacher!" pleaded Mr. Hubert. The expression on Yates' face said he wasn't buying it, so Mr. Hubert quickly prattled off answers, pulling them from somewhere the sun had yet to shine. "Pollution," he spat. "All the oil spills in the Gulf. The tar balls. It affects the ecosystem… maybe."

"*Maybe?*" shouted Yates. "We need something a little more concrete than *maybe*."

"Eco-terrorism?" stuttered Mr. Hubert. At every gunshot, he flinched and tried to lower himself back down to the floor of the alley.

"Muslims?" said Yates. He looked over his shoulder at the crawdad scuttling up the side of the grain silo. "You think Muslims can pull off something like this?"

Mr. Hubert opened his mouth to say something, but had nothing left in the tank. He reckoned, under these circumstances, he could only bullshit so much. He softly lowered himself back to the ground and recoiled beneath the gunmen.

Across the street, in the bank parking lot, two tourists screamed from inside a minivan, their two children banging on the glass as one of the crawdads stood menacingly above them. Yates quit fussing with the science teacher and trained his service revolver as best he could on a spot between the crawdaddy's two bug-eyes. He fired in quick succession, then reloaded and fired again. The two varsity football players, both holding scatterguns, slipped round after round into the barrel, none of which did anything toward stopping the crawdad from picking up that minivan with its mammoth claw and hurling it against the side of the bookstore. It exploded and the screams from within were nevermore.

"There must be a way to stop them!" shouted the quarterback. "Think! How do we kill a regular-sized crawdaddy?"

"Boil them alive," said Malcolm Trufant. He had his daddy's rifle, but had quit firing willy-nilly in order to save ammo.

"That's the best idea I've heard yet," said Tessa. "Let's burn the entire town with them in it. I'll light the match."

Yates eyed her sideways through slits. He turned to the quarterback. "Jordy, where on a regular-sized one of these are they the weakest?"

"The underbelly," he replied. "It ain't got that shell under there."

Yates nodded, then covered his head with his arm as a shower of sparks and embers came down around them. One of the crawdads had ripped the roof from the antique shop and took out two of the remaining power lines in the process.

"We need to move quick," said Jordy's friend, Vern Herman. He gripped his scattergun and held it close to his chest. "We can't get a shot at the underside from behind this here dumpster. We're going to have to get up close."

"I don't think that's a good idea," said Yates. "You can't get anywhere near those things without—"

"We'll be fine," smiled Jordy. He slipped a cigarette between his lips. "I've got luck on my side. I can't be beat."

"What do you mean?" asked Malcolm Trufant.

"I done kissed those poplar boards out at Madame Jolene's," he said. He lit the cigarette, then stared at the flame. "Right before we set her house on fire."

Tessa put a hand to her mouth, which betrayed just how wide open it had become. She had more experience with Madame Jolene than she cared to admit, and knew first hand of the old juju woman's legendary anger. So many things threatened to let fly from her mouth, and she held each one until she could hold back no more.

"Set her house on fire?" she said. She grabbed Jordy's sleeve, her nails digging into his arm. "Why on earth would you set that woman's house on fire?"

"What they say she does out there in that swamp," answered the quarterback, "it ain't Christian." He racked the scattergun and looked over his shoulder. "Come on, Vern. Let's go. Blue forty-two, blue forty-two… Hut, *hut!*"

And with that, the two football players took to the street. Hunched low the first bit of the way, they rose, standing fully erect once they had positioned themselves below the crawdad menacing the hardware store, and pointed their weapons into its underbelly. They shouted the team's battle cry, then took careful aim, but before they could fire, the crawdad behind them, the one perched atop the antique store, swiped its colossal claw and sent them both into the side of the water tower, reducing them to a pair of smudges and smears alongside the town's giant painting of a Tiger, their mascot.

"Oh dear God, what are we going to do?" wailed Malcolm Trufant. He put his back to the dumpster and covered his head with his hands, preparing for the worst.

"George," said Tessa, "I have an idea."

"Can it," he barked. "We got worse things to deal with than whatever you're cooking up."

"George," she said, more firmly this time, and gripped his shoulders, "listen to me. We need to get in your truck. We can stop this. I have an idea."

One of the crawfish was on the move. It scuttled slowly downtown, along Broad Street, passing the alley in front of them. No one moved; no one said a word. First its horrible legs, then that massive tail, ripped up the street, fire hydrants, parked cars… everything in its path. The group of them stood stone silent until it passed, watching it, completely aware of how small they were in comparison.

"Uh… uh…" was all Yates could say.

"If you ain't got no better idea," said Tessa, "then let's go. Follow me."

"What about the others?"

"This ain't a committee!" she shouted. "They can come if they want, but we got to go."

Rather than listen to him try to argue, she grabbed him by his shirt sleeve and yanked him down the alley. Yates looked back at the others, still taking cover behind the dumpster.

"You all coming?" he called. If they could hear him over the gunfire, the screams, the clicking from the crawdads, or the overall din of destruction along the cobbled streets of downtown Maupassant, they gave little notice. Instead, they kept fighting—vain as it was—and Yates left them to it, let Tessa Sherdeman drag him back to the sheriff's department, where he was more than happy to find his truck unmolested.

* * *

Deputy George Yates drove, and not a word was spoken between them as they drove out of town. Once they reached where the state road ended, Tessa told him to take a right, which he did, and then later told him to take a left. He heard her loud and clear, but she needn't have said anything. He knew where he was going.

"A deputy," she laughed. "I bet you really think you've made something of yourself."

"And what do you think you've gone and made of yourself, Tessa?" He kept his eyes on the road. Through the rearview mirror, they could see the glow from the fires of downtown Maupassant. She tilted the passenger side mirror and looked out at the trees as they passed.

"Turn into the woods here, just up to the left," she said.

"I know the way," he grumbled. He slowed to a crawl as they entered the darkness of the swamp. "I been coming out to Madame Jolene's place for quite some time."

"Is that a fact?" She smiled ear to ear. "Don't tell me you drove out here to kiss her porch and all you got out of it was that little badge and a shit pension."

He eyed her sideways, then said, "No. We get calls all the time. Church groups driving out and throwing rocks through her windows. Pastor Dufour led some folks out here to picket and ended up raising such a ruckus that the sheriff sent me out. Not to mention all the looky-loos and folks rousting up an honest-to-goodness scare. No, I've been out to this swamp more times than I care to mention."

"And you never kissed the boards?"

Yates shook his head. "I don't believe in that stuff. None of it."

"Giant crawdads are attacking our hometown," said Tessa. "I think we can change the parameters of what we do and don't believe."

100

"That would be very easy for you to do, Tessa." Yates stayed alert. Even though he was facing forward, his eyes were all over the place.

"Can we call a truce or not, George? I mean, at least until we get out of town." She crossed her arms. "Besides, if you didn't believe in it, you wouldn't be driving all the way out here."

In front of the car, bugs flew this way and that. A few hit the windshield. They seemed to cut a swath through the wilderness.

"I'm serious, George," she said. "Why are you letting me drag you out here if you don't believe in the stuff?"

He shrugged. "We tried things my way. Maybe now we'll try them yours."

"You don't give in that easy," she said. "What's got you coming clear out here to Dorémieux Swamp if you don't believe in it?"

He still didn't answer, so she asked again. Instead, he shot her a glance that said all he needed to say. She fell silent and stared out the front window. Sure, back when they were young, they'd fooled around some. Better yet, they fooled around *plenty*. And in no way did she consider herself dumb enough to believe that any amount of loving would get George Yates the hell out of Maupassant. So, as much as it pained her, she had to drop him and move on.

Say what you want, but neither of them were any closer to leaving town. She realized that, and seeing the grimace on his face, she suddenly felt shitty for what seemed like a long line of bad decisions.

He slowed the truck and she looked right, then left. "Why are we stopping here?" she asked.

"This is her place."

"No, it ain't," said Tessa. "I don't see her house anywhere."

Yates pointed through the window. "That's because it ain't here no more."

She threw a hand to her mouth and gasped. What had once been the tiny, wooden, one-room shack was now a mountain of ash and smoldering debris awash in the glare of the headlamps. Had Yates not pointed it out, she would have completely missed it because there wasn't anything left to see.

"Dear Lord," she muttered.

"They burned the whole thing," said Yates.

"Where do you think she lives now?"

"Let's get out of the car, Tessa."

"It's no use," she moaned. "We came out here for nothing. What are we going to do?"

He opened the door and climbed out of the cab. "Come on," he said.

"Where are we going to go?" she asked. "What are we going to do now?"

"We're going to talk to Madame Jolene, just like you said."

"But how?" Tessa was on the verge of tears. "How are we going to find her?"

"We won't have to," said Yates. "She's found us."

She looked in the direction the deputy was pointing and saw the small, hunched figure standing beneath a loblolly pine, staring at them with her one good eye, her face etched with a none-too-happy expression that asked more questions than it answered.

Tessa sighed and climbed out of the truck.

* * *

The woman called Madame Jolene spun on them and threw a finger to their faces. Her one good eye flickered wildly in jerky spasms while the other floated in a sea of thick milk. At this close distance, Tessa could see the hairs sprouting from the dark mole on her chin, the hairs in her ears, the hairs seeming to pop out from everywhere on the little woman.

"You leave me be," spat the old woman. "Both of you." She turned and shuffled away into the darkness of the thicket.

Yates turned to Tessa. "Now what?"

"We follow her," said Tessa. "We came all this way…" Rather than wait for him, she stepped off the dirt road and trudged into the swamp after Madame Jolene.

"Tessa, wait," he said. He knew she wouldn't. Before she disappeared completely into the darkness, Yates ran into the muck after her.

They came to a clearing in the woods, one that was lit by more than just the full moon overhead, but also by a small fire upon which Madame Jolene had placed a pot of boiling stew. They found the old woman hovering over it, warming her hands before taking up a stick and stirring the dark, brown gumbo.

"Why can't you people leave me alone," she growled without turning around.

"Madame Jolene," said Tessa, "we need to talk."

"I *need* to do no such thing," said the old woman. Her voice dripped with an unidentifiable accent, the lilt of someone from the islands, but enough Creole to make the words a touch indecipherable. She was from another time. "I never wanted to talk to nobody, I only ever wanted to be left alone. I come out here to be by myself, and I get more folks from town than I did when I lived there. No, *chère*, I want you to leave me be."

Deputy Yates would hear none of it. "Listen, lady," he said. "I hear tell this is all some spell you cast. Now I don't believe none of this conjure business or no hoodoo, but I damn near reckon I've seen plenty I didn't believe in before tonight. So if Tessa here says you can help us, then you best help us. You hear?"

A smile slithered across the old lady's face, smoothing out the wrinkles in some areas, cracking new ones in others. She put her crooked finger away and a staccato noise rose in her throat. Tessa feared this to be laughter.

"You don't believe in hoodoo," said the old lady. "Tell me something, Deputy Yates. You go to church on Sunday, do you?"

"Yes, ma'am," he said. "Every single one. And you can bet I've never seen you there, neither."

"No," she said. "I was not there. You don't believe in hoodoo, but you just fine believing in that fancy religion with the shiny altar and the bread and the body and all that business. But I have one question for you, *chère*. When you saw that crawdaddy tear the sheriff in half with his big, bad pincher claw, did you think it was Jesus done sent down that mudpuppy, or did you think it was some old-time swamp hoodoo?"

Yates licked his lips. Tessa could see the deputy figuring on something to say, but realizing he was too deep in it.

The old lady fingered a frog skeleton, then pocketed it. "You didn't go to no church for help, did you?" Her smile brought the sickness back his way. "No, you came here."

Yates reckoned he'd had enough. Few things got his kettle boiling, but blaspheming the Lord was one of them. Sure, a jury of his peers wouldn't take too kindly to his excuse for shooting an old conjure lady, but as far as he figured, what peers he kept were getting burned up with the rest of Maupassant. He gritted his teeth and smiled.

"We ain't been nothing but good to you, Madame Jolene," he growled. "You remember when them fellas came down from Shreveport to give you a what-for? Didn't me and my boys run them off for you?"

"You did," said the old woman. "That, you did. But them was the very same boys who put on bed sheets and come around to kill my daddy. And his daddy before him." She looked thoughtfully into the boiling pot and gave it another stir. Tessa had no idea what was in there, but it smelled wretched. "I'll have you know I could take care of myself against them Shreveport boys. Just like I take good care of myself against you and the rest of your boys. What say them now?"

Tessa closed her eyes. She wanted to intervene, but Madame Jolene kept to a rocky, dark path by needling George Yates. Tessa wanted to be anywhere but here, anywhere but this horrible swamp. But where would she go? Those things overran Maupassant. She'd left it in the rearview of Yates' pickup, along with three of the biggest crawdaddies she'd ever seen. Along with enough flames to send all her memories to rubble.

"We can't keep going round and round with this lady," said Yates. He stepped closer to Tessa and, under his breath, added, "I could put a round in her right now and wouldn't nobody miss her."

"We need her," Tessa hissed. "Don't you dare. Let me try."

"Gladly." Yates stepped aside.

Tessa approached the old lady calmly. "Madame Jolene," she said, "I know you don't want to hurt all the people in town."

Madame Jolene chuckled to herself and stirred her pot.

"I know you don't," said Tessa. "You're a good person. I know folks have been mighty mean to you. You know what? They've been mean to me, too. You think I ain't heard what folks say about me? I swear I think I finally meet a guy with a moral code and next thing you know, my tits are on the internet. I hate Maupassant more than anybody else could possibly hate it."

Madame Jolene looked up, her good eye twitching like mad.

Tessa held her gaze. "But I swear I don't want none of those dumb bastards killed by no giant crawdads. No matter how much I hate them, I don't."

A moment passed. Madame Jolene had nothing to say, kept looking at Tessa and waiting for something, anything. Her one good eye, twitching this way and that. Tessa held a half-breath, then narrowed the distance between them.

"Listen," she said, "I had enough heartbreak in this town to fill ten lifetimes." She cut a quick glance at George Yates, then turned back to Madame Jolene. "And there ain't nothing I'd like better than to be a million miles from Maupassant, from Louisiana and hell, from anything that remotely smells like *backwater*. But the last thing I want, Madame Jolene, is for a mess of people to be hurt while I'm doing it. I'm going to go far, but I'm always going to be *from* here, like it or not. Do you feel me?"

Madame Jolene breathed in, held it a moment, then let it out. She turned her back to them both and looked deep within the bubbling potion on the fire before her. She sighed.

"This is ridiculous," said Yates. "I've had enough. Let's go, Tessa." He grabbed Tessa's arm and made to leave. Tessa jerked herself free. "You can stay here with this old witch all night if you want. But I got to quit wasting time and get back to town. Somebody around here has to have a shred of decency."

"Wait." The word came from Madame Jolene. She spun to face them both. She dropped her stirring stick and stepped away from the pot. "We'll need to act fast," she said. "I'll need both of you to do what I say, when I say it. *Comprends?*" When two blank faces answered her, she restated: "Do you understand?"

"Yes," said Tessa.

"Now wait a minute," said Yates. "Since the sheriff got himself killed, that rightly puts me in charge of—"

Tessa drove an elbow into his ribs and he had nothing more to say. "We understand," she said. "What do you need from us?"

"I need you to get me a fresh-killed mammal," said Madame Jolene. She scanned the edge of the woods, as if expecting one to appear. "It don't matter what—deer, dog, cat—just as long as it's fresh killed. You also need to get me some wolfsbane. You know how to find that, *chère?*"

Tessa shook her head.

"Don't matter," said the old woman. "I think I still got some down in my shop. I'll need you to run down to the bayou and get still water. It has to be still. Make sure no current touches it or it won't work. And I'll need a bottle of corn."

"Bottle of what?" asked Yates.

"A bottle of corn," said Madame Jolene. "Whiskey, son. How far do you take this Jesus business?"

"Your spell calls for a bottle of corn liquor?" asked the deputy.

"No," she answered, "but I do. It helps me settle my nerves if I cast a spell with a bit of a buzz. Besides, if I'm going to have to look at your ugly face the rest of the night, I need to be off my senses." Her throat choked a few times, and before Tessa could rush to help her, she remembered this was the woman's laughter. "And another thing…"

"Yes, ma'am," said Tessa.

The old woman put that crooked finger back in their faces. "I'm only doing this because maybe folks learned their lessons enough. Maybe them Jesus folk is right about two wrongs and all that blah blah blah. I want to be left alone after this, hear? I don't want nobody coming up the swamp to mess with Miss Madame Jolene, follow? But you are right, little one. It ain't my lot to judge. Now let's get them things and chase them old crawdaddies out of—"

And with a horrible shrieking that Tessa had come to know and fear, with the splintering of the wood of eighty-foot pines tossed aside as if they were afterthoughts, with the thunder of footsteps of a hell-bound monster never meant for this world, one of those giant crawdads marched into Madame Jolene's camp and swiped at her with one of its horrible claws. Madame Jolene had enough time to begin a scream, but that was all, for she was thrown against a sturdy beech tree and her back broken immediately.

Yates shouted things, but Tessa did not hear them right away. She ran toward where Madame Jolene disappeared, screaming all the while for the old woman to not be dead. She felt the world shaking beneath her with each step the crawdad took, its horrible tail dragging behind it, but she didn't care. The only hope they had of stopping this madness had been tossed aside like a ruined dishrag.

The crawdad stabbed wildly with its pinchers. Yates jumped this way and rolled that way, each time closer and closer to getting stabbed. He shouted some more, then pulled his service revolver and fired like mad.

"Madame Jolene," Tessa called. "Where are you? Dear God, where are you?"

"Forget her," shouted Yates. "She's gone. We've got to get out of here!"

"Madame Jolene!" Tessa found her. The old woman lie broken in half, as was the beech, her good eye gone cloudy as well. Tessa buried her head in the old woman's chest and pounded at the earth with all she had.

"We've got to go," cried Yates. He grabbed Tessa's shirt collar and pulled her into the forest. Behind them, the crawdad wreaked havoc.

"Where will we go?" she sobbed. "Maupassant is gone! We can't save it without Madame Jolene."

Yates kept running, the pines rushing past them in a blur. He never let go of her arm, and she knew that if she were to fall, he'd drag her all the way to hell and back.

"What does it matter?" he asked. "We've got to put them craw-daddies behind us!"

Tessa Sherdeman no longer cared what was what. Throughout her life, she'd been broken down and put back together so many times that she no longer knew for certain where she was headed. She had little assurances and, for the most part, felt they'd only hinder her from this point on. All she could count on, she felt, was that Deputy George Yates had her arm, and that she kept putting down one foot in front of the other as fast as she could. Where they were going did not matter. Although it had been what seemed like years since she'd kissed those poplar boards herself, her dreams would finally be coming true.

She would at last be getting the hell out of Maupassant.

STONE COLD HORROR FROM THE STARS

Brent Abell

Squinting, Dave Hardy locked on the ten-point buck through his scope, the crosshairs lined up over its heart. The rifle shook a little in his grip from the cold wind howling through the woods and chilling him to the bone. He figured an expensive coat would keep him warm this early October morning, but the frigid autumn air passed right through it; he was freezing.

Fighting off the need to run back to the truck and turn on the heater, he steadied his hands and realigned the sight on the huge deer about a hundred yards ahead. Closing his left eye, his finger began to depress the trigger when the deer looked up and jumped off into the dense thicket.

"Damn motherfucker!" he shouted as he lowered the rifle.

The sound of his voice disturbed the birds in the trees around him. They squawked before taking flight, filling the sky. The air stilled and Dave felt his breath catch in his chest. The pressure in the atmosphere grew heavy around him. Gasping, he fell to his knees and his ears popped as the earth around him trembled. A blast sounded overhead, and the force of it threw him back into the oak tree he had been hiding behind. The back of his head cracked against the tree and the air in his lungs rushed out in a white vapor.

For a moment, the world went black.

When he came to, he found he was sitting on the ground. His eyelids fluttered before finally opening. At first, the light burned his retinas and he snapped them shut again. A pungent smell permeated his nose and he covered it up with a gloved hand in a vain attempt to block the horrible odor. Cracking his eyes open again and glancing around the woods, he saw the line of broken trees, their thick trunks snapped in half like twigs, the exposed wood charred and smoking. Beyond the last smoldering tree, steam rose in the air from what could only be a hole in the ground. There was also a weird popping sound coming from that direction.

His pocket vibrated and he grabbed his cell phone from his coat pocket. He normally didn't carry it with him when he hunted, but hunting season was still weeks away and his buddy had said he would send a text if old man Williams came back home. The last person to get caught poaching on the Williams' property had gotten an ass full of rock salt from a shotgun barrel.

Instead of the warning he was expecting, the message read, "Don't forget Kevin's birthday present."

Still groggy from hitting the tree, he used the gun as a crutch and got off the frozen ground. The area past the trees still hissed, and he noticed there were no other sounds; only the strange noise coming from within the rising steam broke the silence.

Shit, I need to get the kid a present. Wonder what an eight year old would want?

The sounds coming from the hole brought his mind back to his current situation, and he wondered at what could break trees off at the trunk and leave a steaming, hissing hole in the middle of the woods.

Let's go see what we got here, he thought, and started toward what was beginning to look increasingly like a crash site.

Around the hole, the dead leaves and frozen weeds were charred and hot embers surrounded the surprisingly small indention. Leaning over, Dave saw the hole was maybe only two inches deep and about five inches wide. Waving away the smoke, he peered down and saw a small, white stone.

"What the hell?" He reached down and picked it up. It still felt warm through his insulated gloves, but the outside temperature was cooling it down quickly.

The rock was smooth and completely rounded. To Dave, it appeared to be flawless.

Then the idea struck him. A pet rock for Kevin's birthday! He had one when he was a kid and it brought hours of fun and adventure. Of course, he tended to be more imaginative than Kevin at that age, but the rock in his hand was free and saved him a trip to the store.

Dave slung the rifle over his shoulder and headed back to the truck. He checked the time on his phone. It was past noon, and he figured old man Williams would be returning soon anyway. He placed the rock in the same pocket where he kept his knife, patted it to make sure it was secure, then started the two-mile hike back to the edge of the woods where he had hidden his truck behind an old burn pile.

* * *

Pulling into the driveway, Dave could already see Kevin staring out the front window and Michelle standing behind him with her arms crossed. He opened the glove box and dug around until he found an old black Sharpie he kept with him in case he ran into a fan or two. Ever since three of the novels he'd written had become popular, the hometown crowd either walked to the other side of the street when he passed, or they rushed him, asking him to sign a book, a slip of paper, or—on more than one occasion—a boob. Michelle was with him once when a woman asked him to sign her breast. She got pissed and gave him "The Look"—every man in the history of the world had received *The Look* at some point in their lives—and he hated it.

He looked toward the house. Past the bushes, past the front window, and through the sheer yellow curtains he could already see it. *The Look*.

"Shit," he muttered. Staring at the rock, he turned it back and forth and passed it from hand to hand. For some reason that he just could not put his finger on, it didn't feel right.

The phone dinged. He pulled it form his pocket and read the text message: "STOP STALLING AND GET YOUR ASS IN HERE".

Yep, all caps… She's pissed.

Studying the rock again, he took the Sharpie and carefully drew two wide eyes on the smooth, curved surface. Chuckling, he added a wide-open mouth and outlined little teeth since the rock was white. Dave thought Kevin would find the crazy grinning rock with big pearly whites amusing. He hoped it would get Michelle off his back long enough to figure out something else.

"DADDY!" The scream came from outside his truck window and startled him.

Quickly, he shoved the newly decorated rock in his coat pocket and smiled at the bright-eyed boy jumping impatiently outside. Kevin's excitement broke his heart. Hoping his son would like the last-minute present, he opened the door and climbed out from behind the wheel.

"DADDY! Did you get anything?" Kevin asked, and bounded into his father's open arms.

Dave pulled his son into a tight embrace. He picked him up and swung him around in the air a few times before putting him back on the ground. Michelle stepped out on the front stairs and flicked a still-burning cigarette butt into the planter by the drive.

"I saw a big one, a ten pointer, but it got away," he said distantly, and from the corner of his eye he caught the blazing glare boring into him from the stairs. Suddenly, he felt his phone vibrate in his pocket. He pulled it out and looked at his, a frown creasing his face. There were no missed calls. With a shrug, he slid it into his other pocket.

"Maybe next time, Daddy," Kevin said, hugging him again.

"I did find a new friend, though, Dave told his son. "He was hiding in the woods, and when I took a shot at the buck, he came running out from behind a big tree he was so scared." He reached into his pocket for the little white stone.

"What is it, Daddy?"

"Now you have to be quiet. He's scared, okay? Hold out your hand and close your eyes."

Dave laid his fist on his son's open palm and released the pet rock. It nestled into Kevin's grasp and the boy's eyes sprang open. Dave stared at it for a moment. It seemed larger than it had been a few moments ago when he had drawn the face on it, and definitely larger than when he first found it.

"A rock?"

"Not just any rock. Look at the face on him. I had a pet rock like him when I was your age."

Then like chalk scratching across a blackboard, Michelle's shrill voice split the frosty air. "A fucking rock? Really, Dave? That's a new low."

Dave looked down and saw the tears forming in Kevin's eyes. Instead of dropping the rock, he held it tighter and rubbed it against his cheek.

"I like it, Daddy," Kevin sobbed, and then grabbed his father by the neck and squeezed hard.

"Ignore your mother," Dave whispered before letting go of his son.

The screen door slammed when Michelle entered the house. Taking Kevin's hand, Dave led him into the house, where supper would be in silence and the muted tones of "Happy Birthday" to Kevin would be shrouded with resentment and anger.

* * *

Kevin snuggled under his blankets and grinned at the white rock grinning back at him. Three Cheerios and a two-liter bottle cap full of water sat before it, just in case the pet rock felt like eating or drinking during the night. Its eyes never closed or blinked, but that only freaked Kevin out for a few minutes. Once he realized how much his mother hated the pet rock, he loved it even more.

From down the hall, he heard his parents yelling at each other and slamming doors.

"I love you, Jake," Kevin whispered, and petted the rock's top one last time before burying his head under the pillow and falling asleep.

* * *

When the early morning sun hit Kevin square in the face with its blinding light, he jumped up and looked for Jake. The rock was still on his nightstand, but the Cheerios were gone and the bottle cap empty. Cereal crumbs surrounded Jake and water still glistened on the marker-drawn mouth.

Kevin cocked his head to the side and thought about Jake's size. He grabbed the rock and held it for a moment before placing it gently back on the nightstand. It covered more of his hand and it felt heavier than it had last night. In fact, he thought Jake looked like he had grown overnight after eating and sleeping.

Do rocks grow? He climbed out of bed. Slipping into his dinosaur slippers, he picked up Jake and ran out of his room to watch cartoons.

* * *

Dave stepped into the kitchen and watched Kevin wolf down a bowl of cereal in a matter of seconds. Their tabby cat Fluffy sat on the table's edge, ready to pounce at any cereal that might escape the bowl. Forcing a smile on his face, he walked in and ran his fingers through his son's hair.

"About time to get this cut, son. Before long, all the neighbors will think you're a girl." He chuckled and glanced at the table.

The white rock sat there, its large cartoony eyes staring up at him. Looking at it a little longer, Dave thought the smile and big, white buck teeth appeared larger than they had yesterday. It unsettled him because he felt the rock was silently laughing at him. He locked eyes with the rock.

"Kevin, have you named it yet?" Dave asked, his eyes never leaving the rock. Something tugged at his gut, and it wasn't the pizza from last night.

"I named him Jake after the dog in the *Adventure Time* cartoon," Kevin exclaimed, and jumped up from the kitchen table. He reached out for Jake, but stopped short.

Jake vibrated and shook. Fluffy jumped to the floor and tore off toward the living room. The white rock appeared to go blurry with the vibrations, then stopped as quickly as it had begun. Buggy Sharpie eyes still stared at Dave, but now they seemed bigger, the grin larger.

"Kevin, take Jake to your room and get it cleaned up before your cousins come over for your birthday party. Oh, have you seen my pocket knife? I took it hunting with me, but now I can't find it anywhere."

"No, I haven't seen it." He picked up the rock from the table. "Dad, can Brian come over before the party? I want to show him Jake."

"That's fine. Just make sure you get your room done before lunch."

Watching his son bound down the hall to his room, a dark feeling settled over him. He remembered feeling the knife in his pocket when he got home yesterday, but now it seemed to have vanished.

He heard his bedroom door open and his wife begin her morning litany of complaints and prayers to the almighty "God Dammit."

* * *

He covered his ears and tried to fight back the second wave of tears. Once his bedroom door shut, the screaming started in the kitchen. Kevin's red, puffy eyes looked at Jake. The big, round eyes looked back him with understanding. He turned around and began to pick up his Legos from off the floor.

Reaching deep in his toy box to find the squirt gun he could use to defend himself against his cousin Nathan, he stopped. Behind him, the humming he heard began to grow louder and louder. The vibrations from it shook his Star Wars figures from the shelf, and he stuck his fingers in his ears to fight off the noise.

As quickly as it began, it stopped.

Kevin spun around and checked on Jake, afraid the loud noise would have broken the pet rock. Inspecting Jake's sides, he picked him up and looked at his bottom.

"Ugh, Jake, are you getting fat?" Kevin grunted and heaved the rock on to his desk. Jake landed with a loud thump and rolled a few inches. He looked at the place where the rock landed and saw the indention framed by freshly chipped paint.

Jake sat upside down, his huge grin turned into a scary frown.

"Jake, are you bigger?" he asked the pet rock and poked him with his finger.

Something scratched at the door to his room.

"You stay put," he ordered Jake, then went to open the door.

Once the door creaked open a crack, a blur of orange, red, and black rushed into the room and jumped up on the desk. Fluffy arched her back and her fur bristled and she hissed at Jake.

Jake sat there upside down and did nothing, his mouth still turned in a frown.

"Fluffy! Get off there and leave Jake alone!" Kevin shouted, shooing the cat from his desk.

Fluffy ran and dove beneath his bed. Kevin hit the floor and threw up the blanket hanging over the edge of the bed. The scant light reflected off the cat's yellow eyes. Fluffy hissed loudly, striking out at Kevin's hand. Recoiling in surprise, he let the blanket fall back into place as he got up.

When he looked at Jake, he saw that the rock had doubled in size.

"Jake, you were the size of a softball, but now you're almost as big as a basketball! How'd you grow so fast?"

The huge maker-drawn eyes stared and the unmoving mouth grinned up him. Kevin shuddered and left the pet rock on the desk while he ran from the room like wild dogs were nipping at his heels.

Three markers on the desk jerked and slowly moved closer to the rock's smiling maw. Pressing against the white surface, they faded into the rock until they were completely absorbed.

Sated, Jake shuddered and vibrated again.

* * *

"That is so cool, Kevin," Brian Tate said in amazement.

Kevin sat a hot dog and a handful of Doritos in front of Jake and backed away. Brian slid a bowl of water over to the rock, then he quickly pulled his hand away.

"What now?" Brian asked.

"Now we go outside for a few minutes, and when we come back, we'll see if he eats the stuff."

"I didn't know rocks ate stuff," Brian said with a shrug of his shoulders.

"I didn't think so either, but every time I leave stuff out for him, it disappears. Since Dad gave him to me last night, I've fed him about ten times, and each time I'm sure he grew some. He wasn't always a stone basketball," Kevin said, smiling at his two best friends.

"Tag!" Brian slapped Kevin's back and ran to the door.

"No fair!" Kevin shouted, and took off after the neighbor.

Both boys tore out of the house into the yard. They didn't know it at the time, but Jake had begun to eat.

* * *

Dave opened the truck door and felt between the seats, then glanced around the floor boards for his knife. The blade wasn't expensive or an heirloom with meaning, but he wanted to make sure Kevin didn't grab it. If he hurt himself with it, Michelle would never let him hear the end of it. Her mission at the moment was to make certain he never forgot what a shitty gift a pet rock was.

Laughter sounded from the backyard as he shut the truck door. Walking over to the fence, he smiled as he watched Kevin and Brian running around. Dave sighed and was glad Kevin could have a good time and forget the problems between his mom and dad. He didn't blame the kid for his moody behavior; if he had to witness his parent's marriage dissolve before his eyes, he'd had have issues, too. When he first fell in love and married Michelle, everything had been like a fairy tale. His writing career took off with his debut novel, *The Fields*. The money from the paperback rights, foreign print rights, and a monster film option allowed Michelle to stay home and try to finish her degree in accounting.

Once she became pregnant with Kevin, she turned resentful, and as time went on, her attitude toward him and their son soured. He knew she resented them both and off-handed comments from her dad only served to confirm what he already knew.

Dave pushed the painful thoughts back into the deep darkness of his mind and left the boys to play and enjoy their childhood. He needed to get back to work; he had a family to support and a book due to his publisher in a few weeks.

* * *

Kevin and Brian rushed back to Kevin's room and threw open the door. Jake was still perched on the desk, but the hot dog had vanished and a scattering of Doritos crumbs surrounded the rock. Orange powdered cheese streaked Jake's marker mouth. The empty water bowl was tipped over and sat on its side.

"Dude, you have to be bullshitting me," Brian whispered.

"Nope. When I feed him he grows," Kevin replied.

Brian poked Jake and laughed. "I can't believe I fell for you telling me it eats and stuff," he snorted.

"He does eat! And then he grows bigger! When I first got him from my dad yesterday, he was only the size of a shooter marble," Kevin explained.

"I think your dad came in here and made it look like the rock ate everything. My mom says your dad lies for a living because writing is just lying to people."

Tears formed in Kevin's eyes.

"Don't cry, Kevin. I'm sorry," Brian said apologetically.

"Get out! I have to clean my room!" Kevin cried out, and waved his finger at his bedroom door.

Brian didn't say a word as he hung his head and marched out the door and back to his house.

* * *

After lunch, Dave noticed Kevin climb up to his tree house. Alone. Something must have happened between him and his friend, but Dave hadn't wanted to bring it up earlier while they were eating at the table. His cousin Nathan would be at the house soon for the birthday party, but Kevin wasn't showing his usual exuberance toward his cousin's pending arrival. As Dave sat behind the keyboard pounding out the words to his new book, the eerie silence in the house unsettled him. Michelle had gone out earlier to pick up some last-minute supplies for the party, and to get Kevin a better gift because "a rock with some shit drawn on it" was not, in her eyes, an acceptable present. Never mind that the boy carried it around everywhere and loved Jake; she just wanted to belittle him in front of his son.

Gazing out at Kevin in the backyard, he noticed Jake wasn't with him.

* * *

Kevin bounded into the house after Michelle pulled into the drive, some of his upbeat demeanor returning. He watched her carry his cake into the house, along with two shopping bags and a fistful of balloons that swayed in the breeze. By the time he took off his shoes and ran to the kitchen, she had already put the cake on the counter, tied the balloons to the chair, and disappeared with the bags. Judging by their distinct color, he pegged them as Toys R Us bags. "Fluffy! Fluffy! Come here, girl," he called out while untying a balloon from the bunch.

He hunched close to the floor and waited to bop Fluffy with the blue balloon when she came rushing into the kitchen. Last time he did it, she hissed and fought the balloon to its death. The cat looked victorious that day with the shredded green pieces stuck to her claws. He had never been able to get a straight answer from his parents on how bits of green ended up in the litter box the next day.

Five minutes ticked by.

Ten minutes ticked by and still Fluffy hadn't heeded his call.

Michelle opened her bedroom door and came down the hall with four colorfully wrapped presents in her hands. Bright red bows sat atop packages with characters from different cartoons Kevin watched.

"Kevin, who told you you could have a balloon? Those are for your party. Now get off the floor and help me get the kitchen cleaned up," she huffed, setting the presents on the counter.

He sat there and stared down the hall at his bedroom door. He had left it open a little in case Fluffy wanted to get out while he was outside. Now, the hall was silent and he longed for the clicking of claws on the hardwood floors.

"Mommy, where's Fluffy?" he asked timidly.

"I haven't seen her, so get your butt up and help me now, young man. I'll call everyone and cancel your party if you don't hurry and help me," she ordered, anger lacing her every word.

As Kevin got up, he swore he heard a belch coming from his room.

* * *

Dave rubbed his forehead and moaned. Even though his in-laws and their devil spawn were still ten minutes away from arriving, he could feel the headache beginning to pound deep within his skull. His eyes glazed over as he stared at the computer screen in front of him, making his disposition even worse. He knew how this new novella was supposed to end, but it seemed unable to make that last journey from his mind to his fingertips. Alice in Chains played in a low volume from the laptop, so he didn't hear the knock at his office door.

A little face appeared in the space between door and frame. "Daddy, I can't find Fluffy and I'm afraid of my room."

"Afraid of your room?"

"I think Jake hates Fluffy," he said, his voice barely a whisper.

"What makes you say that, big guy?" He hated faking concern, but the story was really eating at him.

"The way he looked at her and moved."

"Jake moved?"

"Yeah, Dad. He started to shake and his smile gets bigger every time I feed him. The bigger smile is creepy and it scared Fluffy away. She's hiding under my bed, but I've been afraid to go and check on her."

The sound of his son's voice weakened him to the point where the problems with the new story were no longer of any concern. "Let's go take a look," he told Kevin, and pushed up from his chair.

Ruffling the boy's hair, he let his son lead him through the door and down the hall to his room. Inside, all Dave heard was silence.

"You go first, Dad," Kevin stammered and backed away from the door.

Dave pushed it open and gave a startled shriek.

Kevin stuck his head out from around his father's leg to see what his father had seen. He let out a small gasp and dove back out of the doorway. Inside, Jake was on the floor with his huge grin and wide eyes… only now he was bigger than the Pilates ball his mother used to work out. A fluffy bit of white fur hung out from the mouth and a red smear dirtied the pristine rock.

"Kevin," Dave stammered, still trying to wrap his head around what they had seen, "I'm going to shut the door and we're going to pretend we didn't see that. Everyone will be here in a few minutes, so let's just go outside, play some games, and eat your cake. We'll deal with this after everyone leaves, okay?"

Kevin nodded, then took off down the hall.

Alone again, Dave stared at the gruesome rock and the remnants of its meal. He picked up the heavy rock and sat it back on Kevin's desk. A sense of disbelief mixed with fear filled him, and when the doorbell rang, he turned away and quickly shut the door.

* * *

Once the door closed, Jake began vibrating again and the maniacal smile grew even wider. The wooden desk beneath it cracked and groaned. When the desk gave way, Jake crashed to the floor. Splinters and shards of wood that littered the floor started to shake violently, then disappeared into the white rock. Blankets rose from the bed and flew at Jake. Toys swirled in the air like a whirling dervish and flew toward the grinning stone. Anything the rock could summon to it became its feast. More and more quickly, Jake entered his cycle of food absorption and personal growth.

* * *

Dave opened the sliding door to the backyard and left the kitchen feeling apprehensive. It wasn't the shrill cries of five kids running around the yard or the sarcasm he heard coming from his mother-in-law as she spoke to Michelle about her husband who "lives in a fantasy world instead of getting a real job." Really, it wasn't even the fact Michelle didn't even bother to defend him and agreed with her mother. Deep down, it was the rock. The pet rock he gave his son had eaten the cat and was getting larger.

"You look preoccupied, buddy," a voice came from behind Dave.

"Oh, hey, John," he replied, snapping out of his thoughts.

"Something wrong?"

"Nah, just thinking about something."

The ground rumbled.

Everyone froze and looked around, surprised by the tremor.

"An earthquake?" one of Michelle's dimwitted brothers asked. "Here?"

Dave turned and, with sarcasm weighting his words, said, "It's Indiana! We live near a fault line!"

Now all attention was on him and he noticed Michelle's eyes burning with anger. He felt the piercing glare digging through his skin, but he didn't care. He already figured out what was causing the rumbling.

Michelle stood on the back deck and raised her hands in the air. "It's over, so let's get back to the party!"

Loud popping sounds and a series of crashes erupted from the house. The rumbling started again and the house shook violently. Instead of ceasing after a few moments, the noise became a roar and the house shuddered in front of everybody. The party goers stared at the bulging weathered boards of the building. Something snapped and the window to Kevin's room exploded outward, showering the yard and a few of the kids with glass and wood fragments.

The structure groaned and the boards bowed outward, the slats splintering. Michelle turned to see what was happening when the back of the house cracked open like an egg. Jake came sliding out from the hole in the wall, its grin now taller than the adults standing with their mouths open in awe at the twelve-foot-tall terror.

When it moved again, Dave pondered how a rock could just glide on the ground so smoothly. He opened his mouth to shout at Michelle, but nothing came out. All the years of their marriage and her treatment of him and their son silenced his words.

Michelle stood there and frantically waved her arms. She screamed curses at the rock. She turned and glared at Dave and Kevin again. "What the hell is this, Dave? You really did it now! My family is here and you ruined the party I planned with this damned pet rock that I don't even begin to understand what Kevin likes about it!"

A noise like a hoarse cry erupted from Jake. The low bass he emitted rolled over the party goers, causing Michelle's family to back away from the stone.

"This is the most ridiculous bullshit I've ever seen!" She yelled at Jake and slapped at his smooth, white surface. She felt him vibrate and she slowly backed away. Fear began to rush through her as the pet rock shifted.

Jake rumbled out onto the lawn, and without wavering from his path, ran over Michelle. Her dying cries were cut short by the humongous stone sitting on her body. Dave saw an arm sticking out from under Jake and it began to twitch wildly. A red pool formed at the pet rock's base and slowly flowed across the patio, staining the concrete.

Dave looked over at Kevin, whose face was empty of all expression. He didn't cry or scream; he remained silent as his pet rock slipped through the yard and crashed through the fence into the Houseman's yard next door.

Michelle's dad, Frank, came over and started yelling in Dave's face. He acknowledged the fact words were coming out of the man's mouth, but all he heard was a buzzing coming from his father-in-law's lips.

"Do something, you worthless son of a bitch! Call nine-one-one or something!" he hollered and grabbed Dave by the shoulders.

Dave snapped back to reality and swung his arms up, knocking Frank's hands off of him. "Don't ever touch me again," he muttered at Frank and walked over to his wife's bloody remains. Kevin ran over and hugged his legs, the tears finally starting to fall.

In the distance, the rumbling continued. The cacophony of squealing rubber fighting against asphalt and metal rending against metal and stone filled the autumn air. Horns blared and the sounds of destruction could be heard all around the city. The shrill scream of sirens echoed down the street as the law-enforcement authorities pursued a giant rock named Jake.

* * *

We interrupt this program for a News4 Alert. The citizens of White Creek are being ordered to stay inside their homes and not to panic. The local sheriff's department and the fire crews are out dealing with the wreckage left behind by what is being described as… Are you kidding me? Who put this on the teleprompter? Really? It is being described as a large white rock that is two stories tall with big round eyes and a large grin. It appears to be heading to Helfrich's Hollow, so please, if you are in the area, leave now and get out of the rock's path. I repeat… CLICK.

Mildred Parker turned off the television and shook her head.

"What's this world coming to, Harry, when the news is telling us a giant rock is rampaging through town." Mildred huffed and looked out the window. Stumbling back, she made the sign the cross and began reciting the Lord's Prayer.

Harry glanced up from his book and saw his wife doing the same thing she'd been doing for the forty-three years they'd been married when something odd happened—or when she over reacted to something. She prayed. The look on her face alarmed him, though.

"Mildred, honey, what is it?"

"Right... they're r-r-right," she stammered and took another step away from the window.

The tremors being felt around town grew louder outside the Parker house. Harry pushed up from his recliner and hurried to the window, where he pulled back the curtains just as a giant, round rock glided over the fire hydrant, sending water into the air like a geyser. He'd left his truck parked out by the curb because he had planned on going to the VFW to throw a few beers back, but the smiling rock rolled right over it, crushing it flat. The white behemoth passed over the cherry red remains of his ST. It made a screeching sound that made what few teeth he had left ache.

Cars were crushed beneath the weight of the huge rock, but as Jake passed over them, the flattened vehicles disappeared into its bottom; it was like the rock was eating everything in its path. Toppled street signs and fence posts became a tidal wave of debris breaking toward the rock, which took in every morsel that came its way. The air around it shimmered as the stone shook, and with each bit it took in, it grew bigger and bigger.

Mildred fell backward onto the couch and closed her eyes. Harry opened the front door and watched in horror as the hulking boulder moved down the street, crushing everything in its path.

* * *

Dave grabbed Kevin and rushed to his Mustang. Pushing past the in-laws, he decked Frank, and feeling a small bit of satisfaction, he got into the car and tore off in pursuit of Jake.

"Daddy, where did you get Jake from?" Kevin asked. His eyes were big like Jake's, but sadness clouded the usually rambunctious boy's gaze.

"I found him when I went hunting yesterday morning. There was a loud explosion, which scared off the buck I was about to shoot, and I found the rock in a smoldering hole. I had a pet rock as a kid and thought you'd love it. I thought it would help open up your imagination," he explained as he drove the car through the twisted and smashed husks of cars that marked Jake's path.

"Where's he going?"

"Shit! He's going back to where I found him… Helfrich's Hollow." Dave muttered the last few words and pushed the gas pedal to the floor.

While his father sped along Reading Road toward Miller's Creek, Kevin stared out the window at the destruction Jake left in his wake. Flames roared, and people stood on their porches and out on the sidewalks with terror-stricken faces. Some cradled bodies that littered the ground while others tried to pull survivors from the wreckage. Even though he was only eight, Kevin could read the pain and questioning expressions on each tear-streaked face.

Next to him, his father was focused only on the road ahead.

* * *

Deputy Larry Moss placed the last barricade across Reading Road and hustled back to his patrol car. The ground beneath him started to vibrate and the rosary beads hanging from his rearview mirror began to sway as the car rocked under the force of the tremors. His radio crackled, but the sound was lost under the increasingly deafening rumbling. Grabbing his shot gun from the dash, he turned around and almost peed himself.

Coming up the road, moving over the faded asphalt like it rode the air, was a giant white rock. Birds exploded from the trees and flew at the rock, smashing into the massive black-toothed grin. As feathers and blood painted the rock's white surface, it vibrated wildly.

The giant rock slowed its advance, eventually coming to a halt, and Deputy Moss froze. Roadside dust, stirred up by the thing's vibrations, surrounded the beastly rock and formed a dirty cloud around it. His mouth dropped open when the white behemoth slowly start to grow. The atmosphere felt denser and he found it difficult to breathe. Raising his gun, he pressed the trigger and emptied the chambers into the happy-looking rock. The rounds struck the stone and chips spewed into the air as each bullet struck its target. Small pieces of the white rock showered the roadside and an unholy cry erupted from the behemoth. Moss dropped his gun and covered his ears.

As suddenly as it stopped, the giant rock started moving forward again. Ducking behind the open door, Moss snatched the radio from its cradle.

"Emergency, emergency! This is Moss out on Reading Road outside of Helfrich's Hollow. That thing is headed right for me. I shot it and it grew! I repeat, it's not stopping! Oh my God..." His radio message was cut off when he dropped the mic and dove to the side of the road. The giant rock paid him no attention as it moved over the patrol car, flattening it into the pavement.

In the distance, an army of local sheriffs and other available law-enforcement personnel within a forty-mile radius was speeding toward the Hollow.

A little further back, a father and son closed the gap to catch the wailing sirens.

* * *

Dave glanced at Kevin. The boy was huddled against the door under a blanket he had gotten from the back seat. Reaching over, he ruffled Kevin's hair, letting his son know everything was going to be okay, before returning his attention to the ruined road ahead.

"Daddy, are they going to hurt Jake?" the little boy asked with a weary voice.

Taking in the wreckage Jake had left behind, he answered as honestly as he could. "I don't know, son. I don't know what's going to happen." But seeing the damage—the broken and uprooted trees and the large indentions in the asphalt where the humongous rock had settled its weight—he knew what would likely happen to Jake, but he wasn't about to say anything that might cause Kevin further emotional trauma.

"What about mommy?" Kevin whimpered.

Tears formed in Dave's eyes and he fought back the urge to release the floodgates. "She's gone, son. It's just us now."

"Why did Jake do that to her?"

"He didn't know, Kevin," Dave answered, trying his best to explain things to the boy in a way he could understand. "He was only moving on."

"You and mommy fought all the time and it made me sad."

Dave barely made out the words through the flood of tears finally flowing from Kevin. Inside, his heart broke and guilt lodged in his throat like a ball.

"I want to you to remember she loved us, Kevin. Every time you feel alone or sad, she'll be there with you, in your heart, to protect you."

"I know, Daddy. I know," he whispered and went back to staring blankly out the window.

In the distance Dave heard the distinct sound of a helicopter overhead and his mind raced. Thoughts blazed through his head; he placed the burden for the blood Jake had shed squarely on his own shoulders. Memories of Michelle, crushed beneath the rock, saddened him, but after ten years of Hell, he was also filled with a sense of relief. The house in ruins, his son scared for a giant rock he picked up, and a town burning in the rear-view mirror weighed heavily on him. He hadn't bought a gift, had tried to be a cheapskate. He had brought the rock into White Creek!

Deep in his gut, he knew the blood of the dead was on his hands.

A figure jumped out in front of the Mustang, snapping Dave back to reality. He slammed on the brakes and jerked the steering wheel to the left. He hit a rut and the car bucked before skidding to a halt beside the crushed remains of what might have once been a police car. Shaken, Dave looked in his mirror. Deputy Moss was running toward the car, his hands waving wildly in the air.

"Stop! You can't go any further!" Moss yelled, still waving his arms in the air.

Are you kidding me? Stop? I just about hit a fucking car that lost a match with a big rock, Dave thought, trying to gather himself. He looked back and saw Kevin staring silently out the window at the flattened car. Dave feared the day's events were finally beginning to hit the boy and he was in a state of shock.

Dave slowly opened the door and got out of the car.

"Dave! What the hell is going on around here?"

"Look, Larry, I need to get down there," Dave said, pointing toward the Hollow.

"Sheriff said nobody is allowed to go in there while they try to stop whatever the fuck that was that tried to crush me in my car."

"Here, drive my car. Believe me, I did this and I have to try something to make it right again," Dave said, and swung open the passenger side door. Kevin didn't say anything, but climbed over the seats into the back.

"Make it right? Shit, did you drive here the way I did? That thing leveled everything along Reading on the way here."

"I don't care. I have to do something," Dave pleaded.

"Okay, I'm gonna get my ass handed to me over this, but let's go." Moss climbed behind the wheel as Dave slipped into the passenger's seat. Larry Moss had never broken a direct order in his entire professional career, but seeing the look in Dave Hardy's eyes convinced him to do it just this once. Without giving it another thought, he tore off down the road, heading deeper into Helfrich's Hollow.

* * *

The buck stopped next to the trees and scanned the wooded area around it. Silence reigned as he checked the brush for his mate and their offspring. Taking a few cautious steps toward the road, the buck froze and sniffed at the air. The ground beneath him shook and the vibrations went up his legs and into his rear flank. His survival instinct kicked in and he jumped across the road.

Jake plowed into the large deer, and its body exploded in a crimson splatter that stained the rock's surface. The bones, fur, flesh, and blood were consumed by the behemoth. In a matter of seconds, there was no evidence whatsoever that a deer had been there.

Jake felt the food enter his system and it fueled his need to grow. He paused for a moment as the vibrations seized him, and then he was on the move again. He was driven by the need to return to where he had arrived. He didn't know why he needed to return, he just knew had to, and he would allow nothing to get in his way.

* * *

Sheriff Jared Castle addressed his men through a megaphone. "Men, keep the thing on this side of Miller Creek! Use whatever force is necessary!"

The rumbling grew louder as the rock drew closer. Twenty police cars encircled the Reading Road Bridge that spanned Miller's Creek. Thirty-five men stood in riot gear, helmets, and had shotguns pointed toward the road heading into the Hollow. Deer, squirrels, and rabbits rushed from the underbrush and the sky darkened as flocks of birds took flight from the trees. The ground shook and the trees to either side of the road began to topple. The men heard the snapping and splintering of wood.

Appearing from around the bend in the road, about two hundred feet from Miller's Creek, the round shape slid toward the line of officers. The smile beaming down on the men looked surreal. As quickly as it began, the ground stopped vibrating and the behemoth rock stared with its big, happy eyes at the rifle muzzles aimed in its direction.

Sheriff Castle lowered his bullhorn and lifted his rifle toward the rock. Spitting out the wad of chew he kept tucked in his left cheek, he yelled through gritted teeth, "Fire!"

The Hollow erupted in gun fire and the rounds raced toward their target. Some shots missed and others hit their mark, sending chips of stone and dust into the air.

"Cease fire! Cease fire!" Sheriff Castle cried out and took off his sunglasses so he could better assess the damage.

He only noticed a few places where the smooth, white exterior was chipped and scarred from the hot rounds. Black carbon streaks marred the surface and smoke poured from the holes in Jake. Suddenly, the trees lining the road began to move like they were being blown by gale-force winds. Castle's jaw dropped when the wooden missiles flew through the Hollow and disappeared into the giant rock. The air around it blurred and he swore the thing grew. Dust and dirt from the road formed a thick cloud around Jake, blocking it from the men's view.

The air grew still and the dust settled. Castle and his men raised their weapons again and fired. The rock emitted a loud shriek and the earth shook as the rock began moving again.

* * *

Deputy Moss and Dave heard the volley of gun fire as they approached Miller's Creek. Moss gave the Mustang more gas and Dave grabbed onto the door to keep from being thrown into the driver's seat.

"Looks like we're late to the party," Dave said, giving Moss a sideways grin.

"Don't count on it," Moss shot back, and spun around the corner.

Moss slammed on the brakes and Dave's head smacked into the dashboard. Kevin rolled from the backseat and thumped onto the floor. The car skidded and fish-tailed to the right, turned sideways, and came to a halt a few inches from Jake.

"Son of a bitch!" Moss bellowed and threw the Mustang into reverse.

"Dad! Jake looks bigger," Kevin shouted and pointed at the rock just inches in front of them. He crawled up and stuck his face against the window.

"Kevin, you're right," Dave said, his mouth hanging open in surprise. "He is bigger."

Moss jerked the gear shift into reverse and put the pedal to the floor. The tires spun and threw pieces of rock and broken wood around in a cloud of dust and burning rubber.

"Larry, get us in front of it," Dave shouted as he rolled down his window. "Now!"

The car tore away from the rock and Moss spun the wheel around so fast the car felt like it was going to go up on two wheels. Once the car settled back onto the road, Moss punched the accelerator and peeled out. The car rushed by the monolith and all three within the Mustang stared out the window at the menacing pet rock named Jake, who just a few hours ago helped a little boy try to cope with his parents' relationship problems.

That same rock had also killed the boy's mother and destroyed part of White Creek on its way out to Helfrich's Hollow, where Dave told his son he had found the strange pebble. Guilt raced through a father's consciousness and sadness brought a son to the verge of tears.

The car swung around Jake and tore off toward the police line.

* * *

Sheriff Castle stared in shock as the car pulled out from behind the rock and sped toward them.

"Hold your fire!" he shouted and lowered his gun.

The Mustang pulled around the police line and the brakes squealed, bringing the car to a halt in a spray of gravel and dust. Castle spun around and started to raise his bullhorn when Deputy Moss and Dave Hardy jumped out and ran toward him.

"What the fuck are you doing, Moss?" he shouted at his deputy.

"I found Dave Hardy and his son, Kevin, not too far from here, and since the rock crushed my patrol car, I needed a lift," Moss explained, still trying to catch his breath.

"What the fuck is he doing here?" Castle screamed in Moss' face, spraying the deputy's face with spittle and bits of chewing tobacco.

"Sir, he might be able to help us. He's the one responsible for the damned thing," Moss answered, tipping his head in Dave's direction.

"You're responsible for this? What the Hell did you do, Dave?" Castle sneered at him.

Dave quickly explained the chain of events that had brought them to this moment.

"Michelle let you give Kev a rock for his birthday?"

"She's dead now, and no, she hated me for it," Dave said quietly.

"Sorry, buddy," Castle muttered, and put his hand on Dave's shoulder.

Dave shrugged of the consoling hand and stared at the rock he'd brought back.

Up the road, the ground rumbled again and Jake started to slowly slide toward the line. Each man brought up his weapon and took aim at the rock. Weird, glowing green goo leaked out from the places the bullets had struck and chipped the massive stone. With nerves on edge, the men stood their ground. Sweaty hands curled around weapon grips and trembling fingers twitched on triggers. Perspiration beaded foreheads and slowly rolled down cheeks in thin streams.

Castle turned and faced the men. "Wait for it," he said, trying to steady their nerves and calm their fears. "Wait for it."

The closer the grinning pet rock came, the harder the road beneath them trembled. The eyes took in each man, and if a rock could glare, Jake was definitely giving them the eye. The ooze dripping down its face gave an eerie glow to the rock's stark whiteness, and its drawn-on mouth seemed to curl up into a sneer.

"Ready, aim, fi…," Castle called out, but the sheriff shut his mouth before issuing the final order.

Unseen by anyone, Kevin had crept from the back seat and now darted out from behind the Mustang and ran toward Jake. He waved his arms wildly and the men could hear the boy sobbing through his heavy breaths. Once he was close to the rock, he dropped to his knees and bowed his head. His wailing grew louder, and as suddenly as Jake had started moving toward the line of police officers, the rock stopped, as though Kevin was the one thing it didn't want to hurt. The vibrations running through the ground quieted, leaving the Hollow in silence, save for one boy's pitiful cries.

The men held their collective breaths, and Dave pushed passed the sheriff and sprinted after his son. Castle motioned for the men to lower their weapons.

Kevin raised his head, looked Jake's marker eyes dead on, and sniffled.

The rock's glare appeared to soften and the maniacal grin to take a softer, more friendly quality.

"Jake, please stop," Kevin whimpered. " You're all I have left besides my daddy, and I don't want them to shoot you."

The rock vibrated and a tremor ripped up the road. Trees swayed from the tremors, and in the distance the sound of falling wood echoed through the forest.

Dave froze. In his mind, he visualized the rock crashing over his son just the way it had done to his wife. The vibrations died off, and Jake sat unmoving before Kevin. He gave Jake a double take and squinted his eyes, not sure of what he was seeing.

Sheriff Castle stepped out from behind the cars and came up to stand beside Dave. "Did that thing just get smaller?"

Surprised by the sheriff's sudden appearance at his side, Dave whispered, "I think it did."

Kevin slowly rose from the asphalt and walked over to Jake. Placing his hand on the smooth, white surface, he whispered to it again. "You're my best friend, Jake, and I forgive you for my mommy. I know she's with me now, but I'm sad and I want you to stop. Please, Jake."

Overhead, the news helicopters were joined by three camouflaged military AH-64 Apaches with full ordinance. The news choppers backed away, give the attack crafts clearance.

Castle looked up at the sharks circling above the tree line.

"Dave, we need to pull Kev back now," he said in an urgent voice.

"I think you're right," Dave acknowledged, nodding.

In front of them, Jake vibrated again, blurring his smooth curves, then stopped again. From his Sharpie-penned eyes, something leaked from the corners and pooled on the ground around him.

Kevin ran up and hugged his best friend, crying and touching his cheek to the white rock. The edges blurred again, and the tremors that ran through the ground felt weaker than they had moments ago. Jake shrank some more, and he was now less than half his two-and-a-half story height.

The Apaches moved into position and hovered in strike formation.

"Dave, grab him now," Castle shouted as he retreated toward the cars.

Dave broke free from his paralysis and ran to his son.

Kevin whispered to the rock and the two completed the bond they began forming earlier in the day. His hands moved over the smooth surface like a boy petting a beloved dog. He felt something tug at him, and the next thing he knew was being swept into his father's arms. Bouncing up and down while his father ran, Jake looked to Kevin like he was nodding his head yes.

Once Dave was safely behind one of the patrol cars, the first volley of missiles was fired from the Apaches. The Hellfire roared at Jake and the chain guns rained down shots. Each was true and struck Jake. The thirty-millimeter rounds bit deep into the rock and the Hellfire blew a huge chunk from Jake's left side when it detonated. An unholy cry erupted from the rock as the other two Apaches fired their payload.

When they hit simultaneously, the sky exploded and bits of rock and metal showered the Miller's Creek Bridge. A burning shockwave washed over the patrol cars. The rolling fire quickly burned itself out, leaving behind a smoldering crater where Jake once sat.

The Apaches, their mission complete, turned and flew off back to the Reserve base a few counties over.

Dave and Kevin stood up and gazed out at the burning road and the smoking hole where Jake had made his last stand. In the distance, more sirens approached, accompanied by every news van in the tri-county area.

"Is he gone, Daddy?" Kevin asked, reaching out for his father's hand.

"Yeah, son, but he'll always be with us here," Dave said, and pointed at Kevin's heart.

"I love you, Daddy," Kevin said and began to sob again, the full weight of the day hitting him head on.

"I love you, too," Dave answered and pulled his son close.

* * *

The sun began to set in the west and the last of the military convoy drove away from Helfrich's Hollow. The military clean-up effort took three days, but Reading Road was once again open. Life was slowly returning to normal in the town of White Creek.

Beyond the cat tails, hidden on the far side of Miller's Creek, three shapes emerged and began walking toward the bridge, each one walking a bike.

"Why'd we come out here again?" one voice complained. "If my old man finds out I came down here, my ass is grass."

"Only because your dad is mayor, Greg!" another hollered and laughed.

The third one followed behind and kept his eyes glued to the ground.

"Hey, Vic, you alive back there?" Greg asked. "Ryan, he still with us?"

Looking at his friends as he pushed his glasses up on his nose, Vic shook his head. "No, I'm dead."

"Seriously?" Ryan responded.

"Look, Greg," Vic said. "I'm watching the ground to see if I can find a piece of the meteor that hit here." He went back to scanning the ground around him.

"My dad says that's what the Army guys who did the clean-up said it was, a piece of rock that fell from the sky and tore through the center of town," Greg said and stopped at the bridge spanning Miller's Creek.

Ryan laid his bike down next to Greg's and both turned to watch Vic pick through a pile of dead grass and leaves.

"See anything, Vic?" Ryan asked, dropping to a crouch.

Vic began to pick through a pile of dead leaves, brushing the decaying remains of summers gone by, when something caught his eye. Under a large oak leaf, hidden by a fallen branch, he felt a smooth, hard object.

Carefully, he leaned closer to the ground and saw a perfect white pebble lying on the damp earth.

Greg and Ryan started digging through the debris on the creek bank, moist, moldy remnants of the spring flooding. Neither one noticed Vic quickly stuff his hand in his pocket and resume scanning the ground.

"This is pointless, they got it all," Vic sighed and stood up. He brushed off his muddy knees and shrugged his shoulders. "I guess the military did get all the meteor stuff cleaned up."

"Yeah, I'm thirsty. Let's go see if Anne is working at Big Top Burger today," Ryan said as he mounted his bike.

"Sounds good to me, man. Need to catch a peek at your woman?" Greg said and began circling his bike around the road.

"Vic, you in?" Ryan asked and started to pedal off toward town.

"Yeah, yeah, I think I am," Vic muttered, patting his pocket.

He thought it odd the change in his pocket didn't jingle, and he swore he felt his pocket vibrate as the three boys biked back into White Creek.

BFF

Kerry G.S. Lipp

The giant green frog fell from the sky like the meteor that meant the death of the dinosaurs. The impact splintered the crust of the earth, its webbed toes digging in, sending shockwaves deep down into the planet's core. It triggered fault lines and created new ones. The pulse the frog set off launched waves stronger than those that turned Pangaea into puzzle pieces.

No one knew how or why, but many thought that whatever gods responsible for sending the raining plague of frogs to Egypt got it dead wrong. The gods didn't send millions. They sent one, nowhere near Egypt, and he was a big, nasty, mean motherfucker.

Lucky for most of the world, but horribly unlucky for North Dakota, the giant frog landed on the main drag of Bismarck. There wasn't much there to destroy in the first place, but buildings crumbled, suffocating dust clouds stirred up, fires blossomed, panic reigned, and the killing started.

Ask any of the billions of people on the planet in any country, culture, or language, how they thought the world would end, and giant frog probably wouldn't have popped up in a conversation, even among the most psychotic of meth heads.

But that's the way it happened.

The United States got it the worst, with Bismarck, North Dakota, a city and state that 99% of the world barely knew existed, labeled as Ground Zero. North Dakota is on the Canadian border, so initially, the Canucks got it pretty bad, too.

The frog's feet were the size of Super Wal-Marts, its webbed toes the size of school buses. They flattened entire city blocks before breaking through the crust of the earth.

Then the chain reactions began.

Around the world, volcanoes erupted, covering cities and towns with nature's napalm. Tsunami's as tall as skyscrapers couldn't put out the fires, but they did drown millions of people. And the frog hadn't even started to attack; it had only landed.

In the hours that followed its crash-landing on earth, the frog, with its deep-planted, trapped feet, shrieked sonic booms that burst the eardrums of the lucky survivors. Their eyes widened and their ears bled while they watched the behemoth struggle to free its feet. Concrete and blacktop sprayed ripples of flying matter from the point of impact like a violent storm surging surf-worthy waves on a crowded beach, but the waves were broken glass and chunks of rock and sharp metal shrapnel flying fast, hitting hard, and slicing deep. Deadly rifts spread like violent squid tentacles. The debris cut the people and property down like Civil War cannons did to the approaching infantry.

People ran, but never fast enough. And people hid, but neither Kevlar nor nuclear bomb shelters could protect them from the deadly and imminent wrath flying at them from the nucleus of Ground Zero.

* * *

Vic held his wife tight with one hand while staring at the phone clutched in his other. The breaking news blared from their bedroom television. He knew they would be calling—and they did. The phone lit up and vibrated. He kissed Marilyn on the cheek, threw his half of the blanket aside, and got out of bed to take the call.

"Vic," he said, holding the phone up to his ear. He was barely able to maintain eye contact with his wife as he watched the tears well in her eyes and spill down her cheeks. She didn't try to conceal the fact that she was crying. He gave her the best smile he could before turning his back to her and looking out the window.

"I'm guessing you've seen what's happening," the voice said. Unflinching, unapologetic, emotionless.

"Yeah," Vic said.

"We need you," the voice said.

"Surprised it took you this long," Vic said.

"It hasn't even been half an…"

Vic ended the call. He didn't need to waste time hearing the general's version of the story. Vic knew that everyone on the planet knew as much as the government did at this point. Nothing. He put his clothes on and stopped when he saw Marilyn softly sobbing, watching him get dressed and prepared. They stared at each other for a few moments.

"I know you have to go," she said. "I know who you are and what you do, and I love you for it."

Vic smiled at her. "I'm the guy who…"

She joined him and they spoke the rest in unison.

"… does all of the shit the rest of the world thinks just happens."

He kissed her long and hard and deep, rubbing his hand lightly on her slowly growing stomach. "And I love you," he said. "I do it for the world, but mostly I do it for you. You are my world." He paused, and she smiled at him. "And I do it for you," he said, kissing her belly. She laughed.

He kissed Marilyn again. He loved kissing her. Vic knew what he did. So did Marilyn. The sense of urgency between them was something few other couples could ever experience. He was a soldier and she was his mate. Every kiss they shared could be their last, and their passion reflected that. *If only every couple could live like that*, he thought, kissing her lips, then her forehead, then the top of her head, losing himself for a moment in the scent of her hair.

He never promised her he would be back because he never lied to her.

"I love you," Vic said, kissing her one last time before turning and walking out.

"I love you, too," she said. She didn't beg him or threaten him to come back safe; she didn't need to. All she said to his back as he reached the door was, "Be careful." He didn't turn around. He never did.

Vic blinked back tears as he left the room. He hated leaving her. Hated leaving them. He didn't believe in empty promises, so all he ever said was "I love you," then walked away. He wished he could turn around. He wished it hard every time he turned away from Mare, but he loved her so much that the tears stung every time, and he would never let her see him cry.

He scolded himself when he realized he had hesitated for a fraction of a second, then he took off down the stairs, out to the garage, and slid behind the wheel of the car.

He would be at the briefing in 20 minutes, and even though he had calmly left his wife, he'd already seen the ruination of part of the world and he was terrified. He was brave, though. And he didn't know if they could stop it, but he wanted to be part of the effort that tried.

Driving had always been therapeutic, and what he saw while he drove the streets told him more than any news broadcast. People on the streets looked frantic, but traffic was moving at a surprisingly normal pace. He would have time to be scared later; for now, he rolled down his window and blasted the chugging guitar riffs, thundering drums, and motivational lyrics of the most inspirational band of all time. Hatebreed's "Never Let It Die" throttled his speakers and he nodded along, mouthing all of the words: "Bonds are strengthened when they've been tested and mended when they've been torn. So give all of yourself that there is to give 'cause in life to have never risked is to have never lived." Vic smiled as he embraced the adrenaline coursing through his body.

* * *

General Kill—that was actually the guy's last name, no one knew his first—met Vic outside, handed him a cup of coffee, and together they walked back into the building.

"So what's happening, Kill?" Vic asked.

"Shit storm. Nobody knows anything. The president wants to talk to us. He's baffled. Hell, we all are. There's been some bad ideas tossed around so far, and I mean really bad, so we've got nothing to work with."

"And are they acting on these bad ideas?" Vic asked.

"You'll see," Kill said, opening the door to the conference room.

Familiar faces greeted Vic with post-apocalyptic grimness. The conference table faced a projection screen that was tuned into a CNN broadcast of the events. Not much had changed since Vic left home, but what he saw chilled him. It was all those bad 1950s B-movies come to life. The giant frog towered high above the crumbling skyscrapers, using its tongue to steal fighter jets out of the sky as if they were nothing more than bothersome flies. A chill swept through Vic's body.

The jets fired round after round at the behemoth, aiming for its eyes, but the optical membrane was so thick, it shielded the creature from the barrage of missiles and bullets. The pink tongue shot out to grab two planes out of the air; there were explosions in the sky as it collided with the fighters. Realizing the futility of their attack, the planes retreated and the frog continued to spread its destruction. Kill was right, just bad ideas so far. But were there any good ideas when dealing with something like this?

"BFF," Kill said. "That's what we're calling him."

Vic stared, confused. "Doesn't that mean best friends forever?"

"Normally, yes, but in this case it means big fucking frog. You know how the military loves their acronyms, and this fucking thing has earned his."

"Jesus," Vic said, and at that moment the big screen switched from the CNN broadcast to a live feed from the White House. The face of the President of the United States took up most of the screen. The past few hours had aged the man dramatically, and there was an uncharacteristic look of defeat etched deeply into his features. The President cleared his throat and began to speak.

"Gentlemen," he greeted, "thank you all for coming on such short notice. I'll make this quick because we need to act immediately. We've got a big fucking problem."

Did the president just drop the "F" bomb? Vic asked himself.

The president continued. "Our first attack and rescue mission has failed miserably. We scrambled fighter jets to try and bring BFF down. As I'm sure you've seen on the news, that frog was snatching them out of the air like he would flies from a lily pad. I'll be honest with you all. I'm out of ideas. We can't move tanks in because of the earthquakes. The jets didn't even scratch him. I'm getting calls from countries all over the globe that are already feeling the effects of BFF. They are demanding we stop it. Some are offering help, and some are offering threats." His words trailed off as his eyes welled with unshed tears.

"I'm… I'm out of ideas, gentlemen. Things are in ruin and it's only going to get worse unless we can stop this thing. We need to act, but I don't know where to go from here, so if anyone has an idea, I'm listening. Please, help me. Help your country. I don't care how bad or how silly you think your idea might be."

"I'm sorry, Mister President," Kill interrupted, "but could you hold that thought? Something's happening. Check your news channel, Mister President." All eyes turned to another television screen in the conference room so they could learn of the latest developments.

"Holy mother of fuck," Vic whispered, then silence descended as they watched the disaster unfold before their eyes.

* * *

The giant green frog blinked just in time to protect itself from the barrage of missiles fired at its face. Its eyelids were as thick as prison walls and as strong as tempered iron. It saw the jets flying through the air as nothing more than flies, and with lightning quickness, its tongue was jettisoned from its mouth, wrapped around the planes, and then were drawn back in before the pilots realized what was happening. Sometimes they blew up and the fire burned, but they were all sucked in, twisted metal and delectable meaty treats within, and it savored them all. There was no end to its appetite, as the massive belly had plenty of room for these loud, buzzing flies.

It sucked in as many planes as it could until they were all gone, which was fine with BFF; it was growing bored. It had been stuck in this same spot for over an hour, and it needed to move. It looked all around, as if considering the best course of action. Which direction held the most promise when it came to more food?

The easiest direction, since that was the way it was facing, was south, so BFF's muscles tensed as it prepared to make the leap, but then it realized just how deeply its feet were sunk into the earth. There was no way it could hop in its current condition; if it did, it ran the risk of ripping off its own legs. It looked around to see if there were any more flies buzzing around, and content that it would not be distracted, it went to work freeing its feet. Its tongue shot out and picked up huge chunks of rock, which it drew back into its mouth before spitting them as far as it could. Boulders the size of whales flew through the air to flatten homes and farm houses miles away. Driven by hunger, the frog prepared to make the jump. After testing each limb to make sure it was free, BFF leapt.

* * *

Vic watched the whole thing live as the news cameras captured the giant frog making the leap. The back legs propelled it forward, and the camera followed the beast's trajectory until it disappeared from view. There was no telling where the thing would land. The commentator was too shocked to speak, so the cameras panned back to the spot the frog had deserted, capturing in great detail all the rolling rubble and smoking ruins left in BFF's wake. After a full thirty seconds, the newswoman was able to shake off her disbelief and continue with her update.

"It appears the giant frog has moved on to another location. While its final destination is unknown, we can tell you that it hopped to the south. After seeing the damage it caused here when it landed, we can only imagine the damage that will be caused when it finally lands again. We'll continue to follow this story and report back as soon as we have a confirmation of the giant amphibian's latest location."

"Jesus Christ," Kill said. "When it hits, it's probably going to rock the world just like it did the first time."

Vic nodded, as did the President and the others gathered around the conference table.

A brief tremor shook the building and Vic's head snapped up. Every muscle in his body tensed as he looked around, waiting for the tremor to pass. Confusion reigned as panic began to sink into all those present. No one knew if that was an aftershock from the frog's initial landing or the result of landing after its current hop.

"Mister President, we *need* to do something," Vic said. "BFF is going to destroy the world."

"I agree." The president nodded, his fingers steepled. "I'm open to ideas."

"Can we nuke him?" Vic asked.

"We've considered that option," the President said. "No one is crazy about detonating a nuke on our own soil, even if it is to stop BFF."

Nods around the conference table.

Someone entered into frame and whispered into the President's ear. "No," the President gasped.

"Mister President?" Kill asked.

The President regained his composure. "BFF just landed on Dallas. The city is in ruins. It's like a countrywide nine-eleven."

"You mean to tell me," Kill said, the disbelief evident in his tone, "that BFF jumped 3 states south. That's… that's thousands of miles. And he did it in what? Minutes?"

"Less than one minute," the President corrected grimly. "Between the initial destruction and the aftershocks, if we don't stop BFF, he's going to destroy the country, and maybe the world before the day is over."

* * *

BFF came down hard and fast, smashing into Dallas with a force equal to the havoc it unleashed on North Dakota. Dust kicked up like a desert storm and chunks of rock and earth flew for miles in all directions, destruction raining down across some of the nation's landmarks. An avalanche of rock destroyed the Ft. Worth airport and reduced Cowboy's stadium to rubble.

With its belly full of the hot, twisted metal of the war planes and the pilots that flew them, BFF turned its attention to the giant lake just ahead. A calm, isolated lake had its smooth-as-glass surface shattered by the massive weight falling from the sky. Waves rolled out in all directions in response to the seismic fissures BFF fired deep beneath on the floor of the lake. The heat of burnt wreckage in its belly ignited an insatiable thirst, and it opened its mouth to let the waters run in and down its tunnel-wide throat.

The surrounding landscape was similar to its previous location, although the destruction it caused was on a much larger scale. It looked to the sky, but there were none of those flies that threw their stingers buzzing around, and all BFF heard was a collective rumble of shaking buildings and screaming humans. It enjoyed watching the structures collapse and those tiny insects running around. Its tongue lashed out and snagged a few of them, swallowing them whole, they were so tiny. It took another mouthful of water, then went to work freeing its buried feet.

Slurping up rocks and spitting them in all directions, BFF watched the insects running away from the falling rocks. The clear pathways between the tall structures were flooded with insects of all shapes and sizes, some running and some gliding across the surface on round objects.

All the water it drank went right through it. While it continued to dig itself free, it released a heavy stream from its rear end. The warmth of the fluid was uncomfortable, and it renewed its efforts to dig its feet free. Once that was done, BFF would move on to a new location.

* * *

"My God," Kill said, "it's taking a leak."

No one in the room spoke.

"He's going to give the entire city warts," the representative from the Center for Disease Control said, horrified.

"That's toads, not frogs, and that's a myth anyway," said the consultant they roped in from the local aquarium.

"Guys!" Vic said. "No one's going live long enough to find out anyway. BFF just hit America's city with a piss tsunami. We've got to do something!"

Chatter, whispers, and murmurs broke out around the table. Disarray, depression, and discord took root and began to spread.

The President's voice, shaky but firm, rang out from the speakers as he tried regain control of the situation. "Just before I received word that one of this nation's most beloved cities had been destroyed by a big fucking frog with the audacity to piss on the ashes, I was about to ask for ideas. I know the destruction is awful, but we need to stay focused. We need ideas. I don't care how bad or how crazy, we need to stop this mother-fucking frog."

Vic's head snapped up, as though a lightning bolt had just zapped his spine. Without saying a word, he lowered his head again, wanting time to think through his idea. The President didn't miss Vic's actions.

"Major Willer?" the President asked. "You look like a damn comic book character with a thought bubble. What is it?"

Vic laughed out loud as he considered the absurdity of it all. At the idea of a giant frog invading the United States, destroying it, and pissing on it. His idea to take down BFF was just as crazy. He pictured it all in his mind and he laughed until tears streamed down his face.

"Major Willer!" the President shouted, snapping Vic back to the desolate reality that they all now faced. "What's so goddamn funny?"

"I've got an idea," Vic said. "But it's way out there."

"There's a gigantic frog hopping across America, Major Willer. What could be more out there than that? Let's have it. Sometimes the only way to kill crazy is to be crazier."

"Okay," Vic said. He got up and started to pace around the room, like a teacher before his class. "You guys ever catch frogs as a kid?"

Almost everyone, including the President, nodded.

"It wasn't hard," Vic said. "You went to the pond and most of them wouldn't even run; they'd just sit there with their throats throbbing and let you pick them up."

"I don't think we've got anything that will pick up BFF," Kill said.

Vic shook his head. "I only did it once," Vic said. "It was gross and I've felt bad ever since, but here it is. I guess everything truly does happen for a reason."

"Get to it," the President said.

"One time me and my friend Carl Edwards caught a frog. Carl had some firecrackers. It was his idea, but I helped. I held the frog while Carl shoved a firecracker up the frog's ass. Once it was stuck up there good and tight, Carl lit that thing like a candle on a birthday cake and let it hop away."

The room exhaled a collective sigh. A couple of them grinned sick grins of sadistic nostalgia. On the screen, the President nodded.

"We've seen that missiles and bullets are not harming BFF," Vic said. "And I completely understand the reservations about dropping a nuke. But if we can figure out way to stick one halfway up his ass, I think we can kill the frog and a good chunk of the blast damage and radiation can be contained."

No one in the conference room spoke as the idea played through in their heads.

"Brilliant," Kill finally said, breaking the silence.

"I agree," the President said. "We just need to figure out how to get it in there."

"There's more, Mister President," Vic continued. "This is the part that you're either going to love or hate."

"Let's hear it."

"We don't have to do it on American soil."

The President cocked his head as he seemed to think it through, and Vic glimpsed a knowing smile on Kill's face across the conference table.

"This is pure speculation Mister President, but if BFF hops again and he continues on his current course, his next hop should take him somewhere near…"

"Mexico City," the President and Kill said at the same time.

Everyone sitting around the table shifted uncomfortably in their seats. Some shook their heads, some nodded, but the grotesque idea made sense. They could stop BFF and they could do it with minimal American casualties. Or at least without adding to the destruction already caused by BFF.

Everyone sat in silence, thinking over not only the idea, but the implications. Vic spoke.

"Think about it," he said. "We're as shell-shocked as the rest of the world, not to mention that our country is Ground Zero. We immediately scrambled planes to try and take down BFF, and it just nabbed them out of the air with his tongue like they were mosquitoes. We don't know how to stop this thing. Just when we are about to mount a second wave of attacks, the big fucker leaps half way across the country and ruins another American city. The death toll must be in the tens of thousands. Maybe even millions. I think we've got sympathy on our side here, gentlemen, and no one needs to know the rest."

"And what exactly is the rest?" the President asked.

"This is speculation, but from what I think we can all gather, BFF landed and hopped after what? How much time?"

"Almost ninety minutes," someone said.

"Okay. And when it landed, all of its feet were embedded deep in the earth. We all watched that damned frog work for a good chunk of those ninety minutes to free itself. Once it was free, for whatever reason, it hopped and landed in Texas. That was how long ago?"

"About fifteen minutes," the same voice said.

Vic was rolling now. "So if we work a similar time table, it's safe to assume that BFF will hop again within the next sixty to ninety minutes. Last time it hopped, it headed due south. It's still facing in that direction, so I think we have to assume it's going to continue south?"

"Do you think we can safely assume that?" the President asked.

"No, I don't," Vic said. "But we have to strike, and if we can get it to continue south, the nuke we drop won't be on the United States. It might do it on its own, but it might not. If we hit it with bullets and missiles from the north, west, and east, maybe we can manipulate its course."

They all chewed on that for a few minutes.

"But we saw it snatching those jets out of the air like flies," Kill said.

"Greater good," Vic said. "Those men don't need to know that it's a suicide mission. We'll tell them something about new discoveries with BFF's peripheral vision. That it can only see certain degrees, and that it's so slow to turn his head, that they'll have all the time in the world to maneuver out of there."

"But that isn't true," Kill said, anger filtering into his tone and his face becoming flushed.

"No," Vic said. "It isn't, but they don't need to know that."

The President sighed deeply and inhaled, getting ready to speak, but Kill beat him to it. "How can you justify that? How the fuck can you send those men to their deaths? These are American soldiers you're talking about."

"Don't get all self-righteous on me now. You guys do it every day, so don't give me any shit. But I get to because I'm going to be the one flying the nuke straight up BFF's ass. I'll be dead, so I don't give a shit how you all deal with the damage control."

Once again silence descended upon the room. Those gathered around the conference table opened their mouths and then closed them without speaking.

"And why would you volunteer for a suicide mission, Major Willer?" the President asked.

"Because somebody has to," Vic said. "And I don't know about you, but I would only trust a volunteer." Vic paused. "And that volunteer is me. I'd trust me a hell of a lot more than I'd trust the guy who drew the short straw."

"Jesus Christ," the President said. "Is this really what it's come to?"

Vic nodded. "Not nukes or an invasion or global warming, or the lower-class revolution that this country has feared for so long. None of that. A big fucking frog. There's no way that…"

"This is how the fucking world ends," Vic cut him off. "And we're fighting back, making sure that BFF *isn't* how the world ends," he said, keeping the emotion off his face and out of his voice. The perfect poker face. He was nervous and full of fear, but he could and would execute. In fact, Vic volunteered because he didn't trust anyone but himself to finish this. He just hoped a nuke up BFF's ass would be enough to finish the job.

It had to be.

"Think about it," Vic said. "BFF has been here for less than two hours and it has already destroyed half the country, not to mention the ripple effect on the rest of the world. If we don't do something, that slimy green fucker will turn this planet into fragments floating through outer space before the end of the day. And I don't see anyone else with any ideas. Believe me, I would love an alternative, but we don't have dick."

No one said a word, and Vic couldn't be sure, but he thought he saw a hint of tears in the eyes of both Kill and the President. Two men he'd rarely ever seen raise their voices. Everyone knew Vic was right.

"What about your wife?" Kill asked.

"She's pregnant, too," Vic laughed, then sighed and shook his head. He could no longer keep the emotion out of his voice or off his face. It wasn't funny, but it was. And that's when the tears and the soft, hopeless laughter heard at funerals or after bad news began spread around the conference table.

"I can't let you do this," the President said, but he didn't sound at all convincing.

"With due respect, Mister President, you can and you will. There's no time to cross-reference a database to find another pilot with my experience who happens to be suffering from suicidal depression or terminal cancer yet still able to fly the plane. We both know that they don't exist and we don't have time to look. I can. I will. And I am your man."

"But why?" Kill asked.

"Because I'm the only one here who can. And we need to move now. We have no time."

"But your wife? Your child?" the President asked.

Vic wiped a tear from his eye and said, "Yeah. And that part sucks, but it's what we have to do. If no one does anything, it's only a matter of time, and based on what we've seen, I would give it a few days, maybe less, before an earthquake, the weather, or even looters get to our families. My child wouldn't even have a chance. I've never met her—or him—but I'm happy to sacrifice myself to give that little one a chance it might not have if we do nothing. Sometimes the dog shits in your yard and you've got to clean it up. Prep the fighters. Make sure BFF hops south and I'll take care of the rest."

"We can't control it," the President said. "What if it hops somewhere

down to check in on their pal BFF, and that the resulting nuclear fallout wouldn't give birth to even greater horrors.

Vic screamed the words to the heavy metal blaring through the jet's speakers as BFF's giant, flexing sphincter came into view. Vic looked out his windows and saw the planes open fire on BFF before breaking formation.

Now Vic was alone. The escorts were gone, the music was loud, and the bombs were ready. Holding the flight stick tight in his hands, he took a deep breath, and in that long breath, reaffirmed the peace he needed to make with everyone and everything.

He flew in low, coming up from the bottom, and with four hot nukes, his jet hit bullseye and kept going, forcing itself deeper into BFF's asshole.

BOOM!

Splat.

Salvation?

GAMS

Tracy DeVore

Blue Ridge Mountains, 1923

Jacob Dugger filled his tin cup under the dripping spigot, then sipped the white lightning, sucking in a hiss as the hot liquid hit his tongue. Good. *Damned* good. Sure, he was sampling more than he ought, but he didn't want to take any chances. The last load had cost him plenty when Floyd called it 'skunky' and wouldn't pay him.

Jacob shook his head and glanced over at Gams, hitched nearby chewing on a pile of sugar cubes without a care in the world. "You believe that, girl? Skunky! That recipe was good enough for my daddy and his daddy, but I guess not for Mister Fancy-Pants Floyd Bartlett."

He dipped a spoon into the cup, raised it to his nose and took a deep whiff before touching a lit match to it. "Ha!" His grin widened at the blue flame engulfing the spoon. "Ain't nobody gonna complain about *this* batch o'shine, no sir!"

He filled two dozen stoneware jugs and pounded stoppers into them, then loaded them into the little wooden cart, gritting his teeth against the pain in his joints.

"I'm sore as a risin', Gams, but we'll be eatin' good tonight." He pulled the halter through her bridle and hitched up his cart, chuckling as he scratched the top of her head. He named her Gams after Floyd told him it meant legs. Gams! What a word! Suited this leggy girl just fine.

"Gee-up!" He tapped the reins, but she wouldn't budge. Danged stubborn beast.

"Let's go, Gams. Get a wiggle on!" He tapped the reins a bit harder. "I know you're hungry, girl, we're all hungry. But we won't have nary a crumb 'til we git paid, so let's go."

Gams snorted and took a few slow, steady steps before stopping again.

"Consarnit, girl! Move!" He slapped the reins and she started into motion, still slow, but at least she was going. Jugs of moonshine clinked together as he walked behind the cart, guiding it down the rutted mountain path. "Durned beast, cain't you go no faster? The sun'll be gone before we get down, then how we gonna see the path? I'm thinking I ought to put you out to pasture, let you fend for yourself."

Gams looked back at him with her big, sad eyes, and he was sorry he said it. She was a good 'ol girl, a hard worker, and strong as a team of oxen, and just as stubborn. Had been ever since he found her in the woods. At first, he'd been damned scared seeing a giant ant—she was bigger than his bird dog!—but she'd been sweet and friendly, and seemed to need him. Heck, she even seemed to grin at him when she was good and fed.

'Course, he never told anybody about her. He reckoned if he did, they might take her away from him, want to run some kind of secret tests or something, like the government did in the mountains here a few years back. 'Course if it wasn't for that, he wouldn't even have his still, so he supposed he should be thanking them.

Just to be safe, though, whenever he brought the 'shine down to Floyd's place, he always unhitched Gams and tied her to a tree up the path a ways, then pulled the cart by hand the rest of the way. Sure, it caused him more work, but he didn't want to lose her. He sure as hell couldn't afford to buy a horse or even a mule. The little bit that stingy speakeasy owner paid barely kept him out of debt, but he knew better than to grumble about it.

Men who crossed Floyd had a way of disappearing.

And ol' Gams, well she seemed happy just staying nearby, waiting for him to come around and feed her; he never once had to tether her. And it was as if she could sense him. She'd be out of sight in that big dirt hill she'd built, but no sooner would he round the bend in the road, she'd be crawling out of that there mound and come right over to him. She wasn't any trouble, never complained or made much noise, so the revenuers had no reason to ever come snooping around. His still was safe. It was the perfect arrangement.

"Aw, girl, you know I didn't mean it. But we got to git down there quick, before Floyd opens up to customers, or neither one of us'll have any supper this week and Sadie will tan my hide." The thought of his stern wife almost sobered him.

Gams picked up the pace, faster, but not too fast. This suited Jacob just fine on the rocky path. The cart tilted on every curve, threatening to overturn.

"I swear, Gams, there weren't so many rocks last time we went downhill. Little buggers must be breeding up here!" He cackled at his own wit, then started into a coughing fit. It didn't last more than a few seconds, but that was long enough to distract him from the path ahead.

Before Jacob could refocus, the cart started a sideways slide and he lost his footing on a carpet of hard little balls.

"What the—"

The cart crashed into a tree and tipped over. Feet skidding and arms flailing, Jacob watched the jugs fly through the air, almost in slow motion, then shatter on the ground. Twenty feet below, he finally lost his balance and landed on his backside with a loud "Oomph!"

He reached down and scooped a handful of the offending culprits.

"Danged chestnuts!" He tossed them aside and glanced up at Gams standing next to the cart. It now stood on its back end. Empty.

He scrambled uphill, fighting the rolling chestnuts, and stared at the busted jugs, their contents spilling out and disappearing into the ground. He dropped to his knees. The wet ground saturated his dungarees, making them stick to his skin like molasses.

"Oh no, Gams, oh no!" He scrambled around, searching for anything he could salvage. One intact jug stood next to the cart.

He crawled over and picked it up, cradling it as he settled himself on the ground and leaned back against the bottom of the toppled cart.

Gams had come unhitched and scooted toward him, dragging the long reins behind her. Edging closer, she sniffed at the sweet, sticky moonshine covering the ground. She leaned down and lapped a few drops that had landed on a raised tree root.

Jacob sifted through nearby pieces of broken jugs, trying to connect them together like a puzzle. He crossed his legs Indian style and placed the bottom half of a jug in his lap, then tried to fit the top half on it gently. It stayed for only an instant before toppling off.

"It's ruin't, all ruin't! Every last drop! 'Cept this one." Jacob looked at the jug in his hand. "Might as well enjoy it, girl. This could be our last meal." He uncorked the sole survivor and took a long swallow. "Sadie'll kill me for sure, and without me, who's gonna feed you?" He took a few pulls from the jug, then leaned his head back and closed his eyes. "If any critter deserves a good meal, Gams, it's you."

Her belly growled loudly, a long, mournful sound, and the licking became more aggressive, but the ground quickly soaked up all the liquor that had spilled.

"Sorry, girl," Jacob slurred. "I'll feed ya when—" Jacob's ears perked up at the sound of running feet and he stretched his neck, peering down the hill.

Floyd Bartlett stumbled into the clearing. He looked mad as hell and drunk as a skunk, his round face all red and puffy from climbing up the path and his bloodshot eyes blazing.

"What the hell is going on here?" Floyd lost his footing and took a sliding nosedive into the chestnuts.

Jacob jumped up as fast as his shaky legs would allow and rushed to Floyd's aid. He was grateful to see Gams out of the corner of his eye, backing into the shadows before Floyd could catch a glimpse of her.

Floyd squatted on all fours, cussing a blue blaze about the chestnuts, Jacob's ignorant ass, and all the wasted 'shine.

Jacob edged over and reached a hesitant hand out to him. "You okay, Floyd?"

Floyd looked up and slapped Jacob's hand away. "A goddamn box of mouse balls has more sense then you, you stupid sonofabitch!" He stood and backhanded Jacob. "Look at this mess! What am I supposed to tell my customers?"

"I don't know, maybe—"

"Shut the hell up!" Floyd slapped him again, this time with his open palm. It stung like fire, but felt good, too, so he let loose another one, as hard as he could.

Jacob cried out, put his hand to his face, and fell backward, striking his head against a broken jug. And he most definitely shut the hell up.

Floyd pressed his boot against Jacob's arm and gave him a shove.

"Get up, you old coot!"

But Jacob didn't get up. He didn't move. He didn't even groan.

"Well, you went and knocked yourself cold, didn't you?" Floyd laughed until he noticed the blood. It was dark as night and hard to see with the sun mostly gone, but there it was. He crouched down and rolled Jacob over a bit so he could see the damage. Glory be, what a dead weight! It was like trying to move a sack of wet fertilizer.

A long, jagged piece of busted jug protruded from the nape of Jacob's neck, and blood oozed out around it.

Floyd let the limp body plop back down, then straightened up and scratched his head, considering his situation. No worries, people would just think Jacob was too drunk to walk, and fell and hit his head. End of story. But what about the product? Floyd didn't want anybody finding all this 'shine evidence just laying around; even though everybody around here knew he dealt with Jacob, the government had never been able to prove it.

He turned, surveying the mess. It might take a minute or two to clean it all up and get it back up the mountain, but he had time. Hell, he had all night. And once he got up there and found the still, he would lay claim to it. That old boy made the smoothest brew this side of anywhere, but that was something he would never have told Jacob. And now Floyd would have the recipe.

He yanked the broken piece of jug from Jacob's neck, righted the cart, then started loading up the evidence.

* * *

Gams stood in the trees and watched. Coherent sentences were beyond her mental capability, but looking at the motionless body on the ground, she instinctively knew her food source was gone. An angry heat boiled inside her. She turned and headed up the mountain.

* * *

The still was just visible in the moonlight when Floyd reached the clearing several hours later, huffing and puffing from the exertion of hauling everything up the steep slope. It had taken a lot longer than he'd expected to round up all those busted jugs.

"Finally!" He dropped the cart and rubbed his blistered hands together, wondering just how in the hell old, arthritic Jacob managed to pull that full cart up and down the mountain each week. Sweat poured out of every pore of Floyd's body. He looked around, taking in his surroundings. Sugar. Corn. A keg of water. Regular 'shine makings. And Lord a'mighty, could this be it? Jacob's secret ingredient? He picked up the burlap bag and sniffed.

Nutmeg! Who would've guessed? Of all the strange ingredients to—

Something moved behind him, just over a large dirt hill. No, not over it. *Inside* it. The hill itself was vibrating.

"What the hell?" Floyd mumbled, standing slack jawed, holding tight to the burlap bag.

The top of the hill rumbled and clumps of dirt rolled down, settling at the bottom.

"What the *hell?*" Floyd stumbled back as the hill exploded and giant ants poured out, their high-pitched voices deafening him. He threw his hands to his ears and turned to run, but they had already blocked his path.

Antennae poked at him from every direction, like live wires shocking him with each touch. God, they were some sort of robot bugs or something! He tried to push through them, but they pushed back even harder and he fell into the still, knocking it over. The contents spilled, plastering Floyd from head to toe in the syrupy residue left over from the moonshine.

The ants closed in, violently licking the gummy liquid from his body, biting at him, chewing on him, until the pain became unbearable.

"Get away from me!" Floyd tried to fight them off, but they were relentless, ripping at his arms, his legs, his hair. He fell backward and the weight of the ants crushed down on him.

Jacob's banged up still lay inches away from Floyd's face. He squinted at the writing on it, barely legible. United States C.W.S. … As his grateful brain slipped from consciousness, his last thought went to his time in the military. C.W.S. … *Chemical Warfare Service…*

* * *

"Fine way to spend a Saturday morning," Billy grumbled, maneuvering through the thousands of chestnuts covering the ground. "You know ol' Jacob's probably just passed out drunk, and he ain't gonna be none too happy about us sneakin' up on his operation."

The sun beat down through the trees and Billy tugged at his collar. "Dang, Virg! I can't believe I let you drag me out here. It's hotter'n a goat's butt in a pepper patch."

"I'd rather be fishing, myself, you know I would," Virgil said. "But I promised Sadie I'd find her man and bring him home. You know what a hellcat my sister can be when she don't get her way."

Billy shuddered, remembering when Sadie flattened him in fifth grade for laughing at her new haircut. "No denying that. I'd rather deal with him than her, to be sure. But what if—" He stopped short when he walked smack into Virgil, who had stopped dead in his tracks. "What's wrong, Virg?"

He followed his friend's gaze and saw Jacob lying on the ground. Several chestnuts had adhered to his body, stuck in something gooey.

Blood.

"Shit!" Billy bent down and shook Jacob, hoping for the best, but he was as firm as a branding iron. "Shit, shit, shit!"

Virgil dropped to his knees and vomited huge chunks of undigested breakfast. The smell of it caused Billy's stomach to flip, but he held steady.

"Well, we gotta let Sadie know." He bent down and hefted Jacob into his arms. Damn, the old man was as stiff as a… Well, a corpse. "You gonna help me carry him to your sister's house or do I have to do it myself?"

A thundering noise started up in the distance, growing louder, and the ground beneath them trembled.

"What's that, a stampede or something?" Virgil looked at him wide eyed.

"Up here?" Billy looked up the mountain path, and sure enough, there was a shadow looming closer, growing larger. "What the heck…"

Coming directly at them was a huge herd of—Billy shook his head and blinked a few times, not sure of what he was seeing—a huge herd of *giant ants!*

Virgil jumped up and scampered down the path, skidding through chestnuts and screaming like a banshee, but Billy was rooted to the spot. As the ants approached him, the one in the lead stopped right in front of him as the others continued on, heading toward town. Billy had to do a double take. It looked like that ant was wearing something… A harness? By God, it *was* a harness! That ant was wearing a harness with the word "Gams" painted right on it. A blood-covered burlap bag hung around its antenna, like some sort of cockeyed crown, and its belly looked as gorged as the Tennessee River after a flood.

Billy's stomach roiled and all sense of reality left him as the ant leaned in close, almost touching him. It ran its antennae up Jacob's cheeks, tapping and tasting, then tilted its head and hooked its mandibles around Jacob's face and ripped the body from Billy's arms.

* * *

Gams watched her children as she dragged her food up the path, back toward the hill. Several of them had converged on the one who had held this one and were enjoying their meal.

The rest marched on, following the scent through the trees and down the mountain, to the bounteous feast beyond.

BEZILLGO

VS.

THE ALLERTON THEATRE

Gary Wosk

When I was eight years old—that would have been back in 1960—my best friend was the Allerton Theatre in the Bronx.

At that time, the movie house was thirty-three, but she was as attractive then as the day they built her. I can still see her large, bold, black-lettered marquee, the inviting free-standing box office, soft interior carpeting, scrumptious snack bar, velvety curtains, and mysterious balcony. Years before, there had been an organ, too. To a boy my age, the theatre was the Eighth Wonder of the World.

And it was a friendly place.

"Hello, Lonnie, good to see you again," was the welcome I always received from the slightly hunched-over ticket taker, Russell Goldman, who was also a projectionist at the theatre until 1934.

Located on Allerton Avenue just up the street from White Plains Road, above which trains made their way to Manhattan via an elevated track, the movie house was the place where I could leave my asthmatic childhood behind and allow my imagination to go wild.

She always gave me what I wanted: a cheap, double-billed thrill featuring low-budget science fiction and horror films even though she was graceful and deserved nothing but classic movies.

My parents, Charlene and Maury Levy, my little brother Michael, and I lived on Arnow Avenue in the Parkside Projects, a community of affordable brick apartment buildings, some as high as fourteen stories, that attracted WWII veterans and their families.

In the summer, which never could arrive soon enough, many of us kids could be seen roller skating, collecting bees in glass jars with lids poked with small holes so the stingers could breathe, playing a chalk game on the ground called Skelly, or throwing a small light red ball against a wall. We also liked to cool off in the outside "showers" of the community's park. About twelve feet below from where our parents watched, four large, rounded shower heads in a cemented area shot up gentle high streams of cold water. That wasn't good enough for us kids. We liked to sit on the drains, clog them up any way we could, and form a shallow swimming pool. Our parents seemed oblivious to our efforts.

There was much more to do in the summer than in winter, when we would go sledding down a snowy hill, but we had to be careful because there was a single chain-link fence at the bottom that could have decapitated us if we hadn't ducked under it. Even when the snow had turned to ice and slush and became patchy, we made a go of it.

There were plenty of kids I palled around with. If there was a choice between building make-shift forts in empty lots or swapping baseball cards or *War of the Worlds* cards that showed military personnel being vaporized by aliens versus watching cheesy movies at the Allerton Theatre, the weird shows won out every time. The trick was getting the parents to give their little sweethearts permission to join me.

"Oh, are you sure these movies won't give my Johnny the willies," Mrs. Chipkin asked my mom. "We usually only take him to go see Disney films."

"My Lonnie has never had any nightmares. Your son will be fine."

I liked Disney films, too, but they tended to be sad. *Old Yeller.* You get my drift.

Allerton Avenue, where the Jews and Italians mingled, bustled with activity. Close to the theatre was the barbershop where my dad took me for my haircuts. My first haircut scared me more than anything shown at the theatre. After placing me in the booster seat, the barber, who resembled a typical small-town *Andy Griffith Show* character, cranked a side handle that lifted me into the dizzying stratosphere. The sound of the electric shearers cutting away at my mane galvanized me with fear.

Other vivid Allerton Avenue memories include the flim-flam man who stood outside the barbershop selling "gold" watches out of a suitcase, and the Jewish deli at White Plains Road that served the best corned beef sand-wiches in the universe. I can still visualize the rows of Hebrew National and other brands of salamis hanging from hooks above the refrigerated display cases near the counter and the mustard jars on the tables.

And then there was Joe Tuckman's Department Store. That's where my parents always bought me Keds, my favorite black-and-white sneakers.

"How do they feel? Run around the store for a while," said the salesman, an older man with a frizzled receding hairline who wore a somewhat wrinkled white shirt and bow tie. And so I did. I became a whirling dervish of energy, making believe I was Superman about to take a flying leap off of a tall building. Around and around the store I went. Of course, I didn't get too far off the ground. I realized I wasn't a superhero when I nearly knocked over an older woman and her grandson, but the shoes felt great.

At the theatre, my imagination knew no bounds either. A mere one dollar paid for the price of admission, popcorn, and a Coke, and if I was still hungry, licorice. The popcorn, for some reason, tasted better in those days, perhaps because they served it in cardboard boxes instead of paper bags. Occasionally, I'd be given some extra money to buy a definitely not kosher hot dog wrapped in a foil bag. By the time I returned to my seat, it was lukewarm, but still tasty. The prospect of indigestion and B movies made my day.

My parents would drop me—and sometimes a friend—off at the theatre in the afternoon. The films weren't exactly classics, but to us they deserved Oscars. Even now, when they are sometimes shown on TV, I miss the opportunities to sit back with a bowl of popcorn and make believe I'm in a time machine returning to the innocence of my childhood.

Hammer's *Dracula* series, *The Blob*, *The Tingler*, *I Was a Teenage Werewolf*, *The Horrible Sun Demon*, and many other works of schlock, as well as anything starring Boris Karloff and Vincent Price, were must-sees. Darn, why did Bela Lugosi have to go and kick the bucket?

The coolest films, however, were those that starred the giant dinosaurs, including *Gorgo*, *The Giant Behemoth*, and *Dinosaurus*, and such Japanese pre-historic monster imports as *Rodan*, *Mothra*, and *Gamera*. They paled in comparison, however, to my all-time favorite, the Japanese creation, *Bezillgo, Fire Monster from the Sea*. Most of the monsters shared something in common. They came back to life as a result of radiation caused by atomic bomb testing, and they loved trouncing people and obliterating cities.

The cartoons and shorts shown before the main events and the movies we really came to see were entertaining all right, but I wanted the projectionist to cut to the chase: Bezillgo in all his glorious carnage.

It wasn't enough that *Bezillgo* was shown frequently on the nightly *Million Dollar Movie* aired on local WOR-TV Channel 9. Far more fulfilling was watching the beast run amok on the big screen. His roar bounced us out of our seats and sounded like the shofar, a horn blown during Jewish religious holidays, but I wasn't about to bow out of the theatre. I only wanted more of the devastation.

Much to my chagrin, no matter where I watched the film, in the movie theatre or on television, the ending was always the same. Bezillgo met his demise at the hands of a noted scientist's experimental invention. Why couldn't they have filmed a happier ending? What were they thinking? What was there to look forward to? Disney movies? *Fantasia?* Yawn.

No, I wanted Bezillgo and his merciless stampede to last forever.

Yeah, I really got caught up in the monster craze. Sometimes, if I went to the movies alone, it would take me longer to leave. There's just something about that lip synching and demolition derby I couldn't pull myself away from.

"Your parents are waiting for you in the lobby, young man," the snack bar woman wearing heavy makeup and a beehive hairdo said. "You don't want them to get any angrier than they already are, do you? You should thank them for allowing you to see such crappy movies."

"Tell them it's the best part. The movie will be over soon," which tended to be in about one hour. They weren't too happy about that.

Oh, yeah, I would have done anything to be in Tokyo when the scaly 267-foot tall, 600-ton, fire-breathing reptile emerged from the city's bay and laid waste to every building in sight. Of course, at the last moment I would have found a safe underground bunker. Equally exciting would have been playing the son of the American reporter in the movie.

The day that changed my life happened in July 1960. It was warm and stormy as the remnants of a tropical storm were approaching. What better place to leave a bored child than at the Allerton Theatre? Besides, my parents needed to clean the house for a party they were planning to give the next day and I would just get in the way. They said it would be okay if I watched *Bezillgo* all afternoon. Heck, if there was a morning show, I could go earlier. I was in Seventh Heaven. Social services probably would have investigated my parents for child abuse if that had happened today.

I was down to my last fifteen cents or so at intermission. I decided to head to the snack bar and buy licorice from the beehive lady, but I was stopped in my tracks by the voice of a man sitting about fifty feet away from me on the other side of the aisle. He was a middle-aged Asian man dressed in a gray suit and a white, open-collared shirt.

"Hey, little boy," the man said in broken English. "I see you here many time last month watching *Fire Monster from the Sea*. What wrong with you? No home? No life?"

I wasn't sure if I should engage in a conversation with a stranger. We were the only people in the theatre and who knew what he was up to.

"*Bezillgo* is my favorite movie," I said.

I began to walk away when he addressed me again.

"Many children like Bezillgo. He is hero to them."

"Who are you?"

"Oh, sorry. My name is Tomonobu Serizawa. I am the producer of *Bezillgo.*"

I wasn't exactly sure what a producer was, so I asked because it sounded important.

"Without me, no Bezillgo monster movie. That all you need to know," he laughed.

The Nobu Company has asked me to make a new Bezillgo movie," he continued. "The working title is *Bezillgo Destroys New York*, and the writer and I are working on script. I just wanted to see how popular movie is in America so I come to theatre every day. I would say reaction excellent, but storm keep everyone away today, except you."

I didn't believe a thing he was saying, which is surprising given that I was only eight years old at the time.

"Did you know that this is lucky day for you?" he said.

"What do you mean?"

"You pay no attention? Sleepy time? During coming attraction announcement say patron in theatre play Bezillgo in new movie. Have raffle. You only patron in theatre. You win. So what you think? Maybe you meet some famous actors, too. You like that?"

My mind was swirling with so many questions. When would the filming begin? How could I get out of school, officially referred to as Public School 96, and travel to Japan if the filming started after the summer? What would I say to all those celebrities? I was getting way ahead of myself. "Here," he said. "Take business card and show it to parents. Explain I offer you chance of lifetime. Have them call me."

When I left the theatre, I came to my senses and realized that this Tomonobu must have been bananas, but this would hardly prove to be the case. Two weeks after my parents made numerous calls to verify he was who he purported to be, I reported to work in a Manhattan studio.

"The other man who play Bezillgo too tall," explained Tomonobu. "And he clumsy. Too much sake. You are perfect size. Easy for cameras to follow."

With that I tried on the custom-made, thick, rubbery costume. It was surprisingly snug, but I was able to flail my arms and legs and move my head around with ease. Most importantly, I was able to breath, but it was still as hot as a sauna. If I dropped any weight, Bezillgo would look anorexic. I couldn't wait to lay waste to the model city of New York. A smorgasbord of destruction awaited me.

Tomonobu could see the fire in my eyes, that is, the fire in Bezillgo's eyes.

"You rehearse first," he suggested. He pointed me into the direction of a smaller corner stage. "This old model of Tokyo from first Bezillgo movie. Have fun. He laughed and so did my parents and some of the other film crew.

After about an hour of practice, including exhaling invisible fire breath that resulted in a minor asthma attack, I told Tomonobu I was ready. "Okay, this is for real, Lonnie. Lights, cameras, action!" and I proceeded to annihilate the place where I grew up. It took about twenty minutes and I felt great.

"That's a wrap. Lonnie, great job," said the glowing Tomonobu. And I was on my way to stardom, or at least I thought so.

Near the end of the first week of shooting, out of the shadows came a familiar face. It was the American star of the movie, wearing make-up for the cameo appearance he had just made as the reporter. The scene was filmed at a studio several miles away.

"Well," he said, "I've been hearing good things about you, young man. What does it feel like to be Bezillgo? To have his unbelievable power?"

"Really neat!" I was as nervous as could be standing before an honest-to-goodness Hollywood star.

"I hope you've told your friends that you're a famous movie star now. It took me years to make it in show business, and here you are, only eight years old. Wait until the media finds out about this. You'll be on the front page of every newspaper and probably interviewed on TV by Jack Paar."

Jack Paar liked to talk and so did my dad, who had a knack for asking people, regardless of their stature in life, awkward questions, which tended to embarrass my mom and me. Whatever entered his mind, he said. We still loved him, though.

"Why would a big star like you want to star in *Bezillgo*?" my dad asked. "You were in *Rear Window* with Jimmy Stewart."

I feared my career was over, but it went better than I expected.

"Well, that's a good question," the actor said. He paused for a few moments. "I guess it's because I like Bezillgo, too, just like your son," which made me feel good to hear.

The filming was over after two weeks, but by then I had had enough. It was getting kind of boring destroying the same city over and over again. I tried to talk Tomonobu into building a model of the nation's capital, but he ignored me.

The man who discovered me in that theatre turned out to be an actor's kind of director. Not to say I was Robert De Niro or anything. He allowed me the freedom to demolish the Big Apple any way I saw fit. Often he would invite my parents and me out to lunch at the "automat" restaurant, and he would tell us about future Bezillgo movies in development. They seemed more like comedies, to tell you the truth.

"Maybe you come to Japan one day and make more movies for me," he said.

A check for $500 made out to me, a fortune back then, arrived in the mail several months later. My parents immediately deposited the amount in my savings account, which they said I could use for film school.

"It will collect interest," my mom explained to me, "and one day it will pay for your tuition." I had no idea what tuition was. Back at Public School 96, my friends were skeptical about my story, that was until I showed them the black-and-white pictures of me with the star of the movie.

"What's next, Frankenstein? The Mummy?" The Werewolf? You should drop out of school and move to Hollywood." They mocked me. Years later, when I was a sports agent for a while, even New York Yankees left-fielder, Masao Matsui, whose nickname was Bezillgo, looked at me in disbelief when I told him my story.

All these years later, my ten-year-old grandson Richard also gave me the "uh huh" treatment. "Let's just watch the movie, Pop," he'd say. "This is the best part, when Bezillgo surprises the islanders in the middle of the night during a typhoon."

"*Bezillgo Destroys New York* unfortunately never made it onto the big screen. The star of the movie was also the executive producer of the film, and he wasn't impressed with the overall product and decided to withdraw his financial support. We remained lifetime friends, however, and he even gave me a bit part on one of his television shows. Whenever I asked him to make a special appearance at the Bezillgo fan club I had started, he was there.

Tomonobu apologized profusely and gave my parents and me free movie tickets and Bezillgo memorabilia for years. Sure, I was disappointed that the movie was never completed, but still, it was a great experience. I bet it would have been good enough to go straight to DVD if it had been made today.

Interestingly, Bezillgo does try to destroy New York City in a poorly made American film by the same name that was released in 1998. In my opinion, it was by far the worst Bezillgo movie ever made. Thankfully, Tomonobu had nothing to do with a film that began to look like a rip off of *Jurassic Park*.

Somewhere, perhaps in a New York warehouse, a film with Lonnie Levy as Bezillgo is sitting on a shelf rusting away in a can. Think *Rosebud*. Perhaps it will show up on eBay one day, and I'll pay whatever it takes to get my hands on it.

And to think, none of this would have happened without the magnificent Allerton Theatre, which closed in 1993. They don't make them like they did in 1927. It's a shame, too, because it would have been the perfect venue for the science fiction and horror films I produce.

CATGUT

Terry Alexander

"Come on, Wayne. Let's dump this shit, and let's get out of here." Al dropped the flexible hose, the brass end crashing through the lake's slick, frozen surface. "Start the pump. Hurry up!"

"Hold your horses," Wayne said defensively. "I can only do one thing at a time." He hit the starter switch on the external pump attached to the large tank. The motor coughed once, belched smoke, and roared to life. Wayne pulled the release lever. The hose began to cough and gurgle. "It's on its way."

"About time." Al watched the thick white fluid surge into the water, the color dispersing quickly in the lake. "Crank it up. We need to get out of here."

"The pump can't go any faster," Wayne snapped. "If I push it too much, it'll bust a piston. It was your bright idea to take this job. If we get caught, they'll toss us in jail."

"You worry like an old woman. We ain't going to get caught." Al shook a cigarette from his pack, patting his pockets for a lighter. He caught a whiff of the toxic fumes and gagged. "This stuff is nasty." He waved his hand in front of his face.

They waited in silence until they heard the sputtering of the empty tank.

"We're empty," Wayne said, stating the obvious.

Al dragged the pipe toward the rock-covered shore. Tiny ripples near the shore caught his eye. He pulled a flashlight from his rear pocket and aimed it at the surface. The beam caught the wiggling bodies of several small catfish, their slick heads above the water gulping air. "Something's wrong with the fish."

"Forget the damn fish. I want to get out of here."

"We made five hundred bucks apiece for three hours work. This is a sweet deal." Al shouldered the pipe and carried it back to the truck.

"I wouldn't be doing this if I didn't need the money," Wayne said, running toward the truck cab.

"Bernie will have another load in three or four days." Al tossed the pipe into the truck before climbing into the passenger's seat.

"Count me out. I'm not doing this again. It's hard on my nerves." Wayne slammed the door and turned the key in the ignition; the diesel engine roared to life. Rear tires churned on the hard dirt, moving the truck along the rough path. The rig bounced onto the gravel road before Wayne switched on the lights.

"You're a wuss." Al rummaged on the floor and pulled a cold Bud from a cooler. He popped the top and drained half the can in a single gulp.

"Say what you want. I'm not doing this again." Wayne drove the small tanker truck onto the highway, speeding toward Bernie Cooper's waste disposal plant.

* * *

Dale Hodge parked his old green pickup under the Chief's Elm. It was a tree Chief Sam Paisley had planted twenty years ago near the parking spot, so the other officers had named it after him. The name stuck, even after all these years. Getting out of the truck, Dale hoped for another slow day. If thing's held to the normal routine, he'd write a few speeding tickets and piss off some summer-time vacationers.

Sharon Plunkett, a holdover from previous administrations, pulled up alongside Dale's truck. "Morning, Dale," she said, climbing from her blue Nova, a forty-year-old classic. Her signature high heels clicked on the sidewalk.

I don't see how she walks in those things. They have to be uncomfortable. "Good morning, Sharon. It's gonna be a great day." He flashed her a broad smile. It was always a good idea to keep Sharon happy. The old girl still had some political pull lurking in the state capital.

"Betty Chambers called me early this morning. She saw head lights coming from Johnson's Point. It may be poachers." She paused before the closed door.

Dale took the hint and opened the door for the older woman. "I'll check it out. What time did she see these lights?"

"Around three, give or take a few minutes." Sharon nodded to the weary-eyed man sitting behind the desk.

"About time you two showed up." Stan Liddell yawned and stretched. "I was beginning to think you'd be late."

"I haven't been late in eighteen years." Sharon cast him a hard look. "Any excitement last night?"

"A couple of raccoons raided the dumpster behind the T-Mart. Damn things are as fat as hogs." Stan rose to his feet. "One had trouble getting out. A few calls about the giant ghost fish came in about eleven."

"Lot of folks are claiming to have seen that fish lately." Dale removed his hat and scratched his head. "Anything on the missing pets? Oscar Rosson said he lost his best hound a week ago."

Stan shook his head. "Drunks see a lot of strange things."

Dale slapped the night officer's back. "Go home and get some sleep. You've earned it." He turned to face Sharon. "I'm driving out to Johnson's Point. Keep things under control while I'm gone."

"I'll call if I need help." Sharon took her seat behind the desk, the police band radio at her side.

"Come on, Stan. I'll walk you out." Dale turned toward the door. "Did anyone call this morning, about three?" he whispered.

"Things were quiet from one 'til about five." Stan yawned.

Dale shook his head. "I wish Sharon's cronies would call the office."

"Force of habit. She's an old fixture in the office, ran the show from the background for years." Stan climbed behind the wheel of his Ford pickup with rusted-out fender wells.

"You'd think an officer of the law would have a nicer vehicle." Dale paused by the cruiser.

"On my salary? You've got to be kidding." Stan started the engine and backed into the street. "See you in the morning," he yelled through the open window.

Dale tugged his ear lobe and glanced at the glass door, debating the wisdom of talking to Sharon and telling her to have the locals call the officer on duty instead of her. After all, she was only the dispatcher.

The highest paid dispatcher in the state—with major clout in the city. If her backers were as powerful as everyone thought they were, he could get fired if he crossed her. "Hell with it," he mumbled. The car alarm beeped as he opened the door and crawled behind the wheel. He would speak with Betty Chambers first, then head out to Johnson's Point.

* * *

Fifteen minutes later he was sitting at Betty's oak kitchen table, nursing a cup of coffee. "How long has this been going on? How many times have you seen this truck?"

"Started a few months ago. I remember because it was cold." She dumped two sugar cubes in the steaming liquid, then pushed her glasses back into place. "I'll see them three or four times a week, and then nothing for a couple of weeks. Then they'll come back." She patted the bun on the back of her head, making sure every hair was in place.

"Why didn't you call earlier?" He sipped from the porcelain cup. "Everyone knows the property is in probate. Anyone prowling around out there is trespassing."

"Thought it was fishermen." She shrugged. "Then I noticed the odor."

Dale frowned. "What odor?"

"A foul stench drifts this way when the wind is right. It was so bad the other night, I couldn't sleep." She blew steam away from her cup before moving it to her lips.

Dale drained his cup. "I'll drive down there and take a look around."

"Be careful. I'll tell Sharon where you're going." The old lady smiled sweetly.

"Thank you, Miss Chambers. I appreciate your concern." *Will it ever end?*

* * *

Deep ruts scarred the trail to Johnson's Point. The cruiser's undercarriage scraped along over the high dirt. *Someone's bringing some heavy loads down here. Damn well wasn't fishermen.* He stopped at a flat stretch of ground fifteen feet from the shore and stared at the crushed grass and wide tire tracks. A set of footprints stopped at the water's edge.

A harsh, rotten smell burned his nose. Dead, half-eaten fish floated in the deep water ten feet from the bank, their bodies bleached of color. He squatted to examine a white puddle on the ground when he noticed the bones in the shallow water and the greasy tuffs of hair floating on the surface.

"Now I know where the pets went." He pulled a cheap pen from his shirt pocket and probed the strange substance. Smoke curled from the plastic tip. "Damn," he cursed as the acidic smell hit his nostrils. "We've got big problems."

Dale broke a long stick from a dying willow. Its gray roots stretched toward the lake. "Wish I had a glass jar or something." He raked at a dead fish floating on the surface, attempting to bring it to the shore.

A massive chalk-colored head broke through the surface of the water. Dale stumbled and fell, drenched by the tremendous splash. His bulging eyes stared at the dirty white creature before him. Dark, soulless eyes, like black saucers, fastened on him.

A massive tail broke the surface, swirling the water, driving the thick body forward. A coarse, rattling grunt came from the creature as it pushed into the shallows. Dale scrambled to his feet, sliding on the grass as he ran to the cruiser. He scrambled for the transmitter. "Sharon. Contact the big shots in wildlife management and the EPA."

"Dale," Sharon's voice squawked through the small speaker, "Justin Tyler just called in. He claims a giant catfish sank Oscar Reynolds' boat. Said the damned thing chased his boat back to the dock. What's going on?"

"Someone's dumping chemicals at Johnson's Point, but that's the least of our problems," Dale said, his words jumbling together. "We need some experts out here ASAP, and contact the other law-enforcement agencies. We've got to clear the lake."

"Dale, we can't do that."

"Sharon, call your buddy in the city. Make it happen." He dropped the mic to the floor. Dale glanced through the dirt-speckled windshield and drew in a deep breath, trying to still his quivering hands. The huge catfish languished in the shallows, cracking its raspy jaws together.

Swallowing the lump in his throat, Dale yanked the pump shotgun from the upright rack and rummaged through the glove compartment in search of slugs.

He found a faded box under the seat, the brass ends green and corroded. He loaded three in the magazine and one in the chamber. He got out of the cruiser and set the butt of the shotgun against his shoulder. Sighting down the barrel, he aimed for the saucer-sized eye. "Hope this works."

Jumbled thoughts ran through his mind. He knew an experienced hunter could down a deer at one hundred yards with a shotgun, but he also knew there was a chance the old shells could lodge in the barrel. Taking a deep breath to steady himself, he tried to convince himself that there was no way he could miss a target this huge at close range. Just as he was about to pull the trigger, the slick head turned. Powerful muscles drove the huge body to deeper water. In a matter of seconds, the ivory mass had disappeared from sight.

"Dale, do you read me, over?" Sharon's voice reached his ears.

He ran to the cruiser, fumbling with the mic. "Yeah, I read you.

When's the cavalry coming?"

"They think I'm crazy," she said. "After they stopped laughing, they said they'd be here in a couple of days."

"What about the lake patrol? Are they going to close the lake?"

"They're still laughing at me. Asked me if I knew how much revenue the lake brings to the local communities." She grew silent.

"What else, Sharon?"

"My contact in the city can't help right now. This is an election year and he doesn't want the voters to think he's lost his mind."

"Call Stan. Get him back to the office. Then find Virgil Prentiss."

"What do you want with that crazy old fool?"

"He's got a boat, and he knows about big fish. I'm gonna need his help."

"Anything else?"

"Yeah. I need the biggest rifle you can find."

"What did you say?" she demanded.

"A .375 Holland & Holland magnum or a 480 Nitro Express." He slipped behind the wheel and started the engine. "Tell Virgil to meet me at the boat dock."

* * *

The twenty-foot pontoon splashed through the white caps. Dale stood by the rail, wiping the spray from his face. "Where is Reynolds' boat?"

"Over by Two Steps." Virgil rubbed his whiskered jaw. "Oscar sets jug lines in the deep water off the rocks. Should be around that bluff." He pointed to a steep cliff thirty feet above the water. The old navy veteran steered the boat around the sheer rock face. What appeared to be two giant steps carved into the stone came into view. A tackle box and some plastic jugs bobbed on the water. "That's the spot."

"Are those jugs hooked to the boat?" Dale asked. "Think we can pull it to the surface?"

"The lines aren't strong enough and I don't have the horsepower." Virgil shook his head. "Reynolds usually attached about seventy five feet of heavy string on every jug. The water's about fifty feet deep here. Leave 'em where they are. It'll serve as a good marker for the Lake Patrol."

"There's something over there," Dale said, pointing. "Barely under the water. It's big." He held his hand over his eyes to cut the glare. "Get a little closer. I want to see what it is."

"I don't see nothing," Virgil mumbled.

"Right there." Dale leaned from the side of the boat.

"Don't lean over the rail." Virgil yanked the police officer to the center of the boat just as a massive head broke the water's surface. The beast's wide mouth snapped closed on the bill of his ball cap, snatching it from his head. The wide body turned in mid-air and splashed into the mirror-like surface.

Dale sputtered and wiped the water from his face with his sleeve. "What the hell was that?"

"That's your ghost fish." Virgil jammed the throttle open. "We gotta get back to shore."

* * *

The giant trolled the deep water, the smaller fish fleeing in fear at its passing. Long whiskers dragged through the silt, searching for food. Hunger gnawed at its insides. A hunger that never ended, that could never be satiated.

A dark shadow passed overhead. Vibrations tingled through the whiskers. It sensed food. The wide tail propelled it from the bottom, gaining speed with every movement. The ivory missile burst from the water, striking the center of the small outboard.

The impact lifted the vessel into the air. Wood and fiberglass crushed under the pressure of its massive jaws. A lone passenger splashed into the water, momentarily stunned as his body slammed into the surface. The gaping maw opened. Before the man had a chance to recover, raspy, sand paper-like teeth mashed down on his ankle. The pain revived him, but it was too late. By the time he realized what was happening, the fish had dragged him to the bottom and started to grind the body to red sticky paste.

* * *

"My God, where have you been?" Sharon met him at the door. "There's been another attack. Ben Morton. Witnesses say it was a giant fish. One person swears it was a shark."

"Damn, that's just great. Did you call Stan?"

Sharon nodded. "He's on his way here."

"Have you found a rifle?" Dale lifted the coffee pot from the warmer and filled his stained cup, then turned to Virgil. "Care for a cup?"

"Is that all you've got?" he asked.

Dale nodded.

"Fill me a up." The old seaman accepted the offered mug.

"Excuse me," Sharon said, glaring at the fisherman, "but we were talking." Then to Dale, she continued. "No, I haven't found any large bore rifles."

"Call Dusty Russell. He'll know if there's any around. Try the big shots again, tell them we need some help down here. Now."

"Yes, sir." Sharon hurried to the phone.

"Dale, there's a big fish out in the lake, and it's pissed off," Virgil said. "How are you going to handle this?"

"Have you seen anything like it before?" Dale sipped at the bitter brew.

Virgil shrugged. "Saw a giant squid once, and a shark that had to be eighty feet long. It was chowing down on a twenty-foot whale, but that was in the Pacific Ocean."

"Didn't you work on a whaler once?"

"Yeah," Virgil said. "Didn't like it. Too much blood and guts, and the smell is awful."

"Can you fix a harpoon? We may need one if we're going to stop that monster."

"You're kidding. You want to go after that thing? There ain't many boats on the lake that can mess with that fish." Virgil shook his head.

"It's a joke, right?" Stan burst through the door. "I heard it on the scanner. It has to be a prank."

"Afraid not." Dale exhaled a deep breath. "Sharon, any luck on the rifle?" he shouted.

"Dusty knows a man who has a .444 *Winchester*. He said it'll drop a grizzly bear."

"Tell him to get it and all the ammunition he can carry." Dale turned to the two men. His gaze centered on Virgil. "Take Stan, make as many harpoons as you can."

Virgil massaged his forehead. "Okay. We'll be needing some heavy gauge steel."

"Go to the salvage yard, take what you need," Dale's voice turned stern.

Virgil nodded. "Come on, Stan. There's no point in arguing." He pulled the younger man toward the door.

"Sharon, call the highway patrol, local law enforcement, and the lake patrol. I want that lake shut down," Dale ordered.

"Right away." Sharon brushed a tuft of loose hair from her face.

Dale sat on the corner of his desk, sipping from the battered cup. Waiting was the hardest part. He should be doing something, but for the present all he could do was sit on his ass. The cell phone in his shirt pocket rang. He pulled the slider free. "Hodge," he said, gruffly.

"I've been trying to call your office for ten minutes, and I keep getting a busy signal." Dusty's familiar drawl sounded in his ear. "I've got the rifle, promised Bob you'd return in one piece."

"How much ammunition did you get?" Dale asked.

"Near twenty rounds. What's going on? Did you spot a bear?"

"Drop it by the office," he said, intentionally not answering the man's question. "I'm going by my house and pick up a few things." He started to close the slider then hesitated. "Oh… And stay off the lake." He snapped the slider closed.

"Dale, they're closing the lake, but it's going to take a while," Sharon shouted.

"Hold down the fort. I'll be back in a few minutes." He jammed his spare hat on his head and walked toward the door.

"You can't leave me here alone. I can't handle all this."

"Sharon," he snapped. "Take care of things while I'm gone. Call my cell if it's an emergency." Stan and Virgil had taken the police cruiser. He climbed behind the wheel of his pickup and headed home.

Dale returned twenty minutes later dressed in black fatigues. He carried two pistols, one strapped to his thigh, the other in a shoulder holster. He glanced at Sharon. Her tight bun had fallen, loose hair framed her face.

"Where have you been?" she demanded. "The whole place is going mad. The phone's ringing off the hook, State Senators, County Commissioners, the Governor's office even called. He wants to activate the National Guard."

"It's okay, Sharon, calm down." He noticed the rifle and bullets in the center of his desk.

"You don't understand. There's been another attack." She flipped the hair from her face.

"I thought they were clearing the lake?"

"It's a big lake. Your ghost fish capsized another boat. Three people drowned." Sharon closed her eyes. "Wildlife Management and the EPA are on their way."

"It'll be dark in a few hours." He glanced at the afternoon sun.

"What's that got to do with anything?" Sharon shouted, mascara ran from her tear-filled eyes.

"I know where it's going." Dale stroked the day's growth of stubble along his jaw.

Sharon glanced out the window. "Virgil and Stan are back." She jumped at the shrill ring of the phone. "I haven't had a moment's peace today."

Dale met the pair at the door. "Show me what you've got."

Stan opened the trunk. "Did the best we could." Stan lifted a handmade harpoon. The steel shaft ended in a sharp spear head. "Attach this to a wooden handle, pass a rope through this ring, and hold on."

Dale took the weapon from Stan. "It's heavy. How far could you throw one of these?"

"Gonna have to be close to score a good hit," Virgil said. "We heard on the radio that the Governor has called in the National Guard. Be smart. Let them deal with it."

"Yeah, this is out of our league," Stan agreed. "Let The Guard handle it."

"I know where it's going. If I'm right, we can end this tonight. If I'm wrong, we'll let the weekend warriors handle things." Dale eyed the two men. "Are you going to help me or not?"

"Speaking personal, I'd like to sit this one out." Virgil removed his sweat-stained ball cap, running his hand through his gray hair. "I saw a big tiger bite a sailor in half once. I'm not anxious to get onto the water with something this big."

Sharon's face appeared in the door. "We're getting calls from the TV stations. They're sending reporters down here. They want an interview. What do I tell them?"

"Local or national?" Dale asked.

"Both. What do I tell them?"

"Tell them to call Wildlife Management and the EPA. They have all the answers." Dale stared at the pair. Both men suddenly took an interest in the condition of their shoes and refused to meet Dale's gaze. "I'm going out, but I'm going to need some help."

"You know I'll help," Stan mumbled, "but I'm not happy about it. We could get killed out there."

"Can't let you landlubbers do this on your own." Virgil jammed his cap on his head, his hair frizzed around the sides.

"Take five or six of these, go to the narrows. After the fish comes through, anchor your boat in the center."

"Hell! That thing could tear my pontoon apart." The old man puffed out his cheeks.

"I'm hoping we'll kill it at Johnson's Point. If it gets past us, it'll be up to you." Dale met the older man's eyes. "Simple as that."

"That's a hell of a plan." Stan shook his head. "Is it too late to change my mind?"

* * *

"Any more sightings?" Dale toweled the sweat from his face.

"None for a couple of hours." Sharon's disheveled hair hung limply around her shoulders; her eyes were puffy, and mascara lined the wrinkles on her cheeks. "My friend called. He's going on television at eight to give a rousing speech. He thinks it'll guarantee his re-election."

"Stan and I are going to Johnson's Point. Harvey can keep an eye on the town. We'll be back before daylight. I hope." Hit with a feeling that he'd never see Sharon again, Dale hugged the older woman. "Thanks for all your help."

* * *

"This plan sucks. Virgil's right. This could get a man killed. I can't believe I'm going to hide behind that big cottonwood on the Point and throw harpoon's at a pissed-off *giant fish*." Stan emphasized the last words.

"I'll be on the shore with the rifle. It'll be focused on me." Dale spoke softly. "Each harpoon has thirty feet of rope. Tie the free ends to the tree and make sure the knots hold."

"This is crazy." Stan hefted a large bundle to his shoulder and waded through the deep water to a huge cottonwood. "I want you to explain to my family how I got killed."

"When it comes into the shallows, start tossing these things and aim for the head." Dale dropped his bundle to the ground. "Don't miss. I want that damn thing to look like a porcupine."

"Are you listening to me?" Without waiting for an answer, Stan unrolled the bundle and tied the ropes around the base of the large tree.

Dale moved the pickup behind a clump of trees. He hid in the undergrowth near the rutted tracks. *Now we wait.* He snuggled behind a patch of wild roses. The hours passed slowly. Dale checked his watch impatiently. The glowing hands told him it was almost three o'clock.

Where is the damned thing? What if I'm wrong? What if it's out in the deep water munching on a big bass? Dale debated the wisdom of his plan, wondering if he should call it a night. The walkie-talkie crackled at his side.

"Dale, are you there?" Virgil's haggard voice squawked the speaker. "It just passed through the narrows. It might be a trick of the moonlight, but the damn thing looked bigger to me."

"Thanks, Virg, wish us luck." He clipped the radio to his belt.

A set of headlights turned off the highway, driving down the rutted trail. Dale crouched behind the thorny growth. The throaty roar of a diesel engine cut through the night. The bright beams highlighted the briar patch for an instant. Dale's heart beat quickened as the truck turned and the driver killed the headlights. A set of back-up lights danced on the still water as the tanker backed toward the inky surface.

The door creaked open and a booted foot stepped to the ground. "Catgut, where are you?" a man's voice spoke to the night. "Where you at? I've got something for you" He pulled a pet carrier from the cab. A low whine came from the cage.

It took Dale a moment to recognize the voice. *That's Al Whitten. What the hell is he doing here? Has he made that monster into a pet?*

"Come on, Catgut. It's feeding time." Al struggled with a hose attached to the truck. "I know you love this stuff." He connected the hose to the tank outlet. The free end splashed into the water. A huge shape rose from the depths, swimming into the shadows. The moonlight reflected from the smooth skin. "I can't believe what this stuff's done to you."

Al waded into the lake. He advanced to the open mouth of the gigantic fish, standing in water above his waist. "That's my boy." He patted the brute's smooth head and side. The wide tail splashed the surface. "You're a good boy. Don't worry. I'll feed you in a minute." He turned toward the shore. His hand closed on the pump's starter switch, water streaming from his clothes.

"Don't move, Al." Dale stepped from the concealing shrubs. He thumb-cocked the hammer on the Winchester. "See you managed to get here. I had a hell of a time convincing the Highway patrol not to close the road."

"What in the hell are you doing here, Dale?" Al lifted his hands above his head. He turned slowly. "You're screwing up a sweet deal."

A loud grunt came from deep in the creature's gullet. It plowed through the water into the shallows.

"Catgut wants his supper." Al nodded toward the massive fish. "He gets cranky when he's hungry."

"Move out of the way, Al. I'm stopping your monster." Dale lifted the rifle to his shoulder. The truck's back-up lights gave him a perfect shot at the wide head. His finger found the trigger, slowly taking up the slack. The weapon bucked in his hands, the blast driving the butt plate into his shoulder. The report echoed from the trees and set Dale's ears to ringing.

A large red flower blossomed on the ivory head. The tail churned mud into a brown froth. It surged forward, the massive body coming to rest in less than two feet of water.

Moonlight glinted off the harpoon as it sailed through the air. The sharp barb buried into the beast's smooth hide. Dale worked the lever action. The empty casing sailed over his head and he slid a fresh round into the breech.

"What are you doing?" Al splashed into the water. "Don't do this. I'll turn myself in. Just don't hurt him anymore."

"Dale, Dale, come in." Virgil's frantic voice rang from the two-way radio. Dale ignored it, intent of stopping the creature before him.

"Leave him alone. Take me to jail, but leave Catgut alone." Al placed himself between Dale and the beast. "I did this, this is my faul…" His words were abruptly cut off when a harpoon tore through his body. Al fell to his knees, tugging at the iron shaft, a line of blood flowing from his mouth.

The ghost fish closed in on his body. It rolled to its side, mouth open, and snagged the wounded man in its maw. Rolling back onto its belly, the beast tossed its head back and its throat muscles working furiously. Dale watched in horror as the dying man was slowly swallowed whole.

Snapping himself out of the daze, Dale emptied the rifle. He dropped it to the soft ground and drew the pistol from his shoulder holster. With surprising speed, the fish managed to turn itself around and the V-shaped tail drove it toward deeper water. The rope tightened, the ancient cottonwood bending and creaking in protest.

The monster's frenzied movements slowed, its struggles grew weaker. Thick blood stained the water. It surged forward a final time, the taut lines popping like a shotgun under the stress. The suffering fish dove beneath the surface, only to emerge seconds later; it rolled to its side.

"It's all right, Stan. Get over here." Dale flexed his sore shoulder.

"Are you sure that thing's dead?" he stammered. "I'm not getting in the water unless it's dead."

"It's dead."

Virgil spied the lights in the distance. "Dale, looks like we got company. Do you think Wildlife Management will throw us in jail for taking this fish illegally?"

"We'll have some explaining to do. I better call the station, tell Sharon she can lock up the place, and go home." Dale pulled the slider from the thigh pocket of the camouflage blacks.

"Yeah, it looks like our night's not over yet, but someone on the force should get a little sleep." Stan splashed into the water, hurrying to the shore. "Do you think there are more of these things?"

"Dale, this is Virgil, come in." The old sailor's panicked voice reached the sheriff's ears.

Dale took the radio from his belt and spoke into it. "We got it, Virg. We killed it."

"Damn it, boy, listen to me. There's more than one. Did you hear me? There's more than one."

Stan screamed in anguish and disappeared beneath the rippling water.

NATHAN'S FOLLY

J.M. Scott

Nathan Cross stared at the glass of wine and swirled the rather heavily poured sampling of Grenache. *It is cut with something*, he thought, *perhaps a Syrah or a Tempranillo*. The bottle had a good bouquet to it; fleshy, with a hint of allspice and orange blossom. It was clearly light oak and had a twist of either vanilla or sweet wood. He took a hesitant sip and smiled. It was sheer luck that he had happened upon the winery, and even more good luck that it had been open. Many of the businesses on his way into Monterey had closed early due to a natural disaster of some sort that had rolled through the area. He had become lost, his GPS useless with all the detours and closed off streets.

Several construction crews shoveled debris into the backs of city trucks, and fire engines were parked in what he estimated to be one mile intervals. The bright red vehicles reminded him of his youth. His father was a fire fighter, and as a child he would ride around with him and operate some of the controls on the truck. His favorite thing to do was raise and lower the extendable ladder.

"How is it?" the waitress asked.

Nathan hadn't seen her approach the table. He'd been too busy trying to expand his palette. The interruption was a little irritating, but he knew she was just doing her job. He decided not to launch any verbal barbs at her. A nonthreatening reply would suffice.

"It's good."

"And the scenery?"

He looked up at her. "Even better."

The waitress stared intently out the large window. Part of the view

179

was obscured by the winery's logo. "Crazy, isn't it?"

Nathan had no idea what she was referring to, so he asked, "What's crazy?"

"The quake," she replied. "It's been the only interesting thing to happen around here in a while. You go day to day hoping for a little excitement, then something like this happens... It's just crazy. You know what I mean?"

"Oh, yeah. The quake. Is that what happened? I'm not from around here."

"It's been all over the news. You must have been in a cave or something."

Nathan laughed. Because of the nature of his trip, he'd avoided the internet or anything else that would betray his location. Besides, the job was too important to allow himself to get distracted by current events. Admittedly though, he was curious as to what she was talking about.

"So, how big was this quake?" he asked.

The waitress looked around to see if her boss was watching. He wasn't, so she pulled up a chair and sat close to Nathan, real close. He almost spilled the delicate purple liquid on his jacket as he moved to counter the assault on his personal space and cringed at the thought of having to remove a stain from his favorite article of clothing.

"You're lucky," she said.

"I am? And why is that?"

"Because I study geology at Monterey State University. I'm in my third year."

"Oh, good. Good," Nathan said.

"You see, the upper crust of the Earth is made up of several plates that are constantly shifting. They bang into each other, separate, and even move parallel to one another. We have a tendency to think of world events in our own time frame, measuring things in minutes, hours, and even days."

The waitress must have been genuinely excited. She reached out and placed her hand over Nathan's.

She continued. "Geological time is different. It's measured in millions of years."

Nathan checked his watch. He had to get going soon, so he'd have to cut this conversation short. "This is all really fascinating, but I have to..."

The waitress pressed on as if he hadn't said a word. "Every now and again, geological time and our time intersect. When they do, it causes an event like the one that happened yesterday. Off the coast, we had a giant separation between two tectonic plates. Gasses were released, precious metals were thrown into the sediment, and things from the deep…" She left him hanging a moment, gave him a flirtatious smile, obviously enjoying their interaction."… well, these things from the deep, they just might come a-calling."

"Things?" Nathan asked.

"Yes. Things," she replied. "There have already been reports of missing divers."

"Really?" Nathan said incredulously.

The waitress nodded.

Nathan made a point of looking at his watch again. "Well, thanks for the chat. It's been a real pleasure," he said sincerely as he got up.

The waitress stood with him.

"I like talking to people. Especially from here. They're more interesting. I have a second job at a sea food restaurant, but the people there don't talk much. They just want to eat."

"Well, uh… Thank you."

As the waitress walked away, Nathan couldn't help but think about what she'd said. He put her at about twenty-two, a little too young for him. *Besides, she couldn't even tell me a damn thing about the wine.* All the same, she was cute and seemed to be able to spin a good yarn. *Things from the sea,* he scoffed with a shake of his head.

A middle-aged couple and their children sat at a table a few feet away. Their teenage daughter was typing furiously on her cell phone while the younger boy was pretending that his plastic toy shark was swimming through the water. Nathan sneered at them. The wealthy always carried an established presence and look that he found distasteful. The mother was older than she wanted people to think she was (that, or the stress of the life style she married into was beginning to take its toll), but Nathan wasn't fooled; he saw right past the heavy layers of makeup and designer glasses to the stress-lined face beneath. The father, the intended recipient of Nathan's disdain, looked like a zombie in khakis. He had died long ago.

"When are we going to the islands?" the daughter asked.

Neither parent could be bothered to grace her with a response.

Nathan balked at the idea that the rich worked harder than the average man. It had been his experience that the entitled were usually made up of self-indulgent fools. They were handed privilege, and for the most part, put less effort into their jobs than the typical blue collar worker. The upper affluent members of society sent their kids to the best schools, set up trust funds for them, and financed their drug habits all with a relative impunity from responsibility.

Nathan hated the banality of their conversation, each one so wrapped up in their own existence that they weren't even aware there were others at the table, and put them from his mind. He needed to focus; he was working after all, and even though he was being forced to do the job to pay off his gambling debts, he knew that murder was a complicated game. He hadn't been given time to plan things out to any great extent, so he didn't know what his chances were of actually getting away with the crime. He was flying blind, which is why he had made it a point to arrive early so that he could get the lay of the land. He had a few hours before he needed to meet up with his intended targets. He knew exactly where they would be, so when he had spied the open winery, he decided to stop in and have a couple of drinks.

The waitress returned, handed Nathan his tab, and gave him a playful smile. "You're a good person," she said. "I can tell."

He thought the comment odd, but it was of no consequence.

A framed image on the wall caught his attention as she walked away. It was a movie poster from the 50s that depicted a giant sea creature attacking a bridge.

Nathan stared at the strange piece of art for a few seconds, briefly recollecting the waitress' words. He shook off the distraction with a knowing grin; *yeah, she was good*, he thought. He examined the bill and noticed that his rather chatty server had not charged him for his first glass of wine. She had also written her name and phone number at the bottom of the slip of paper. She had dotted the "i" in Lisa with a little heart.

Cute, he thought, pulling a wad of cash from his pocket. He separated out a single hundred dollar bill from his bankroll and tossed it on the table. Stuffing the receipt in his pocket as he walked out of the establishment, he smiled at the waitress and winked. She had been a wealth of information and mildly entertaining. If he decided to stay in Monterey overnight, he might give her a call, but he really didn't think it would happen. Once his job was complete, it would be best if he left town. He'd have to pass on the affectionate offer, but reassured himself that, with enough persistence, Lisa would find someone to take her out for the night.

Walking toward his vehicle, Nathan took note of the time. He needed to retrieve the ammunition that he had locked in the trunk of his car. Even though his gun was unregistered, he made sure to keep the rounds separate just in case he was pulled over. The least he could do was try to follow California's ridiculous gun laws.

Sweat beaded along his forehead as he sat in the front seat of the car and clumsily loaded the bullets into the gun. The closer it came to having to carry out the job, the more nervous he became. He had never considered himself to be an upstanding citizen. After all, wasn't it because of his gambling debts that he found himself in this predicament? The thought of killing someone was something that had never crossed his mind, no matter how messed up his life had become. But here he was, getting ready to do it. To actually *kill* someone. Well, attempt to. He didn't know if he'd be able to pull the trigger. Even though he harbored an extreme prejudice against the rich, he still didn't know if he'd be able to go through with it.

He paused for a moment and considered the consequences: kill or be killed. It was enough to bolster his confidence, and as he turned his thoughts toward his intended marks, he was surprised to find that he was actually smiling. Not only did he get to assassinate a high tech CEO, he would also be taking out the man's son as an added bonus. From what he'd been told, the teen was attending a religious university in Nebraska. The kid was tall, had little to no personality, and wore his hair so that his bangs covered the top half of his face. Nathan didn't understand the stupid boy band look, but it didn't matter. A rich guy and his bible-thumping son. *It couldn't get any better*, he thought.

Once he arrived at his destination, he waited patiently at the dive site. While he stared out the window of his car, he took in the beauty of his surroundings. The cove looked as though it had been painted onto a giant canvas. Waves slowly rolled onto the multi-colored sand that covered the beach. Even though it was low tide, the beach was relatively clean. Looking at it, Nathan found it hard to believe the area had been rocked by a small earthquake.

He got out of the car and strolled down to the beach. As he did, he looked down and noticed a series of strange holes leading to and from the water. They were deep, and there was a definite pattern to them, although he had no idea as to what could have made them. He pushed them from his mind and tried to focus on the task at hand.

Earlier in the day, a young man at a local dive shop had, for a hundred bucks, told him the people he was looking for had filled up two 80cu aluminum tanks. That was enough to give the divers at least three hours of recreation. That was, of course, if they scheduled some time to allow for proper decompression.

The only difficult part of the job that Nathan could foresee was making sure that he accurately identified the man and his son. The plan was simple. Wait for them to exit the water and shoot them on the beach. He could have chosen a better venue for the job, someplace a little more private, but he was pressed for time. If he didn't report back to the man that was forcing him to do the job within twenty-four hours, he would be the one with a contract out on him. He thought about his disadvantages. As divers, they would have knives, but their equipment was so incredibly cumbersome they'd never be able to effectively wield the blades once they were out of the water.

Nathan saw three figures breach the ocean's surface. They looked like clumsy seals flopping around noisily. The divers exited the water, took off their fins, and dragged their heavy equipment up to a staging area on a nearby patch of grass. They were out of sight, which helped Nathan's situation a little, but they could still be potential witnesses. He hoped he wouldn't have to take them out as well.

A nearby hotel obstructed the view of the beach from the street, which is one of the reasons why he had chosen this particular spot. That, and because it was a frequent starting point for divers, according to his paid source.

Nathan breathed a sigh of relief when he changed vantage points and saw the three men make their way to the street and start loading their equipment into a parked car. Watching them as they drove away, he hoped no one else would happen by, either on foot or in a vehicle, until after the job was done.

He turned his attention back to the waves just as two heads popped out of the water.

"These may be my birds," Nathan whispered. He figured the easiest thing to do would be to ask them their names once they hit the shore. To his good fortune, the older of the two removed his mask and hood, and then shouted something to his partner. They were too far out for Nathan to make out the words clearly. The two continued toward the shore, and once he was able to make out what they were saying, Nathan hung on their every word.

"All I need is to hear their names," he said.

As if on cue, the older man, noticing that the teenager appeared to be struggling, asked, "Jacob, did you lose one of your fins again?"

"Yeah," the younger diver barked, "and get off my back, dad."

Nathan reached into his jacket and caressed the small caliber handgun that rested comfortably in his shoulder holster. "Bingo."

The two divers were now waist deep in the water, the father slightly ahead of his son due to the youth's carelessness with his gear. Nathan approached the shore.

"You know, I'm really tired of buying…" the older diver's words drifted off when he realized something was wrong with his son. The kid's eyes had gone wide, and he was shaking as though undergoing a violent seizure.

The teen was pulled under and resurfaced almost immediately. "Help!" he managed to cry out as he spit out a mouthful of water.

"Jacob!" The older man started toward his son, fighting against the surf as it rushed the shore.

"What the hell," Nathan said.

The younger man was lifted out of the water, held aloft by what appeared to be a giant claw. Whatever it was attached to started to rise from below the surface. Water cascaded off a large oval-shaped shell, and as it cleared, Nathan saw two black eyes the size of bowling balls staring back at him.

He was too shaken to draw his gun. Everything he knew about the world or how it worked was being tested. Never believing in the boogie man, aliens, or as anything like that, he was having trouble accepting that a giant crab was rising out of the ocean.

"You have got to be kidding me?" he said. It felt like he was dreaming, the sight was so incredibly surreal. A mixture of emotions flooded his system—fear, awe, disbelief—but it was when he saw the beast step toward him that he felt the first sense of danger. He watched as the young man it held was cut in two by the massive claw, each half falling into the water.

He finally found the courage to draw his firearm. When the creature shifted, he fired. The bullets careened off the hard exoskeleton, the hot lead as useless as a thrown rock.

Suddenly, there was a loud roar, low and piercing. The glass from the windows on the nearby hotel shattered and blew inward. As the dust settled, people raised their heads to peer out from the open rectangles, the curtains dancing over them like wandering apparitions. Then, Nathan heard the first scream. It came from a rather large woman standing on her balcony.

The creature ignored the gathering crowd and turned its attention to the remaining diver, who was too shocked by the sight of his son floating in two pieces to move. As the claw lowered toward him, the man recovered enough to try to scream. His mouth was open, but no sound came out. The creature reached down and pinched his torso near his beltline. The man finally let out with a shriek and drew his knife. He stabbed at the hard shell that covered the claw, but nothing happened. There was no damage. Not even a scratch.

He looked at Nathan. There was a desperation in his eyes; the man knew that he was about to die. Raising its massive pincer, the creature pulled the man toward its mouth. Nathan watched helplessly as the man was pushed into the undulating mandible head first, and in a matter of seconds, his fins, with his feet still inside, landed on the beach.

Nathan couldn't believe his luck. Both of his intended victims were dead, and not a single shot needed to be fired.

The creature moved. It pounded its way onto the beach. The hotel patrons panicked. Some disappeared deeper into the building seeking protection, while others watched the spectacle taking place below.

Mini waves created by the force of its legs pushing water forward washed over Nathan, driving him backward. He stumbled.

The beast stepped over him, and Nathan turned and watched its progress as it attacked the hotel. It swung a massive claw at the structure. Pieces of concrete fell on the escaping masses of tourists and smashed the cars parked on the street.

The devastation happened quickly. Nathan didn't know which way to run. A part of him wanted to get just far enough away so he could still witness the destruction of Cannery Row. He was behind the creature now, and in no apparent danger, so after holstering his gun, he stood and ran down the beach to put some space between him and the marauding beast. While he ran, he saw the couple and their kids from the winery scurrying toward their expensive SUV. The vehicle was far enough away from the chaos that they must have thought it was a good idea to get in and drive away. The creature tore a large section of the hotel free with its claw. It threw the mass of steel and stone over its head. Nathan saw the bus-sized projectile fall in slow motion and land on top of the escaping SUV, crushing it flat.

"Wow, a khaki sandwich," Nathan said with a nervous giggle. Although he felt bad for the children, he thought the parents got exactly what they deserved. He continued down the beach.

He saw a tattered piece of wetsuit rolling in the current, and then something else caught his attention, something shiny and out of place given the circumstances. It had washed up onto the shore.

He made his way over to the object. It was an expensive-looking dive computer still strapped to a man's wrist.

Nathan crouched down and undid the watch from the severed arm. He turned the watch-sized computer over and saw the man's name and address engraved on the metal backing.

"Definitely my marks," he said.

Suddenly, something grabbed him from behind. He jumped and reached for his gun.

"What the hell are you doing?" Lisa said.

Realizing he was in no danger from her, he let his hand drop. "You startled me."

"Told you," Lisa said, pointing. She stared at the creature as though she couldn't believe she had been right.

"I know. You win. Now, let's get out of here."

"How?" Lisa asked.

Nathan rolled his eyes. "With my car," he said patronizingly.

The creature moved away from the hotel and started to make its way along the coast toward Fisherman's Wharf. The sound of car alarms and police sirens invaded the once peaceful community. Nathan had to admit that the sight of Monterey's finest made him a little uneasy. He watched the police officers step from their vehicles, draw their weapons, and engage the creature.

Nathan formulated a plan. It was simple. He would slip away unnoticed during the commotion. After all, he did have evidence that his targets were dead. He looked at his watch and considered his timeline. If he left now, he'd have plenty of time to make his rendezvous.

He was only vaguely aware of Lisa babbling about something. He heard the words, *no access* and *tunnel*.

"What are you talking about?" Nathan asked.

Irritated that he hadn't been listening to her, Lisa put her hands on her hips and repeated what she had said. "I said that the earthquake has the roads all messed up on Highway 1 toward Pebble Beach. There's no access to Monterey from the south. The only way in or out of town is through the tunnel to the north."

Nathan remembered driving through the tunnel earlier. "So?" he said.

"That's where the monster is headed. If it destroys the tunnel, we're all stuck here for a while."

Nathan's frustration grew. Creature or not, he had to report back or his life was over. He couldn't imagine what kind of God would hate him enough to put him in this kind of situation. He expected that there would be a couple of hiccups with the assassination, but a giant crab? He was so angry that he wanted to punch someone, but the only person near him was Lisa, and she didn't deserve that kind of treatment. He'd have to do something. Something drastic.

"I've got to stop that thing. Stop it or get around it somehow," he said. "You went to college. How do you think a monster that size could be destroyed?"

"I study geology remember? I have no idea how to kill something like that."

Then, Lisa got an idea. "Wait a minute."

Nathan listened intently.

"At my other job they serve crab. When they get a really big one, instead of dropping it in boiling water, they take a knife and puncture it just under its apron."

"Apron?"

"It's kind of like its belly. And it's slightly under its mouth." Lisa pulled out her smart phone. She was having trouble getting a signal, but when the device did connect, she referenced a picture from the internet of a local species of crab. She used her index finger to show Nathan the spot. "That's how you would kill it."

"Great. Now all I need is a giant knife."

Nathan heard the siren first, and then saw the fire truck as it rounded the corner and came to a halt in the middle of the street. The fire fighters hastily disembarked to help the injured people on the street.

"Follow me," Nathan said. "I need you to operate some equipment."

"What equipment?"

"That." Nathan pointed to the truck.

"No way," Lisa countered. "I'm a college student. I don't know anything about fire trucks."

"You don't have to. I'll take care of everything."

"And why would they give us a fire truck?"

"They won't. We'll have to take it."

"I can't steal anything. I'm not a thief."

"There's a first time for everything," Nathan said as he started toward the truck. When he realized she wasn't following, he turned back to her. "Look, you're going to have to check your morals at the door for just a little while. Your community is dying. The cops are useless. They wouldn't listen to us anyway."

His words seemed to have the desired effect as Lisa visibly calmed.

"On the ladder to that truck there's a three inch pipe and a spray nozzle. It's used to spray down tall buildings. Trust me. My father was a fireman."

"So, are we spraying it with water?" Lisa looked confused.

"No. We're going to extend the ladder and ram the pipe into its belly, or apron, or whatever the hell you call it."

"You're crazy."

Nathan eyed the retreating monster. "Maybe a little, but all I need for you to do is raise the ladder. I'll drive. When we're close enough, we'll jump and give that thing a belly ache from hell."

Lisa looked about frantically hoping somebody would step in and offer some assistance. She wanted to help, but was scared.

Nathan knew she was more than capable. She just needed a little push.

"Remember when you said I was a good person?"

"Yes."

"Well, I am, I've just made some mistakes, and I was given a choice. I came here to do a job. That's why I have the gun." He opened his jacket and looked at his shoulder holster.

Not knowing what to say, Lisa held her hands to her mouth.

"I didn't do what I was sent here to do, but the job is done all the same, thanks to that thing. Now if I don't meet with a very unsavory character soon, he'll put out a contract on me. Either way my life is in jeopardy. So I have to try, and you're the only one that can help me."

She listened to him, but still was not swayed.

"Besides, didn't you say you were up for an adventure?"

Lisa cocked her head, thinking, and raised an eyebrow as a smile played at her lips. She could see that he was being sincere, and even though it was against her better judgment, she finally agreed to help him.

Relieved, Nathan started to put his plan into action. "I'll run down how to use the joysticks on the ladder as soon as we grab the truck. Don't worry, it's easy."

With his plan in place, and Lisa in tow, he made for the truck. Luck was on his side when he realized the engine was still running. Nathan opened the door and got behind the steering wheel while Lisa climbed into the passenger seat. Once she was safely buckled in, he stepped on the gas pedal. The truck engine roared, and they were on their way to kill the beast.

While on the road, Nathan explained to Lisa how the joy sticks worked. She nodded as if she fully understood, but the expression on her face said otherwise. He knew that if she didn't, she'd figure it out eventually.

Meanwhile, the creature was making its way toward the tunnel. People scurried out of its path and tripped over each other as they made their escape. The monster roared and slapped at the vehicles on the road. It seized a yellow Porsche in its claw and threw it across the highway. The sports car flew into the side of a gasoline truck, causing a massive explosion.

Nathan followed the destruction until he caught sight of the beast. Cars and tourists were strewn about the battlefield. The seaside town known for its exquisite beauty had been turned into a war zone, the allure of white sands and rolling waves replaced by an unwanted terror.

Shaking his head at the destruction, Nathan was forced to slow his speed as he made his way through the obstacle course the street had become. Time was not on his side because the monster was almost to the tunnel. If the throughway became plugged up in any way, he wouldn't be able to make his meeting. He shivered at the thought of what the mob would do to him.

He stopped the fire truck and told Lisa to go to the back and man the ladder controls. She would have to make adjustments so they could hit the right spot. He was putting a lot of faith in her ability because he knew they would only have one shot. He hit the sirens and sped forward.

Lisa was a little awkward at the controls, but managed to raise and extend the device. She saw the flaming gas truck in the distance. She called to Nathan, who stuck his head out of the window. She pointed to the inferno.

"Make sure you jump before we hit the fire," Nathan shouted.

Lisa made the sign of the cross along her torso as she prepared to jump.

The truck's sirens blared, and Nathan pulled at the air horn. The creature took notice of the commotion to its rear and spun to engage the new threat. They were almost at the flaming wreckage. Heart pounding, Lisa made one final adjustment to the ladder before abandoning her post. She waited until Nathan had to slow down a bit to get around a stalled sanitation truck before making the leap. She hit the pavement and rolled until her body finally came to a halt. Breathing heavily, she moved her limbs to make sure she hadn't sustained any injuries other than the scrapes and road burns. She struggled to her feet and took cover behind a flipped over car so she could watch Nathan's assault on the creature.

"Good luck," she whispered.

Once he had maneuvered around the truck, the way ahead was relatively clear. The only thing between him and the giant crab was a wall of flames. Nathan floored the gas pedal. The sirens were still blaring and he leaned on the horn, hoping the noise would distract the creature. The monster issued a loud bellow that cracked the windshield of the fire truck. Nathan was getting ready to make his own getaway when the crab charged.

Time to go, he thought. Flinging the door open, he went to make the jump, but was jerked back into the seat. "What the…" He looked around and saw that his jacket had become entangled on a piece of equipment jutting out from the rear of the cab. There was no time to free himself. He settled back into the driver's seat and shut the door just as the truck collided with the fire. He felt the cab heating up and prayed the truck wouldn't stall. If this didn't work, he knew the fire wouldn't be the worst thing he'd have to face. He still had about two tons of raging claw to deal with.

The creature saw the truck barreling through the flames. It swung its giant pincer in a downward arc, but the vehicle managed to slip past the attack. The pipe at the end of the ladder missed its mark; the creature was too tall. Nathan slammed on the brakes while at the same time turning the wheel, and the truck started to spin on the slick pavement. The vehicle caught the creature's legs on one side. Thrown off balance, the crab fell.

Watching the monster crab collapse under its own weight, Nathan stepped on the gas pedal again. It took a moment for the wheels to grip the pavement, but when they finally did, the truck leapt forward. The make-shift harpoon struck home, burying itself deep within the crab's belly. The weakened windshield shattered and safety glass rained down around Nathan as the creature roared and fell to one side. Its legs shook wildly. The force of the collision threw Nathan forward and he felt his jacket rip. He wasted no time crawling through the opening left by the shattered windshield and scurried over the hood. He darted across the street and was running down the road when the fire truck exploded. The force pushed him to the ground.

Lisa ran to his aid. His clothes were smoking, so she helped him up and patted him down. They turned to watch the creature burn.

"Well, what do you know," Nathan said, a note of disbelief in his voice. He truly didn't expect he'd be alive at the end of all this. "We did it."

Lisa laughed, but stopped abruptly when she noticed Nathan's gun.

He looked down at the firearm. Removing it from his holster, he tossed it over the small embankment into the ocean.

"I would never any good at that kind of job anyway. Let's get out of here."

Lisa hugged him.

"Feel like going for a ride?" he asked.

Since she didn't have a lot going on other than school, Lisa decided to take a chance.

The two made their way back to Nathan's car and immediately hit the road. There was a massive amount of debris on the highway, but Nathan was confident he could navigate through the wicked obstacle course. The trick was to get out of town before the police closed everything down. There was a massive amount of confusion, which gave Nathan a small opening that he took advantage of. Finally, they were on their way out of Monterey.

Nathan figured that when he had his meeting, the less he said the better off he would be. There was no way to explain what had happened. Even he didn't believe what he'd seen, and he'd been there. The media would make a few incorrect generalizations before they got the story right, so he wasn't too worried about what his "boss" might or might not know about the incident.

He and Lisa drove into the night. Before they reached their destination, Nathan wrapped the dive computer in a towel that he had in the trunk of his car.

Before heading on to the pre-arranged meeting, he stopped by a road-side motel, got a room for the night, and left Lisa to recover from their ordeal. Then he was off to meet The Man.

* * *

The location for the meeting was an abandoned warehouse, and when Nathan walked in, he found himself in near-complete darkness. He stood there, waiting.

"Any problems?" a voice asked from the shadows.

"No," Nathan replied.

"Really? I heard some reports of a disaster of some kind in that area yesterday. You didn't see anything?"

"Nothing that concerned me."

"Your gun," the man said.

"Not with me," Nathan replied.

"Hold up your arms."

Nathan complied. Someone seized him from behind and patted him down.

"Nothing," the man behind him said.

"Now back to business," the shadowy figure commented.

There was silence as the man seemed to think things over, weighing the truth of Nathan's words. Finally, he said, "Look on the table, Mister Cross."

A light came on in the center of the floor, revealing a table upon which sat a black-lacquered box.

He pointed to the box. "What's that?"

"For you."

Nathan approached cautiously and lifted the lid, half-expecting it to be booby trapped in some way. What he saw amazed him. Nestled in a bed of molded red velvet cloth was a dagger, the hilt of which was in the shape of a cross. Nathan retrieved the weapon and wrapped his fingers around the handle. It felt good in his hand, and had obviously been crafted just for him.

"Thought it was fitting," the voice said, "in the event that we could entice you to work with us again sometime."

The man obviously didn't know that Nathan hadn't killed anyone, but that was a secret he intended to take to the grave.

Nathan looked to where the voice was coming from. "Thank you. Now I have a gift for you." Without waiting for a response, he placed the dive computer on the table.

"What's that?" the man asked, obviously confused.

"Your proof."

The shaded figure stepped forward to retrieve the device, and then quickly retreated back into the shadows. After a moment, he said, "Nice, but how is this evidence that the mark is dead?"

"It's a dive computer. If you flip it over you'll see the correct name inscribed on the back."

"You could have purchased this yourself and had it engraved," the man said. "Nevertheless, I'll accept it. You know what will happen if I find out you've deceived me, don't you?"

"I know," Nathan replied. He was beginning to sweat. Even though he knew the executive and his son were dead, he still couldn't help but worry.

"Until we meet again, Mister Cross," the man said. His parting words were immediately followed by the echo of footsteps as he walked away.

Nathan had no intention of doing anything ever again that would have him crossing paths with such an unpleasant individual. He picked up his new acquisition. He left the building and climbed into the car.

As he drove along the empty highway, images of what he'd been through continued to play through his head. He had yet to banish them by the time he got back to the motel, and he doubted he would ever be able to remove them totally from his memory.

When he arrived back at the motel, he found Lisa was still asleep. He stood over her briefly, watching her in peaceful slumber, and smiled. The nightmare would have been worth it if only she would stay with him. He didn't know if she would, but he hoped. And while the future was uncertain, there was one thing he knew for sure: He'd be steering clear of the ocean and would never visit the coast ever again.

GRONK!

Doug Blakeslee

Its nose dug into the silt and mud, rooting up the fish and small crustaceans, consuming them with a gulp. It wiggled across the bottom of the lake, searching, eyes closed to let other senses do the work. Water rushed over and around its massive body, unable to penetrate the layer of oily fur. Great webbed hands paddled and its tail flapped to move it through the murky waters. Nothing escaped its keen senses, locating and exposing prey for consumption. But it wasn't enough. There was too little to fill its massive stomach and endless appetite. It needed more. Something larger than its normal fare. Something tasty. It knew where it had to go. It pushed off the bottom, moving upwards with great strokes, water swirling in its wake. Mouth open wide. Hungry. Consuming.

GRONK!

* * *

Sunlight sparkled off the waters of Vancouver Lake. Steve Wilson pulled down the brim of his trooper hat and squinted across the rippling surface. He donned his sunglasses, finally able to see without the glare. Wind whipped up waves on the normally placid surface of the lake in the early dawn hours. A small, rocky beach encompassed the body of water, leading into a reed-filled marsh to the west and south. He squatted down and looked at the mess before him, a pile of water-bloated flesh and chewed bones; a pulpy mess that was once human. Only the upper half of the body lay on the ground, raggedly torn just below the rib cage.

"Dang shame," said his partner, Dale Merchant. "What do you suppose tore him in two?"

"No idea. Something big," Steve drawled. "Go check out the motor-bike and call in the license."

"Will do."

A red and white Henny-Packard ambulance backed into the lake parking lot from the packed dirt road. It was wide enough to let two Hudson Hornets pass with inches to spare or drag race along the mile long stretch. His '49 Hudson Commodore black and white sat parked along the side of the road, along with the mayor's '54 Buick Skylark convertible.

Useless car for this part of the country. Rains too damn much. Not like Texas. He caught himself wishing for the state of his birth. The flat expanses, hot summers, and minimal rainfall. Not like here, with the persistent greenery, high peaks of the Cascades to the east, and the rainy season from September to June. *Two weeks of hot weather, then it's barely ninety for the rest of the summer.*

The mayor, Joseph Sohns, clucked and fussed, waddling towards him in an off-the-rack gray-striped seersucker suit. A photographer for the *Columbian* screwed another bulb into the camera flash. "Deputy Wilson. I thought the lake was off-limits to swimmers," huffed Mayor Sohns, waving the fat cigar between his yellow-stained fingers.

Steve jerked a thumb towards the posted signs that were partially submerged in the lake. "Got signs along every access road and trail leading down here. The sheriff's office sends out a patrol or two at night. Not our fault that he ignored the signs."

"That's not an excuse. The sheriff said he would assign a deputy full time, and I want to know why this is not happening."

"Look," he drawled. "We don't have enough men to post someone out here full time. Half the deputies quit after the election. We barely got enough to cover the highway and back roads. This mud hole isn't a priority."

"A man drowned last night and it's not a priority?" Sohns' face turned a bright shade of red as beads of sweat dotted his thinning black hair.

"He didn't drown. Something cut him in half."

"Nonsense. He drowned and some wild dogs ate him."

"Mayor, I've seen people eaten by dogs. They don't leave a body in that shape."

"Perhaps he was cut in half by a barge. The blade would cut a man in half easily, and then the tide washed him here."

Steve looked over at the Columbia River, a few hundred feet away through the swampy ground. "That's a big tide and no way it would flood this far."

The photographer hovered over the scene, taking pictures as the ambulance drivers covered the body and lifted it onto the stretcher. Dale jotted something down in his notebook as he examined the battered red dirt bike. Mayor Sohns wrung his hands, pacing nervously, and pointedly looked away from the body.

"A mess. This is an appalling turn of events."

"I'll talk with Doc Housen later today and see what his autopsy turns up." Steve looked back at the lake and noticed a glint of light off something metal on the far side. "Anyone living out here?"

"No one lives out here," snapped the mayor.

"What about Arnold Pellswit?" said Dale.

"That old hermit? Hasn't that ol' coot died yet?"

"Nope. Still hangs out here, fishing and trapping for a living."

"Is that his shack over there?" asked Steve.

"Yeah. He's supposed to have a still around here somewhere. Sells it as a cleaner to a few of the garages."

"I'll go see if he saw anything. Dale, run down the owner of that motorcycle and see if it matches the victim."

"Will do."

"I expect a full report, Deputy Wilson." Mayor Sohns whirled around and stomped off towards his car, the reporter tagging behind like a stray dog. The ambulance pulled out of the side lot, gravel crunching and popping as it accelerated away.

"Idiot," Steve muttered under his breath.

* * *

High, dark clouds obscured the sun, threatening to unleash a late spring rain as Steve reached the hermit's dwelling. Moss and mold crept up the sides of the shack. Pieces of corrugated tin and scraps of wood were nailed together haphazardly to form the sides and roof. From the top rose a thin metal pipe. A piece of rough-cut plywood rested on rusted hinges, and a length of heavy rope nailed in place served as a handle. Someone had written "No Trespassing" on the door in white paint, now faded by the weather.

Patches of reeds and grass grew around the structure, interspersed with rusted drums, bags of trash, and accumulated flotsam. A wooden chair with a hole carved in the seat and bucket acted as a crude, noisome outhouse, enclosed by three walls and a tin roof. Cords of wood, covered by an oilskin tarp, were stacked against one wall.

"Hello? Anyone home?" Steve called out.

Silence.

"Mister Pellswit?" His knock rattled the flimsy door.

Silence.

The door was unlocked as Steve pulled on the rope handle, allowing light to spill into the dark, dank interior to reveal a sparsely furnished dwelling. An old spring bed with a thin mattress and blankets was positioned in the corner, a steamer trunk at the foot, and there was a wood stove in the middle of the floor with a pot of a cold, thick *something*. Body odor pervaded the dwelling.

Something rustled in the cattails and tall grasses.

"I thought I told you lot to leave me alone!"

Steve turned in the direction of the voice. Its owner was ancient. Deep lines creased a face tanned by exposure to the elements. Wisps of white hair dangled from the sides of his bald pate. His hand gripped a gaff hook, while the other held a stick with a long line and hook. An empty fish stringer lay on the ground, dropped as he emerged from the foliage.

"Mister Pellswit?"

"Who wants to know?" His eyes darted around.

"I'm Deputy Wilson. Want to ask you a few questions."

"What do you want, Deputy?"

"A man drowned in the lake last night. I wanted to know if you heard anything."

"Nope. Ain't heard nothin'."

"No yelling or screaming?"

"No." He shuffled a bit, turning towards the lake only a dozen or so yards away. Steve noticed the decrepit rifle on his back.

"You always carry a .22 around?"

"Got a problem with dogs 'round here. Damn things always barking and trying to steal my fish."

Steve nodded at the empty stringer. "No luck today?"

"No luck at all this week. Damn bluegills ain't bitin'. Sure enough bones on the shore, but not a damn thing in the lake. Have to go to the river nowadays. Long damn walk at my age."

"Sorry to hear that. Hope you have better luck today."

"Anything else?"

"You've had other visitors?"

"Some out-of-town feller and his girl. Said he was a perfessor from up north. Testin' the water for parasites and askin' about the fish. Ain't no bugs in the water 'round here. Not the type that's chasin' away the fish."

"Pardon?"

"Nothin'. Ain't nothin' concerning you," said the hermit.

"What about the fish?" asked Steve.

"All gone. Ain't natural." He scowled. "Ain't no concern of yours."

Crazy old coot. "Did he say where he was staying?"

"Up the road a spell. One o' them fancy places near the highway. The Evergreen I think."

Steve nodded. "Thanks, Mister Pellswit. If you see anything unusual, please give us a call."

The hermit gave him a hard look and nodded curtly, glaring as he ducked into the crude shack. The old man closed the door immediately, and Steve heard the sound of a wood brace being set in place.

* * *

Mud plastered his shoes and the cuffs of his pants as Steve trudged down the path. Rain pattered down, a light drizzle that left small spots on his jacket and the brim of his hat. Another mile and he would be back at the car. Rounding a corner in the path, he paused and whistled. On either side of the path, something had flattened the reeds and grass. Something big. He stepped forward carefully, hand on his revolver, to look up and down the clearing. It ran from the lake and curved out of sight to the left. Towards the river. *This wasn't here earlier.* Mud and plants lay scattered and crushed at regular intervals, uprooted in large clumps and tossed backwards. *Something weird is going on here.*

* * *

Steve wrestled the Hudson off the side of the blacktop, bumping it over the shoulder and into the parking lot. High above the row of faded white bungalows a green neon tree buzzed. Underneath it was a sign, painted in a dark green, that proclaimed *The Evergreen*, along with an illuminated red VACANCY sign. Half a dozen cars were parked in front of the various units. His car lurched to a stop, and he listened to the *ping-ping-ping* of the cooling engine before getting out.

"Hi, Deputy. How can I help you?" Ruth Anderson popped her head out the door, her silver and grey hair covered with a cap to hide the curlers. A cigarette hung from bright red lips, matching the heavy blush on her cheeks.

"Ruth." Steve tipped his hat. "Looking for one of your guests. Came down from Seattle. A professor, I think."

She clucked her tongue. "Is he in trouble? Mister Anderson and I don't want any trouble. Staying in separate rooms, but insisted they be adjoining, if you know what I mean."

"They?"

"A pretty, young thing. Dotes and pampers that old man. He's old enough to be her father, if I'm not mistaken. Disgraceful, really."

"No trouble. I just need to ask him a few questions. What room is he in?"

"He's in 106. She's in 105. Connecting units," she said.

"Thanks, Ruth."

The curtains rustled after she ducked back into the main lobby. Steve walked across to the indicated rooms, noting a late-model Buick in the space for 106, and knocked at the door.

A weedy-built man with slicked-back black hair and dressed in a disheveled checkered flannel shirt and jeans opened the door. His eyes widened at the sight of the deputy and he took a step back. "May I help you?" he stammered.

"Morning, sir. I'm Deputy Wilson. Could I ask you a few questions, Mister—?"

"Pearson. Derrick Pearson. Professor of Biology at University of Washington." He ran a hand through his hair. "How can I help you, Deputy?"

"I understand you were out near Vancouver Lake the other day. Could I ask your business there?"

"Am I in trouble?"

"No, sir. I'm merely following up on a lead. We had a man drown there last night, and one of the locals mentioned that you were there."

"My assistant and I were taking samples for testing. It was recently brought to my attention that the wildlife in the area has been severely depleted. As a scientist, it is my duty to investigate these types of mysteries to ensure it poses no threat to humanity."

"Poses a threat?"

"Professor Pearson has a penchant for overstating the situation, deputy," said a female voice behind him.

Steve turned to find a short brunette standing in the doorway of Room 105. "Ma'am." She was dressed in a similar manner as the professor.

"Deputy, this is my assistant, Lisa McDonaldson." The professor frowned briefly.

"Pleased to meet you," she said. "The professor and I are merely doing field work for the university."

"How long are you going to be in the area?"

199

"Until our work is done," said the professor. "Such studies take time."

Steve nodded. "Thank you for your time. Please be careful when you're out there." He tipped his hat and walked back to the car. In the rearview mirror, the couple entered the professor's room, slamming the door behind them. *Ruth Anderson is going to light up the rumor mill with those two.*

* * *

Its prey slumped down on the log, waving a stick at the big, swift water and wiping at its skin. "Dang fish. Ain't bitin' for nothin'," said the thing. It watched the thing from the reeds that hid it well, giving it a place to bask in the intermittent sunshine and wait for a meal to wander by. It required more food, as nothing dwelt in the small water anymore. The large, flowing water had food, but it was unfamiliar and uncomfortable in that place. Other food was needed, like the meal from the night before. Big food. Warm food. A new taste, even with the strange second skin that didn't taste like food.

It moved slowly, pushing aside the reeds and grasses with a swipe of its clawed appendage. The thing hadn't move, its head slumped to the chest and stick dangling in its hand. Inattentive. Easy prey. It waddled forward, limbs kicking up the small stones and rocks on the shore of the big, moving water. The thing jerked up and looked back, eyes wide and mouth open.

"Ah, the devil!"

GRONK!

* * *

"Deputy Wilson, this is entirely unacceptable! Another man has drowned! When is the sheriff going to do something?"

Steve sighed. "Mayor, Arnold Pellswit didn't drown. Something tore him apart." Blood painted the log a bright red. The hermit's body lay strewn from the dead wood back to the grass, bits of bloody flesh and bone in small heaps, carelessly dropped by whatever had eaten the man.

"Nonsense! There's nothing here that could do that sort of terrible damage! He was out swimming and got caught by the propeller of a boat." The photographer from the *Columbian* snapped another picture of the scene. Dale walked around the area, tagging each bit of the remains, unconcerned and relaxed.

"Why would he go swimming in overalls and in this weather? He didn't seem like one for personal hygiene."

"He was a crazy old coot."

"Not buying it," said Steve. "There's something odd going on here, and it's not just these deaths. Something made a path from the lake to the river through the grass. Something big." He pointed to the swath of grass and reeds, crushed and flattened.

"Kids and their hot rods. Coming out here to drink and smoke and carry on. Just like that couple up at Ruthie Anderson's place. Disgraceful!"

"You shouldn't listen to rumors, Mayor. Besides, there's no remains of a bonfire or tire tracks."

"And you need to pay attention to these drownings!"

"Steve, company," hollered Dale.

He looked up and noted the two figures standing near his partner. "I'll be back in a minute."

The mayor huffed and fished out his lighter, flicking the lid open and closed.

"Professor Pearson. Miss McDonaldson."

"Deputy," said the professor. Both wore denims, heavy shirts, and hip waders smeared with dried mud and bits of greenery. His assistant carried a grey plastic case that was battered and scratched from years of use.

"I'm gonna have to ask you folks to leave. We've got a crime scene here and don't want to offend any sensibilities."

"Thank you for the concern, Deputy, but I've seen dead bodies before," Lisa said, setting down the case.

"That may be, ma'am, but I can't let you any closer." Steve paused. "But maybe you could answer me a question."

"What do you need to know?" asked the professor.

"Have you seen any signs of dangerous animals that may live in this area? Like a big cat or packs of dogs that might tear apart a person?"

"No. There's no apex predator in this area. The territory is small and too close to an inhabited area." Professor Pearson looked at the body, then to the river.

"That sounds very definitive."

"You asked." He turned towards his assistant. "Come along, Miss McDonaldson, we have our samples and need to examine them."

She frowned at him, then gave Steve an apologetic look.

"If you see anything out of the ordinary, please let me know," Steve said.

"I doubt that will happen," said the professor.

He watched the pair disappear back up the trail toward the road. "Dang, he's high strung. Wonder what she sees in him." Behind him, the mayor raised his voice, yelling at Dale. "I don't get paid enough for this."

* * *

"Shouldn't we tell him about the sturgeon carcasses?" Lisa heard the angry voice from the other side of the dune.

"Of course not. Let the deputy have his body and we'll worry about the sturgeons," said Derrick.

"Do you think it killed that man?"

"Improbable. Clearly a pack of feral dogs attacked him. It has nothing to do with our experiment."

"I don't know. Things are out of control."

"Nonsense. Everything's well in hand." He gave her a smug smile. "We should go check by the lake again."

"Very well." She cast a worried glance back at the dune before turning away and walking after her partner.

* * *

Mayor Sohns huffed and puffed up the hill, sweat beading his fat face. Strands of his wispy black comb-over flapped in the evening air. The flashlight illuminated the muddy path that wound around the lake and led towards the hermit's cabin. "Damn fool. Getting himself killed." Behind him, the photographer grunted as the pair slogged through the mud.

"Now we have to get someone to run that still before those gangsters come back," the mayor griped.

"Do you think they killed Arnold?"

"No, we had an agreement. The old fool got careless and got himself eaten by a pack of dogs. Maybe I'll run the still myself; that'll be one less person to split the profits with." He fished out the lighter and flicked it open.

"What are you going to do with your share?"

"Retire to Florida once my term ends. Get out of this wet, miserable city." They stepped into a small clearing, little more than a dozen feet wide. Two sheet metal tanks sat in the middle, copper tubing twined between then. Charred wood lay under one of the tanks, remnants of a fire long gone cold. A blue tarp covered a rough, irregular stack nearby. Crates of clay jugs and mason jars cluttered a crude wooden table. Some contained a clear liquid, as did the bucket under the end of a spout. "Still intact. Now all we need to do is restart the fire."

The reporter opened his mouth, then paused. "Did you hear that?"

"Hear what?"

"Something's in the bushes over there." He pointed off to the left at a clump of reeds and grass.

"Better not be any of those delinquents trying to get at my still." The mayor pulled out a small silver handgun. "Go check it out."

"Hello?" The reporter stepped tentatively towards the waving foliage. "Who's there?"

GRONK!

It charged out, snapping and waddling in a frenzy of fur and webbed feet. With a snap, the surprised man sailed through the air from a flick of the creature's massive head, coming to rest against the covered woodpile.

"What the hell is that?" the mayor screeched, pulling the trigger of the pistol, muzzle flashing in the dark, shots echoing across the still night.

GRONK!

Sohns let out with a scream as he turned and slipped, splatting heavily into the mud. Both the gun and lighter disappeared from his grip. "My suit!" His eyes went wide as the creature lurched forward, webbed feet planting into the ground as it straddled him. The animal's bulk passed over him with inches to spare, filling the air with the scent of wet fur, rotting vegetation, and fish. "Oh God, oh God, oh God." He briefly saw the night sky as the rear feet passed, then the large tail swung into view, rising toward the stars.

GRONK!

* * *

Steve ran into the clearing, .38 unholstered, hammer back, safety off. The mayor's body lay in a muddy depression, broken and twisted from the great blow that had snuffed out his life. His companion had fared little better; the reporter's head lolled at a ninety degree angle from his shoulders. He looked at the cold still, and then at the path leading through the clearing. "What in name of Sam Hill is going on here?"

"A giant specimen of *ornithorhynchus anatinus*," said Lisa, struggling through the path of crushed reeds. "At least that's what it looks like."

"A what?" Steve looked at the three-foot-wide prints in the mud. "Those look like duck footprints."

"Platypus, Deputy. One of the few monotremes left in world and the only surviving member of its genus." She knelt down in the mud, unwinding a measuring tape, and spreading it across the print.

"Miss, I'm not a dumb man, but I ain't no scientist."

"It's an egg-laying mammal from Australia. Lives in the water, eating fish and crustaceans. Small crabs and lobsters. Males have a spur on their hind legs that contains an extremely painful venom." Lisa scribbled in a notebook.

"Venomous? Like a rattler?"

"Not as deadly, but this size might be. It's newly hatched and shouldn't be wandering around."

"Might be? What the devil is it doing here?"

"Professor Pearson created it. He has a theory on evolutionary biology and radiology. He thought that the proper application of radiation to the eggs would create a slight amount of growth to the young. We planted the eggs in the lake and let them incubate naturally. They're born helpless in the wild. This one is obviously not helpless, and it's very hungry. They can eat twenty percent of their weight every day."

"Eggs? There's more than one of those things?"

"We found the nest and only one hatched."

"Miss McDonaldson, are you telling me that a giant platypus, whatever that is, ate every fish out of the lake? And that it's only a baby?"

"Yes, Deputy. The side-effects of the radiation accelerated its growth beyond our expectations."

"And you got some sort of monster?"

"It's not a monster, but a great breakthrough!" said the professor, stomping into the clearing. "Imagine chickens the size of cows. Eggs the size of your head. It would solve the world's food problems in just a few short years."

"Derrick…"

"Don't start, Lisa. We've had this discussion. The creature needs to be captured and studied."

"This isn't what we planned. It devoured every fish in the lake and attacked people! If more of those eggs hatch, they'll cause even more damage."

"A small price to pay. Think of the accolades and the grant money. We can establish a proper laboratory."

"I hate to interrupt, but that thing has killed four people, maybe more. I'm gonna get some men out here and hunt it down," said Steve.

"You can't! I won't allow it." Professor Pearson tackled him, catching him off guard. Both men crashed to the ground. Steve's .38 plopped into the mud.

"Mister, you're making me angry." Steve balled up a fist and swung blindly at the professor. He was rewarded with a sharp exhalation of air from the thin man as his fist made contact. The professor threw a punch that connected with his chin, driving his head back. "Get off!"

Suddenly, the heavy weight on his chest was gone as the professor scrambled free.

GRONK!

Lisa let loose with a high-pitched wail of terror, stumbling back and collapsing on the wet ground.

The platypus waddled down the path, webbed feet pushing its fifteen-foot-long body along at a rapid pace, mouth opening and closing under the bill-like beak, tail wagging in the mud behind it. Water beaded and slid off the oily fur.

GRONK!

"That thing's huge! I've seen full-grown gators that aren't that big."

"Fascinating. An adult would be over twice that size. Even its vocalization has been changed." The professor clambered up from the mud. "Amazing."

"Derrick! Look out!"

Steve scooped up the pistol, shaking away the mud and water, and pointed it at the oncoming monster. *Click.* "Hell." *Click. Click.*

Professor Pearson scrambled through the mud, leaving furrows as his hands and feet clawed feebly to move him out of the way. He reached the still as a clawed, webbed flipper speared him and the tank. Clear liquid sprayed out, soaking the creature and dulling the sheen on the fur.

"No!" Lisa sobbed.

A glint of metal caught Steve's eye. The mayor's lighter. Closed. He scooped it up and flicked open the cover. It sparked twice, then caught. He ran forward, cupping his hand around the small, flickering flame.

Small, beady eyes focused on the movement and light.

GRONK!

The moonshine-soaked fur flared up with a bright blue flame that lit up the clearing. Steve grabbed the bucket from under the tap and heaved, sloshing more moonshine onto the creature. Air whooshed as flames engulfed the monstrosity.

It thrashed, bill and tail whipping widely from side to side. Metal buckled. Twisted. Split. Moonshine poured out and pooled under the creature. It didn't take long for the flames to ignite the liquid. A bonfire of blue flame roared into the night sky, accompanied by the crackling of skin and a wailing cry.

GRONK!

* * *

"Shame about the mayor. Who'd a thought he was running booze," said Dale. He stood at the edge of the clearing, one hand on hip, the other pointing at the scene.

Dawn revealed the extent of the devastation. A large patch of charred ground, dried and baked by the heat of the conflagration. Metal melted into pool of slag amid shattered jars and jugs. White blankets covered three heaps in the midst of the clearing, surrounding the larger blackened hulk. A lingering odor of burned hair and pork filled the area.

"No wonder he didn't want anyone out here," said Steve. The morgue attendants lifted one of the draped forms, carefully setting it on a stretcher. *That would be the professor.*

Lisa sat at the edge of the clearing, rocking back and forth and mumbling something under her breath. She stared past the remains of the creature with unfocused eyes, looking at the lake.

"What's she saying?" Dale gave her a pity-filled glance.

"Something about..." Steve followed her gaze. "...eggs."

THE SHAPELESS THINGS TO COME

Christofer Nigro

I could scarcely believe my eyes upon seeing the chaos before me in the laboratory. I understood how respected and valued Dr. Harold Pymfield was to the company as regards the emerging field of bio-physics, but I personally believed this chap to be a veritable madman. I was just a mere lab assistant, a peon in the hierarchy, so my voice would hardly be heard if I protested his work. In fact, it would likely have led to my dismissal for insubordination, if anything. And as much as my job utterly terrified me now that I was assigned to assist Dr. Pymfield with his secret project, I needed it to pay the bills. I had just married Ethel, she was expecting in a few months, and as the man of the house I simply could not afford to quit. But looking at what was going on before my eyes…

"I assure you that it won't happen again, Mister Brand," Pymfield anxiously stammered to the company bigwig as he simultaneously wiped at the patches of blood and various chemicals staining his white lab coat. "It was just a miscalculation in how fast they would grow, and the main fault can be attributed to the incompetent number cruncher the accounting division assigned to me. Just get that sorry square out of here, and let me do the calculations myself. If you do, I swear that my project will bear lots of fruit with… well, a minimum of costly mishaps."

Mr. Brand's lips appeared a bit tremulous as he looked down for a second and then up at Pymfield again. "Look, just be a trite more careful in the future, Doctor Pymfield. If something like this happens again, you can safely wager than any help we may assign to you is going to start asking for hazard pay, and we're going to have considerable difficulty keeping a hush on what we're doing here from those nosy media moguls."

"I told you, Sir, it wasn't my fault!" Pymfield protested loudly. "I appreciate all the funding and faith you've put into my project, but let's not start building an undeserved reputation against the quality of my own competence when it's these other fools your company assigns to my crew that…"

Despite his realization that Pymfield's talents were unique and highly valuable to the company's potential growth, Mr. Brand didn't get to where he was at the top of the hierarchy—first in the petroleum field, and then branching off into the various realms of scientific development—by tolerating back-talk from *anyone* working for him. He signaled for the anxious scientist before him to cease and desist his protestations mid-sentence with a quick wave of his hand.

"Doctor Pymfield, I will thank you to mind your manners when speaking to me. You're a brilliant man, no doubt, but nobody in this world is indispensable. The most skilled people on this planet in any field that BrandCorp branches into can be considered a liability if they're not team players—especially if they fail to realize who is the employer, and who is the employee. Do you understand what I'm saying here, Doctor Pymfield?"

The young scientist moved his hands over his sweat-soaked, dark blonde hair and clasped his eyelids shut for a moment, as if forcing himself to regain control of his emotions. "I'm sorry, Mister Brand, I meant no disrespect, really. I'm just a bit excited at the prospects of my research, and whenever a promising bit of work hits a… setback like this, I'm sure you can understand that those who put so much into it can become a bit overwrought."

Mr. Brand looked around at the spectacle of broken flasks, overturned tables, pools of blood, and the bullet-ridden body of a gerbil the size of a cow laying insensate just a few feet away; its dead, bloated body was twisted in a grotesque manner akin to a fetal position. He winced visibly as screams of agony and remaining terror could be heard echoing from the nearby company infirmary like a ghastly cacophony from an episode of *Thriller*. Scenes and sounds like this were not to be heard even in a midnight viewing of Universal Studio's *Frankenstein* when it played on Shock Theater the previous Saturday morning. I knew this, because I was at such a household last weekend with a group of friends who regularly gather at the home of the only one among us who owns a television set for these monster movie marathons. But this… *this* was going on before me in real life, and I could scarcely believe it.

"Pardon me for having concerns above and beyond your own 'overwrought' feelings in the matter right now, Doctor Pymfield," the tall, heavily built, and immaculately dressed CEO coldly retorted. "Do you see this mess? All those gallons of blood on the floor didn't come from that thing of yours that security had to shoot dead; nor did the multitude of broken flasks containing experimental blood, for that matter. And those screams you hear coming from the infirmary? Well, those are from two lab assistants of yours who are overwrought over missing body parts, not the mere result of one's pet project not quite going as planned."

"Of course, sir," Pymfield replied, noticeably forcing his voice to speak in a low, artificially somber, and reproachful tone. "I do not lack compassion for the harm this accident inflicted upon innocent employees. It's just that we were so close... so damn close to finally getting it right. But when Delois injected the boom formula into that rodent, we didn't expect the growth surge to be so quick, nor for the animal to react so aggressively once the growth parameter maximized."

I finally found it necessary to intercede here. I felt that I owed it to my fellow lab hands to 'respectively' call Pymfield on his mindless pursuit of scientific advancement to the detriment of caution and vigilance. Not to mention good old-fashioned ethics. "Um, Mister Brand, may I say something here?" I asked with caution, trying not to flinch when the large-framed CEO looked at me with a daunting glare.

"Yes, I suppose you may, Mister... Burger, correct?" he replied with no attempt to cover his annoyance at my unasked-for interjection.

"That's *Burton*, sir," I politely, but firmly corrected. "And thank you for allowing me to speak. I really appreciate having a voice..."

"Yes, yes, I know. Now kindly stop wasting time thanking me for conferring this privilege upon you and make use of the permission I just granted," he said, with a smirk accompanying his irritated tone.

"Of course, sir." I quickly followed with a barely suppressed cough of anxiety. "Sorry. But anyway, with all due respect to Doctor Pymfield, whose scientific acumen greatly exceeds my own... well, I think maybe he should have anticipated that a radical acquisition of mass to an organism might cause a corresponding reaction in their mental state... leading to, well, sort of... aggressive reactions to everything around them, especially other living beings."

Now it was Dr. Pymfield's turn to give me a discomfiting glare, as if he had just caught me urinating in his can of Mocha Cola. His response was seething with a fiery tone indicative of barely concealed rage. This made me wonder if the rumors of his being a wife-beater might have any validity to them. Not that his personal life was any of my business, mind you.

"Mister Butter, are you suggesting that I'm somehow... shall we say, absent-minded? Or lax in my professional judgment?"

"That would be *Burton*, sir," I corrected, trying to keep any hint of incivility from my tone. "And, to be frank with you, sir, I just think that you may have... well, jumped the gun a bit. With all due respect and concern, you've been working a minimum of twenty consecutive hours at a time since this project began months ago, and that is bound to cause periodic lapses of judgment in *anyone*. Perhaps if you took some time off, and had more rest each day, your performance would improve."

Dr. Pymfield then scowled and waved me to silence. "Mister Burton, with all due respect to *you*—a type of courtesy I'm not required to give, considering your position—since when did you become my therapist? Is making such diagnoses a qualification you have that you may have forgotten to include on your resume when you applied for a job with this company? Because if so, you are quite overqualified for such a lowly position in the science division. So on your behalf, I would recommend an immediate transfer to the psychological medicine division of BrandCorp."

"I didn't mean to come off as presumptuous, sir," I nervously added. "And I never meant to imply that I had medical evaluative qualifications. I was simply giving a suggestion out of concern for..."

"Mister Burton," the scientist curtly interrupted. "Perhaps it would be more constructive if your concern was focused upon maintaining your job to the best of your ability, while I focus on doing the same with my own. Overstepping one's boundaries on the job never creates an agreeable working environment."

I opened my mouth to respond to that, but then decided it was better to remain quiet when I saw the look that Dr. Pymfield gave me. Mr. Brand simply watched the completion of our distressing little exchange with his right index finger on his massive lips, as if deeply pondering something.

Satisfied that he had achieved a moratorium on my perceived boundary-stepping, Dr. Pymfield then quickly resumed his conversation with our lord and employer. "Mr. Brand," he said hurriedly, before the CEO could interject. "I can assure you that I'll get you good results on the growth possibilities of the boom formula, which I developed from that subterranean substance the retrieval team collected. I doubly assure you that I can do it in a relatively short time, with no more casualties and mishaps—or at least, keep such things well within acceptable parameters, of course."

Acceptable parameters? I thought to myself, as I began to shudder. *What, exactly, did he mean by that?*

"Here's the deal, Doctor Pymfield," Mr. Brand finally decreed. "The board is genuinely impressed with what you were able to do with the boom food we acquired. Transforming it into a liquid and tablet form that supersedes the limits of the quasi-culinary version was a true stroke of genius."

"Thank you, Sir," Pymfield proudly stated. "I knew the particle bombardment procedure I developed would do the trick. Unlike the, ah, 'quasi-culinary' version, we can inject the boom juice, or crush a boom pill into a morsel we feed a fully adult animal, and the organism will dramatically accrue mass and reach maximum size parameters within *seconds*. I'm also working on a method to reverse the process, so…"

"You didn't let me finish," Brand interrupted. "Needless to say, despite this breakthrough, the board has come to the conclusion that your zealousness, lack of rest, maverick nature, and your personal problems at home leaking into the work environment have combined to occlude the effectiveness of your judgment. You're a potential loose cannon, Doctor, and we can't have that here."

Pymfield scowled, blatantly biting his lip and choosing his next words carefully. "I understand your concern after this debacle, sir, but accidents do happen in the pursuit of science."

"But some accidents are far worse than others," Brand icily replied. "Some are less excusable and far more costly than others. So here is the other side of the deal I was attempting to explain to you. As of this weekend, we're going to have your lab moved out of Central City and into a small desert facility in Nevada. A small staff of assistants will be provided for you, as will all the facilities you may need to carry on your experiments on behalf of the company. You will follow a new series of protocols that will be specifically written for you, and you will follow them to the letter. Is this understood?"

Pymfield gritted his teeth together so hard I feared they might shatter into countless little fragments of enamel. But much to my regret, he ultimately won the several-second battle he waged within himself to keep his ego and temper at bay for his response.

"All right, sir," he said with carefully feigned courtesy. "Not that I think all of that is necessary, but if you declare it a requirement for my continued services, I will comply. Much is riding on this project, and I can just sense that something *big* is going to come out of it."

Dear God, did Pymfield just make a very inappropriate innuendo? I had to wonder.

"There's one more stipulation before we proceed with this deal, Doctor Pymfield," Brand firmly stated. "Mister Burton will be one of the staff assigned to you, and he will be acting as our lab manager, keeping an eye on the proceedings."

"What!" both Pymfield and I shouted in unison.

"You both heard me," was Brand's stiff reply. "The advice you gave earlier was quite astute, Mister Burton. You clearly deserve to be the head assistant, and the eyes and ears of this company for the duration of Doctor Pymfield's project. I'm thankful that you spoke up like that. The board will feel much better knowing that you'll be there as our watchdog."

"That—that is very generous of you, sir," I hastily lamented, "but considering what happened earlier, and having a baby on the way, I don't think it would be a good idea for me to take such a dangerous assignment, and to be away from home for so long…"

Brand cut me off with that macabre gaze of his that had his bushy eyebrows forming a sinister mask over the front of his chubby countenance. "Mister Burton, relax. It will be but ten days, and our new protocols will insure a safe working environment. Even so, your position as lab manager will provide you full hazard pay, as well as a generous life insurance compensation package for your family should you… well, meet with some unfortunate mishap. So fret not, all will be well for your family regardless of the outcome of your participation."

He smiled that disquieting beam of his, his teeth looming large and yellow. I found his wide smiles utterly disgusting. He then pinned Pymfield with a sharp look, almost daring him to protest, before taking his leave. It was clear to us both that the big boss wasn't going to take 'no' for an answer.

Pymfield then looked at me with that disturbing scowl of his and projected his index finger just two inches from my forehead. "Remember what your boundaries are, Mister Bugger, and we will have no problems working together," he said, then gritted his teeth as he walked out in a huff.

"That's *Burton*!" I corrected with a twinge of irritability at his retreating form. At that moment, I bleakly accepted the following week would begin a long and arduous assignment that would be difficult to endure. Little did I realize what an understatement that would turn out to be, and that years later, I would still not be sleeping nights as a result of all that would ensue at the relocation assignment.

* * *

I experienced a profoundly ominous feeling as I drove along the back roads leading to the desert encampment of the BrandCorp laboratory. The company provided a vehicle that could handle the terrain, as my little '47 Chevy never would have made it. Since I didn't believe in the supernatural, I dismissed the seeming premonition as simple nervousness at being several miles from the nearest town, and many more miles from my family. For God's sake, Ethel was pregnant, and here I was taking time away from her side to spend supervising a malcontent like Pymfield. The extra money would be an immense help, especially if I did well enough on this assignment for the promotion to become permanent. I just couldn't get that bad feeling out of my mind; deep down I knew nothing good could come out of this.

The crude little map Mr. Brand's secretary doodled for me proved quite accurate, and I soon found the small man-made path leading to the isolated laboratory. Its white walls were heavily weathered from the frequent sand storms that corroded its exterior, making it resemble a dilapidated warehouse rather than a new, state-of-the-art lab where advanced science was being conducted. I couldn't help but wonder if the outer appearance had meta-phorical connotations for what was going on inside. I parked near the side entrance where I was to enter. I gulped audibly as I stepped out of the vehicle and approached the facility. The outside heat was quite stifling, and I prayed that Mr. Brand wasn't too cheap to spring for air conditioning.

The side door was unlocked, and I casually walked down the short corridor leading to the single large lab. Approaching the inner lab door, I heard a loud commotion coming from the other side. It sounded like a man screaming, while other voices—Pymfield's foremost among them—shouted frenzied orders. Wondering what was happening, I made the bad decision to see what assistance I could offer.

As I entered the lab, I saw the first thing on the assignment that I will take to my grave: Pymfield and a lab assistant I didn't recognize standing around another assistant who was bellowing in agony and horror as a dog-sized creature with a long snout filled with razor-sharp teeth extended its head out of a cage and gripped the hapless man's leg. Blood was dripping from the creature's mouth. The man's lab pants were stained a dark scarlet. Another cry ripped from the man's throat as the animal viciously shook its jaws, tearing his flesh apart. Pymfield and the other lab assistant each held heavy wooden sticks as they desperately tried to batter the creature's head and free the BrandCorp employee who was slowly having his limb torn off. I gasped in terror, loud enough for Pymfield to hear me.

"Burton, get back against the wall!" he shouted at the top of his lungs. "Now!"

I had no qualms about immediately doing exactly that. "Dear God, Pymfield, what the holy hell is going on here?"

"One of the shrews we fed a boom tablet to grabbed hold of Mister Garrett!" he hastily answered. "For God's sake, I told these fools not to get too close to that cage!"

"You also said you had sedated those animals, Doctor!" the other assistant Lewis, pointed out.

"I miscalculated how long the sedative would last, given its physiological alteration!" Pymfield hollered back. "You saw the animal, Lewis. It looked as if it were asleep when Garrett walked past the cage! But I still told each of you not to approach any closer than five feet, just as a precaution. This is what you imbeciles get for not listening to instructions!"

The argument was then cut off by Garrett's newest screams, along with his yelling in a half-choked voice, "Get this thing off of me! Get it off!"

"Oh dear Jesus…" I quietly uttered, looking around for something to grab and assist Pymfield and Lewis in extricating Garrett's already-mutilated leg from that horrid creature's jaws.

"Garrett, stop struggling, I can't get a clear shot at its head!" I heard Pymfield shout.

Garrett's response was an even louder bellow of white-hot agony as the gigantic shrew, struggling to divest the man's leg of more of its flesh, released a spine-chilling squeal. I could see that his limb was already torn to the bone, and the cracking sound I heard was the shrew's teeth beginning to crush it.

"Move aside, Lewis, you're getting in my way!" Pymfield commanded as the pandemonium continued.

Not waiting for the assistant to move, Pymfield pushed Lewis aside and rushed forward to bring the stick down on the top of the creature's head. It let out a loud screech, and reacted by increasing its maniacal twisting of Garrett's horribly torn leg. The beleaguered lab assistant began emitting screams the likes of which I never knew a human was capable of producing as an unnerving cracking sound was heard from where the animal's teeth were locked onto his leg.

"God damn it!" Lewis hollered. "Doctor Pymfield, do something, for God's sake!"

"I am, I am!" the scientist shouted back. "Just shut up and stay out of the way. You're distracting me!"

Pymfield then moved forward again and struck the animal twice more on its skull, this time leaving an open gash that squirted a thin fountain of blood onto the floor. The animal made a tortured hissing sound, and with a combination of rage and reflex, it jerked its head two more times and ripped Garrett's leg from his body.

When I saw that, I dropped the heavy glass flask I had picked up to hit the creature with and vomited on the floor. I was far too horrified to be embarrassed.

Pymfield struck the shrew's head one last time, completely crushing its skull. It collapsed, its body twitching at the bottom of the cage as sticky brain matter oozed from its shattered skull. Garrett's leg was still gripped tightly in its teeth. A torrent of salivary foam gushed from its mouth to add to the stream of the man's blood already dripping from the creature's clamped maw.

Garrett writhed on the floor, howling in horrific agony. A crimson spray from the mangled stump quickly coated the floor.

"Hurry and get a tourniquet, Lewis!" I heard Pymfield shout as I continued to vomit my guts out. "Wrap it tightly around the area above the wound! And get me that Bunsen burner, quickly!"

Oh my God, I thought as my gastric fluids continued spewing from my mouth. *He isn't going to do what I think he's going to do with that Bunsen burner, is he?*

Spitting the last few chunks of vomit from my mouth, I gasped as loudly as I could, "Doctor... call... call an ambulance... that's what we have to do..."

"No!" he spat in response. "An ambulance won't be able handle this terrain. Besides, we can't reveal what's going on here! Don't worry, I can get him stabilized. Then we'll have a company transport drive up here and get him back to the BrandCorp infirmary in Vegas!"

"But... but," I choked further. "You're... not a... medical doctor."

Working desperately to save the injured man, Lewis ignored my pleas—despite my being the lab manager—and tightly wound the rubber tubing above the stump, hoping to slow the flow of blood so the man wouldn't bleed out. The task was made all the more difficult because Garret was still kicking and screaming with extreme frenzy.

"For Christ's sake," I said, wiping my mouth on my sleeve. "Get him a pain killer. The man is in terrible pain!"

"I have to get this tourniquet on first!" Lewis retorted, making it clear that I should do something useful and get the pain killer myself since I was obviously finished vomiting.

I forgave the tech his insubordination and rummaged through the lab looking for morphine and a syringe. I didn't know where to look, of course, so I basically began tearing the lab apart. *Jesus, what a way to begin my first day of work out here.*

Pymfield affixed the long tube that connected the Bunsen burner to the gas faucet and lit a strong, searing flame. He then rushed over to the still struggling and bellowing Garrett, who stubbornly refused to pass out from the pain and shock as I hoped he would. Lewis leaned on top of him to secure his upper extremities. Pymfield stepped on his remaining leg to hold it down while he touched the flame to the bleeding stump, hoping to cauterize and disinfect it. Garrett's screams increased in volume as the smell of burning flesh and the sickening sound of its sizzling suffused the room.

I felt the urge to vomit again, but I used every iota of my will to force myself not to do so. I finally located a syringe and a bottle marked 'fluidic morphine' in the same storage window. I quickly filled the hypodermic needle with the powerful pain-killing opiate and gently pushed the plunger to force out any remaining air. Then, doing my best not to look at what Pymfield was doing, I rushed over to where Garrett was being held down.

"Garrett, calm down," I said to the wounded tech. "I'm going to give you something to help with the pain." I stuck the needle into his right arm to dispense the painkiller into his bloodstream. I was familiar with measuring dosages accurately, so I knew I gave him a sufficient amount to quell the agony within seconds.

Sure enough, as the formidable opiate fully entered his system, he ceased screaming and fell into a stupor. His flailing limbs went slack, and Lewis let out a sigh of relief. A few minutes later, Pymfield sat back, confident that he fused the flesh on the surface of Garrett's stump so that he wouldn't bleed out. He then ordered us to bring him several rolls of sterilized gauze, which he swiftly wrapped around the stump to further protect it from infection. Garrett just lay there gurgling and moaning incoherently as the twin effects of the shock and the large dose of morphine worked on him. Despite being shielded from the outside desert heat, I perspired heavily. Shock began to set in and I suddenly started gasping for breath. I couldn't believe what had just happened, despite working in a lab where Pymfield was doing his thing.

I became further unnerved when I looked at the large cage a short distance away, at the body of the giant shrew with its shattered skull still oozing blood and cerebral fluids; it was no longer twitching, and Garrett's severed leg was still clutched in its jaws. Further back in the cage, two other giant shrews—these ones apparently still under the effects of whatever sedative Pymfield gave them—were stretched out on their sides, appearing to calmly watch us.

"My God, there's more of them?" I asked.

"I injected four of them," Pymfield replied as he caught his own breath. "One of them hemorrhaged to death, but the other three grew to giant size as projected."

"Yes, and then ate the remains of the one that died," Lewis added.

"Shut up, Lewis," Pymfield replied, clearly annoyed. "Thank you for informing Mister Butler of that needless detail. Now help me get Garrett to the cot in the other room where he can convalesce."

"It's *Burton*," I choked. "And, Doctor, you said that you were going to call the company to get a transport out here for Garret, correct?"

"Yes, but I didn't say I would do it immediately," he replied with an equal degree of annoyance. "We have work to do first. He'll be fine in there, now that the bleeding has been stopped."

"When you're done moving Garrett in there," I said, "we need to talk, Doctor."

"Whatever you say," was his curt response as he and Lewis carried the sedated, but thankfully still breathing Garrett into the other room.

* * *

I moved a chair as far from the cage and the beady, staring eyes of the two remaining giant shrews as I could and still be in the room before sitting down. I made a mental note to insist that Pymfield destroy those infernal beasts the moment he collected whatever data he needed to glean from them. This man had to be stopped, and I had already decided to call the board and make an official complaint. I wanted off this terrible assignment, but at the same time, I felt obligated to fulfill my responsibility to keep an eye on Pymfield for the project's duration. I also remembered my desire to earn as much money as I could for my wife and unborn child. The thought of which obligation was greater kept warring in my mind; was my responsibility to the company—and perhaps, the world—greater than the prospect of not seeing my child grow up and leaving my wife to raise our baby alone?

My dark ruminations ended when Pymfield walked out of one of the adjunct rooms that served as makeshift lodgings and approached me. Seeing his lab coat stained with blood not his own infuriated me, as it caused me to heave.

"You wanted to speak to me, Mister Burton?" he asked me in a contemptible tone of voice. "Am I going to receive a time-wasting lecture about safety precautions, or perhaps about the folly of tampering with the natural order, or some similar cliché?"

I ignored his sarcasm; it had taken only a few minutes, but I was fed up with this damnable project. "When did you enlarge these shrews, Doctor Pymfield?"

"Earlier this morning, around 8:00 am," he said. "We have a mere ten

ATTACK! OF THE B-MOVIE MONSTERS

days on this project due to the cost of the relocation, and I didn't want to wait until your estimated noon arrival before getting underway on the next testing phase."

"So you began working without my being here to monitor your progress?"

"Yes, I did, because two extra hands were all I needed."

"That is not the point, and you know it, Doctor. You were given explicit instructions by Mister Brand himself that this project was now being conducted under my watchful eye, and I can't watch things and make sure all is going well if I'm not here. And you knew ahead of time that I got lost in traffic and wouldn't arrive until noon."

"Those were four invaluable hours that the project couldn't afford to lose. If we fell behind schedule because of your inability to handle traffic or follow a map, I'm sure Mister Brand and the rest of the board would have been furious. Pardon me for taking my job and my obligation to this company seriously, Mister Burton."

I glowered at the scientist as my patience wore thin. "I take my obligations to the company, and to the safety of all those involved, *very* seriously, Doctor Pymfield. That's why whatever time you think you saved starting work before my arrival resulted in Garrett losing his leg. Now call a company transport to pick up Garrett immediately, or I'll phone the board and advise Mister Brand that this project is going to cost more than it's worth on many levels."

Pymfield returned my fiery gaze with one that burnt even hotter. "That decision would cost the entire company, including the four of us in this lab, a lot of money. It would deprive the world of the many benefits this project may produce for it."

"Not to mention a whole slew of nightmares, as if the world needs any more of those."

Pymfield clenched his fists as he often did when enraged while struggling to keep his temper from exploding like an animal euthanized in a vacuum chamber. "Listen to me closely, Burton. Do you want all the losses that occurred during the course of this project to have been in vain? As it stands, Garrett and his family could really use the windfall that the successful completion of this project will provide for them."

I thought about that, as well as my need to provide for my family. I quickly realized that Pymfield and Brand were not alone in being tempted by the lure of the dollar. I'm no communist, but I felt the need to put everything in perspective, even if the resulting thoughts flowed more 'red' than the plethora of blood I just witnessed. I had no idea which sickened me

218

more. But then I offered what I felt at the time to be a good compromise between my need for money and my concern for the wellbeing of everyone involved.

"Here's the thing, Doctor Pymfield. I will put a moratorium on filing any official complaint if you call that company transport for Garrett immediately, *and* if you agree to only work under my direct watch from now on. You can take it or leave it."

Clearly mulling over the offer for a moment, Pymfield made another grudging decision. "All right. Agreed, Mister Booger."

"That's *Burton*!"

"My apologies for continually forgetting that, Mister Burton. I'll call the transport now, and I'll have Lewis look after Garrett until it arrives. In the meantime, you'll have to assist with the implementation of the third phase of the project."

"The third phase? Already? But with the failure of the second phase…"

"Oh, it didn't fail, Burton. After the first shrew died following its consumption of the tablet, the next dosage was properly adjusted under particle stimulation. The other three grew as expected. The mishap involving Garrett had nothing to do with the efficacy of the boom formula."

"But…"

"Mister Burton, did you not want to see this project ended as soon as possible? If so, you may be going home in time to see your baby born, and with a lot more money to contribute to the household as a result of our success. Or, if you prefer, we can miss the time table, which means no money—or we can request more time for the project, which, if approved, will mean perhaps several more weeks or months together in this god-forsaken locale, rather than resuming the preferred company of our families. So, my esteemed head assistant, by all means make your decision."

Damn him, I thought to myself, as I considered all that he said. "All right, Pymfield. Let's get moving *after* you call for that transport, okay?"

"With pleasure."

* * *

I felt a bit better after the call was made. Lewis popped out of the room for a few minutes to let us know that Garrett seemed to be resting, so long as he had periodic morphine injections. Taking that for as much comfort as I could, I diligently assisted Pymfield as he explained his plans for the third phase of his horrifying project. I kept wishing the excited tone he projected while discussing any aspect of the venture would cease, as it was all too obvious how impressed he was with himself.

"See this device here?" He pointed to a large machine with an extended, crimson-colored lens-like projection.

"It's hard to miss."

"It's the particle generator I discussed. I was able to construct it months ago, courtesy of the funding from this company. It's my theory that it taps into extradimensional sources to cull particles that are not readily identifiable by physics as we know it. They provide a subtle, but crucial, alteration to the chemical make-up of the boom formula in its liquid and tablet forms, enabling the altered substance to produce a substantial accruement of mass— presumably from that same theorized extradimensional source as the par- ticles—immediately following injection or consumption by a living subject. The tablet, of course, can be mixed with conventional feed for that purpose, or dissolved in a liquid and then imbibed. The previous version of the boom formula, in the form of 'boom food', would only effect recently born organ- isms, never adults, and the growth only became evident as the organism ma- tured. Can you not imagine what a breakthrough this alteration is?"

"Yes… I think I can."

"And it wouldn't have happened if not for this particle generator of mine."

"So you keep saying."

"Was that sarcasm, Burton? Understand that this accelerator of mine is thus far the only way to produce the specific type of particle I mentioned. It occurs nowhere in the space/time continuum with which we are familiar. It's another X variable added to the one represented by the boom food, which was found in the subterranean depths of the world we know, albeit of unknown origin. And I made a point to patent the design of the generator before going to work on developing it for BrandCorp."

"I get all that, Doctor. Can you explain to me what phase three will entail?"

"Most certainly, since I am as eager to get on with it as you are. This phase is designed to test whether microscopic organisms can be affected by the boom formula."

The look of incredulity that crossed my features must have been palpable. "I don't understand, Doctor Pymfield. You want to increase the size of microorganisms? To make them visible to the naked eye? What sort of benefit would that have for the world?"

"You are predictably short-sighted, Mister Burton. That explains why you are a lab assistant, and not a scientist, despite the fact that we are nearly the same age."

"I beg your pardon?"

"Listen to me! If we can enlarge such organisms, we can study their organelle structures without the need of a microscope. We can actually vivisect these enlarged structures and learn exactly what lies inside and determine with precision how they work. We may be able to more efficiently test the effects of newly developed antibiotics and other deterrents on such organisms. We can test the very parameters of what scale all forms of life can exist on, and how to apply these discoveries to improving the human species. And that is just the short list of possibilities."

"You'll have to forgive my 'short-sightedness' on the matter, Doctor, but I think my questions are pertinent. I have the distinct feeling that not all the possibilities you mentioned are altruistic or designed to improve the human species, but rather will be used by certain people in power to wage war on other people inhabiting foreign lands."

"Forgive me for what may be a personal question, Mister Burton, but do you perhaps have communist leanings you are reluctant to share openly?"

"Hell no! Pardon my French, I meant, 'No, Sir!' I am nothing but loyal to our country and the foundation for which it stands. You had no call to question that!"

"Well, you did express a bit of concern over the possible uses our country may make against foreign adversaries. Would you prefer we just share this data with them for the 'benefit of the people?' Forgive me for wondering, but that does sound a bit 'red' to me, Mister Burton. Have you been reading the rantings of Karl Marx in your spare time?"

"Of course not! Isn't that being a bit paranoid? Using the 'communist' accusation as a way of silencing any concerns you don't want to hear?"

"I suppose I'm just paranoid about the threat posed by the Russians, then? Are you suggesting that doing my share to give my country an edge against such a threat and bolstering the strength of American capitalism is somehow a bad thing?"

"You know that's not what I was saying, Doctor Pymfield!"

"Do I? You didn't exactly make yourself perfectly clear, Burton. And if you don't want me—or others you work with, and work *for*—to think such things, then maybe you should cease making these types of objections to our work here. Consider that friendly advice from a concerned colleague— and a loyal American."

Sighing audibly, I couldn't help feeling just a bit intimidated into retracting my objections, but my livelihood was on the line, and it's not like that wasn't an important consideration for every man who needs to support his family. The world is important, but... I thought it was too big to be the primary focus of my concerns. I realized that I needed to keep telling myself that.

I looked up nervously at Pymfield. "Okay, I get your point, Doctor, as silly as it is to suggest that I'm a pinko. Anyway, I'm still going to do my job and keep an eye on you. So can you kindly tell me how you're going to get microorganisms to consume the boom formula?"

"Gladly. Look and learn, Mister Burton. Observe this petri dish. On it is a drop of water containing an amoeba. A fascinating microorganism, to be sure. No definite shape, a simple, but highly efficient system of organelles surrounding its nucleus, and the ability to use its shapeless mass to form pseudopods to surround and consume particles of food. It's also quite the predator of the microscopic world, often subsisting on other living organisms that share its general scale as a major part of its food source. It more than deserves to be our initial microscopic test subject."

"Yes, I took fifth-grade biology as surely as you did, Doctor. And I can see why you'd consider an amoeba to be your ideal subject for the third phase. But you still didn't really answer my question about how you plan to..."

"You didn't let me finish, Mister Burton. Interrupt less and listen more if you want to learn. I have developed microscopic sacs of protein residue and injected particulates of the boom formula into them. I will use a stopper to introduce those protein sacs into the water. I think our starving amoeba will be glad to consume them. Then we will observe the result."

The bad feeling within me now permeated my psyche to the point where my physical being was feeling the effects. My stomach churned with gastric acid, burning like liquid fire. I prayed I would not have to vomit again. I watched as Pymfield squeezed several droplets of water from the stopper into the petri dish. The impish grin on the scientist's face as he did so made me feel even more ill. I found myself praying that nothing would happen.

"Damn it!" Pymfield exclaimed after two minutes of close observation under the microscope. "Our test subject voraciously consumed the protein sacs, but the boom formula isn't having any discernible effect, though I can clearly see the particles being consumed in the vacuoles."

"Well, you can't expect every experiment to be a success, Doctor. Why not just call it a day as we wait for the transport to arrive and take Garrett out of here?"

"No! Setbacks are to be expected, but you don't quit because of them! Quitters never succeed! You compensate for setbacks."

"I didn't suggest that we quit for good. Only until we've had a chance to study the results we viewed so far to learn why the microorganisms are not receptive to the boom formula."

"Not receptive? We haven't even attempted to enhance the effect of the projected growth with a particle bombardment yet, now have we? The particle generator can be used directly on an organism that consumed the formula. I'm going to put that to the test right now. If this succeeds, there's a chance these mystery particles will be named after me!"

"I don't see that having any discernible effect either…"

"And do you know why you haven't seen a discernible effect of using the particle generator, Bourbon? It's because we *haven't actually used it yet*."

"My name is *Burton*! I think you do that on purpose just to…"

"Concentrate on the task at hand, will you? That is part of your job as my assistant. I'm going to power up the generator and project the particle bombardment directly on the amoeba, with a specific focus on its food vacuoles. You might want to stand back; the particle beam may emit small amounts of radiation."

I did as he instructed, counting the seconds until this would be over. I didn't see the particle generator having any type of immediate effect on a microorganism, and I was hoping that a failure with this part of the experiment would stifle Pymfield's implacable zeal. I was also hoping for the transport vehicle to arrive so that poor Garrett could be taken to the company infirmary in the Vegas BrandCorp facility.

After donning a pair of protective goggles, Pymfield stood a bit closer to the device as he hit a few switches on a back panel to activate the machine. It started with a low humming sound; the scarlet tip of the projector began to glow a fiery red that seemed to get exponentially brighter with every passing second. The projected beam was invisible, save for the incandescence of the projector tip as the mystery particles were snatched from their realm of origin and forced into our universe. Pymfield stood behind the control panel, carefully and methodically manipulating the buttons and switches to make sure the beam was aimed properly. Several seconds passed with no noticeable effect, even as the generator continued to emit a squelching sound more piercing than one you might hear on a radio when it gets stuck between stations.

"I'm sorry, Doctor, but it's not working!" I did my best to shout over the increasingly shrill thrumming of the generator. "Let's call it a day, like I suggested. The transport vehicle will be here any minute, and we should help them tend to Garrett when they arrive."

No sooner had I finished that sentence than my mouth suddenly gaped in horror as the table holding the petri dish abruptly collapsed. The sound of the table crashing to the floor didn't startle me half as much as when I looked down and spotted the reason for the collapse.

I saw what resembled two large, gelatinous, transparent tendrils arise from beneath the rubble. Quickly flowing into view was an enormous blob of clear gelatin, with several dark, shiny structures visible in its interior, all surrounding one particularly large, centrally located structure that was darker still in hue. It made a discomfiting slurping sound as more tendrils flowed from the central mass, feeling about the floor and the surrounding tables as if to acclimate the organism to a completely new environment. Several flasks and chemical cases were knocked to the ground by the probing giant pseudopods as the bizarre blob-like entity lifted itself into view with a horrible gurgling sound.

"Gods alive!" Pymfield shouted. "Burton, it worked! The intense particle generator frequency I used stimulated the boom formula to enlarge the amoeba to far greater proportions than I imagined possible."

"For the love of God, Pymfield, what have you done? We need to get the hell out of here!"

No sooner did I make that declaration than the flowing gigantic amoeba pushed its shapeless mass upward and projected one of its huge pseudopods directly at me. I leapt aside just in time, as the temporary cytoplasmic limb proved strong enough to annihilate the table that was directly behind me with a single blow. The damned thing was ravenously hungry after being enlarged to such an alien scale, and it was trying to consume any living thing in sight.

"Oh my God! Pymfield, do something!"

Attracted by the ruckus, Lewis left Garrett's bedside to see what was happening. Unfortunately, he had no clue what he was walking into.

"What's going on out here?" was the last thing he shouted before screaming at the sight of the car-sized mass of flowing cytoplasm with its glistening interior organelles clearly visible to the naked eye.

Just as he turned to flee, the amoeba flung a pseudopod at him and wrapped itself around the hapless lab assistant like an octopus grasping a fish. It effortlessly lifted Lewis and plunged his body into its transparent, ever-flowing mass. The man thrust his limbs about in unremitting horror as he floated about inside the giant organism's cytoplasm, his flesh rapidly beginning to dissolve as the creature's digestive fluids did their ghastly work.

"Dear Lord, Pymfield, you bastard! We have to get the hell out of here now! But we can't leave Garrett!"

"Then go in there and get him! I'll do my best to distract this beast!"

Showing that he had nerve despite his dangerously unscrupulous aspects, Pymfield quickly seized two flasks of acid and splashed the corrosive liquid on the creature's metamorphic mass. The liquid sizzled on contact with the giant amoeba's outer cellular membrane, which caused it to contract inwardly in pain. Such an attack wasn't sufficient enough to stop it, though, and as I ran towards the now open door to Garrett's room, I had to stop in my tracks as the full mass of the amoeba moved with amazing speed to intercept me. *How is this thing surviving in a non-aquatic environment in the first place?* I found myself wondering. *What changes in its cellular nature were wrought by its enlargement?* The implications of these questions were too unsettling to ponder any further as I saw it readily change shape to slide through the much smaller portal of the doorway.

Peering inside, I saw the still slightly sedated Garrett look up from his cot. I couldn't help but shed tears as I realized the last sight this man would see after everything he'd already been through was one more inexplicably horrifying thing that no man should have to experience. The slithering gurgles made by the amoeba's flowing cytoplasm awakened Garrett from his semi-slumber. Even through the drug-induced haze clouding his mind, he knew what was happening; the look of sheer terror on his visage was another image that would live on in my nightmares for the rest of my life. He managed to muster enough strength to let out with a mind-numbing scream, but it was rapidly cut off as the amoeba's projecting pseudopodia grabbed him. He struggled weakly as the creature pulled him towards its main mass and hungrily enveloped him within its cytoplasmic substance. Garrett's thrashing form joined the partially dissolved remains of Lewis. The lab tech's tongue protruded from his mouth as he tried to scream, but there was nothing I could do for the man. The amoeba's deadly efficient digestive process was already working on the soft tissues.

The gelatinous creature spasmed convulsively as it was struck by a powerful stream of water generated by the laboratory power hose that Pymfield now wielded.

"This won't hold it back for long, Burton! Get out of here. Now. I'll be right behind you."

Scarcely believing that Pymfield could actually have a selfless bone in his body, I did as he ordered and fled the lab. I found myself stopping outside the side entrance in the hot desert sun to shout back at the doctor.

"Pymfield, that's enough! Hurry and get out! We have to find a way to destroy that creature!"

At that moment, the BrandCorp transport van pulled up on the sandy pathway behind me. The two occupants had no idea they were putting their lives in danger by answering our call, and I had to warn them. I ran toward the vehicle, screaming at them to drive away as fast as they could and alert the local authorities. Suddenly, losing my job didn't seem nearly as important as seeing my baby born.

Before I reached the van, Pymfield came rushing out of the doorway, having held off the amoeba as long as he could with the power hose. He stopped and looked aghast as he saw the company vehicle. The driver and his passenger disembarked from the van despite seeing me frantically running towards it, apparently unaware that I was trying to warn them away.

"Okay, where's the patient?" the first one asked me.

"You've to get out of here!" I shouted urgently. "There's a monstrous creature loose in that lab, and it's only a matter of time before it…"

My sentence was cut off as a huge cylindrical pseudopod burst through the window. Within seconds, the cytoplasmic creature flowed its entire mass out of the small rectangular portal like water flowing out of a spigot. Sensing more food in its midst, it lifted a tongue of its amorphous body upwards and rapidly headed in our direction.

"Holy jumpin' shit stains!" one of the men yelled. "What in God's name is that thing?"

The amoeba formed a huge pseudopod and thrust it towards us at blinding velocity. It wrapped around the shocked man faster than he could react, and then pulled him off of his feet as if he were weightless. A horrifying gurgling sound issued from the thing as it pulled its meal into its mass. The man's death throes while floating in the center of the creature's cytoplasm made it clear to us how unbelievably painful the creature's digestive process must be as it started to dissolve the soft tissue.

"Oh my God!" the second man hollered. "That thing just ate Clyde! I'm hightailin' it outta here!"

The man turned and jumped back into the van, making sure to close the door behind him before desperately trying to start the vehicle. It was obvious he wasn't concerned with our fate in his panic.

I ran towards the scientist, who stood near the side entrance, clearly in shock. When I reached him, I forcefully grabbed the collar of his lab coat.

"Doctor Pymfield, we have to stop that thing before it finishes its meal and heads for Vegas! Let's face it, the project is over! Use that great mind of yours to save people rather than doing them in for once!" The scientist's eyes moved around as if contemplating my words. "Can you think of anything to stop that thing?"

"I—I think so! I'm not yet certain if the process can be reversed, but it's possible that further intense bombardment with a focused beam from the particle generator will fatally overtax its system."

"Or it could make it grow even larger and more dangerous!"

"It's my theory that there is an upper limit to how big any organism in our universe can grow and still survive. Simple laws of physics, man!"

"Which *you* seem to have proven can be circumvented! I don't think this is a good idea…"

Incessant screams made us turn toward the van. The amoeba's mass had enveloped the vehicle before the driver could get it moving. He managed to shut both windows, but its cytoplasmic substance flowed around the vehicle, feeling for a way in. Within moments, it found a gap in the side windowsills just wide enough for it to seep through. Its substance eerily filled the interior of the van within seconds, swallowing the struggling form within and dissolving the body sufficiently so that it changed shape within the amoeba's protoplasmic interior, collapsing in on itself as the creature flowed back out of the vehicle. The amoeba then began moving toward us, hoping to complete its unholy desert feast.

Realizing that Pymfield's hypothesis was the only thing that could possibly save us, I put my misgivings aside as we both ran back into the laboratory and readied the generator. I moved the projector into position as Pymfield quickly hit the proper sequence of buttons to generate the intense frequency he intended. The device was slow coming to full power, and I mentally commanded it to hurry the hell up. The amoeba flowed into the entranceway. Quickly detecting the presence of the two life forms within, it started toward us like a colossal heap of ambulatory mucous.

"Oh God!" I yelled as the machine began humming to maximum power.

Not a moment too soon, the projector's transparent tip began to glow its characteristic ruby red. The beam was then released, and the amoeba's nebulous shape began undulating in every direction, as if having the protoplasmic equivalent of an epileptic seizure. Its mass appeared to expand like a balloon filled with water before finally bursting outward, its giant organelles splattering on the surrounding walls. What was left of the bodies of four men also covered the walls in a fantastic spray of gore. Their partially dissolved clothing landed on the floor all across the room with a wet slapping sound.

I fell to my knees and vomited again. I was overwhelmed, first by a sense of extreme relief, and then by complete madness as I began cackling uncontrollably, unable to stop as the entire nightmarish events of the day continuously replayed themselves in my mind.

Pymfield simply raised his arms in triumph and exclaimed, "Yes! The experiment was an unqualified success, despite another setback! I'm quite confident that human trials can begin next! My name will be in all the history books!"

Or at least in the comic books, I thought as I continued to laugh and rave like a lunatic.

GOING TO WORK

Colin McMahon

"One knight, a father, and son go fishing. They each catch one fish and return with a total of three. How is this possible?"

"I've heard this one. It's a grandfather, father, and son," Homer Davidson said, trying—and failing—not to sound bored. He looked up from his bowl of Cheerios to his roommate, Tobias Grossman, sitting on the other side of the pale green table in their equally pale green kitchen.

"Nope. That's the one that goes: two fathers and two sons each catch one fish and return with a total of three." Tobias flashed him a good-natured grin. Homer never understood why his roommate was always so happy. Sure, Tobias had an interesting job, but still… Other than his job, the man never did anything remotely exciting. He ate the same mind-numbing thing for breakfast every day—toast. Not French toast, but regular, boring, crisped bread, and always with the same mundane strawberry jam. So what if he used his combat knife to spread the red goo, it was still dull.

Homer tried to refocus his mind on the riddle as he ate another mouthful of his cereal. The taste distracted him. Cheerios were getting old. They were so similar, each one the same; never any variety. Maybe Fruit Loops next—or better yet, Lucky Charms. On second thought, no Lucky Charms. Fruit Loops were one thing, but even he had his limits on how adventurous he wanted his breakfast. Might as well begin every day with a red bull and a cup of sugar.

"You're thinking about it too much," Tobias interrupted his thoughts.

"Or maybe not all," Homer conceded. "What is it, man? Pen and I have to leave for work in a few minutes." He watched Tobias smile as he cleaned his knife on a napkin. Always so clean. Just once Homer would love to see Tobias wipe his knife on his pants. It's not like anyone would notice it against the camouflage pattern.

"No, no! I want you to guess. The answer is so simple."

Homer rolled his eyes. "Not everyone is as good at deductive reasoning as you, numb-nuts. Did a fish hop in the boat?"

Tobias sighed. "You're not even trying!"

"You're right. I'm not. I've got better things to do." Homer didn't like to start the day with a headache, so he didn't bother trying to ponder the riddle. Let Tobias have his confounded logic puzzles with their bizarre tricks. They took way too much time to solve, and the payoff never felt rewarding afterward. It was time to move on with the day.

He turned in his seat and called down the hall. "Pen, you ready for work, baby?"

There was a moment of silence before his bedroom door opened and Penelope came trudging out, still trying to pull on a sweater over her undershirt. Completely blind, she staggered down the hallway. It was a good thing that he and Tobias kept that corridor vacant or she definitely would have hit something. Unfortunately, the same could not be said for the kitchen, which is where her luck ran out.

"Ow! God damn it!" She cursed, jumping back while tugging the sweater into place. She looked to have a major case of bed head, and the static from the sweater caused a few strands of her long blond hair to stick out like she'd been electrocuted. "What did I hit?"

"The table," Homer replied simply. Pen's face contorted with exasperation and she rolled her eyes. Homer allowed his gaze to drift momentarily back to Tobias. He recognized that gleam in his roommate's eyes. "So, ready to go?"

But his roommate was faster. "She hasn't heard the riddle yet!"

Homer winced. Escape plan failed.

"Oh, is it a new one?" Pen asked, her face breaking into a smile.

"It's Monday, isn't it?" Homer replied darkly.

"Hey, is that a crack at me? Because if it is, I definitely told you one last Thurs—" The walkie-talkie strapped to Tobias' belt erupted in static and his trade-mark grin vanished. He wheeled around, scooping the device up to his ear with one fluid motion. *Saved by the bell*, Homer thought. Work was the only thing that could make Tobias forget all about his stupid riddles. He watched as his roommate stood up and began pacing, all the while speaking furiously into the walkie-talkie. He could have listened in to find out what had Tobias so agitated, but he saw his chance and fully planned to take advantage of the opportunity. If they didn't get out of here now, they were going to be late for work.

"Right," he said, pushing away from the table and getting up. "Ready to go, Pen?"

"Uh, yeah, I guess, but what about—"

"Great!" Homer took her by arm and steered her out of the kitchen. He hurried her down the hall toward the door and escape. Passing the living room, he glanced inside when he heard voices, then realized somebody had forgotten to turn off the television. It took a moment for him to realize the news was on, which was strange because it was time for the morning talk shows. He didn't have time to stop and see what was so important that they would interrupt their regularly scheduled programing; they had to get out of there before Tobias finished his conversation. They paused at the door only long enough for Pen to slip on her shoes. He checked his watch. They still an hour before they each had to be at their respective jobs, but—he glanced toward the kitchen— there was no telling how much longer Tobias would be otherwise engaged. As if on cue, Tobias' voice drifted down the hall. "Hey, Homer, Pen!"

Damn it! He didn't want to answer, hoping by not saying anything Tobias would think they had already left, but the words were out of his mouth before he could stop them. "Yeah. What?"

"Have you seen my gun?"

Thank God that's all it was. "The M4? You left it on top of your dresser." Homer checked his watch again: fifty-eight minutes! Looking up, he saw Tobias dash from the kitchen to his bedroom.

"Ah, so I did! Have a good day at work, you two! I'll see you tonight— unless I'm held up or put in the infirmary. I'll call if I am."

Always so damned cheerful! "Yeah, great. Please do." Homer opened the door for his girlfriend. "I'll want to know if it's okay to turn off the hall light before going to bed. Later!" He tried to hurry Pen out the door before his roommate remembered that damned riddle.

"Bye, Tobias. Have a good day at work!" Pen didn't even have time to say her goodbye before Homer all but pushed her out the door. Tobias started to call out something else, but the thick wood of the door muffled his words. *Free! Score one for me*, Homer thought, an accomplished smile spreading across his face. One last glance at his watch: fifty-seven minutes. He could breathe now; they had gotten out in time.

Both Homer and Penelope walked to work every day. It was just one of many advantages of living in the city, and Homer's favorite, second only to the numerous well-placed locations of Ben and Jerry's. Pen worked at Farrow Laboratories, and he had the thrilling position of assistant regional supervisor at Randall's Box & Shipping Company. Farrow was a lot closer to the apartment—only fifteen minutes—so he always dropped off Pen first before hitting the "trail" (his nickname for his walking route). In reality, Randall's was only a few blocks away, ten minutes by straight shot, but Homer was never one for the straight shot.

His route took him all over town. Between crossing the Sticklon Bridge to say "Hi" to his friend, Walter, and grabbing a coffee at Dunkin, which was located on the third floor of the Galleria shopping center, Homer's route always took him at least half an hour. There was a definite joy in it, however; he reveled in the odd encounters he had that sparked a sense of adventure—no matter how mundane—that made his day just that much more exciting. That was how me had met Walter, a homeless man who could always be found camped out near the bridge. Compared to most of his colleagues who took the direct route every morning and never looked particularly happy, Homer always arrived at work with a smile on his face. His coworkers would be so much better off if they stepped off the beaten path every now and then.

He couldn't do a thing about them, and he didn't wish to dwell on their misery because today was a beautiful day. The sun was out, gleaming off the freshly blanketed snow and giving a warm edge to the otherwise chilled air. The roads, he noticed, were unusually quiet. It was almost as if there were fewer people in the city this morning. Winter had that effect on the population, but today seemed more desolate than usual. Whatever the reason, Homer didn't care; he had the road to himself and the most beautiful woman he knew at his side.

"Is there something in my hair?" Penelope asked. She kept running a gloved hand through it and shaking her head. "I thought I felt something when I was in the shower, but then I got soap in my eye and couldn't find it again. Jesus, it had better not be a bug!"

"In the middle of January?" Homer turned to her, eyebrows raised. Nevertheless, he proceeded to scan the back of her head. "Hold still a moment." He grabbed her hand so that he could get a better look. "Nothing. You're fine."

She gave him a playful smile. "Just fine?"

"Well… maybe a little better." He had to duck at she took a light-hearted swing at him. "Ow! Hey, stop being such a child!" He paused a moment, looking around for a place they could sit for a bit. Work could wait. When Pen got like this, he wanted to take the time to enjoy it. She was far too serious half the time, a side effect of her job.

"I'm dealing with a child," she scolded. "What are you looking for?"

"Just checking to see if there's a Starbucks or a Dunkin around."

"You know there isn't."

"You never know," he said, his tone indicating he knew something she didn't. "These things always sprout up overnight, so there could be."

Penelope rolled her eyes. "Uh... Yeah. Sure thing. And even if one did, we don't have the time to stop. I got a phone call from the lab. They want me in as soon as possible."

"Are you giving a presentation or something?" Homer asked.

"No, it's kind of strange really. We've been conducting a few experiments, but we're in the observation stage right now. Not sure what they need me for."

Penelope's voice carried an edge it didn't normally have, but Homer shrugged it off. She was always doing things at work that he didn't understand—or that she couldn't talk about. Top secret and all that. Today seemed to be the latter; it was one of the few downsides of dating a scientist. He still couldn't even pronounce her actual title: something Latin with way too many syllables. Oh well, if she couldn't talk about it, best to switch the topic of the conversation to something more engaging.

"Maybe they just want a pretty face doing the observing," he mused. That got a smile and a slight blush. He was doing well. They continued talking, mostly about dinner plans and whether or not to drive up to see Homer's mother that weekend (he was in complete favor of hitting the gas in the opposite direction) until Farrow Labs came into view.

"She's your mother; you really need to spend some time with her!"

"Yeah, I know, but you've met her, Pen. You know how depressing she is. How could she be any different? All she does is sit in that house all day, watching the news and drinking wine. Occasionally there might be a grilled cheese thrown into the mix. When grilled cheese is the highlight of your life, how great can it be? Pen... Penelope?" Homer stopped and looked back at his girlfriend. She had stopped and was staring straight ahead, mouth hanging open. Homer turned his head to see what she was looking at, putting up a hand to shield his vision from the sun, and what he saw set off an alarm deep inside him.

To say that Farrow Labs had an air of intimidation to it would be an understatement. Homer always found the grim grayness of the windowless walls to be particularly off-putting. It made the place look like a giant battery. Supposedly, it was for energy efficiency. Maybe it was, and maybe that wasn't what really bothered him. Maybe it was the twelve-foot-high electric fence that seemed to almost hum in anticipation when he stepped too close. Hardly what he would call inviting. To Homer, it looked like a prison, and on normal days, he hated leaving Pen at the gate. The sight that greeted him was evidence that today was anything but a normal day.

Four large army trucks were parked in front of the facility, and soldiers had set up a protective barrier around the entrance of the building. Homer wasn't sure, but he thought he could make out tendrils of smoke rising up from the far side of the building. Had there been a fire? A terrorist attack? He knew that Pen's biggest client was the government. What if Al-Qaeda or some equally insane group had just blown up a bomb or something? Christ! Pen could have been inside!

Homer looked to his girlfriend. She was still staring at the smoldering building. Her eyes were wide, but it wasn't what he expected. There was no look of surprise, just knowing fear. Whatever had happened, she already knew the cause. Suddenly, a thrill surged through him; every morning he longed for an adventure, and now he was getting one. But was this the kind he wanted?

"Come on." He grabbed Pen's hand and hurried toward the nearest guard.

The man turned to face them and coldly put up a hand. "This facility is off limits to civilians and all non-essential personnel at this time." Very officious and monotone. He then produced a clipboard with a single piece of paper clipped to it. "Name?"

"Doctor Penelope Hazlett," Pen replied. Her voice sounded feeble, and Homer thought he could detect a slight tremor. He gave her hand a reassuring squeeze.

"Your name is on the list," the soldier acknowledged. "Please proceed. They are waiting for you." He turned to Homer. "Name?"

"Uh, Homer Davidson?" *It never hurt to try*, he thought.

The soldier narrowed his eyes as he scanned the clipboard. "You're not on the list. I'm sorry, but you'll have to leave." The soldier's expression was distracted. It was Penelope's turn to offer him some reassurance, and she squeezed his hand.

"Could I just see her to the door?" he asked.

The soldier gave him a blank stare. "I'm sorry, sir, but you'll have to leave now. It's for your own safety. Return to your home, turn on the television, and wait for updates."

The television? Homer's mind flashed on the scene he had seen on the news that morning instead of the morning talk show anchor. If only he had taken the time to listen to what was being said. What had happened? Was it another 9/11? Could that even be happening?

The soldier stood his ground. "Sir, you must leave. Now." Just a hint of menace, barely detectable.

Pen released his hand and started walking briskly toward the front gate. He watched her move from his side and ease past the soldier. Even though she was only a few feet away from it, she had crossed a boundary line that made it feel like they were miles apart. He didn't like it. Not one bit.

She turned to look at him. "Just go. I'll be all right." She gave him a smile that was meant to be reassuring. "I'll call you as soon as I know what's going on." *As soon as she knew what she* could *tell him*, Homer found himself thinking bitterly.

"What *is* going on?" Homer heard the pleading in his voice, and he hated himself for it. He felt like a child again sitting at the kids' table, out of the way so as not to cause a scene among the adults, and he had hated that, too. Pen putting him there was one thing, but this soldier... this government lackey... Homer would get the truth out of him.

"I'm sorry, sir, but I have only been instructed to direct civilians to their homes." The soldier did not look sorry. Not yet he didn't.

"But I have to go to work!" He knew how desperate he sounded, how crazy, but he couldn't stop himself. "I can't just go back home. What's going on? I have a right to know!"

Pen tried to soothe him. "I'll call you as soon as I can. I promise." What he wanted was for her to come back to him, to take his hand and take him back home where they would both be safe. Pen was backing away now, each step taking her further away from him and closer to the building. Homer started after her, but the soldier blocked his path. "Please go, Homer," Pen said, and for the first time he heard fear in her voice. Not a fear of what she was heading into, but a fear of what might happen to him should he continue to press the issue, and that scared him even more. "Go home. Go to work. Just go, and I'll call you later."

"You should listen to her," the soldier stated.

"Fuck off," Homer replied, still feeling like a kid mouthing off to the playground bully. Even as his mind rebelled, he realized they were right. He would accomplish nothing here by getting the guard riled up, and knew that the only thing to come of it would be getting himself into a heap of trouble. Worse, he could also get Pen into trouble with her bosses. It was best for all involved if he did what they said. He still wasn't sure where he was going to go, home or work, but either way he'd be able to tune into the news. If they weren't covering the situation any longer, he would just have to wait until Pen called. "You're right," he said, quickly adding, "I'm sorry." He looked at Pen. "Call me when you can. I love you!"

As if ashamed to admit her feelings in front of the soldier, she mouthed the words back to him, then she turned and hurried away.

Homer's sense of trepidation flared again when he saw a group of soldiers hurry from the building to greet her. They conversed briefly before moving as a single unit toward the building. He waited until she was swallowed by that menacing beast before turning away. As he walked, he was hit with a sense of loss and betrayal. Why couldn't he have at least walked her to the door and said his good-bye? It would have allowed them at least a moment's privacy. She could have chosen not to go in, could have chosen to stay with him, but there was more to it, and he knew that. As he walked, he continued to examine his feelings, and then he had it—He felt denied. Denied the chance of what he sought each morning as he took the long way to work: a true adventure. He was also being kept from the woman he loved, but she had made her choice. What did that say about him? He hadn't tried to talk her into leaving with him. What kind of boyfriend just walks off to leave the woman he loves to God only knows what? He should have stayed. He resisted the urge to turn around and go back, but then he remembered the look in her eyes… the fear. She had wanted him to go.

Homer continued to run everything through his head as he strode up the unusually vacant sidewalk. Today was turning out to be very peculiar, and he needed to know why. Luckily, there was one person who might be able to tell him, one person the military couldn't silence: Walter. Whenever anything odd was going down, Walter usually knew about it. He had his finger on the pulse of the city, probably one of the few advantages to being homeless. Almost always on the street, the man heard things the average person missed because they were wrapped up with the pressures and stresses of their day-to-day existence.

With a plan in mind, Homer checked his watch. At this time of day, Walter would be hanging around the Sticklon Bridge. Homer knew this because he always exchanged pleasantries with the man on his way to work, and Walter always had a joke ready for him. Most of the time the jokes were funny, other times not so much. There was something else, too, Homer remembered; Walter was always trying to warn him about something, but what? Homer never paid too much attention to that part of the conversation because he, like everybody else, had their own problems to deal with. Well, today was different. Today, he would listen because he needed answers, and he had a feeling Walter was better than the television or radio broadcast because there was nobody around to censor him.

Moving quickly, Homer raced down the sidewalk and turned the corner that would take him down by the river. The bridge was close and he was anxious to find out what was going on. Sure, he would end up being late to work now, but it was worth it. In fact, work was quickly becoming a distant memory. Homer turned to look into the windows of the passing shops. That's when it hit him. Had he and Pen really been that absorbed with themselves earlier? How had it taken him this long to see?

Everything was closed. Everything!

Suddenly, the air filled with thunder. At least he thought it was thunder. What else made a noise like that? The answer came quickly as several jets streaked overhead. Homer's eyes widened. Had those things had been armed with missiles? Suddenly the cell phone in his pocket vibrated. Thinking it might be Pen, Homer fumbled the phone from his pocket and slammed it to his ear before he realized he hadn't opened it.

"Pen?" He didn't even need to check the caller ID to know it was her. "What's going on?"

"Where are you?" Her voice was strained, containing barely suppressed panic.

"I'm about to turn on to Sticklon. I was going to see—"

"Get out of there. Now! Helicopters will be landing soon to evacuate anyone who hasn't already left. Find one and get on it!"

"What's going on?" Homer screamed.

"Hold on."

Homer heard the muted voices as she spoke to somebody in the room. Even though he couldn't make out the words, he had no trouble picking up on their sense of urgency. Then suddenly Pen was back. "Oh God, Homer. I just received an update. It's practically on top of you!" He knew then that whatever was going down was bad; it wasn't like Pen to lose it like this. That hitch in her voice... She was crying!

He spun around, not sure what he was looking for. Someone... Something... Anything! And then he heard it.

The roar. So loud the ground vibrated and the windows rattled. So loud, yet sounding so familiar. What... It came to him in a flash of memory. Homer had been to the zoo many times as a child. He loved the place so much he had even taken Pen there last summer on a date. His favorite animals were the lions and the crocodiles; she had liked the penguins. The roar, it sounded like a bizarre mix of all three, only so much larger.

Homer turned in a slow circle, like someone lost who was trying to get their bearings. He could hear explosions now, and beneath the sounds of the blasts there was something else. Screams. Homer wheeled towards Sticklon Street, and for the first time that day he saw people. They poured into the street from the surrounding buildings, running in a blind panic. He tried to put it together in his head—Pen's fear of whatever they had unleashed, the roar, the screaming masses—and he couldn't do it. There were still too many unknowns, but he knew how he could find out. Pen had said it was almost on top of him, so it had to be near the Sticklon Bridge.

"Homer!" Pen screaming his name through the phone brought him out of his thoughts, and suddenly he felt guilty. How long had she been calling his name??

"I'm still here," he answered. "I'll find a helicopter, Pen." And then he remembered Walter. "There's something I have to do first."

"No! Just get out of there! Run!" Pen didn't try to conceal the fact that she was crying now, and Homer felt so angry with himself; if only he could lie to her, tell her what she wanted to hear, but he couldn't, not without know what was happening.

"I'll be all right, Pen. Call you back in five minutes, I promise. I—I love you." And before she could say anything that might make him change his mind, he hung up.

There was no more time for thinking; he needed to act because if he didn't, he just might turn tail and run—just like Pen pleaded with him to do. Another roar ripped through the morning air; he could feel the vibrations in his legs. It was now or never, and without thinking what his next step would be, Homer surged forward. This was stupid, so stupid, but he had to see what was making that sound.

Pushing against the rushing, panicked crowd, he slipped around the corner onto Sticklon Street...

And stopped.

"What the hell!"

The bridge was gone. Jagged pieces of road ended in steep drop-offs Cars had been abandoned in the street, and there was one balanced precariously where the roadway had met the bridge, but with the span gone, there was nothing below it. Buildings were crumbled, smoldering wrecks. It looked like a war zone, but there was no sign of what had caused the damage. It took a moment for everything to sink it, and when it did, he realized he really was in danger. *Oh God, what am I doing?*

Homer scanned the horizon. On the opposite side of the river, like lemmings perched on the edge of a cliff, he could see a group of people gathered. They were too far away to see clearly, but Homer thought he could make out Walter's tattered form front and center, but considering the scenario, it could have been anybody.

Realizing there was nothing more he could do, he thought it best to retreat and honor the promise he made to Pen. It was time to find a helicopter and get out of here.

A breeze came out of nowhere, stirring up dust and debris, and with it came a foreign sound. Homer looked up and saw a helicopter descending. The side door was open and somebody was waving to him. Shielding his eyes against the sudden wind storm, he tried to see who it was.

The helicopter touched down and the figure jumped out and dropped into a crouch before darting forward in Homer's direction.

"Homer," the figure called out, and Homer was surprised to hear that all too familiar voice. "Hey, Homer! I thought that might be you." Tobias grabbed him by the arm and started to lead him back to the waiting helicopter. "Let's get you out of here! Crazy day, huh?"

"What's going on?"

"Later. We have to get you to the Evac-Zone."

"Evac-zone?" He looked at Tobias and was not surprised to see his roommate grinning. Figures. The Sticklon Bridge destroyed, downtown in shambles, and God knows what roaming around, and Tobias still wore that stupid grin.

Homer let Tobias lead him across the rubble and help him into the helicopter. Once he was safely strapped into place, he looked around. There were several other people in the vehicle, but he didn't recognize any of them.

"Hey," Homer started, "what about Pen?"

"She's fine. She and the boys at Farrow are feeding us intel on the creature. Hopefully we'll find a weakness before it knocks down every McDonald's in town. I don't know about you, but I am dying for some chicken nuggets." How was Tobias doing this? How was he possibly thinking about food, let alone chicken nuggets, right now? The helicopter started to rise from the ground, and Homer looked out the window as they ascended.

On the other side of the river, another helicopter had come down and people were being helped on board. Among them was Walter. The man was safe. He continued to survey the ground below when an explosion rocked the helicopter. Some people let out screams, and Homer whipped his head around to see what happened.

A building had exploded. Flames licked at the bricks as thick black smoke rose skyward.

As the smoke cleared, Homer finally saw it. It looked like a dinosaur, but not any Homer could name. It stood on two legs with a massive tail swinging behind its body. It was hunched over and bent down in a predatory stance. Homer could see the thick muscles in the beast's legs. In a lot of ways it looked like a larger version of the T-Rex from *Jurassic Park*, except the head was all wrong. It was wider and flatter, with three very large, sinister-looking horns, like a mutated triceratops. Its eyes were wide and constantly moving as it searched for food.

Tobias leaned past him to look out the window. "Ain't she beautiful?"

Homer spared his roommate a glance before turning his attention back to the creature just in time to see it lurch forward and smash into another building, an electronics store that Homer had always thought was too overpriced. *No great loss there.*

On the other side of the river, the helicopter started to take off, and in so doing drew the attention of the creature. It raised its massive head and used its front claws to push itself off the ground. Once it was erect, it took a deep breath, held it a moment, then expelled it in a stream of fire. It actually breathed fire!

Homer watched in horror as Walter's helicopter was engulfed in flames. He waited, expecting to see the machine rise above the flames, but then it exploded. In his mind he could hear all those people screaming, then suddenly nothing. The creature roared as the fiery remains rained down around it. It dropped down into its predatory crouch again and appeared to be sniffing for something. Occasionally it would find whatever it was looking for because Homer saw it press its snout to the ground, its tongue working to draw whatever it was into its massive mouth. As the helicopter he was riding in veered away, Homer caught sight of what the creature was doing... and wished he hadn't. He would never be able to unsee the upper torso of a woman slip from the creature's mouth and fall to the ground below.

Feeling sick, Homer closed his eyes and settled back in the seat.

"Have you ever seen anything like this before?"

It took Homer several seconds to register Tobias' question. He looked at his roommate as if seeing him for the very first time, then slowly shook his head. "Have you?"

Tobias nodded, and for the first time Homer could remember, the man wasn't smiling. "It's all part of my job."

Homer suddenly understood why Tobias always had the same thing for breakfast every morning, why it was always the same old toast and jam.

I WAS A FIFTY-FOOT HOUSEHUSBAND

Nicole Massengill

"It's a necklace," I said, staring down at the pendant and chain that Sandy had just placed in my hand.

She stared at me with raised eyebrows, one hand resting on her hip. "Oh, don't start with the macho stuff now."

"I'm spending my days working diaper duty, vacuuming, and watching *Ellen*. I think I'm allowed some macho male behavior," I said, mirroring her stance.

"No one's making you watch *Ellen*."

I shrugged, smiling. "I like her humor."

"And I thought you'd like this pendant. Seems right up your alley."

She was right—it was. The pendant was in the shape of an eagle and cast in a rich, dark metal that was already warming comfortably in my hand. She knew me well. She always had.

"But I can take it back," she said, reaching for it.

I closed my fist around it and jerked my arm behind my back. "No. No taksey backsies."

"No takesy backies, huh?" She smiled wryly at me.

"Yeah, I've been doing this for all of a month now, and I've already got the lexicon of a five year old."

"Well, I won't be playing takesy backsies unless my department does first."

I brought my hand around and looked back down at the bird, my thumb stroking the detailing on one wing. "Sandy," I said, warningly.

"Hey, I kid, I kid," she said, holding up her hands. "That's just plain old standard metal. Nothing to get excited about. Phil promised. You remember Phil, right?"

Phil. The semi-balding, egotistical, pipe-smoking asshole who regularly got to spend more time with my wife than I did. The same asshole who made a crack about aprons and cookie baking last time I came by the office. Yeah, I remembered Phil. I smiled anyway, though my teeth were gritted behind it. As she turned around, commenting about something new they'd recently gotten into at the lab, something was niggling at the back of my mind, and I tightened my grip on the eagle. Still, I dismissed it and took Sandy's comment at face value.

After all this time, I should have known better than to take anything my wife said at face value.

* * *

"Mph!" The pain was sharp, intense, and went all the way through the muscles and into my bones, as if my legs had been caught under a fallen wall. I sat up, swinging them out from under the covers, and placed my feet on the floor, rocking them into the aging carpet.

"What's wrong?" Sandy asked groggily, placing a hand on the small of my back.

"Cramp," I managed through the agonizing spasms. Then, just as suddenly as it started, the pain was gone, save for a slight ache I could feel when I placed pressure on the floor. I breathed in and out, shakily. "Just a cramp. Go back to sleep."

She murmured something and rolled over, stretching her legs before pulling them toward her chest, forming a fetal ball. I watched enviously for a second before looking over at the clock—3:23 am—and rubbing my hand over my eyes, wincing when the sleep crust scratched at the corners.

I stood up slowly, easing myself off the bed, not so much as to avoid jostling her, since she was already out like a light again, but to try to avoid making my legs cramp again. I could feel them pulling and straining as I made my way towards the bathroom at the end of the hall. The thing I noted first was that the aching didn't end with my legs; I could feel it all over, and it wasn't like a good workout burn, but more the achiness that goes along with the flu. That, I thought as I peeked into the kids' room, was the last thing I needed. Julie had a ballet recital that week, and heaven knows Sandy wouldn't be making it—hardly ever did when the lab got busy on a project. Plus, when one of us got sick, it went through the whole family, and I needed a toddler with the sniffles like I needed another hole in the head.

It was when I stretched and rolled my shoulders, trying to pop my back, that I noticed how my shirt tugged uncomfortably; it seemed too small despite having fit just fine just a few hours prior. I shrugged it off though, too tired for it to really register like it should have. Somehow, I doubt it would have done me any good if I'd noticed at that point anyway.

* * *

"I'm going to be a little late for dinner tonight," she had said while we made the bed the next morning. I'd grimaced, more at the way my t-shirt was riding up a little, pinching my arms and shoulders, than the knowledge that it would probably just be me and the kids again. She must have noticed, though, as a look of guilt had crossed her features before she'd added, "But not very. Maybe by a half hour," she'd said, looking down, and then added nonchalantly, "And Phil's coming."

The sound of ripping fabric had filled the space between us in that small bedroom. She'd looked at me, somewhat horrified, then at the sheet, before I'd lifted up an arm to examine the damage, ripping out a few more stitches in the process. I'd simply shrugged and walked to the closet.

I didn't expect her to retell the story that night at dinner, for which she'd been almost an hour late. Granted, it was to relieve Julie's tears about outgrowing her favorite sweater, but still... "See, baby, everyone has growth spurts. Even Daddy," Sandy said, trying to reassure her as she wiped at her pink face. Upon hearing of my experience, an odd expression fell over Phil's face, and he chuckled.

"Better late than never, huh, short stop?" he said, laughing. "Maybe your wife will finally be able to wear her high heels."

"That's not very funny," Julie said, earning sputtering from Phil, a scolding from Sandy, and a low five under the table from me.

A few minutes later, though, Phil looked at me with the same expression as before. It was unsettling, although at the time I couldn't explain why. I might have ignored it, had it not happened again, and again; slight glances here and there, interested, but clinical, as if I were one of his specimens laid out on the microscope slide. One of the times I caught him staring, he'd seemed a little flustered, but only for a moment, and then Sandy was asking Phil about a couple of men who'd come by the lab that afternoon asking after him. She hadn't seen them before, and they'd been abrupt with her when she asked what they wanted. Said it wasn't any of her business, and did that ever piss her off, although she didn't say it in so many words since young ears were still present; that was her lab, and she'd be damned before someone came in and acted like she didn't belong there.

Phil shrugged. "Just a side project." He reached for another piece of chicken. "They shouldn't have come into the lab to begin with. I'll give them a call and make sure it doesn't happen again."

She didn't look very convinced, and afterwards I overheard them hissing at each other in the study. I stood in the foyer, just outside the door, for a moment before knocking and bringing in the cups of coffee.

* * *

That night, after taking off my plaid button up, I noticed the dark marks, yellowish brown, on my chest where the necklace had been lying. The necklace itself hadn't changed color, just the skin underneath. I decided to leave it on for the time being. It's not like anyone would notice, since it was under my shirt anyway.

* * *

The next morning the spot on my chest had grown larger and darker, and my wedding ring had gotten too tight to wear without cutting off the circulation to my finger. I took it off for the first time in three years. I took the necklace off as well.

* * *

The following Saturday was the last time I saw my wife. She'd been frowning more, ever since the night Phil had come over. I didn't really know what to think, but I knew there was something on her mind. I would catch her glancing in my direction, then looking past me, then back to me, and biting her lip.

I guess maybe I was afraid of what she would say, so I never asked.

That morning she'd been on the phone. I'd caught part of the conversation—not enough to put together, just the biting tone—on my way once again to the bathroom, where I'd spent a good portion of the day feeling like my insides were rearranging themselves.

The girls were, mercifully, with a sitter.

I was about to go check, brave the areas of the house that were not wonderfully cool bathroom tile, to see what was bothering her, when the pain pulled me down again. A door slammed shut and I heard the car peel out of the driveway... and then I blacked out.

When I came to sometime later, I was bathed in cold sweat. My head was spinning, and I wasn't certain how much of what I remembered was real and how much I had imagined, so I yelled for her, hoarse and embarrassingly weak. I got no answer. I stumbled drunkenly through the house, checking every room and calling out her name, but she was gone, and she had taken the rather thick books that had been sitting on her desk. She'd also taken the necklace, although that was something I wouldn't realize until later.

* * *

She'd been gone for two days.

The kids were asking about Mommy, and I didn't know what to tell them—I offered up sincerely worded comments like "Mommy's working late," and "Mommy's got a new project," and "Mommy's got a deadline," but that doesn't mean a thing to a two and five year old. All they knew is that Mommy was here one day and gone the next and she hasn't read you a bedtime story in *forever* and Daddy's here… but *Mommy*…

I wished I could tell myself all those wonderful little half-truths (whole truths? Full out lies?) that I told them, but her cell phone wasn't working. I tried it the night she left and got her voicemail. I didn't bother to leave a message. I assumed she would know why I was calling.

But she didn't come home the next day, or the next, and her cell phone kept ringing and ringing.

And my body kept screaming.

Pulsing rushes of pain so intense I thought I would pass out took me by surprise and left me gasping.

The first time the girls noticed, I thought both of them were going to burst into tears. Well, Lori *did*. Julie was a big girl and distracted her baby sister while I stared down at the plate I had dropped, feeling like my skin was going to rip itself apart, just like the seams in my clothes.

I didn't have any more clothes, none that weren't torn and shredded. I'd burst through my slippers the day before, my toes going straight through the fabric before I could even start to slip them off.

I kept expecting at any minute that my bones would do the same thing to my skin.

* * *

Things finally broke that evening.

My left hand was the first thing to go.

245

There'd been a blessed reprieve for a few hours, no aches, no twists of muscles and sinew, so I took the opportunity to play with the girls.

Barbie dolls were spilled out across the floor, most of them blonde, because wasn't that the way with Barbie collections. Lori, I think, had better luck telling them apart than I did, although whether that was actually the case or was just her and Julie teaming up on me, I don't know.

The pain caught me off guard, thrumming throughout my body like usual, but more intense than what I'd been feeling. My hand started to spasm and I dropped the doll and miniature t-shirt I'd been trying to work with and pulled it in towards my body. All I could think of was the taste of blood in my mouth and the way I felt my hand shifting against my stomach as though it had a mind all its own. It was only a second later, when I felt a small hand on my shoulder, that I realized I was screaming, and all I could think was that I had to get away from the girls because the sound was enough to give them nightmares for the rest of their lives; they didn't need to actually see what it was doing to me. Somehow I managed to stumble into the bathroom and lock the door before falling over onto my side, my shoulder slamming against the tiles.

There was a banging on the door and Lori sobbing, "Daddy, Daddy!" I tried to stifle my screams and couldn't, and I knew I was only adding to the distress they were already feeling.

I looked at my hand and I thought, *God, I'm turning into a Sid and Marty Kroft reject*, because my skin was whole, not burst through like I'd feared, but the ring finger was at least twice as big as my index finger, and the index finger was twice as large as my normal-sized pinkie, which was popped out of joint and twisted outwards.

With some sort of numb, detached, wow-isn't-this-horrible sort of feeling, I realized the ache that had had been isolated to my hand was starting to spread through the rest of my body. My abdomen was the next thing to go, inflating and distending with a sickening lurch, and if I hadn't been about to throw up from the pain, I could have sworn I was suddenly and ravenously hungry. That was neither here nor there, though, since my right leg had suddenly decided that it wanted to join in the fun and stretched lengthwise by a few feet, extending itself long and thin, the muscles pulling taught before slowly filling out.

The next thing I knew, my back was pressed into the cabinet and my knee was shoved against the wall. I could feel the muscles and bones shifting, shifting outwards, and all I could think was, *No, no, no*, before everything started cracking and breaking.

The last things I heard as the wood and drywall splintered around me were two small, pained cries.

And then nothing.

* * *

For a while, I was entombed within a mental grave; a fog blurred my vision, and through it came a muffled, distorted wailing. And strangely enough, I could feel a cold rain soaking my body. I think at one point I smelled diesel, but I can't say for certain, because almost as soon as my senses came back, they were gone again. And there was quiet, too much quiet.

* * *

I woke up cold and naked, bones aching and crying out with each small movement, but nothing compared to what it had been before. I prayed that somehow it was all a hallucination, but I was naked, the floor under me was metal, and as I opened my eyes, I realized the walls surrounding me were, too. I thought the room, or holding pen, or whatever, was too short. When I looked up, I saw the ceiling arching over me, with steel supports angling upwards from the walls, and all that came to my still-foggy mind was how weird that construction was for a space so small. I reached out a hand and stopped when I met resistance in the form of wire cords. They ran down from a bracelet on my wrists and were secured to the ground. I was really starting to hate jewelry at that point.

"Good morning." The voice was tinny and loud, echoing off of the walls and sounding completely and utterly wrong. Too high pitched.

I heard steps, also amplified and coming from some hidden speakers, and then Phil came around from beside my knee, tiny like a mouse. For a second I wondered what he'd done to himself before realizing it wasn't him, but me.

Phil just stood there, an amused look on his face as he studied me. It was the same smirk I'd seen him wear almost every time I'd seen him, self-important and smug.

"Well, now… How are we doing today?" His voice was mock friendly, with just a dash of bite. "Don't worry about answering, by the way. I'm sure even you will realize how completely impossible making comprehensible speech will be at this point, enlarged larynx and all." He tapped his throat.

I struggled, face heated, pulling against the wires, feeling them give just a little, but not enough. I didn't say a word, didn't make a sound, because at that moment I couldn't stand to hear what my voice sounded like.

"I think you'll find this to be completely unnecessary," he said, stepping just out of range as I kicked my legs as much as I could. "There's no point in struggling."

I stopped struggling because I had felt them give, not much, but maybe just enough, and I wanted to know what was going on. I glanced around the room.

"Oh, really?" He looked at me almost sympathetically, and I have no clue what he assumed I was thinking. He was holding that damn pipe again, which stunk and smelled up the house and left traces on Sandy's clothes every night. "I'm sorry," he said, shaking his head. "Do you really think anyone will be looking for you? We were quiet thorough, you know."

I didn't want to know what that meant. The way I'd taken down the house—*Oh God*—and the way I'd grown, how could they not *know*?

It must have shown on my face because he just stared at me for a minute, his expression unreadable, before laughing, like it was the funniest thing in the world. "What?" he said, wiping a few stray tears from his eyes. "Did you—did you have this image of yourself rampaging through the city or something? Maybe finding Sandy and spiriting her away to Sears Tower?" He chuckled a little, calming. "No. No, that's not how it works." He stepped just a little closer again, fiddling with his cuffs instead of looking at me. "This could have all been averted, you know. I tried, really I did. And then this…" Phil laughed again, pointing towards me. "… this really wasn't *intentional*." He shook his head again, and that was becoming damn irritating because he was standing there, barely the size of my hand, waxing condescending. "Circumstances," he said, as if that explained everything. "I'm sorry about this, really I am."

I didn't believe a bit of it.

"You know, even when she was getting too nosy…" He paused for a moment, whether for thought or dramatic tension I didn't know; I could never be sure with Phil. "I really did try to divert her attention. You have to believe me. But then the mix up with the metals, you see, and… well…" He shrugged, smiling, "She'd already been digging for too long anyway. Even I couldn't pull her out at that point. So I let the dirt fall in."

Before I even realized what I was doing, my hand was free, the wires snapping, and I had reached out and grabbed Phil. The man struggled in my hand, smaller even than the girls' Barbies. I pushed down that pain, so much worse than the growing, the distorting, but not soon enough because Phil's eyes bulged, just a little. I watched him, and I watched myself.

Hundreds of scenarios played out in my mind, unbidden. A hundred plots, the same hundred outcomes, all ending in destruction. Like favorite t-shirts ripped, conversations stilled, a bathroom and a hallway and a box of Barbies crushed and… And suddenly I didn't care anymore. Not about him, not about anything.

And my hand was wet.

GIANT MUTANT TIGER SLUGS

VS.

SALTY ANGEL GIMP WARRIORS IN LEATHER

Jay Wilburn

The priest knelt on the thin carpet in the corner between the leather fetish videos and the *Classy Ladies of the Eighties* blow-up dolls. He bowed his head and prayed for mercy while ignoring the screams coming from the front doors.

Freddie Pop and Douglas Finn pressed their weight against the doors. Alice fell away, screaming as she grabbed at her wrist. Smoke boiled up and flesh melted from her fingers in glossy filets. She shook as bone and dissolving muscle replaced her functioning hand. The slime ran down her surviving arm and onto the knuckles of her other hand. Her skin blistered and split. She fell unconscious on the floor under the rack of sex toys.

The two men dodged another splurt of slime blasting through the door to land on the tiled floor. Freddie turned and pushed with his back. The nametag for the Smut Shoppe tore his polo shirt as it caught on the edge of the door. Douglas loosened his tie and pulled it from around his neck. He fed it through the handles of the door and, with Freddie's help, tried to knot it. The slime dripped on it and the material fell to the floor in pieces.

"We need something more durable," Freddie shouted.

"I have a chain, but it's out on my truck," Douglas grunted.

Freddie shook his head. "I'll open the door if you want to go for it."

A growl from outside was all the answer they needed. Something heavy smashed against the caging on the outside of the door with enough force it set the building to vibrating.

"Don't you have handcuffs or chains in here?"

Freddie shrugged. "The cuffs are all break-away fakes. There's a town ordinance against selling real ones. As it is, the cops are giving me a hard time at least twice a week just for being open. No need to add to the troubles."

"I should have just kept driving through this crazy town. What are those things?"

Freddie screamed as a trail of goo dribbled over the top of the door and sizzled through the material on his shoulder. "Do you think this has happened before, man? I don't know what they are." His eyes darted around the shelves and racks, searching from something to use to secure the door, but his choices were severely limited. Then he spied something and had an idea. "Wait. Can you reach that whip on the shelf above your head?"

As the slime started to eat away at his skin, Freddie let out with a howl and clawed at his shoulder.

Douglas turned and looked up. He reached for the braided leather coil on the hook. The doors bucked against them.

Freddie threw his raw shoulder against the glass, making the caging rattle on the other side. "Don't let go, man. Hey, Preacher, you want to lend a hand? I'll keep your secrets from the town. Now is the time for more leaning and less kneeling. You hear me?"

The priest stayed in the corner with his hands folded. Alice began to seize on the floor, and her eyes rolled up in her head. White foam bubbled from her mouth and she started to expel thick, green paste from her nostrils. It pushed through the foam and oozed between her chattering teeth.

A glossy stalk slid through the space between the shaking doors. The fleshy growth was as thick as a man's forearm. It was like an organic periscope, peering this way and that with the cat-like eye at the end of the stalk. As it rubbed against the edges of the doors, it made a wet slapping sound. The eye bobbed up and down as it looked between both men.

"Get it," Freddie hissed. He slid his feet back, away from the base of the door, as the pale slime leaked underneath near his shoes.

Douglas lunged for the hook, letting the door swing inward. Freddie caught a glimpse of the striped head and body of the creature attached to the stalk. He thought he saw others twisting and snaking around each other, pressing against the doors as they tried to creep inside.

Freddie swallowed. "Oh, God, help us."

Douglas managed to catch hold of the whip and yank it loose from the hook. His elbow hit the shelf underneath, scattering packages of *Lusty Laos Kim-ginas* across the floor to where the thin carpet met the smoking, peeling tile. One of the *Kim-ginas* landed in a pool of the goo near Alice's twitching foot. It sizzled through the plastic packaging and began to rapidly dissolve the latex form.

Without wasting another second, Douglas fed the whip through the handles of the door nearest him, but he could not reach Freddie's side. The doors pitched out further and he could see the mass of giant slugs the other man had been watching in terror. He renewed his efforts to get the doors closed while the slugs pressed forward, eager to squeeze through the gap and what lay beyond. "Oh, Lord," he cried out, "push. Help me get them closed."

Both men slammed into the doors and pushed. The stalk prevented the door from closing all the way, but they continued to push with all their might. Sensing it was trapped, the eye bulged as the stalk thrashed wildly about. An inhuman squeal sounded from outside. The doors bucked against the men's weight. The stalk extended further into the store, and they could see the indentations caused by the edges of the doors. Freddie and Douglas locked eyes and nodded at each other before once again throwing themselves against the doors. The doors suddenly came together as the stalk snapped. Strings of white fibers oozed from the end as it flopped to the floor, the pupil of the eye widening as if in surprise.

Douglas slid his hand through the door handles, trying to grab the whip. The doors bucked again, and he realized the danger he had put himself in. Freddie reached through and managed to get hold of the braided leather. They passed it back and forth, wrapping the handles securely before tying it off.

The metal moaned and screamed as it bent from the outside. The glass between the men and the caging cracked. The crack spread rapidly, covering the entire sheet on Douglas's side with jagged, white spider webs.

Both men backed away from the doors. The leather squeaked under the strain, but it held. The light on the other side was blocked by the brown and black striped bodies slithering over the surface of the doors. Slime dribbled over the leather coils. Smoke rose up from the makeshift rope.

"Here we go," Freddie sighed.

The vapor dissipated, but the whip held. Slime continued to ooze through the thin openings around the door. Big droplets fell from the top of the door onto the leather. It bubbled over the whip and fell to the floor.

The cow hide darkened, but did not break, but the tile beneath melted to the concrete foundation.

Douglas pointed down. "Freddie, your shoe."

Freddie instinctively jumped back, then looked. The earlier emissions had spread out, and now the tip of his shoe was smoking. He lifted his foot to inspect the damage, half-expecting to see his toes melting. The leather had darkened, but it was still intact.

Douglas stared. "Are you okay?"

"The creepy slime doesn't do so well with leather. How did you know my name was Freddie?"

"It's on your nametag. I'm Douglas. I usually don't introduce myself in places like this, but under the circumstances…"

"Pleased to meet you, Douglas."

Alice's body finally went still, but a gurgling sound still issued from her clogged mouth and throat. The wash of goo reached her ankle and began to sizzle. The skin split and peeled back. A blister swelled under the flesh and exploded in a splatter of green on the tile.

Freddie grabbed her under her armpits and pulled her away from the doors. Her foot stuck to the tile. Freddie pulled harder. Douglas reached down and pulled at her calf above the sizzling, smoking ankle. The leg snapped at the ankle, leaving the foot still attached to the floor. Freddie yanked her back and dropped her. Her head bounced on the floor, but she did not react. He felt for a pulse.

Douglas looked from the bubbling foot to the glossy bone at the end of her leg. He turned and threw up on the edge of the carpet.

Freddie pulled a leather French maid's outfit off a rack and removed it from the hanger. He placed the outfit gently over Alice's face.

Douglas looked up at the ceiling and wiped his mouth. "Did you know her?"

"She was a regular."

"What was her name?"

Freddie shook his head. "She wouldn't want me to say. Her husband has a fairly conservative image."

Glass exploded from the frames and shards sprayed across the floor and onto the video shelves. A copy of *Hung Demons vs. Busty Angels* fell to the floor next to Alice's severed foot. The case shook as the slime from the creatures dissolved the back cover and melted the movie inside.

The wet, slithering sound of the long, striped bodies crawling over the metal mesh filled the video store. Under the slimy motion, Douglas heard a clicking and a chorus of shrill squeaks. When he dared to look, he saw the massive slugs twisting over one another as they covered the doors. The metal grating blackened and sizzled as the bloated bodies passed over it. The holes in the exposed caging no longer aligned evenly. The metal twisted and distorted so that some holes melted together and others sagged open wider. The entire sheet of compromised metal began bulging into the store through the broken door.

"Freddie, what do we do?"

"Based on my vast knowledge of giant acid slugs?"

A piece of glass on the floor popped, flinging droplets onto a sign for Dwarfsplotation titles and into the carpet, where they immediately began to burn.

"Is there a back door?"

Freddie's eyes went wide. He ran behind the counter. Douglas followed for only a few steps. He stopped by the register and looked back. He took in the scene before him: Alice's body, a slug with one eye stalk staring at him as it pressed against the failing metal, and the back of the priest as he cowered in the corner.

"What about him?" Douglas asked.

"Forget about him. Get over here quick and give me a hand."

Douglas ran around the corner and into the stock room. He saw light shining through the broken wood of the exterior door. Freddie was using a cardboard box to try to slide the metal gate closed. The limited view of the outside was obstructed as giant slugs climbed over the door, their collective weight pushing Freddie back as he tried to avoid coming in contact with the eye stalks that wiggled through the cracks in the wood. Slime leaked through the holes and ran down the painted wooden surface, and where it connected with the box, steam billowed up as it ate into the cardboard.

Douglas grabbed a shelf loaded with stock and pulled it slowly across the floor, the metal squealing as it scraped over the concrete surface.

"Hurry," Freddie groaned.

Douglas pushed harder and the shelf tipped, but didn't go over. Large cardboard boxes tumbled from the shelves, bursting open when they hit the floor. One remained on the shelf, but opened, spilling its contents down onto Freddie in a rainbow of color. They hit his head and rolled down his back. Some were soft, some were hard.

"Come on," Freddie yelled.

Bracing his feet against the floor, Douglas pushed against the shelving unit, strained until it tipped and lodged itself against the door. It wouldn't keep them out for long, but it would buy them a little extra time.

Freddie tried to push the gate closed again, ducking the stalks that slid through the splits in the wood. He jumped back suddenly when thick loops of slime dripped down the broken door and oozed over the metal shelves. As soon as the goo made contact, the metal began to change color and smoke rose up from the smooth surface

"Jesus, are you okay?" Douglas asked.

"It burns, but I think I'm okay. But I can't get the gate closed with the shelves against the door. We need to find another way out or we're done for."

They backed away from the door, and Douglas' foot came down on something soft and squishy and he lost his balance. Looking down, he saw what he had stepped on and let out with a shaky laugh. The floor was littered with vibrators and dildos.

"Shit," Freddie mumbled.

"What?"

Freddie indicated the blockaded door with a tilt of his head. The metal was already beginning to sag under the corrosive secretions.

"Damn." Douglas looked to the other man. "How are your fingers?"

Freddie looked at his hand. The flesh was inflamed and blistering. "Hurts like hell. So does my shoulder. Not as bad as Alice, though."

Douglas sighed. "Her name was Alice?"

Freddie glared at Douglas. "Don't, man, just don't."

Ignoring him, Douglas started to pace around the room as he frantically looked for another means of escape. "Is there another way out?"

Freddie shook his head. "We're fucked, man."

Douglas stopped in the center of the room and ran a hand through his hair. He did a slow turn, studying the walls. He almost missed it because it was hidden behind a stack of boxes, but he hurried across the room. "What's that?"

He started pulling the boxes away from the wall, gradually revealing a utility ladder bolted into the cinderblock. He followed it up to a recess in the ceiling, and a hatch. He turned to Freddie. "Where does this go?"

"Where does it look like it goes?"

"The roof?"

Freddie nodded.

"If we can get onto the roof, we might be able to cross over to another building. These things can't fly, can they?"

Freddie shrugged. "They're slugs. They're probably crawling over the entire building—including the roof."

Pieces of the metal from the shelving unit broke away from the main structure and clattered to the floor. The acid-like substance started to eat away at the floor where it landed.

"It's the only chance we got."

"That shit eats through everything—including metal."

Remembering what they had used to secure the front door, Douglas said, "Not everything."

Freddie watched as another piece of the shelving fell to the floor. "What are you thinking?"

"Do you carry anything made of leather that we could wear?"

Looking Douglas up and down, Freddie laughed. "Crotchless panties, extra-large. Assless chaps, one size fits all."

Douglas rolled his eyes. "Don't you have anything full body?"

Freddie started to shake his head, but then stopped as a smile played across his face. "I have some suits that might work."

Something crashed at the front of the store. They ran back through together and skidded to a halt behind the register. The monsters with their bobbing stalk eyes slithered through the shattered glass and over the fallen pieces of grate that had covered the entrance to the shop. The leather whip binding the handles together dripped with steaming acid, but was still intact.

"We're too late," Freddie whispered

Douglas climbed onto the counter. "Get the suits ready."

"Where are you going?"

Douglas rolled to his feet on the other side and ran along the wall. "Somebody's gotta get the preacher. You get three suits ready."

The slugs crawled over Alice's corpse. Their slimy bodies pushed against and between one another and shoved others to the outside of the pile. Freddie caught glimpses of bone as the slugs tore open the liquefying sheets of skin and muscle. He ran back into the storage room.

A few of the slugs attempted to cross the room along the ceiling. The tiles broke apart and the slugs fell from the hanging frame onto the shelves of videos, smashing through them with their monstrous weight. The ones advancing toward Douglas along the walls fared better.

Douglas grabbed the priest's shoulder and shook him. "Come on. We have to go right now."

The priest shook his head, then bowed it again, as if in prayer. "God will send his angels if he wants me to live. This is punishment for my wrong-doing."

Douglas looked back at the approaching creatures. Fumes from their combined acids made his eyes water.

"We got no time, man. Preacher is in a flood. God sends a truck, a boat, and a helicopter. Preacher drowns. He asks God why He didn't help. God says I sent a truck, a boat, and a helicopter. What the hell did you want? So, me and Freddie are your helicopter and your time is up. Let's go."

The priest fell forward onto his face. He groaned into the carpet. "I'm so ashamed. God is letting me die here for how I lived."

Douglas reached down and pulled on the back of the priest's jeans, but he would not rise. Something crashed behind them. He looked back and saw the register on the floor. One of the beasts was slinking along the top of the counter, ruining the finish and blocking their exit. "Maybe I should close my eyes, bend over, and kiss it goodbye, too."

One of the slugs screamed and jerked backward between the shelves.

Douglas saw the wings first. Something walked out into store, moving between them and the giant slugs. It was shaped like a man, with black wings spread behind its dark armor. A helmet covered the head and face as a sword was lifted into the air. Slime flowed down the blade until the silver finish washed off and the plastic underneath curled.

The black-winged angel bellowed, "What are you doing on your face, Preacher? Stand up and follow."

The priest sat up and stared at the figure, who reached up and started to peel off its face. When it was done, Freddie stood there grinning, a black leather bondage hood in his hand.

"Why does it have wings on the back?" Douglas wanted to know.

"It was part of a promotional push for *Fetish Angels*, volumes one through fourteen. They didn't sell well. The real leather was expensive. Now, let's get out of here."

The blade of the sword dropped from the hilt. Freddie looked at the ruined blade as though he couldn't believe what just happened to it, then tossed it aside. He crossed the floor and grabbed the priest's arm and pulled him backward a couple feet, but the man still wouldn't stand.

As Freddie tussled with the priest, more slugs slithered into the room. The one in the lead seemed to glare at them from its single eye stalk. Douglas grabbed the priest by the other arm, and together they dragged him across the floor toward the stock room as the one-eyed monster pursued them.

"Move faster," the priest hissed.

"Now you're motivated," Douglas grumbled.

The striped shape on the counter turned toward them and rose up like a cobra. Freddie let go of the priest and stepped in front of Douglas. The slug hit Freddie in the chest, making his leather wings flap with the impact. Freddie grabbed the slug by the stalks, right below the eyes, and pulled it from the counter. In one fluid move, he turned, the weight of the creature carrying him around, and tossed it at the other approaching monstrosities.

Another slug had gotten too close, and now tried to twist itself around Freddie's ankles. The man quickly brought his foot down, pinning it to floor. The slug squealed and hissed.

The priest started to climb over the counter, but Douglas grabbed him and pulled him back. "Don't touch the slime. Now hurry, before it spreads." Warning issued, he shoved the priest back toward the counter.

The man of God wasted no time climbing over the scarred surface, but once his weight was settled on the counter, the glass, weakened by the acid, gave way. As the priest struggled to get up, Freddie shoved Douglas, and the two men made their way over what was left of the display case.

"The suits are in the back," Freddie shouted over the noise. "You'll need to strip to get in them. Let's go."

The priest followed, clutching at his wrist. Blood oozed between his fingers. The one-eyed tiger slug slid over the remains of the counter and along the floor in pursuit of the three men. Glass shards sliced the soft body, but didn't seem to slow the beast.

Once they were safely in the stock room, Freddie slammed the door and backed away from it. It barely fit the frame and Douglas could already see it reacting where the slugs pressed on the other side. He could hear the ones outside the back door screeching as the acid devoured the metal. Freddie slid boxes in front of the door. The priest looked from the leather suits to the other men.

Douglas pulled off his shirt and started unbuckling his belt. Freddie dropped to his knees and rubbed at the slime caked on his thighs. He wiped his gloved hands on the cinderblock next to the failing door. Douglas jerked down his boxers and stepped into the winged suit. The priest shook his head.

Freddie yelled, "God, it burns."

Douglas sucked in his gut to avoid catching himself with the zipper. "Is it eating through the suit?"

"They work fine. That damned slime is still hot, though. Father Baker, you better put on the armor of faith here or you will die one layer at a time, screaming to death just like Alice."

The metal grate of the back door clanged loose from the frame on one side and fell against the shelf as the creatures continued to melt their way through. Bits of wet wood, pieces of the back door, fell to the floor, revealing the slithering stripes on the other side. One bulbous eye peered in at them through an opening.

The priest pulled his shirt open without unbuttoning it, scattering the plastic buttons across the floor. The blood from his hand soaked into one of the sleeves.

Douglas wrestled with the hood, trying to find the eyeholes once he had it zipped. "Did that sword come with the costume?"

Freddie helped the priest pull the gimp suit up over his shoulders. Father Baker mumbled to himself as he brought the zipper up.

"No," Freddie answered. "That was a collectable from *The Elf Wars* box set."

Douglas frowned, but it didn't show on his hooded face. "Is that a porn series?"

"Do I have to pull up the hood?" the priest moaned.

Freddie shrugged, causing the leather wings to flap. "Do you want giant slug acid eating your face off, Father?"

The priest sighed. "I'm considering it and don't use my name in here."

Freddie tilted his leather-clad head. "Would you prefer Jonathan? Or maybe Johnny Boy?"

"I prefer not to be identified at all."

"Then I guess you better zip up that hood unless you want to be seen running out of this building in that outfit."

Father Baker pulled the hood over his head and started fumbling with the zipper.

"And, no, Douglas, *Elf Wars* is a cartoon fantasy series from the seventies. Not everything I'm into is porn. I just sell it to you guys to pay the bills."

Douglas held up his leather-encased fingers. "Fair enough."

With a groan through the zippered mouth of his hood, Father Baker complained, "This is a new low. I need to reevaluate my life."

A muffled noise that sounded like metal crashing to the floor came from the main section of the store, and that was followed by the unmistakable sound of glass shattering. Freddie cracked open the door and looked out. The front door had finally given way and the rest of the counter had been destroyed. The floor was a steaming pool of slug sludge. More of the creatures were pouring through the door and falling on top of each other. One had a skeletal foot stuck to its slimy side. Douglas joined Freddie at the door and looked for the one-eyed slug, but he did not see it. The shelf by the back door collapsed, the acid finally weakening it to the point where it couldn't support its own weight, and the slugs started to slide in from the outside.

Freddie slammed the door. "Get to the ladder and climb."

Douglas ran ahead and started up the ladder. Father Baker followed, threatening to climb over Douglas in his haste to get away from the approaching slugs. Freddie waited at the bottom, swinging a mannequin's arm from side to side like a club in an attempt to hold the slugs at bay.

Douglas pushed on the hatch above his head. A sliver of light showed around the edge, but a combination lock held the latch closed. Slime oozed into the opening and dripped down the rungs.

The priest shook a drop off his gloved finger. "Oh, God."

"What's the combination?"

Freddie tossed his make-shift weapon aside and started to climb. "Hurry up."

"What's the combination?"

The lock and latch fell away in three pieces, hitting the floor below as it melted. "Never mind," Douglas said, then pushed the hatch open a little wider, but the weight on top prevented him from throwing it over.

"They're too heavy."

Douglas felt the metal bending around his gloved fingers. Father Baker climbed up beside Douglas and started pushing, too. Freddie clung to the ladder, but as the slugs drew closer and started to climb the walls, he, too, was forced to climb. He reached out and grabbed the shelves, first on one side, then the other, pulling them over in an attempt to slow the creatures' ascent. Paint buckets exploded on the floor, splashing the monsters with neon colors, an improvement over those tiger strips. They hissed, but kept coming.

A time-weathered paper bag near the base of the ladder split open, spilling sparkling white crystals onto the floor.

Freddie maneuvered into position between the other two men and managed to get one hand on the hatch and added his efforts to their struggles.

On the floor below, a slug crawled over the spilled crystals and issued a scream that startled all three men, and they almost lost their grip on the ladder. The slug writhed in pain. They looked down at the bloated, serpentine shape. A second tiger slug slithered onto the crystals and abruptly stopped and reared back, knocking others out of its way as it tried to retreat. The skin of its belly split in long, black fissures. The stalks sagged and the eyes closed as the slug gave voice to its pain. The others stopped short of the crystals and began crawling up the shelves.

"Freddie, what is that stuff?"

Freddie thought for a moment, trying to remember what it was, and then he had it. "Salt. It's rock salt!"

The slugs circled around the crystals and started to climb the walls. The men renewed the efforts, pushing with everything they had until the hatch finally gave with a resounding crash. The dark angels clambered up the ladder and onto the roof—and found themselves surrounded by dozens of the creatures. They were trapped.

Without thinking about what he was about to do, Freddie disappeared back through the hole in the roof and came up a couple seconds later lugging a large paper sack. He ripped the top off the bag, reached inside, then scattered a handful of rock salt around them. A few of the slugs scuttled aside as the salt struck them. Others approached from the side. Freddie threw out another handful. As if sensing the danger, the slugs backed away before it struck them. Some of the creatures sought escape over the side of the building.

Throwing down handfuls of rock salt, Freddie made his way to the edge of the roof, Douglas and Father Baker following closely behind him. "We'll have to climb down the gutter pipe. Is it clear down there? Doug? Is it clear? Talk to me."

Freddie threw out another handful, forcing the more persistent creatures to retreat.

Douglas' voice sounded strained through his hood. "The alley is clear-ish."

Father Baker added, "The rest of the town? Not so much."

"What does that mean?"

"Just look."

Freddie stared out across the section of town that included the massage parlor, the Methodist and Lutheran churches, Mom and Pop's Place, and the chain supermarket running M&P's out of business. The slugs filled the streets and covered the sides of the buildings. One lowered itself slowly, twisting on a string of slime, from the steeple of the Methodist church. Someone inside a car covered with the striped bodies screamed. Thick clouds of steam rose from the vehicle's surface.

A man ran across the parking lot of the massage parlor. One of the creatures dropped down from the building's gaudy façade and landed on his back. The man fell face first to the asphalt as other slugs clustered around his body. Douglas braced himself for the scream, but never heard it, as it was muffled by the mass of bodies. The creatures sloughed away the man's flesh and kept going until there was nothing left, not even bones.

Freddie let out a scream. A slug had wrapped around his leg. Frantically, he dumped a handful of salt crystals on the creature's head. The giant slug exploded, splattering the men with guts and slime. Startled by the sudden death of the slug, Freddie stumbled backward and toppled over the side. He grabbed for the gutter pipe, but missed. Douglas lunged and managed to catch hold of one of Freddie's legs with both hands. The leather on leather allowed for a secure hand hold, but the added weight almost sent Douglas over the edge as well. Father Baker grabbed hold of Douglas and screamed as his leather glove pulled at the cut on the palm of his hand.

One of the slugs crept up Douglas's leg. He felt the pressure, but there was little he could do unless he let go of Freddie. It reached his knee and the heat built under the leather. He shimmied and shook, trying to dislodge the monster, but it held on, its eyes bobbing around his sweaty crotch.

"Stop squirming," the priest said, but Douglas didn't listen. He continued to dance a jig as best he could to free himself of the creature. Father Baker lost his grip, and suddenly Douglas pitched over the edge. The priest lunged, but was too late; his forward momentum carried him over the edge, too.

They spun once in the air as they fell one story to land on the central air units. The grill of one was forced into the metal casing, tearing loose the fan blade within. As they rolled off, Douglas caught his foot on the piping and tore it loose from the wall, dousing Father Baker with a brief spray of fluid. The men were slow to recover, and in the time it took for them to gain their footing, a line of slugs started to make their way down from the roof.

Groaning from the pain as he got to his feet, Douglas said, "God, I think it hurt worse landing in this tight suit. My ribs."

Father Baker tried to get up, but dropped back to his butt holding his ankle. "I don't think the wings worked."

Using the wall of the building for support, Freddie managed to stand. He looked back at the other two "Where do we go now?"

Douglas looked toward the parking lot, where striped bodies were crawling over one another. Where their bodies touched the pavement, steaming cracks opened up, making the roads hazardous to navigate. "We could try for my truck. We might be able to get out of town." He scanned the street. "Which way is quicker?"

Father Baker watched the slugs approaching them from on high, eating the whitewash off the side of the building. "East," he said absently. "Takes you past the chemical waste dump. That way—" he pointed north, "—takes you out past the farms for about fifteen miles. West is best. Maybe eight miles, but it winds through mountains once you get past the sewage treatment plant, the reservoir, the cosmetics labs, and the elementary school."

Douglas looked at the other leather angels. "Which way do you think these things came from?"

"I'm not going," Father Baker said, ignoring the question. "There are people suffering here, and I can't just run away and leave them to these things."

"I'm staying, too," Freddie said. "This is my town. We'll understand if you wanna go; you're passing through. You got family somewhere, right? A wife?"

Douglas rubbed at the smooth top of his leather hood. "These things are laying waste to the roads, and I probably wouldn't get far before the tires on my truck gave out. I'll stay, but we need another plan, something other than wearing these gimp suits and trying to fly."

Father Baker turned his attention from the slugs and looked toward the main drag. "What about more rock salt? A lot more."

Freddie considered the idea. "It's out of season. We might be able to get a dozen bags between M&P and the hardware store."

"People might have some stored in their garages," Douglas suggested. "We could go door to door."

Father Baker shook his head. "Not with the way we're dressed. We'd be shot."

Freddie opened his mouth to say something, but a loud screech caused the words to dry up before they left his mouth. He looked up just as a slug dropped from the edge of the roof. Father Baker pushed him back and the creature landed between them. It split open on the concrete. The corrosive guts splattered and immediately began eating away at the sidewalk.

Before the slugs could launch another aerial attack, the men, forgetting all about their aches and pains, ran toward the front of the store. "Thanks, Preacher," Freddie said, "your next three rentals are on the house."

They paused at the mouth of the alley. Freddie looked around, not exactly sure what he was looking for, but figured he would know it when he found it. "Is there someplace where they might have rock salt stored in bulk?"

Douglas stepped out of the alley, then quickly jumped back, trying to corral the other men back the way they came. "Go back. Go back."

Jon looked over the other man's shoulder. The one-eyed slug rounded the corner, followed by a swarm of others, effectively cutting off their escape route. Some of the slugs were splattered with brightly colored paint. The men turned and ran, staying close to the wall of the comic book store as the ones climbing down from the roof reached the sidewalk. They jumped over the body of the dead creature, and continued toward the back of the store.

A slug dangled and twisted from a thick rope of slime attached to a tree branch. Its eyes rolled up in the bulbs of its eye stalks and ignored them. Another twisted from a light post.

Douglas skidded to a halt. "What are they doing?"

Father Baker ran nearly ran into Douglas as a thought came to him.

"The Shed."

"What shed, preacher?" Freddie asked.

"The County Shed. South side by the substation. They keep the snow-plows there, and we stocked up on rock salt after the last winter's freeze. It was a big vote, and it was delivered right before I rotated off the board."

"We should have invested in burying the power lines like Alice proposed," Freddie grumbled.

"Are we really going to do this now?"

Douglas ignored the brewing spat and looked back at the alley. "How far is it?"

The priest coughed. "Other side of town. This isn't New York City, but it isn't close."

Watching the one-eyed slug draw closer, Douglas said, "Then let's go."

They ran down the slope, slogged through the drainage ditch, and climbed back out next to the supermarket. Jon slipped and grabbed his ankle. The other men grabbed him and pulled him along. Screams came from inside the market as slugs climbed up the inside of the glass. The leather-clad, winged men ran past the dumpster and continued up the side street. As they weaved through town, they witnessed the destruction caused by the slugs, and only a handful of people stopped to stare at the hooded leather angels going by; those that didn't were too busy fleeing or dying.

As they made their way toward the shed, they noticed that there were fewer slugs pursuing them. They also noticed that there were more and more hanging from the ropes of slime and twisting in the wind.

Once again, Douglas asked, "What the hell are they doing?"

Father Baker stopped and leaned against a telephone pole. He reached down and rubbed at his ankle through the leather. "It is hot as hell in here. And I think my ankle is swelling, but I can't tell."

Freddie gripped Douglas by the shoulder to get his attention.

Douglas looked at him. "What?"

Freddie pointed and Douglas followed the line of the man's finger to a giant slug dangling from the power line. As they watched, the creature swelled into a ball. Its belly opened like a zipper and released a flood of goo that carried dozens of smaller slugs. It spilled onto the road, forming a large puddle, and the smaller slugs wasted no time slithering toward the heart of town. The street sizzled beneath them.

A high-pitched squeal came from behind them. They turned, attempting to locate the source of the sound, and saw it was raining smaller slugs as two other suspended bodies split open. The noise continued, and then they saw a squirrel dart out from beneath some bushes. Its fur was burned away in several places. Four tiny slugs clung to its side. It ran around in a circle, then collapsed in the center of the street and died. The smaller creatures strayed from their course and head toward the slowly dissolving carcass. Those that were already attached to the rodent's body appeared to grow noticeably in size.

Douglas let out with a startled gasp. "They're growing as they eat."

The massive mother slug crawled down the pole, its body whole, as if she hadn't just given birth, and hissed and stared at the men.

"C'mon," Father Baker said, and started in the direction of the shed. The others followed.

The shed was padlocked, but they found a split in the sheet metal that they could peel back and slip through. Once inside, Father Baker unzipped his hood and scratched at his sweaty hair. "I don't know anything about this stuff."

Douglas unzipped his hood and looked at one of the pieces of equipment. "This is a spreader." He opened a panel and looked at the engine.

"Can you get it running?" Freddie wanted to know.

Douglas scratched at the heat rash that had broken out on his throat. "It's been drained for storage. I can run the spreading mechanism, but it will take some work to get it to drive."

Freddie slapped a hitch on the back of a flatbed truck. "Can we tow it?"

Douglas looked and nodded while Father Baker slid open a long door to reveal stacks of large, brown bags of rock salt. "Let's get started before the town runs out of squirrels and people."

Without waiting for a response, Father Baker heaved one bag of salt awkwardly onto the flatbed. Douglas released the clutch on the spreader and Freddie helped him roll it slowly to the back of the truck. As Douglas attached the hitch, Freddie helped the priest move the heavy bags. Douglas stood on the hitch and bounced on it to test the connection.

"Bring a couple of those to the bin on the spreader," Douglas said, "and let's load it up."

Freddie carried one bag on each shoulder as Douglas opened the loading bin on the back. Freddie's eyes went wide and he dropped the bags. "Look out!"

In his haste to heed the warning, Douglas tripped over his own feet and fell. Jon ran from the storage section and Freddie rounded the vehicle as Douglas rolled over and looked up into the one eye glaring above him. He tried to kick at the slug, but it had already pinned him with its weight. The maimed slug crawled up Douglas's body toward his exposed face. Douglas folded his forearms over his eyes as slime leaked over the leather.

The creature reared its head up, away from Douglas, and growled.

"Some help here."

Freddie called out, "Father, get the salt. Hurry!"

Douglas moved his arms and saw Freddie holding the eye stalk with both hands, trying to pull it off. He tried to slide out from beneath the slug, but he couldn't move.

"Hurry up! It's starting to burn."

Father Baker threw the bag down on the slug's back and clawed at the paper. "I can't get it open with these gloves."

Freddie started clawing at the bag with one hand while holding back the slug with the other. "Find a knife or something to rip it open."

Trying to do two things at once, Freddie couldn't hold back the slug with one hand and the thing's head began to move lower toward Douglas' face. Douglas grabbed at the hood, but he couldn't get it back into place. He pushed at the slug with his gloved fingers and felt the creature pushing back as the heat on his legs continued to build.

"Freddie!"

Freddie managed to rip a small hole in the bag. He fished out a few crystals and rubbed them into the monster's eye. It roared and flung itself backward, off of Douglas' legs. Startled, Freddie's feet went out from under him and he landed flat on his back next to Douglas on the gooey floor. The slug whipped its head from side to side and bucked its body in an attempt to dislodge the bag of rock salt. The slug's moist body had soaked through the paper and the corrosive secretions began to eat away at the bag. Father Baker raced back to the two men. He thumbed out the razor on the rusty box cutter he'd found. Freddie grabbed the priest's boot.

"Wait, let it happen."

The priest looked down at Freddie until the monster screamed. He looked back and saw the crystals falling onto the slug through the holes its slime had eaten through the bag. Its body began to swell and split in black gashes.

Freddie reached over and started zipping up Douglas's hood. Father Baker pulled the mask over his face and pulled the zipper closed. The one-eyed beast exploded, spreading guts into the rafters.

Douglas climbed to his feet and swept the slime off his suit. "Let's get this done. He's not going to be the only one."

They loaded the flatbed, filled the bin, and precut the tops of the bags. As they finished fueling the truck from the gas cans, the metal building began to rattle. They looked up and saw the walls and ceiling changing color, growing darker in spots. Freddie pointed at the floor. Tiny slugs slid under the eaves and through the cracks around the base of the wall.

"The door is padlocked," Father Baker said, climbing behind the wheel of the truck.

Freddie climbed onto the flatbed as Douglas cranked the spreader. "Ram it."

The priest started the truck and lurched forward. Freddie hoisted a bag and moved to the spreader above the hitch.

"We're not going fast enough," Douglas said. The mask muffled his words and nobody heard his concerns.

The doors collapsed off their hinges before the truck reached it. The massive slugs slithered inside. Most were covered in pink, blue, green, and red paint. Douglas activated the spreader. Freddie started pouring the bag into the bin as crystals sprayed the walls of the shed. Freddie climbed back onto the flatbed and the slugs began to scream. They drove out of the shed while the creatures exploded inside. Others sizzled and fell off the roof as Douglas reached back and aimed the spray up at them.

Father Baker drove slowly up the street. Freddie maintained a steady feed into the spreader. Douglas turned the mechanism on and off as they passed clusters of the creatures. The slugs fell away from the battered frames of houses. They dropped, screaming, from their ropes of slime before they could reproduce. Douglas adjusted the angle of the sprayer as needed.

"This thing wasn't designed for this," Douglas said with a shake of his head.

Freddie loaded another bag into the spreader. "Just keep going."

Father Baker turned and drove down another street.

The larger creatures thrashed and exploded in the wake of the leather, winged salt men. The smaller ones popped like firecrackers.

The truck rocked as one of the tires popped. The rubber peeled completely off the rim of another. The remaining tires spun on the slimy road, trying to gain purchase. Father Baker revved the engine; eventually the tires found traction and they were moving again.

Freddie walked along the bed and leaned around to the window. Father Baker started to roll it down before he realized the glass had melted and there was no window.

"Pastor, are we okay?"

"I'm having to drive faster to keep our momentum. We won't be able to hit Pine or Cloister because of the hills. Once the tires are gone, we won't have the traction to tow."

"Just get us as far as you can."

As the monsters fell away and fled, people started looking out through broken doors and melted windows. They waved at the dark angels unleashing salty death on the mutant slugs.

Another tire fell off in pieces as they drove up Main Street. The truck sputtered and stopped in front of the Sex Shoppe. Douglas shut off the spreader. He stood up in the seat and looked out at the melted metal in the parking lot.

Freddie called, "Douglas, you okay?"

"If it wasn't for the license plate, I wouldn't even know it was my truck."

Father Baker opened the driver's door and stood on the running board. "We ran out of gas before we ran out of tire."

Freddie patted the stack of bags. "We still have plenty left and probably half the town left to do."

Climbing onto the flatbed, the priest limped toward them. Douglas heard the roar building behind him. He turned and saw the lines of people crunching forward over the salted street carrying guns, knives, rakes, and shovels. Douglas climbed over onto the flatbed, too.

"What do you make of this, Freddie?"

Freddie shrugged. "Gratitude?"

The crowd cheered as they approached the dead vehicle and the men in winged gimp suits. Father Baker unzipped his hood and exposed his face. He raised his leather-clad arms above his dark wings.

"What the hell?" Freddie whispered.

The priest shouted, "This work is not yet done. Grab bags and slay the monsters that plague us. Get salt from your homes. There's still more in the County Shed. If you have a vehicle that works, rid our town of these things. Go out through the farms and into the mountains. Pine and Cloister still need to be canvassed. Let's take back our town from the giant, mutant slugs."

The crowd cheered as more men and women gathered to take bags of salt through the rest of the streets.

Freddie passed down the last bag and grunted as he unzipped his hood. "I need a drink. Are you sorry you stopped, Douglas?"

Pulling back his mask, Douglas said, "I'm glad I stopped at your establishment first."

Freddie looked at the priest, who was staring at the two steeples in the distance. "What about you, Preacher?"

Father Baker sighed. "Well, it depends on what you have to drink. If my church is still standing, we'll split something next Sunday. If not, I'll take whatever you got."

Freddie patted the priest's back, then they sat down side by side on the end of the flatbed. "It's a deal, but let's not wait until Sunday."

They stared up at the steeples together and ignored the screams echoing from deeper in town.

VERMIN

Kevin Bampton

Roger climbed down from his pick-up and limped across to the town's only store. The people of East Creek relied on Peterson's for all their needs. Seemingly bigger inside than out, it was the kind of place that sold almost everything.

The bell above the door tinkled as he entered the well-lit, airy shop. After old man Peterson passed away, his daughter had taken over, and she had made it a much more inviting place to visit, with little touches and changes that included brighter lights and music from a radio on the counter.

"Hello, Roger," Lily said over the sounds of Elvis filtering through the speakers. "How are you?"

"Not too bad, Lily. Leg's a bit stiff again today. Must be the damp weather. It doesn't agree with shrapnel."

"I don't know how you deal with it every day. I know I couldn't."

"The price of freedom, I guess. A lot of guys didn't even make it on to the beach on D-Day. I'm alive and thankful for it. This just reminds me how lucky I am."

Lily nodded as she came round to the front of the store with an old kitchen chair. "Have a seat while I get your things" she said, taking his list.

"That's very kind of you. Thank you."

Lily walked around the store, referring to the list and taking items from the shelves, and in no time a pile of food and home items appeared on the counter.

"More poison! Haven't you got rid of those mice yet?"

"Most of them are gone, but a few seem to be immune to the last three types I've tried. They appear to be thriving on the stuff. And they're difficult to trap. Found a tail in a trap the other day. I saw its owner running off in the distance."

Lily disappeared for a moment, and when she returned, she was lugging a five-pound bag of something. "Try this. Maybe it will do the job. And speaking of catching things, any more kids using your land as a lover's lane?"

Roger stood and walked to the counter, a smile on his face. "Not in the last few weeks. The weather's not been too good for them. Too muddy for the boys and their pretty cars."

Lily opened her mouth to reply when a loud shriek came from the radio. Lily and Roger winced and covered their ears. The noise cut off as suddenly as it had begun.

"Whoa! That hurt!" exclaimed Lily, "What was it?"

"It was loud, I know…" Roger's next words were drowned out by the sound of a heavy, rumbling engine. They both looked through the window as a large, grey diesel lorry trundled by, rattling the pane of glass.

"That's twice they've been past today. I think they must be lost."

The radio crackled back to life and the sounds of *Viva Las Vegas* once again filled the store.

"Ah, so Elvis hasn't left the building then" said Roger with a grin. He paid Lily and took the first box out to his car. Lily came out from behind the counter, picked up the other box, and followed him out. As she loaded the box into the back of his truck, Roger took a deep breath and said, "So, will you be at The Homestead this evening?"

"Of course! I never miss a dance night."

"Good. Um, I don't dance," he said, tapping his leg, "but I hope you'll allow me to buy you dinner."

"Oh." Lily flushed lightly. "Yes. That would be wonderful, Roger. Thank you."

They stood in silence for a moment, then Roger moved to the driver's door.

"I'll call for you. Seven thirty?"

"Yes. Yes. Definitely." Lily moved back, both excited and embarrassed in equal measure.

Roger climbed into the truck and drove away, leaving Lily standing in front of the store with her hands clasped to her chest. Realizing how much like a school girl she looked, she spun round and dashed back inside, her mind already deciding what she should wear that evening.

Driving home, Roger's mind filled with thoughts of Lily. He smiled as he saw a wolf through the trees and birds fluttering into the sky. His good mood was dampened, however, when the grey lorry he'd seen in town sped around the curve in the road. It was on the wrong side and heading straight toward him. Forced to swerve onto the grass, he braked sharply to avoid hitting a tree. He hissed through his teeth as a stab of pain shot down his injured leg.

"You're gonna get yourselves killed driving like that."

Reversing back onto the road, he continued home, mindful of the fading pain in his thigh.

* * *

At 7:45, Roger pulled into the parking lot of The Homestead, Lily at his side. He had planned to arrive with the radio playing, but all he could get from the speaker was a low hum punctuated with an occasional crackle.

So much for atmosphere, he thought as he climbed from the truck. For this special occasion, he had taken his only suit out of the closet. It was light grey and starting to show its age. Lily was wearing a pale blue dress with complementary shoes, bag, and hat. Standing next to her, Roger felt like a scarecrow.

Inside, the band had just started their first number and a few people were getting up to dance. They waved hello to Sheriff Acton, who was ordering his supper. Roger led Lily to a table, where they were met by Lily's Uncle Jack, a retired government scientist.

"Hello, Jack," said Roger pleasantly as they shook hands. "How's the water?" Jack had a reputation for every so often checking the town's water supply at the reservoir next to Roger's farm. What for? Nobody knew.

"Hello, Roger. I do hope you're looking after my niece. And lay off the water, the beer is better."

Roger smiled and helped Lily with her seat before picking up the hand-written menu and asking her what she would like for a starter.

* * *

A few miles away, amidst the protective cover of trees lining Lover's Lane, a car pulled to a stop.

"Here we are," said Lee. "Nice and quiet." Only the sound of crickets and the occasional bird call broke the silence.

"Okay," replied Lucy, "but we can't stay long or my dad will be out looking for me. If he finds us here, I'll be grounded for a month."

"He won't, honey, he won't. Nobody knows about this place except us." Lee slipped an arm around Lucy's shoulder and she snuggled closer, raising her face to his. He leaned in and kissed her softly on the lips as his free hand slid onto her thigh. As Lucy pulled his roving hand away from her leg, she noticed that the crickets had stopped.

A sudden crash on the roof of the car caused them to jump apart. Lucy let out a short scream. "What was that?"

"I don't know. Probably just a tree branch come loose. I'll take a look." Lee opened the car door, climbed out, and looked over the roof. He was yanked upwards out of Lucy's view, a short screech escaping his mouth before it was cut off with a loud crunch.

Lucy screamed in terror and turned to her door, ready to run. She screamed again as the glass shattered inwards.

* * *

Roger sipped his soda and watched as Lily danced with her uncle. She was graceful on the dance floor, and he wished his damned leg had healed better. Not that he had been a great dancer before the war, but at least it would have been an excuse to hold Lily a little closer. He leaned back and stretched his leg, massaging his thigh with a fist.

"Bad leg?" asked the man sat beside him.

"Something like that, Dave. It comes and goes," Roger replied. He had been sitting beside Dave since the man had arrived halfway through the evening. Dave drove the delivery van for a local food wholesaler. Ex-army, like Roger, he was a regular about town and often stopped overnight at The Homestead. Always presentable and polite, he was well liked by the regulars.

"Wouldn't do me any good. Couldn't drive with a bad leg."

"You'd get used to it. The body adapts over time."

The music finished with a howl of feedback that left the band looking puzzled. Lily and Jack came back to the table.

"Wow, sounds like my stereo did last night," Lily said.

"Really? What time?"

"About eight-ish I suppose. Not long after sundown anyhow."

"Hmmm," Jack said, looking for a moment to be deep in thought, but then he shook it off and looked at Roger. "Another beer?"

"Not for me, Jack," Roger replied. "Two's my limit. Doesn't sit well with the painkillers."

"Suit yourself. Same again, Dave?"

"Yes, please" the driver replied.

Jack crossed the dance floor to the bar, a concerned look on his face.

He placed the empty glasses on the counter next to where Sheriff Acton was sitting, wiping his mouth with a napkin.

"Just finishing up, Sheriff?" Jack asked.

"Yep," said Acton, putting the napkin down, "and just one more drive round town before I'm finished for the night." He turned as his plate was taken away. "Thank you kindly, Maggie. That was a fine meal."

"You're welcome, Sheriff. Any time. Have a good night."

"You, too. Be safe all. Goodnight"

Acton strolled out to his patrol car, unlocked it, and slid behind the wheel, sighing deeply as he settled into the seat. Another half-hour turn around town and then home to bed. That would leave his deputy, Clayton, to watch over the switchboard at headquarters. The engine turned over with a twist of the key in the ignition, and he pulled slowly out from his parking spot, unsure of which way to go first.

"Think I'll check out Roger's place first, make sure the kids aren't doing anything they shouldn't be doing, then work my way back round to home. No sense in making this any longer than necessary. Lover's Lane, here I come." The car accelerated out of the parking lot into the darkness.

* * *

The sheriff drove along Lover's Lane toward the glowing red taillights at the end of the track. He smiled when he recognized Lee's car.

"Not the first time I've caught you with a girl down here, Lee," he said with a knowing chuckle. "Probably won't be the last, either."

His smile faded as the patrol car's headlight revealed the condition of the other vehicle. A large shapeless lump was draped over the roof, and just beyond the wreckage, something large was moving through the undergrowth.

"Holy shit!" he exclaimed as he slapped on his high beams.

A giant mouse, pale grey and at least six feet long, was pulling what appeared to be the body of a girl through the dense foliage. The Sheriff grabbed his shotgun and jumped out to confront it.

"Hey! Hey," he shouted. The mouse glanced at him, and then continued tugging at the unconscious girl. He raised his shotgun and stepped forward, firing as he did. The first blast hit the rodent in its left rear leg. It squealed and let go of the girl. It turned to face the sheriff. A second blast caught it in the face as it lunged forward, dropping it to the ground. Acton grunted and stepped forward again, then turned sharply as he heard the sound of feet rushing at him from behind. He attempted to raise his shotgun, but the mouse was already on him, driving him to the ground even as its teeth ripped into his throat.

* * *

Roger was awoken from a sound sleep by a furious banging on his front door. Pulling on a bathrobe, he limped downstairs to see who was raising a ruckus at five in the morning. He found the sheriff's deputy standing on his porch, looking stressed. On the road behind stood a group of men, including Dave and Jack.

"Clayton! What the hell? It's barely dawn!"

"Sorry to wake you, Roger, but I need your help. We've got three people missing. A lad by the name of Lee Barlow, his girlfriend, Lucy, and the sheriff."

"What? Give me five minutes."

Roger got dressed quickly and was out the front door in record time. He walked to where Dave and Jack were waiting beside his pickup. Clayton followed behind, waiting until they were all grouped together before handing a two-way radio to Roger.

"I've got the last radio contact from the sheriff logged," Clayton said, "so we'll start from there. You three okay looking for the kids?"

"Yep," Roger said. "We'll check Lover's Lane first, then work our way back toward town. Meet up at the station in a couple of hours?"

Clayton nodded, then hurried to his patrol car. They watched as the deputy drove off with Michael and Tony, two regulars from The Homestead he'd roped in to help, before crowding into Roger's pickup and heading toward Lover's Lane.

"We'll start by the main road and head in from there. Should take us about five minutes to get to the turnoff," Roger told the men. "We can work our way along to the end, then cut across the field and head back up to the highway from there."

"Damn, I hope those kids are okay," said Dave.

"They probably got so comfortable they fell asleep," Jack said. Their parents are gonna give 'em hell when they get home, that's for sure. But kids will be kids. They've got more freedom than I ever had at that age. But I would've been doing the same if I could've."

"I still try," Dave said, earning a laugh from the other two.

"Here we are," said Roger as he swung the pickup off of the main road and onto a well-travelled dirt track. He slowed to a crawl and switched on his high beams. They all looked carefully around them as they advanced down the track, searching for any sign of the missing kids.

"What's that?' Jack asked.

"Where?" Roger wanted to know.

"Looks like a light shining through the trees."

Roger stepped on the gas and the truck accelerated, stirring up a cloud of dust. He followed it around a bend in the road, where he stepped on the brake at the site of the sheriff's patrol car abandoned in the center of the road. The driver's door was still open, debris from inside spread across the ground.

"This doesn't look good," Roger said, taking a pistol from the glove compartment. "Stay here." He got out of the truck and glanced around before moving forward slowly. He brought the gun to point as he rounded the patrol car and looked inside. There was a pool of blood on the floor of the cruiser. Looking further along the road, he could see another car with one door open. Stepping away from the patrol car, he started forward to get a better look when something wet squelched beneath his foot. He looked down, then jumped back in horror.

"What the hell..." It took him a moment to realize he was looking at a large, furry animal of some kind. It took a moment longer for him to realize what it was. A mouse. A giant mouse.

"Guys, grab the shotguns in back of the truck and get over here fast," he shouted to men waiting in the pickup.

They came running, stopping short when they closed in on Roger.

"Awww, my...!" Dave exclaimed. "What in God's name is that?"

"*Mus musculus.*" said Jack after a moment.

"*Mus* what?"

"*Mus musculus.* The common house mouse. Or in this case, the uncommon house mouse. It's massive. At least a thousand times the size it should be. Look at it. Perfect in every way, just much, much bigger."

"Not *quite* perfect," Dave said once he had recovered from his shock. "Look at its tail. It seems to have had half of it chopped off. Must have been a hell of a big carving knife."

"No," said Roger, recognition dawning on him. "Not a carving knife. A trap. A regular mouse trap. This thing is one of the mice from my barn."

"You have mice this big in your barn?" asked Dave, raising an eyebrow.

"No. Ordinary size, but resistant to all the poisons I've laid out. This one lost its tail a week ago. Saw him running from the trap. It's the closest I'd gotten to trapping any of them. They all seem to be smarter than the average mouse."

"Looks like a shotgun blast finished this one off," Jack said.. "The sheriff, I suppose, but where is he?"

"Let's check that other car. It might belong to those kids. Did anybody think to get the plate number from Clay?"

Both men shook their heads before the three of them walked slowly down the track, on the alert the entire time.

"Footprints," said Jack. "Big mouse footprints. More than one set, by the look of it."

"You mean there's more than one of these?" asked Dave.

"Looks that way. Look at the blood on the roof. Passenger window is smashed and... Oh!" Jack had glanced in only to find the lower half of a woman, legs and skirt covered in blood. Everything from the waist up was gone.

"Here!" called Roger. He had found the bloodied remains of a man. Amongst the gore they spotted the tin star of the sheriff. The continued to search the area, and it wasn't long before they found what they took to be the remains of Lee, the last of the missing people.

"These things are man eaters. I'll call Clayton and get him over here."

* * *

Clayton and his team arrived within twenty minutes. They climbed from the cruiser and walked along the track to where Roger was waiting.

"You're not going to like this, Clayton. Down this way."

"Oh lord, no..." Clayton said quietly. Roger reached out a hand to steady the deputy, who swayed forward slightly before righting himself.

Taking a deep breath, he took control of the situation. "There's a camera in my car. Let's record the scene and gather what we can before moving all this back to town for further examination. Jack, I think I'm going to need your professional help with this."

"Certainly," said Jack.

* * *

People were going about their business when Roger and Clayton drove into town. At Jack's request, they stopped briefly by the store to pick up Lily. After bringing her up to date with the events of the morning, they closed up shop and headed to the police station. Small town that it was, they didn't have a hospital, but they did have a makeshift morgue in the station's basement where they could store the bodies until they could be transferred. Not that an autopsy was needed; the cause of death was obvious. Clayton hadn't wanted to leave the bodies in the wilderness until the medical examiner could arrive. He knew it wasn't standard operating procedures, but this was the sheriff, and he wasn't about to leave him to the mice.

"Park your truck in there," Clayton told Roger, indicating the station's garage, "and let Jack get to work."

Once inside, the men lifted the mouse from the pickup and transported it downstairs to the morgue, where Jack and Lucy proceeded to examine it. Roger and Clayton followed behind them, making numerous trips to relay the bodies of their "missing persons" to cold storage until autopsies could be performed.

"I'll call the doc over in Clarkesville to come and get the examination done." said Clayton. "I won't mention the mice, it might put him off." He walked through to the office, sat down, and sighed deeply before picking up the phone.

* * *

"So what have got?" Clayton asked. He'd been in and out of the room over the last two hours, and each time he came in, he'd ask the same question.

Roger looked at Jack. "Floor's all yours."

"Basically, we're looking at giant mice. I've had a good look at this fella and, with the exception of its size, it's a regular mouse. Roger has identified it as possibly being one that was in his barn a few days ago. Only then it was normal sized. The one he saw had the same tail damage. Somehow they've mutated, grown to the size of horses, and now they're hunting us."

"But their size? Could it have been the combination of poisons I was using?"

"You've been using poison?"

"Yeah, all kinds to try and get rid of the damn things."

"Mice can adapt pretty quickly to a threat. You may have killed some, but the others... What were you using?"

"I can get you a list of those," said Lily.

"Do that. But that doesn't explain the size. I can't think of anythi..." Jack trailed off into deep though for a moment. "Unless... Roger, does the reservoir water seep onto your land? By your barn?"

"It does. It flooded over a couple of weeks ago. Why?"

"I need to get some paperwork from my office. Now. Lily, will you drive me?"

"Of course."

They left the station with the promise of returning as quickly as possible.

"Well," Clayton said. "How do you think we can deal with the rest of these things, Roger?

Roger thought for moment. "In all honesty, I can't come up with anything that doesn't involve setting traps or hunting them, neither of which is an option while we have a town full of people."

* * *

Lily drove Jack to his lakeside home.

"We'll go the long way round. The land is more open out there. I don't fancy any of those things jumping out at us," said Lily.

"Good idea."

"What's that?" Lily asked, pointing at something in the road ahead. "Jack, it's that grey lorry. The one that's been driving round town. It looks like they've had an accident."

"Pull over," Jack instructed. "They might need help."

Lily pulled the car over to the side of the road and Jack climbed out. He walked carefully toward the van, shotgun held ready. The rear doors were open and covered in blood. Inside he could see some electronic equipment and what appeared to be a radar dish. Moving round to the front, he peered in through the broken windshield. A man in blue overalls lay in the cab. His head was missing.

"This happened a while ago," Jack said to Lily. "Probably early this morning."

They moved to the rear of the lorry and looked inside.

"This wasn't just thrown together. This is expensive equipment. I haven't seen anything like this since I retired."

Lily glanced at Jack. "So government then?"

"Most likely. I worked with something like this in the lab. On mice, in fact. We administered a neural inhibitor to them, then subjected them to microwave blasts in an attempt to control their behavior."

"Why on earth would you want to do that?"

"It had potential applications in mind control, crowd control, that sort of thing. But instead of being able to control them, we lost control. They went mad, became savage. We eventually worked out that a protein in their food was reacting with the inhibitor. It wasn't what we wanted or expected." He paused for a moment, a thoughtful expression on his face. "Maybe Roger's poison is having a similar effect, but instead of driving them mad, it's altered their natural growth pattern. Come on, let's get my test results, then fetch that list of poisons. We need to get back to town, and we need to take this lorry with us."

* * *

Back at the sheriff's station, Jack explained his thoughts to the group.

"The equipment is far more advanced and more powerful than anything I worked with in the past. Add in my findings from the reservoir tests that I've been performing... Well, it looks like the government has been conducting illegal human tests. On us. Whatever they put in the water, it's mixing with the poisons you've been using. Combine that with the microwaves pulses they've been bombarded with, and it appears the growth center in their brains has been altered dramatically and given us some sort of super mouse. A super mouse with a grudge against humans."

"If that is the case," Dave said, "how do we deal with them?"

"If I can repair the equipment, I think I can reverse the polarity of the microwaves and use it to shrink the mice back to normal size. That is, if I'm right about what made them grow in the first place of course. It would be risky, dangerous even."

"Well, then," said Roger, "we'd better get on with it. Jack, you get to work on the equipment. Clayton, we'll need some up-to-date maps of the area. We need to pick a secluded location to trap the mice and figure out a way to lure them in."

"I'll get them from the town hall."

"You're going to need bait," said Dave, grinning like the Cheshire Cat. "And guess who happens to have a truck load of cheese?"

Roger smiled broadly. "Perfect."

* * *

After several hours of work, they were ready to go. They loaded Dave's cargo of cheese onto the back of Roger's pickup as Jack finished up his work on the microwave equipment. He continued to make some final adjustments as they pulled away from the town square.

"Try not to bounce us around too much, Dave," Clayton said from the back of the lorry. "Go slow and keep on Roger's tail. He's picked a spot where we can set up the ambush. If this works, we'll need the mice contained so we can destroy them."

"Why's that?" asked Dave

"They've tasted human flesh," Jack replied. "We can't risk that blood lust being passed on to their young. Imagine them breeding. Imagine a thousand ordinary-sized mice with that desire. No, that can't be allowed to happen."

Twenty minutes later, Roger swung off the road onto a dirt track. Five minutes after that he pulled up and signaled Dave to pull up alongside. Ahead of them was a large, shallow pit.

"Swing up to the highest point so Jack can aim the dish down to the center of the hollow. We'll drive down and set up the bait."

The two vehicles set off again. Roger drove the pickup down into the hollow. He and Lily climbed out and looked around. The only movement was the grey lorry driving round the rim.

"All right, let's get this cheese unpacked and join up with the others as quickly as possible."

They opened cartons of cheese and spread it around the ground, then rejoined Jack just as he was making the final adjustments to the equipment. The stage was set; all they had to do now was wait.

* * *

Two hours later they were still sitting in the grey lorry, staring down at a pile of cheese. They'd baited the trap, but their intended prey had yet to strike.

"Maybe they won't come," said Lily. "They might realize we're trying to trap them."

"Maybe," said Jack. "But their natural instinct to find easy food will take over."

"I have an idea," Roger volunteered. "I'll take a small amount of cheese in the pickup and drive around a bit, then come back here. The noise and the smell should lure them in."

"No," Lily cried out. "It's too dangerous."

"No more than waiting round here. And I'll be on the move all the time. I won't take any chances. I promise." Roger climbed out of the cab, walked to his pickup, and drove down to the cheese. He loaded a few large pieces into the back and drove off.

He got to the edge of town without incident. Then, just as he was turning a corner, he caught sight of a mouse. It was trying to get into a back garden.

"Wow! So that's where you've been. Let's get you away from there before you do too much damage."

Roger leaned on the horn and gunned the engine, which got the mouse's attention. Roger drove slowly along the road, watching the mouse the entire time. Its nose twitched as the smell of the ripe cheese drifted through the air. As Roger passed by on the other side of the road, it started running towards the pickup.

"That's it. Come get some free lunch."

Roger stepped on the gas, and immediately the mouse gave chase, squeaking loudly as it ran. Another mouse rose up on the side of the road, then another and another. Roger swerved to avoid yet another as it tried to leap onto the truck. He turned back towards the woods and accelerated, keeping the eight giant mice just out of reach of the food they so much desired.

As Roger approached the hollow, he could see Jack readying the dish. Dave was on the roof of the van with Clayton, who turned and shouted down to Jack. He drove the pickup at high speed straight down into the hollow and right into the mound of cheese. He threw open his door and jumped out, his bad leg buckling beneath him. He tried scrambling up the slope, but the earth crumpled beneath him. By the time the mice swarmed the pit, he hadn't made any leeway. Dave and Clayton jumped down and ran to help, grabbing Roger's arms and dragging him up to the van.

"Now!" cried Dave.

Jack threw a switch and a fierce humming, crackling noise filled the air. Clayton helped Roger to his feet as Lily jumped from the cab to join them. The five of them watched as the mice fell onto the cheese, tearing at it with their teeth and claws. One of the mice reared up on its hind legs and twisted in the air. The others started to writhe on the ground as they felt the effects of the microwaves penetrate their bodies. Slowly but surely they started to shrink. At that moment, an explosion rocked the grey lorry and smoked poured from the open doors. Jack staggered from the back of the vehicle, coughing loudly. The high-pitched hum that indicated the dish was emitting the radiowaves began to wind down until it fell completely silent.

Roger looked down at the mice. The plan had worked, somewhat, for the mice were smaller, about the size of Dobermans. They just needed a little more time for the process to be completely reversed, but that wasn't to be.

Clayton reached into the patrol car and pulled out a couple of shotguns. Tossing one to Dave, the two men walked slowly to the edge of the pit and opened fire on the disoriented mice. They kept firing until nothing moved.

Roger struggled to his feet, wincing against the pain in his leg. He leaned against the lorry as Lily checked to see that Jack was okay.

"It's over," said Lily. "We did it."

"We did," replied Jack. "Strange to think that after all that, their downfall, their biggest weakness, was cheese."

SIEGE OF THE SILURIDS

Gerry Griffiths

From a taped interview with marine biologist Vernon Murdock, conducted sometime after *The Pier 39 Slaughter*—

Interviewer: *Why did you choose this particular species of fish to bioengineer?*

Murdock: *There are over two thousand different types in the* Siluridae *family, which meant that I would have a better selection.*

Interviewer: *These fish have unique defense mechanisms, am I correct?*

Murdock: *Yes. Some Silurids have impenetrable body armor and can walk on land, as they have lungs much like a human. Some have the capability to discharge deadly electrical shocks, and others have venomous barbs.*

Interviewer: *Sounds to me the military would be most interested in turning them into a bio-weapon, much like they tried with dolphins.*

Murdock: *That was not why I bred them.*

Interviewer: *But yet you created the deadliest predator on the planet.*

Murdock: *My intent was to put an end to world famine.*

Interviewer: *And that is why they were fifty-feet long?*

* * *

Vernon Murdock merged with the meandering tourists onto Pier 39 near Fisherman's Wharf and entered the waterfront complex crammed with its gift shops and over a dozen restaurants.

Everyone detoured by a walkway barricaded by yellow cones so a maintenance worker could wash down the passage with a high-pressure hose.

A few yards away, carpenters were adding a new section to a building. One of the men was stacking lumber against a wall, and another used a nail gun to anchor a window frame. The foreman held up his lunch pail, signaling to the others it was time to break for lunch.

In the center of the pier, a group of spectators had gathered around a small stage where a performer was riding a unicycle while juggling four plastic bowling pins.

Vernon glanced down a passageway that led to the westerly walkway and saw tourists gathering to watch scores of California sea lions languishing on platforms as they basked in the sun where fishermen once moored their boats. He saw a woman holding her nose and overheard her say to the lady next to her, "Oh, my. They sure do stink. Let's go!"

As he came around a corner, Vernon looked over the railing and spotted two fishermen standing on the deck of their moored boat, glaring at the sea lions. He was close enough that he could hear what they were saying.

"Pretty sad, you ask me," said one of the fishermen. "And they wonder why the restaurants charge so much. Damn seals come in and eat all our fish."

"Putting us out of business is what they're doing," said the other fisherman.

"I'd give my right nut to be rid of those damn things."

Vernon strolled by a teenage boy hoisting a crab cage out of the water by a rope. Five tourists were assembled around the boy waiting to see his catch. The boy knelt and opened the cage door and dumped out ten small crabs.

"They don't move around much," one onlooker commented.

The boy poked a crab with his finger. "It's dead." He poked another one. "They're all dead. Darn, you can't eat them if they're already dead."

Vernon walked over to The Sea Lion Cafe and waited outside.

Soon Vernon's sister, Jess, showed up with her boyfriend, Devon. Ray, Devon's uncle, had also come along. She gave her brother a hug, and after exchanging pleasantries, they went inside. The hostess escorted them to a table with a fabulous panoramic view of the flotilla of private boats and the sixty-plus sea lions lounging on the numerous platforms. The city of San Francisco towered in the background.

Vernon waited until the hostess left before saying, "I think some of them may have survived."

"What do you mean?" Devon asked.

"There have been strange anomalies occurring in the past several months. Large populations of dead fish washing ashore, even great whites and killer whales that have been gutted. There have also been reports of fishermen gone missing. I've been tracking the events as they have been happening along the California coast."

"I thought you said the fish were destroyed when the tank breeched," Jess said.

"They were. Some of their eggs must have gotten out."

"Jesus, Vernon. Do you know what you've done," Devon said. "Out in the ocean, who knows how big they've become."

"Do you have any idea where they are," Jess asked. "Because if you do, we need to—"

"There hasn't been any great white activity at the Farallon Islands, which can only mean one thing," Vernon said. "They're headed this way."

"But why?"

"They've come to—"

Vernon paused and turned to look out the window when he heard a raucous bull sea lion causing a stir on one of the platforms. The boisterous animal was drawing quite a crowd of tourists. Vernon recognized the clamor, having heard it before, and knew it had nothing to do with luring a mate.

The male seal lion was petrified.

The other young bulls and cows joined in, barking and wailing in such an uproar that some of the tourists were actually placing their hands over their ears. And that's when Vernon saw the creature lurch out of the water and land on the bull sea lion's platform.

"Look!" he shouted.

It was a fifty-foot silurid. Even though most of its body and tail were still submerged, Vernon was pretty sure of its size.

The fish was female, of that much he was certain; he could tell by the shape of the flat head and the distinct black diagonal markings etched along the algae-green dermal plates on its flank, like notches on the handle of a gunfighter's pistol. It had two nasal and two maxillary barbs and two pairs of chin barbs on each side of its mouth that whipped about its face. There was a wound on the top of its head and tissue missing on the dorsal fin, possibly an injury caused by a large ship's propeller.

Vernon watched in horror as the female silurid opened her mouth and bit down on the bull's upper body. He could only imagine the power of the bony jaw as the silurid chomped the sea lion in two. Blood and flopping organs gushed out all over the platform.

Just like a Ray Harryhausen creature feature, another silurid lurched completely out of the water and landed, this time straddling two platforms right on top of a raft of sea lions. It was another female, smaller than the first, forty feet in length, with identical markings. The main difference between the two was that the second fish was pregnant. Vernon could tell by the bloated, extended belly.

Some of the tourists were screaming and running away, while others stayed behind with their cameras, catching the excitement like it was a big Universal Studios attraction and not realizing the real danger.

The pregnant silurid squashed the sea lions beneath her and slashed others with her venomous barbs. Each sea lion thrashed as the spines of the silurid's pectoral fins punctured their black hides and injected them with deadly serum. The attacked animals quickly slumped and tumbled into the water.

Vernon heard a strange noise much like that emitted from a flickering neon light. It took him a moment to realize it was coming from the two giant fish. The silurids were electrocuting the sea lions with their electric organs. He could actually see the quick blue bursts shooting out like short lightning bolts.

He saw the two fishermen standing in their boat, pumping their arms in the air as if cheering on the silurids. That is until one of the females turned her attention toward them and charged their boat.

The humongous fish slammed against the starboard side of the fishing vessel and cracked the hull like a hard-boiled egg. Both men were flung overboard and fell into the water. The silurid dove after them.

Outside, people were stampeding down the pier, yelling and screaming.

A third silurid came out of the water and climbed up onto a Chris Craft, using it as a stepping stone to clamber over the railing. The wooden railing snapped and buckled under the weight of the gigantic creature as it pulled itself up with its powerful pectoral fins. The force of pushing off the boat's bow crushed the hull and it slowly sank.

This fish was different from the other two, as it was a male. Vernon could tell because the fins were pointier, its head was flatter, and there was a distinctive black strip down its flank. Its eyes were the size of portholes and had a gray filmy look, an indication that the fish might be sick.

Vernon was amazed when the silurid got onto the asphalt gangway and began to *walk* by raising itself on its stiff pectoral fins and twisting its body and tail to give it forward momentum. It was slightly larger than the females. Vernon couldn't be sure, but he guessed the creature had to weigh ten tons—and it was coming directly towards them.

"Let's get out of here," Vernon yelled and got up. His companions bolted from the table and ran out of the restaurant. Devon and Jess went one way as Ray and Vernon split up. Vernon dashed into the center of the pier, where some of the tourists were still not aware of the carnage taking place not too far away.

The juggler was still performing on the stage, flipping his bowling pins as he balanced himself on his unicycle. He cut a bowling pin out of the rotation and tossed it to his lovely assistant, who was dressed as a court jester. She caught the pin and threw it into the audience. A man snatched the bowling pin out of the air and lobbed it back at the juggler, who had to speed across the stage to retrieve the pin before it hit the floor. The assistant overthrew a bowling pin, and it soared over the spectators' heads.

Everyone turned, laughing, but not for long. Laughter turned to screams when they saw the pin roll to a stop beneath the massive chest of the male silurid. The incredible beast opened its mouth and expelled a mournful croak, then grunted like an obese man getting up from a chair.

"What in God's name!"

"That can't be real!"

"Run! Everyone run!"

The male silurid belly flopped onto the stage and ate the assistant. Quickly dismounting his unicycle, the juggler attempted to run backstage, but he was impaled through the back by a six-foot long spine. The juggler dangled for a moment like an offering on a shish-kabob stick before being thrown into a curtain.

With blinding speed, the male silurid swatted its tail and swept two men off their feet. They crashed down and rolled along the asphalt. The fish flanked the men so that Vernon could no longer see them, but he could still hear their screams as they were crushed.

Vernon ducked around a corner and watched the gigantic creature lurch toward a barricade of yellow cones and a cart full of souvenirs. A woman was crouched down behind the concession stand, hiding. An enormous pectoral fin brushed against one of the spoked wheels and rocked the wagon, causing the woman to scream. The silurid smashed the wagon into kindling.

In one quick swoop, the giant fish grabbed the woman by her head and shoulders, holding her in its mouth. She wriggled her arms and kicked her feet in a futile attempt to get free. The silurid tilted back its head and, in two gulps, swallowed the woman.

Devon and Jess slipped into a corridor between two restaurants to avoid the rabble and hurried down a passageway. A maintenance man was fighting off one of the sea creatures with a high-pressure water hose. The man courageously stood his ground, blasting the monstrous fish in the face. He glanced over and saw Devon and Jess.

"You folks better get out of here!" He had only taken his eyes off the fish for a split second.

"Watch out!" Jess screamed, but it was too late.

In one swift motion, the fish lunged, and with its massive body, crushed the man against the side of the building. The high-pressure hose dropped and wriggled crazily like a snake squirming on a hot surface, causing the erratic nozzle to go wild, shattering rows of plants in clay pots.

The mighty fish spun around on the slick pavement.

Devon and Jess jumped out of the way so as not to be struck by its powerful tail fin. They sprinted over to the construction site, where there was framework to an addition to an adjacent building. The mammoth fish took pursuit, its ponderous body slapping the pavement, causing the pier to shudder with each forward plunge. Devon pulled Jess under a brace nailed between two upright studs. They stepped back into the interior of the new addition. The behemoth smashed headfirst into the pine wood structure, knocking out a section of studs and wedging itself within the frame. An overhead ledger prevented the fish from raising its head, giving it no other alternative but to wiggle its way further into the construction site.

Devon and Jess backed up until they had reached the outer wall of the restaurant, leaving them with nowhere else to go. More studs cracked and snapped, allowing the creature's head—which had to be over ten feet wide—to gain another five feet inside the framed addition. It was six feet away, close enough that the barbels could reach inside and touch them. The couple pressed their backs against the wall. Jess knocked a barbel away with her fist when it came close to landing on her shoulder. Another receptor grazed her cheek to taste her flesh.

The double plate under the head groaned as the humongous fish muscled its way in. It slowly opened its mouth, expelling a foul reek far worse than anything rotting inside a dumpster.

"Oh God!" Jess said. She reached down and picked up a two-by-four and began walloping the barbels.

Devon looked around for a weapon and saw a nail gun left on the step of a ladder just five feet away. "Keep fighting it off," he said and side-stepped toward the ladder.

Jess reared back and swung the board. The intended barbel swayed out of the path of the two-by-four and Jess lost her balance when her swing missed the target.

The board flew from her hands as she fell.

She was on her knees looking up when she saw the fish's slimy tongue dart out of its mouth. It was thick and gray, as big as a twin-size mattress. She rolled over to get out of the path of the tongue and was struggling to get to her feet when it twisted and curled around her ankles.

"Devon!" The incredibly strong tongue tightened around her legs and began retracting back into the creature's yawning mouth.

Jess screamed as she was dragged over the asphalt. She reached out in desperation for something to grab, anything that would prevent her from being hauled into the monster's cavernous mouth. Her foot was inches from its slobbery lips.

"God, no!"

Devon stepped up, aimed the nail gun, and fired a quick burst into the beast's milky eye. The fish let out an agonizing howl from deep inside its gullet that sounded like a chorus of lost souls in hell. He shifted his aim and continued to fire more rounds into the creature's tongue until it released Jess.

Groaning with pain, the colossal fish backed out of the framing and took off down the pier, crashing into walls as it lumbered around the corner of a building.

"Are you okay?" Devon asked, holding Jess.

"I think so."

"My God, Jess. What the hell was Vernon thinking?"

* * *

Vernon reached the sidewalk on the Embarcadero and paused to catch his breath. People were still scampering off the pier, many of them screaming. He could hear snippets of conversations as harried strangers clustered on the sidewalk to get their bearings, taking a brief moment to exchange their traumatic experiences, everyone suddenly bonded by a common event. He had never seen so many frightened people.

Glancing over his shoulder, he could see the carnage over the railing. Large chunks of blubber and pink flesh littered the platforms, slaughtered remains one might expect to see on the deck of a whaling ship. Blood splattered the concrete barriers and the pilings. The surface of the marina was covered with a thick, oily, crimson blanket of blood. There had to be over fifty sea lion carcasses drifting like a logjam in the water. He had never seen anything so horrific.

A woman a few feet away suddenly screamed and Vernon turned. Two giant fish were heading directly for the main street. One fish was coming up the pedestrian ramp while the other was actually able to climb aboard and straddle two fishing vessels as it clambered over a railing with its extended pectoral fins and flopped onto the sidewalk near the ferry's ticket booth.

It was like being cast in a B-horror movie. They were enormous. Seeing them completely out of the water, the fish had to be over four car-lengths long. Each one was covered from its nose to its tailfin with armored plates and looked like an invading war machine from another world. They seemed quite adaptable to land and were remarkably fast for their size, as they used the strong muscles in their abdomens and their powerful tails to propel their enormous bodies across the asphalt.

Hundreds of people were running in the streets as though they were being chased by a flash flood. Vernon watched the fish near the ferry ticket booth barge onto the street and into the traffic. Terrified motorists slammed on their brakes to avoid the creature, crashing into and rear-ending each other. A big delivery truck plowed into the back of a small sedan and ran up over the car, compressing the roof and squashing everyone inside before it flipped over onto its side and flattened the driver in a BMW convertible. A rickshaw driver reared up on his bicycle, and the couple he was towing toppled backward onto the pavement.

The fish crossed onto the street and charged head-on into the frantic tourists. It twisted its body and swished its tail, blocking the mass exodus. The bodies began to pile up as each person that came in direct contact with the fish was electrocuted. A few were lucky enough to escape being seared to death, only to be impaled by the fish's deadly barbs.

Three police cruisers barreled down the street from the opposite direction and came to a screeching halt. The officers sprang out of their vehicles, drawing their weapons as they dashed toward the monstrous fish. Two of the men walked right up and started firing point blank into the fish's head. The .38 slugs struck and lodged in the armored plates, but were not powerful enough to penetrate it. One cop ran up and began blasting a pump shotgun.

The fish glared at the man, and with a quick flick of its head, it snatched the man in its mouth and swallowed him whole.

Vernon turned as the other mammoth fish lumbered off the pier and came straight for him. He glanced across the road, saw a man sitting in a big rig tractor uncoupled from its trailer, and bolted into the street. He ran between damaged cars and across the cracked asphalt to the truck. He jumped onto the running board and hauled himself up so he was at eye level with the driver.

"Get this thing rolling!" he shouted before dropping to the ground. He ran around the front of the truck and climbed into the passenger's seat.

Black smoke billowed from the exhaust stack as the truck driver revved up the idling engine. The driver dropped the transmission into gear and pulled the big rig away from the curb. Picking up speed, the truck headed straight for the fish, making its way up the street past the *Ripley's Believe It or Not* museum. Tourists coming out went bug-eyed when they saw the unbelievable fish terrorizing everyone.

"Ram it!" Vernon shouted to the driver as the truck roared down the street.

The fish stopped when it heard the loud engine, and turned just as the heavy bumper and grill smacked into its side.

In low gear, the truck was like a military tank, pushing the ten-ton fish across the street and down Pier 45. The pier was narrow and had a building on the left.

The fish's tail was dangling off the right side of the pier, trailing the water when it struck the bow of the *USS Pampanito*, the submarine tourist attraction moored to the pier.

The fish broke free of the truck's bumper and was tossed off the pier, smashing into the starboard side of the submarine. As long as a football field and weighing over 1,500 tons, the sub still listed dramatically to port under the impact. The fish submerged as the submarine rocked in the water and the truck backed up to prepare an assault on the other fish. There were so many bodies lying in the street, it looked like a crop duster had just flown over and gassed everyone. More police arrived in cars and helicopters. Twenty men carrying automatic weapons and dressed in combat gear piled out of the back of a black van and split into four-man teams to gain advantage over the rampaging monster. They formed a semicircle and began firing. The gunfire was horrendous. It sounded as if the whole marina was under siege. Every projectile either lodged in or bounced off the heavy armor. The men stopped to reload.

Vernon watched from the cab of the truck as the cunning fish charged up the middle, and with one powerful swipe, killed an entire team with its tail. Continuing the attack, it stuck out a barbed pectoral fin and slashed two men at once across the chest, slicing through their Kevlar vests with its razor-sharp barb and coming out their backs, separating their heads and shoulders from the rest of their bodies.

Two men were caught by surprise and beheaded as another team was gorily disemboweled and left standing with their entrails spilling out of them like pink serpents.

As the men fled, the fish was upon them, crushing and shocking them to death.

"Hit it!" Vernon yelled.

The big rig slammed into the fish like a wrecking ball, striking it with such force that it was temporarily stunned. The impact had gashed the fish's side, causing the creature to abort a basketball-sized orb out of her vulva.

The truck driver shifted gears and backed up for another run at the beast.

Vernon spotted blood draining from the wound. The thing definitely looked like it was in pain. The fish slapped its tail on the pavement and two more golden orbs slipped out.

Revving its engine, the truck made another run at the behemoth.

The fish had had enough. It retreated and dove into the marina, leaving behind the three orbs that were crushed beneath the truck's big tires.

The fish sounded and then was gone.

* * *

They had decided to regroup at Ray's houseboat in Sausalito to put together a plan of action.

"I know one thing for certain," Vernon said. "One of them is pregnant. I saw it discharge some eggs. There's one male and two females. I suspect both females are bearing eggs, but one is farther along than the other. My guess is that they're heading up the channel to the Sacramento River to fresh water. I'm betting they're returning to Lake Recluse to spawn."

"That's almost two hundred miles," Jess said.

"You know," Devon said, "I blinded one of them in one eye with a nail gun, although it already looked like it had a cataract."

"That was the male. I think it may have a form of macular degeneration. It's losing its sight. It has to do with their accelerated metabolism."

"If it becomes blind, it will be helpless, won't it?" Devon asked.

"Not likely. If it were to go blind, it would rely on its weberian apparatus to detect its prey. Much the way a blind man's sense of hearing becomes more acute after he's lost use of his eyes."

"We need to pass this information on and alert the Coast Guard," Ray said.

"I wouldn't advise it," Vernon said. "Too many boats and the fish will disperse. More than likely, they'd head back out to sea. If they do that, we'll never be able to stop them."

"Maybe you're right," Ray said. "Back in '85, a humpback whale came into the San Francisco Bay and got disoriented. It swam up the Carquinez Strait and was headed up the Sacramento River, but got stuck in a dead-end slough. I'm sure you heard the story."

"Yeah," Vernon said. "Humphrey."

"Talk about a media circus. There were boats everywhere."

"They mustn't elude us and be allowed to breed," Vernon warned. "Every generation will be larger than its predecessor and exponentially so. In no time, they'll rule the oceans and won't stop until they've destroyed all marine life on the planet."

Silence descended upon the room.

"You know, Vernon, a lot of people died today," Devon said solemnly.

"Devon, please," Jess said.

"I know that," Vernon said, "and I know I'm responsible. I plan on making a public statement later, but first we have to stop them."

"And how do you propose we do that?" Devon asked.

"I've got the answer. Follow me." Ray got up and opened the front door of the houseboat. They followed him onto the deck. Once they were all assembled, Ray led them along the dock and to the boathouse. He opened a set of double doors and stepped aside, allowing them to see what was within.

"There's my baby," Ray said proudly.

"Isn't that one of those river patrol boats like they used over in Vietnam?" Vernon asked.

"Sure is. You're looking at a Mark II PBR thirty-one-footer with a Fiberglass hull and fully loaded. I was planning on taking her out for Fleet Week."

Vernon walked alongside the vessel, admiring its features.

"She's got dual 220 horsepower diesel engines with twenty-eight hundred rpm direct drives to two Jacuzzi water jet propulsion pumps. She can do twenty-eight knots and cut a one-eighty degree turn inside her own length in two feet of draft," Ray boasted.

"That is impressive," Jess said.

"How are you doing for fire power?" Vernon was staring at the fifty-caliber machine gun.

"There are twin fifty-caliber machine gun turrets in the bow and a fifty-caliber mounted at the stern. We have M-60 machine guns port and starboard, and a forty-millimeter Mark 18 grenade launcher."

"What about ammo?"

"Uncle Ray's got enough to fight off an army," Devon piped in.

"That's right," Ray said. "Fifty-caliber belts, tracers, grenade rounds. Even have some Claymores. And for our fishy friends, we have armor-piercing rounds."

"My uncle is what you might call a militant survivalist."

"I wouldn't go that far. Survivalist maybe, but militant... Hell no! There's a difference between them and me. They're paranoid. I'm prepared."

"If you don't mind me asking, where did you get all this?" Jess asked.

"Let's just say it wasn't on the *Home Shopping Network*," Ray replied.

* * *

An hour later, Fleet Week was officially underway, but would likely be cancelled by the mayor due to the silurids' attack on the city.

A nuclear submarine spearheaded the flotilla, with forty sailors in dress whites standing topside at parade rest. It passed under the Golden Gate Bridge, followed closely by two heavily armed Aegis warships. Coast Guard vessels patrolled the bay and assisted with the maneuvers, clearing a path through the clog of sailboats as the Blue Angels made a spectacular approach over the bay. Ocean-going tugs were in the procession, their high-pressure nozzles shooting high arcs of seawater into the air. An aircraft carrier was next to cruise under the span, its antennas and radar dishes jutting skyward from the flight control tower, almost tickling the underbelly of the bridge's steel girders. A string of F-18 fighter jets were lined up on the port side of the flight deck, as was most of the crew. As the aircraft carrier navigated past Alcatraz Island, a small boat pulled ahead of the seagoing airbase's bow on the starboard side.

The PBR raced up the bay doing twenty knots, leaving a long, white wake. Vernon was at the helm, with Jess standing lookout. An American flag was mounted on a steel pole attached to the transom. Ray and Devon were squatting by a bulging tarpaulin near the stern, getting the boat battle-ready.

"Grab that end," Ray said, helping Devon to remove the tarp, exposing the single .50-caliber machine gun.

"I know how to shoot, but I've never fired anything this big before," Devon confessed.

"Just remember what I showed you," Ray said, grabbing the ballistic shield so as not to be thrown overboard as the boat's bow slammed over a swell. "This weapon is air-cooled, belt-fed, and can fire eight hundred and fifty rounds a minute with an effective range of two thousand meters. Fire too many rounds and you're going to experience what we call a *cook-off*. That means the gun has overheated."

"What do I do then?"

"You'll have no choice but to let it cool down. I suggest if that happens and we come across these things, you grab a backup weapon. One of the rifles or a grenade launcher."

"Okay."

"Also, these belts do have the armor-piercing shells—illegal as hell—and phosphorus tracers. Don't ask me where I got them."

"You think it will be enough to stop them?" Devon asked.

"I guess we won't know until the time comes. Come on, let's load this puppy," Ray said, opening an ammo box.

A while later, Devon was familiarizing himself with the .50-caliber, swiveling the machine gun back and forth and sighting in on imaginary targets. He made sure to keep his thumb off the trigger, as Ray had loaded live ammunition into the belt feed and the weapon was ready to fire. Ray knelt beside one of three military green footlockers tucked next to two like-colored five-gallon gas cans. He opened the lid on the footlocker.

Devon craned his neck and looked up as a large shadow passed over the PBR. They were cruising under the three bridge spans known singularly as the Benicia-Martinez Bridge. Off the starboard side he could see white smoke billowing from the stacks of a structure surrounded by large petroleum holding tanks.

"Phew," Devon said, wrinkling his nose.

"That's the Benicia Refinery. They process everything from jet fuel and propane to asphalt."

"No wonder it stinks."

"Yeah, it's pretty industrialized back here," said Ray.

Devon glanced to his left and saw hundreds of brand-new automobiles in a parking lot right off the shore, a temporary staging area before the cars were transported to dealerships.

"There are ten land mines in here," Ray said, directing Devon's attention to the inside of the footlocker.

"Claymores, right?" Devon asked.

"That's right. Just in case, you never know. What you do is you attach a trip wire to the thin bar on one of these, point it in the right direction, and the enemy gets peppered with seven hundred and fifty ball bearings. It's very important that you face them in the right direction or you'll be the one getting plastered. There's more ammo in the other lockers."

"Gotcha. Whoa," Devon said as the PBR approached a mass of towering ships moored together in the middle of the channel.

"Those rust buckets are the Mothball Fleet. Navy auxiliary ships left over from World War II. I think there's about forty of them. There's even a battleship in there. The *USS Iowa*," Ray said.

"Too bad you couldn't get your hands on that."

* * *

"We should check out that slough," Vernon said, pointing at the narrow inlet.

"Okay, everyone, look alive!" Ray yelled over the boat's powerful engine.

Vernon took the boat slowly up the restricted channel. The mud flat banks on either side were covered with salt-marsh growth, a combination of tall reeds and scraggily brush that reached to the height of ten feet in some places.

Ray jumped inside the twin turret up front. He held the grip and threw back the bolt on the dual-barreled .50-caliber machine gun, making sure not to stand on the long-strand ammo belt laid out at his feet. Next to Jess and Vernon, within easy reach, a couple of M-l Garand rifles leaned against the bulkhead.

Devon peered over the aft of the single turret .50-caliber's gun sight and stared at the boat's trailing wake. He could feel the Fiberglass around him vibrate as the twin diesel engines rumbled below and the water pump discharged seawater out the stern ports. His hands were sweaty. He was nervous, but not scared, at least not yet. He wondered if this was how a big game hunter felt stalking his prey. The anticipation, knowing that something was out there, but not knowing if and when it would show itself.

Vernon continued to nudge the PBR up the slough. The waterway had been gradually tapering off until it was only forty feet wide. There was still enough wiggle room for the PBR to execute a one-eighty degree turn.

After less than a mile, the inlet came to a dead end. There was thick brush and a massive U-shaped mound of sedimentary mud that had built up into a ten-foot high wall. It could have easily been mistaken for a levee.

"I'm afraid this is the end of the line," Vernon said.

Ray pointed the muzzles of the twin .50-calibers at the shore and made a cautionary sweep. "Better swing us around."

Vernon reversed thrust on the pump and the stern slowly swung toward the muddy bank. From where Devon stood, it seemed near to impossible that the PBR could actually turn itself around in such tight quarters. There was less than a foot leeway on either end for the bow and stern to clear the shore as the boat pivoted in the water.

Devon peered down over the gunwale and could see the weedy bottom three feet underwater. The PBR was almost wedged in the slough.

Feeling a strange sensation come over him, Devon thought it was the tremor from the boat idling in the water, vibrating through his body, but then the landscape moved. "What the—"

Devon turned and saw a porthole of mud open up. An eye the size of a manhole cover stared back at him. He quickly scanned the immediate surroundings and saw the sludgy hillock shift into three distinct mud-covered shapes. Here and there gobs of caked mud began to dislodge from the mound and slide down the slope, revealing patches of hexagonal dermal plates. A venomous spine sprang out of the mud like a pot grower's booby trap.

"Get the hell out of here!" Devon yelled.

The terrain sprung to life. A barrage of mud splattered the PBR as the three gigantic fish broke from the shore and lunged for the water. Two of the silurids made their escape and dove into the slough, slamming against the port gunwale and almost capsizing the small craft. The third fish charged the vessel.

The beast rose and opened its enormous mouth, which was large enough to park a mid-sized sedan.

Devon hit the deck just as the fish lurched forward and bit down. The sharp tip of the eagle on the flag post punched into the roof of the fish's mouth, lodging it open.

Devon manned the machine gun, swinging around until he was aiming right down the fish's throat before pressing the trigger with both thumbs. As the .50 caliber machine gun barked a steady rhythm of staccato bursts, spent brass cartridges flew everywhere. Phosphorus tracer projectiles seared the internal organs, igniting the creature from within, leaving smoldering exit wounds as huge meaty slabs of flesh exploded from its body.

Wincing in agonizing pain, the silurid backed off the boat, taking the flag post with it, and thrashed on the shore.

Nearby brush had already caught fire and within seconds there was a spectacular raging bonfire with the silurid at the center of its core. The crew had only a moment to relish the sight as the PBR executed its turn. Ray opened up with the twin .50 calibers as Vernon gunned the swift boat and they sped down the slough. "That way," Ray yelled, pointing off the starboard bow. He opened the breech on the smoldering machine gun and fed in a fresh belt of ammo.

The bow of the PBR bounced up as the light craft skipped over a series of choppy swells.

"Faster, so you can level out!" Ray yelled over his shoulder.

Jess peered over the partition and saw the two silurids swimming up the channel a quarter of a mile away. "I see them!"

Ray immediately opened up and strafed the water, giving the illusion of a thousand stones skimming across a lake. Devon and Vernon scanned the water ahead, hoping to catch a glimpse of the fleeing fish.

A dark shadow fell over the boat.

Both men turned and gazed up at the bow of an ocean freighter as it bore down on the PBR. The housed anchors on either side of the bow's centerline looked like a pair of sinister eyes staring down on them. Devon could see the draft markings on the red paint below the hull's waterline. He knew if they attempted to cross in front of the ship they would share the same fate as JFK's PT-109 and be sheared in half.

High above, the ship's horn blared a warning.

Ray quit firing and yelled, "Hard to starboard, Vernon!"

The crew held on as the swift boat suddenly banked to the right. Devon could hear the rumbling engines through the hull and the churn of the ship's props as they skirted by the wall of steel.

The PBR jetted up the channel, avoiding the freighter's powerful wake. Jess staggered forward and stood next to Vernon as he gave the boat full throttle. "Do you see them?" he asked.

Jess pointed at an inlet. "They're heading for Big Break!"

* * *

They looked like a pair of beached whales scuttled in the cove's shallow tidewaters. Only a hundred yards away, the silurids were easy targets.

"Grab a weapon out of the gun locker!" Ray yelled, and threw back the breech on the twin .50-caliber machine gun.

Devon stepped from behind the aft .50-caliber and grabbed an M-16 carbine from the locker. "Jess, take this."

Jess grabbed the weapon. Devon chose an M-60 machine gun.

"Steady now!" Ray said.

Vernon eased the boat closer.

"When I start firing," Ray said, "give it everything she has and you guys open up."

"Say *when*."

"Now!"

Ray pressed his thumbs down on the dual triggers and the twin turrets blasted off a quick round. The projectiles paved a deadly path up the water toward the waiting fish.

Vernon gave the boat full throttle and the PBR shot across the water. Ray's upper torso shook as the machine gun vibrated in his hands. And then the gun seized up.

"Damn cook-off!" Ray yelled out.

Devon was coming up one side of the control cockpit, Jess on the other side of the coxswain station as the boat sped toward the silurids. The male and female had moved together, their shoulders touching. There was no threat of electrocuting each other as there was an insulating gelatin-like layer covering the skin beneath their armor plates.

Ray went aft and grabbed an MK-19 grenade launcher from the locker. He joined Devon and Jess up near the bow. They were closing in fast.

Ray shot off a grenade. The round lobbed in the air and splashed ten feet in front of the silurids and broke the surface like a depth charge. A high plume of water rose in the air and rained down on the giant fish.

As Ray loaded another grenade, Devon opened up with his M-60 machine gun. The bullets struck the male silurid, ricocheting off its armored body. Jess fired the M-16 carbine at the female. Again, each strike bounced off the thick, impenetrable plates.

Ray launched another grenade. This time the bomb landed on top of the silurids and slid down between them before erupting. The concussion was enough to shove the fish apart. There was blood and pieces of shrapnel embedded in their flesh where plates of armor had been ripped from their bodies.

Before Ray could load another grenade, the whale-sized fish charged. They came at the boat like a pair of unstoppable Sherman tanks even though they were taking direct hits to their faces from both machine guns.

The PBR hit the male silurid head-on, running up its body before becoming airborne. Soaring over the fish, the swift boat rotated in the air and came crashing down into the shallow water.

* * *

Devon found himself near the shore in two feet of water. Blood trickled down the side of his face where he must have hit his head when the boat capsized. He quickly looked around to get his bearings. The PBR was on its side in the water not too far away. He could see Ray staggering thirty feet beyond, apparently dazed. Debris floated in the water. There was no sign of Vernon or Jess.

"Help," a voice called out.

Devon struggled to his feet and waded over to the boat. When he stepped around the bow, he saw Jess and Vernon. Jess was pinned under the boat and Vernon was trying to keep her head out of the water so she wouldn't drown.

"Devon, thank God," Vernon said. "I can't get her out."

Devon pressed his shoulder against the hull and pushed, but the boat wouldn't budge. "Maybe we can pull her out."

"Not without hurting her. She's wedged in pretty tight."

Jess' head slipped from Vernon's fingers and went under the water. Vernon frantically grabbed her by the hair and pulled her back up. Devon knelt in the water and positioned himself so Jess was able to breathe.

"We need Ray," Vernon said. "What the hell is he doing out there?"

They glanced over in Ray's direction and saw the man stumbling in the water.

"I don't know," Devon said.

"Will you two shut up and get me out," Jess snapped.

Vernon grabbed her under one arm, Devon under the other, and together they yanked. To their relief, and despite Jess' screams, they were able to slide her out from beneath the wreckage. Jess draped one arm over Devon's shoulder as he assisted her to the shore.

Once they were safely on land, they looked across the water and saw the two massive silurids, belly down in the shallows, watching the strange man staggering aimlessly back and forth not too far away.

"Ray looks confused. Must have hit his head," Devon said.

Vernon had found an M-1 Garand rifle on the bank and was wading out toward Ray, who was a few yards away from the capsized boat. There was a large film of blood accumulating on the water's surface around the female, signifying that the creature was injured. She was listless, so the wounds had to be severe.

The male silurid hadn't budged a muscle. One of its eyes was destroyed, and the other glazed over, milky white, the lens of its eye covered over with the cataract. The island-sized fish was blind. Vernon knew the lack of sight was not a deterrent. The fish's other senses made up for its inability to see. It knew exactly where its prey was.

As Vernon slowly approached, he could hear a faint crackling on the surface of the water as it came in contact with the fish's body. He was close enough that he could call out to Ray without having to yell. "Ray, get back here. I'll cover you."

Ray was leaning forward with his hands in the water. "Don't come any closer unless you want to get us both killed."

Vernon stopped and glanced down. He was standing in about two feet of water and could see his boots. Six inches in front of him was a trip-wire just below the surface. He followed the wire to a flat object lying on the sandy bottom. He had no problem making out the words even though the letters were upside down: *Toward the Enemy*. He quickly looked to his left and right and realized what Ray had been doing. The man had been stringing out the Claymore mines.

Ray slowly straightened up. "I want you to get the bastard's attention

300

and then run like hell."

"Say when," Vernon said, raising the barrel of his rifle.

"NOW!" Ray raced back, leaping over the submerged tripwire.

Vernon put his sights on the male's right eye and fired.

The fish's eye exploded in a grisly display that looked a lot like blood-tinged soapy water sloshing out of a pail, and even though the bullet struck home and should have found a path into the creature's brain, the silurid seemed unfazed by it. The assault, however, did have the desired effect: it provoked the monster into attacking.

Vernon waited until the fish started in his direction before he turned tail and ran for his life.

The male silurid pushed itself up out of the water using its pectoral fins, and hovered there for a moment as if to fuel its muscles. Then, as if ejected from a catapult, it launched itself at the fleeing form.

Vernon and Ray were splashing for shore when a series of explosions threw them off their feet. As Vernon went down, he caught a glimpse as the deadly volley of metal pellets riddled apart the silurid's face, sounding like a hundred wet rags slapping against a concrete wall.

More mines exploded in front of the female silurid. Huge chunks of flayed flesh were flung through the air and rained down on the water and peppered the shore.

"Looks like that's the end of that," Ray said, staring over at the gruesome carcasses in the middle of the cove.

"Not quite," Vernon said.

While Ray went to check on Jess and Devon, Vernon searched the wreckage until he found what he needed. He traipsed back through the water lugging the two five-gallon cans of gasoline and a flare gun tucked in his belt.

* * *

San Diego—Southern California—Two Months Later

Vernon was exhausted after a long day at the consortium. Marine biologists, ecologists, and oceanographers, known and unknown, had been in attendance at the Scripps Institution of Oceanography to listen to Vernon's presentation, *"The Behavioral and Adaptive Characteristics of Siluroidei."*

But not everyone was anxious to hear what Vernon had to say. There were protestors picketing the entrance gates and hecklers that had managed to crash the meeting hall. Ever since that fateful day at Pier 39—best known by the news media as *The Pier 39 Slaughter* and hailed as the worst animal attack on humans in history—Vernon had been receiving a barrage of threatening phone calls, mostly late at night, both from those who had been terrorized on the pier or by those who had lost loved ones.

After Vernon had concluded his speech and stepped away from the podium, security guards accompanied him to an awaiting chauffeured car that drove him from the premises and safely transported him to the Hyatt Regency Mission Bay, where the institute had booked him a room.

Upon his arrival, Vernon checked his wristwatch. It was nearly ten-thirty in the evening. Having taken the elevator up to the fourth floor, Vernon strolled down the hallway until he reached the door to his suite. He shifted the strap of his computer bag higher on his shoulder and dug into his pocket for the access card. Slipping the plastic key card into the slot, he waited until the light turned green before pushing on the door handle and stepping inside.

He flicked on the wall switch, illuminating the lavish space. To his right was a bedroom with a white curtain that could be drawn for privacy. It separated the sleeping area from the larger sitting room. Setting the computer bag on the bed, he kicked off his shoes. He was in need of a drink, and was on his way over to the small fridge stocked with sampler alcoholic beverage bottles when someone knocked on the door. He approached the door cautiously, as he wasn't expecting anyone.

"Yes?" he said, and peered through the peephole.

He saw a fisheye view of the top of a man's head, apparently staring down at something. "Room Service," the man said, but did not look up.

"I didn't order anything," Vernon replied.

"Compliments of management," the man answered.

Vernon took a deep breath and sighed. "I'm really tired. Just take it away."

"I'd rather not, sir. I'll get in trouble."

"Just tell them I'm not interested."

Vernon watched the man, expecting him to go away, but instead the man just stood there with his head bowed.

"Oh, for God's sake," Vernon said and turned the door handle.

The door burst inward, knocking Vernon backward onto the floor. Two men rushed in, each wielding a baseball bat. They were dressed in plaid shirts and jeans and looked like a couple of truckers.

Vernon scampered back like a crab in flight. He managed to get into a crouch before the first man swung, striking him in the shoulder. The other man came in quick and took a wild swing at Vernon's head. Vernon ducked and kicked the man in the gut.

He braced himself for another attack, and caught a glimpse of a third man standing in the hall. He was wearing a hotel uniform. Realizing he'd been spotted, the man grabbed the wheeled serving cart and scurried away.

As the one man dropped his bat and doubled over, Vernon brought his knee up and smashed his attacker in the face. The other assailant attacked from behind, swinging the bat and struck Vernon across the shoulder blades. As Vernon crashed to the floor, the injured assailant struggled to his feet.

Vernon tried to protect himself by folding himself into a fetal position as the men began beating him with their bats. He yelped as one strike caught him across his left shin and another one walloped him in the ribs.

"Get off of me," he managed to cry out through the pain. "What the hell is wrong with you people?"

"This is what you get for playing God!" The man swung his bat with one hand and connected with a glancing blow off of Vernon's skull.

Vernon rolled with the blow, coming to rest on his back. He was afraid to move and could only stare up at the ceiling. Both men were standing over him, their bats poised.

His head was throbbing with pain and he closed his eyes. That's when he heard heavy footsteps enter the room. Then a series of crackling noises that were accompanied by strangled voices and screams. He felt something thud to the floor to either side of him.

Vernon slowly opened his eyes and was surprised to see the trucker-types laid out on the carpet, both men twitching and shaking spasmodically. Electrical wires were sticking out of their chests. He followed the leads and saw that they were attached to stun guns held by two men dressed in black business suits.

As he glanced around, he counted a total of four men standing in the room, all of them wearing similar clothes. The first thing that came to mind was that they were government agents. "What's going on?"

One of the agents knelt and slipped a black cloth hood over Vernon's head.

"Hey," Vernon protested, his voice muffled.

Another agent flipped Vernon onto his stomach and secured his hands behind his back with a pair of handcuffs before hoisting him to his feet and hauling him out of the room.

THE WORM PEOPLE WANT YOUR LIMBS

Jonah Buck

July 8, 1968

Jack Hudson watched the landscape through the plane's grungy window. Craggy, snow-capped mountains thrust out of the ground in folds and ridges, and hardy grasses clung to the thin layer of soil above the permafrost. Braided streams twisted across the chilled land like agitated serpents.

Summer was a brief, surreal experience in northern Alaska. In a few months, the entire region would be buried under mounds of snow again. There was no sign of habitation anywhere, just endless wilderness. Jack felt like a starship captain surveying some primeval world. The lumbering aircraft's other passengers mostly slept, ignoring the half-thawed scenery.

Minutes trickled into hours as the plane struggled to conquer the Alaskan vastness. Jack continued to gaze out the window. He was looking for a particular shape among the dismal hillocks and murky lakes. There was a particular mountain, one that did not appear on any maps or records. An ancient volcanic eruption had blown out one slope, giving the mountain the appearance of a misshapen apple with a large bite taken out.

After another hour, Mount Celeste slowly rose over the horizon until it dominated the landscape. Clouds veiled the volcano's heights. The peak loomed over its companions like an Alaskan Olympus. A tiny blotch of concrete, the Mount Celeste Radar Defense Facility, clung to the mountain's base like an unnatural cyst.

As a geologist, Jack loved Alaska. Part of the Pacific Ring of Fire, the state had more volcanoes than anywhere else in the United States. There was something poetic about the constant battle between crackling ice and molten fire, as if long-forgotten gods were jostling for dominance in one of the few corners of the world left untouched by man. But for all its beauty, the potential for a very real battle lay just over the horizon. If Soviet missiles and bombers surged into the western hemisphere, the shortest route lay directly over the Arctic, across Alaska and Canada, which is why the Distant Early Warning (DEW) Line was constructed.

A joint project between the United States and Canada, the DEW Line was a series of radar stations straddling the northern frontier. Hundreds of miles away from civilization, the individual installations operated in profound isolation. Simply keeping the outposts supplied with enough fuel to prevent the inhabitants from freezing to death required a massive logistical effort. Coordinating the tangled supply chain required almost as much effort and expense as an active military campaign. Located amongst icy scablands shunned by even the native Inuit, none of the stations were self-sufficient, but that was about to change.

Given Alaska's volatile geology, small geothermal plants could supply all power onsite. The process was simple. Sinking a borehole directly over an underground magma chamber provided a stable heat source. Then, groundwater naturally filtered down the shaft and vaporized into steam. The boiling vapor rose up the shaft and spun a turbine, generating electricity. Excess steam could be diverted through pipes under the floors to comfortably heat an entire base. Mount Celeste's facility, one of the larger DEW stations, would be the first outpost to install a geothermal system. Jack was extremely proud of the ultra-efficient generator under construction there. After all, he designed it.

There was only one problem.

A week ago, Aerospace Defense Command lost contact with Mount Celeste. All transmissions simply ceased, leaving a gaping hole in the radar net. Even if the cause was almost certainly equipment failure, Jack felt uneasy.

Kelsey Stilson, the company's top geologist, was overseeing the geothermal system's construction. Her work was top-notch, but there was more. Aside from her immense skill and knowledge, she was also charming, witty, and vivacious. They'd been friends since college, and Jack was thrilled when they ended up working together. When he was placed in charge of the project, he dispatched Kelsey because he knew she could handle the technical details better than anyone else. Now he was wondering if he had made a mistake he would regret for the rest of his life.

Defense Command was taking the Mount Celeste incident seriously. Maybe it was just a burp in communications. Maybe Russian Spetsnaz units had overrun and torched the facility. Maybe the geothermal steam conduit exploded and braised everyone stationed there. The military was covering all its bases. Not only had they asked Jack to investigate the project, but twelve Army Rangers, fresh from Vietnam, also rode in the plane's belly. They were professional and courteous, but Jack didn't like the implications of their presence. Two communication techs, loaded down with all the gear necessary to reestablish contact, rounded out the passengers. The older of the two techs wore thick, Army-issued glasses. His partner bore a vague resemblance to Marlon Brando. Glasses Guy and Brando were playing cards to pass the time.

At thirty-five years old, Jack Hudson used to be a young gun at the Atomic Energy Commission. Equipped with dual degrees in engineering and geophysics, he started out designing next-generation nuclear waste depositories and hidden fallout shelters for Washington's elite, but eventually transferred into the Defense Energies division. Fed up with the red tape, Jack finally split off and joined an experimental engineering firm and developed his geothermal generator. His career came full circle when the government snapped up his design and asked him to install it in DEW stations.

"We have the facility in sight," the plane's intercom crackled. "Our instruments aren't picking up any sort of beacon. It's a communications graveyard down there. Be advised, the station looks like it sustained some fire damage. Prepare for descent."

Jack fidgeted. *Fire damage? The hell?* Rangers stirred to life like hunting dogs catching a scent.

The intercom popped back to life. "Looks like some battle damage near the barracks. Radioing it in to command."

As the plane banked toward the runway, Jack got his first good look at the base. The facility was shaped like a capital "H", with two main buildings connected by a covered corridor. A large concrete structure, the unfinished geothermal plant, stood to the southwest. Mount Celeste was an active volcano. Though it wasn't likely to erupt in the foreseeable future, the base's namesake rested over a large magma chamber filled with molten rhyolitic rock. Digging over the volcano kept costs down because they didn't need to drill nearly as far to reach a suitable heat level.

What happened here? What happened to Kelsey? Jack's stomach climbed upward and his heart sank lower as the plane bled altitude. Even from the window, he could see the facility's scorched radar tower presiding over burnt-out snow crawlers.

Grabbing weapons, the Rangers prepared to disembark. Their leader, Captain Fontaine, examined his men and snapped off a final debriefing.

The intercom coughed back on. "Command wants the area secured and a report ASAP. Get the radar equipment operational again and investigate the geothermal equipment. ETA: one minute."

Landing gear pivoted into place with a *whump*. Jack was having trouble switching mental gears. He expected a technical glitch, not… whatever this was. Coils of anxiety squeezed his chest. Privately, Jack had looked forward to the trip. He'd missed Kelsey when she was away. They had been exchanging a lot of correspondence since she departed, talking about the geothermal plant and more mundane things. Her letters, filled with doodles and quirky observations, often mentioned the beauty of Mount Celeste silhouetted against the Alaskan midnight sun. Jack was having trouble seeing that beauty right now.

Captain Fontaine ambled up to Jack. Keeping a firm handhold on the cargo netting, he leaned over and half-shouted over the engine noise. "Doctor Hudson, a couple of my men will escort you to the drill site after the facility is secured. Is there anything we need to be aware of? Dangerous chemicals? Explosives?"

Thumping down on the tarmac, the plane's engines roared in protest as the pilots throttled down. Fontaine barely lurched as the plane bounced onto the runway.

"No, nothing like that, but… I have a colleague supervising the drilling process. Could you look for them?" Jack tried not to sound like he was pleading.

"If he's here, we'll find him," Fontaine nodded. The plane coasted forward, sidling toward a refueling hut. Propellers snarled and spat like chained beasts.

"She, actually. Do your men have medical supplies in case… in case something happened?"

"This place has a basic infirmary, and Sanchez can patch people up well enough. Look, this doesn't look good. I'd keep my hopes—"

The intercom popped back on. "Prepare to disembark. We have— wait, what is that? Oh, Christ. He's headed right for us." The aircraft lurched violently left.

Fontaine stumbled as the plane bounced up onto the grassy tufts lining the runway. Shouts issued from the cockpit. "Cut power to engines three and four, dammit! We don't have the speed to get air born again. Get those props quiet before—"

Jack mashed his face against the window, trying to see what was happening. He caught a brief glimpse of the slashing propellers, but then a dark fluid squirted against the reinforced glass, obscuring his view. For a second, he thought that one of the hydraulic lines had ruptured. As the liquid beaded, he realized that the window had been sprayed with blood.

The Rangers had the cargo door open and were pouring out before the plane even came to a complete halt. Both pilots cursed wildly. Captain Fontaine threw open the door to the cockpit.

"What the hell just happened?"

"I don't know. Some guy came out from behind the refueling shed and came right at our propellers. The crazy son of a bitch hurled himself in."

"You ran into him?"

"No. We tried to swerve out of the way, and he just augured right into the blades. The bastard fed himself to the number three engine. Christ, he was like a guided missile!"

Fontaine swore. "Was it someone from the station?"

"He was dressed in an American uniform, so probably, yeah. The guy just kamikazied into our propellers," the pilot muttered in disbelief.

"Is the plane still operable?" Red lights were blinking all over the cockpit, like a galaxy of angry stars.

"Engine three is pretty chewed up, and engine four probably took some debris. You ever heard of birds hitting the propellers and taking down a whole plane? Well, we just hit one hell of a bird. We're certainly not going anywhere until I can make repairs."

"Get it fixed. I don't care how." Spinning around, Fontaine gestured at Jack. "You, sit tight with Berwyn and Sanchez. They'll guard the plane."

Fontaine stood at the rear ramp, operating his radio. The other Rangers dispersed to examine the installation. Both communication techs stood near the runway in a shared plume of nervous cigarette smoke. Static-filled status reports issued out of Fontaine's radio in a jumble of jargon. The words spilled out like a bizarre liturgical chant as each voice reported in with updates.

"... breached barricade here. Shell casings are everywhere. No tangos..."

"I read you five-by-five. Negative, the fire was definitely set intentionally. Incinerated bodies..."

"... infirmary is FUBAR. There's a body strapped to the operating table and some, I don't know, *things* in specimen jars."

Tuning out the radio chatter, Jack tried to maintain hope that they would find Kelsey. That was increasingly difficult amid the overwhelming smell of blood and offal. The rotational force of the propellers spewed pieces of the dead man in all directions, much like shit hitting a fan. Everything from the man's waist up had been chewed to red rags and liberally distributed over the length of a football field. Sanchez, the medic, examined the intact portion of the remains. Jack tried not to be sick. The body looked as if a large shark had chomped down on the man's upper half and bitten him in two.

"Look," Sanchez pointed. "I don't like this."

A pale blue glow emanated through the cadaver's skin. Blobs of blue, luminescent jelly were also mixed in with the man's scattered remains. Stranger yet, the corpse's legs were twitching spasmodically. Jack remembered a science experiment in school where they had applied electricity to dead frogs, producing a jerky, galvanic dance from the unfortunate amphibians. Jack had hated that experiment.

"What is this, some sort of radiation? Sanchez?" Fontaine reached for his radio as the twitching grew more pronounced. The disembodied legs flopped around on the ground like dying carp. Both of the communication techs watched in mute horror, incredulous, cigarettes dangling from their lips.

Sanchez tugged at his pencil-thin mustache. "Radiation doesn't do this."

"Hudson? Your project?"

"The geothermal equipment just generates electricity from steam. Nothing dangerous," Jack confirmed.

The other Ranger, Berwyn, uneasily scanned the surroundings for threats. Bloodied boot heels thumped against the ground in a ghoulish staccato. Fontaine toggled his radio and updated everyone. The dead man's muscles continued to rebel against death, growing more violent as the body quickly cooled in the frigid Alaskan air. Lizard-tail twitches arched the legs in violently divergent directions.

Crunch! Jack watched in disgust as one of the legs hyper-extended backwards at the knee, kinking the appendage at a gruesome angle. Sanchez made the sign of the cross and muttered rapidly in Spanish. Invisible suspension ties seemed to be snapping one-by-one within the body's musculature, warping the corpse's internal integrity as they disengaged.

A voice buzzed over Fontaine's radio. "I found a survivor!" Jack tore his attention away from the uncanny spectacle on the tarmac. *Who had they found? Kelsey? Please let it be—*

"He's one of ours, but he's just standing here, staring into space," the tinny voice continued. Jack's heart sank.

The Ranger's voice crackled. "Private, what happened here?" A pause. "*Private!*"

"What's going on?" Fontaine demanded. Knocked akimbo by the rolling seizures, the severed legs abated their crazed jitterbug into a mere shudder, as if whatever demon possessing them had been exorcised… or

309

it needed a pause to catch its second wind.

"I think he's in shock. He's got some light burns and cuts, but he looks alright. Hold on, he's looking at me now. Private, can you hear—oh, Jesus."

"Crowe, report."

"*Worms* are crawling out of his face, Captain! Right out of his god-damned skin! I don't even... He's walking this way. No, stay back or I *will* fire. Stay back, dammit!"

Shots rang out from the radar station. "Everyone, find secure positions and coordinate fire," Fontaine ordered. "Do not assume survivors are friendly, repeat—"

More gunshots echoed through Mount Celeste. "Target is still mobile. Falling back!"

Jack struggled to take in the tangle of reports squawking through the radio.

"... message scrawled on the infirmary wall. I think it's written in blood."

"... outta nowhere! Leeches or something were bursting..."

"... retreating past the barricade. Wait, someone's coming... Oh, fu—"

Nearby, something squirmed out from the top of the now motionless legs, wriggling its way through the shredded meat and flopping onto the tarmac like a newborn seal. Jack stared at the blood-soaked bundle of twisted flesh.

"What in the blue hell is that?" Glasses Guy asked.

Staring at the gore-crusted creature, Jack was reminded of a condom laying forgotten in the gutter. The flat, translucent creature shivered on the cold runway. Nubby caterpillar legs lined its underside in tumescent bulges. His scalp prickled at the grisly sight. The animal was unspeakably wrong.

Like a deep sea fish, a faint bioluminescent glow effused the worm's body. The light was the same sickly blue hue that continued to emanate through the dead man's skin. Two knots of muscle anchored metallic-looking pincers to the creature's body. Its quivering, unnaturally thin body reminded Jack of an oversized tapeworm. He couldn't see any eyes on the mysterious animal's viscera-splattered body. Two membranous flaps perked up on the worm's "head," flaring open like a pair of bat ears. *Sensory organs,* Jack surmised. With the fangs, the creature resembled a vampire's intestinal parasite.

"What is that? What was it doing inside that guy?" Brando stammered as another creature plopped out of the ruined legs. Flesh rippled like a grain sack invaded by mice. Jack could see the body's still-glowing skin undulating as more, *many more*, glowworms inched their way toward freedom. Soon, dozens of worms were huddled on the tarmac.

Under different circumstances, the grim exodus might have been fascinating. Jack had no idea what the animals were. Mutated larvae? Experiments gone awry? Hell, aliens?

Sanchez backed slowly away. Fontaine had stopped shouting into his radio, shocked into silence by what he was seeing. More gunshots rattled out of Mount Celeste's installation as the Rangers retreated to safer positions.

Jack once saw a dog's heart infested with parasitic roundworms, and the image rose unbidden to his mind. These creatures looked more like something that would live in a dinosaur's guts, though. Plus, there were *hundreds* of them. *Good Lord.* More worms spilled out of the ruptured corpse like maggots strained through a meat colander. Jack forgot everything, even Kelsey, as the glowworms turned to face the confused and horrified men. With their sensor flaps unfurled, it was like staring down a nest of cobras.

There was a pause before the sickle-fanged monstrosities attacked in a coordinated wave, like the barbarian hordes of old sweeping down on a Roman phalanx. Berwyn, closest to the tsunami of invertebrates, emptied a rifle clip into the formless mob, but to no avail. The worms swarmed Berwyn. He squashed several with his foot, only to pull his leg back sharply. Multiple worms attached themselves to the thick sole of his boot, using their pincers like pitons. Effortlessly, they slit the shoe open and whipsawed their bodies into the malodorous darkness within. Shrieking as the creatures amassed all around him, burrowing into the flesh of his lower legs, Berwyn looked as if he was standing on a malevolent magic carpet. The worms used their pincers to crawl inside his body. Individual glowing patches squirmed under the man's skin like a species of sentient rashes. Dozens of worms packed themselves into the Ranger. Jack thought the screaming man would burst like an over-filled balloon. Instead, he fell to the ground as his muscles seized up. The tiny monsters quickly swarmed over Berwyn's prostrate form.

And there were still more worms.

Like a salvo of heat-seeking missiles, the hundreds of remaining worms zeroed in on Jack's group. "*Run,*" he yelled. Jack sprinted in the opposite direction of the boiling heart of worms, away from Berwyn's pitiful screams. The only shelter available on the open tundra was the geothermal station. Everyone ran for the concrete sanctuary. Unnaturally flat, the worms flowed across the ground like a living shadow.

Glasses Guy tripped on a tangle of fibrous tundra grass. The worms washed over him, covering every inch of his body as they attacked his soft flesh. Jack had the preposterous impression of hooligans sneaking under the canvas sides of a circus tent. Maybe he was losing his mind.

They were almost to the geothermal station now. Jack was breathing hard as he tried to keep up with his military companions. Many of the worms had stopped to burrow into Glasses Guy, but a few continued to slash through the grass after additional prey. Fontaine, well ahead of Jack, slammed open the station's door and swept his pistol across the dark corridor within. Sanchez leapfrogged past him and gestured that the plant's interior was clear as well. The two Rangers turned around and frantically waved Jack and the remaining tech forward. Jack took the last few steps at a dead rush, right on Brando's heels. Fontaine slammed the door shut.

Brando stared at the blocked door, panic in his eyes. "Oh man, those worms got Earl," he moaned. "What were those things? I mean, what the hell?" His voice cracked.

"Stay frosty," Fontaine ordered. "Doctor Hudson, you designed this place. Are there anymore entrances to this facility? We need to seal them off right now."

Bent over with his hands on his thighs, Jack nodded. "There's two more. Another service door on the west side and a big, roll-up loading door over there."

The Rangers quickly fortified the building.

Radio chatter squawked inside the cavernous room, bouncing off the cement floor and walls. All but two of the Rangers made it to safe areas, but they were spread out in small groups across the DEW station. The pilots had locked themselves in the cabin.

Aside from the gigantic drill platform and the gaping hole in the center of the floor, the building could have passed for a derelict warehouse. None of the pipes or equipment had been connected yet.

Fully extended, the drill was ready to plow deeper into the earth at the flick of a switch. A hopper could automatically feed more drill lengths down a ramp to the primary apparatus, allowing continual excavation. The shaft itself was little more than a pit, ten feet in diameter, leading down into a pool of infinite darkness. Wooden sawhorses provided a modicum of safety. At the bottom far below, the super-massive drill bit was built like a giant egg beater. Heavy blades crusted with hard diamond whisked away rock as the drill bit spun while a constant slurry of water and lubricants kept the drill bit from grating apart or melting.

NASA was on the verge of placing a man on the moon, almost a quarter of a million miles away, yet all the engineering capacity of all the industrialized nations of the world couldn't dig a hole ten miles deep. The cold vacuum of space was more easily conquered than the Earth's interior. One Soviet project was trying to drill beyond the Earth's crust, into the semi-plastic molten mantle. So far, they'd failed. Unforeseen problems multiplied in proportion to depth. Ignoring the heat and pressure, trying to dig that far was the equivalent of standing on the roof of a house with a steel ribbon and threading a needle on the ground. Great swathes of geological theory were based on calculation and extrapolation rather than intimate observation. Anyone could watch a healthy human and speculate on how the internal organs functioned. Short of cutting someone open, proving those theories was more difficult. Gleaning secrets from under layers of compacted rock was even harder.

Jack stood near the edge of the shaft and stared down into the darkness. Foul-looking slime rimmed the edge of the shaft, as if a large creature had heaved itself out of the earth. *Or a whole bunch of tiny creatures*, Jack thought. He ignored the ooze for now.

There was a body near the drill. The corpse was in pretty bad shape, but the man's green jacket identified him as a member of the radar team. Something had torn apart the dead radar operator. His jacket was shredded and matted with blood. Fontaine swore and covered the body with a tarp.

Jack searched the area. Two large lockers, each bigger than a train car, sat abandoned. Special equipment for the drill was kept there. Someone had set up a desk and a privacy nook in one corner of the room. With a pang of sadness, Jack realized they must have been Kelsey's. The barracks didn't have a section for women, so she'd set up her own space inside the geothermal station. An empty coffeemaker stood next to a stack of papers on the desk. Curious, he picked the pile of handwritten notes. He briefly glanced at the top sheet as he flipped through the stack, but then he snapped back to the first paper.

"Captain Fontaine? Captain! We need to get this drill raised right now."

"Why? What's the problem?"

"I found my project manager's notes. The last entry… They drilled down a lot further than they should have."

"So?"

"We're directly over a magma chamber filled with rhyolitic lava. Some types of lava are more viscous than others. Rhyolitic magma behaves more like a liquid."

"I'm not hearing a problem yet, Doctor. We green-lighted this geothermal plant specifically because of the lava."

"Yes, but they didn't just sink the shaft below the targeted zone; they aimed the drill straight for the magma chamber. If they punched into that high-pressure bubble, it would send molten rock right up the borehole like an artificial volcano. I think it was a last-ditch attempt to destroy the base, but the electricity went out at the last minute. The main circuit breaker is down now, but if one of your men restored power…"

Fontaine made a face. The entire facility might be burnt slag within a few minutes of reactivating the drill. "How do we raise it without power?"

"There should be some equipment to manually raise it in one of these lockers. We just need to make sure it doesn't start grinding rock if it's accidentally turned back on."

Something banged into the western door with a crash. Everyone jumped. More thuds sounded from the other side of the door, the sound of fists banging on metal. Someone from Mount Celeste was trying to get inside.

"McKee," Fontaine pointed at the technician Jack had mentally been calling Brando, "help Doctor Hudson with those lockers. Sanchez, check all the doors. We need to make sure this building is secure until help arrives. It's gonna be awhile."

Each locker was the size of a New Orleans shotgun house. Like the door to a garage, the storage locker had a handle toward its base. Grumbling, the remaining technician bent over and hefted the door open.

"*AAIIIHHH!*" McKee screamed as a hunched human form burst out of the darkness inside the storage unit and grabbed the communication specialist. Jack jumped backward in surprise.

Worms sprang out of the infected man in their haste to colonize a new victim. His Adam's apple bobbed grotesquely as invertebrates crawled up the inside of his throat and flowed out of his mouth like an outpouring of vomit. Covered in squirming horrors, the man looked like a gorgon with hypertrichosis.

Zombie-like, the worm man grasped the struggling technician. Invertebrates flowed down the man's arms and tunneled their way into McKee's flesh. The worms tethered the two men together as they burst out of one flesh and burrowed into another. There were so many worms sprouting out of the man's skin now that he was simply a bipedal mass of stringy bodies. The helpless technician was being engulfed by the amorphous, writhing mass.

The creatures must have used their conquered flesh to incubate several new generations of ghastly spawn, filling their host to bursting with hideous offspring. Now they were on a Malthusian migration to a new body, trans-mitting themselves like a living plague.

Everything happened in just a few hectic seconds. Clawing madly at his trespassed flesh, McKee lunged frantically backward. With a final, fear-crazed lurch, the technician butted up against a wooden sawhorse, inches from the borehole. His foot slid on the ooze rimming the circular chasm, and he teetered on the slimy precipice. For a split second, McKee stood arched back like a gymnast fighting for balance during a difficult routine. Then, gravity took over. With a scream, McKee, the sawhorse, and the worm man all tumbled into the pit.

Fontaine rushed over and aimed a flashlight into the darkness. There was no sign of the technician, just a vertical tunnel leading down to hell's foyer. Warm, foul-scented air rose out of the shaft like a belch.

"Shit," Fontaine said.

The intense heat at the base of the shaft would boil the marrow out of McKee's bones before he hit bottom. Jack wasn't sure if that was a mercy or not.

After firing an update into his radio, Fontaine helped Jack raise the drill. One danger removed, they discussed a plan of action. With contact lost, a full rescue team would arrive from Fairbanks in a few hours. Jack would read through Kelsey's notes and search for useful information while Fontaine and Sanchez guarded the impromptu citadel. Sharp, percussive bangs continued to echo through the half-empty building as one of the worm people pounded on the door. Jack tried to ignore the unnerving arpeggio while he pored over the documents.

At such high latitude, the sun dipped precipitously close to the horizon but never fully set, bathing Alaska in the gloomy rays of the midnight sun. As the pseudo-twilight settled over the tundra, Jack prepared his findings. Scientifically, the notes were astounding, but the increasingly desperate undertone clawed at his soul. Had Kelsey shared the same fate as the rest of Mount Celeste's residents? No, he refused to believe it. She clearly outsurvived most of the personnel, as evidenced by her notes. Furthermore, Kelsey was a clever, experienced outdoorsman. Surely, she was camped out somewhere upslope with a box of supplies, waiting for rescue.

Jack tried not to think about her sparkling blue eyes, or the charming way she laughed, or her goofy jokes. He thought he was doing her a favor when he made her the project manager, not stranding her in a literal hell hole. As he filed through the notes, Jack swore to himself that he'd find Kelsey and get her out of here.

"What have you got for us, Doctor Hudson?" Fontaine asked.

"Ms. Stilson," Jack swallowed hard, trying to snap out of his guilty misery, "came up with some solid theories about the worms and how they work."

"Let's hear it then."

"The worms initially came from the pit. Our engineers pulled up the drill to fit a new head, and they discovered unknown organisms attached to the grooves. The Mount Celeste staff kept a few in specimen jars in the infirmary to ship out for study."

"Does it say if they were slimy when they came out?" Sanchez interrupted. "See that stuff McKee slipped on? I can't figure out where this crap came from. And the radar man over there is *covered* in it," he pointed at the tarp-draped figure nearby.

"The notes don't mention what that is, but I assume it's from the worms. Anyway, the specimens from the infirmary escaped and lodged themselves in some of the personnel here."

"How did the radar man die? Do the notes mention that? He was damn near torn in half. Don't tell me the worms did that," Fontaine glanced at the too-short shape under the tarp.

Bang! The poor bastard outside hadn't given up yet. More angry knocks rattled the door.

"Kelsey must have cleared out before that happened," Jack said. Sanchez and Fontaine exchanged a look. "The notes don't explain, but I imagine he was killed by industrial equipment, like the guy who ran into our propellers."

"Do we know why the worms attack people?"

"Not for sure, but Kelsey thought they might be thermosynthetic organisms."

"Thermo*whatnow?*"

"A purely theoretical type of organism. Plants are *photo*synthetic; they take the light from the sun and convert it into usable energy. Animals eat the plants, taking some of that energy, and we eat the animals. Pretty much any living thing you can name ultimately depends on photosynthesis in one way or another."

"And these worms do what, exactly?"

"Obviously, there's no sunlight deep underground, but there is considerable warmth. These creatures have evolved to use heat energy as the driving force of their survival. They convert warmth into bodily fuel. Their thin bodies and mandibles allow them to anchor into tiny fissures and soak up energy. Those flaps on their heads? Heat sensors. The way they glow? A byproduct of thermosynthesis."

Fontaine nodded. "So when some of them were pulled to the cold surface, they immediately sought out the nearest warm objects: human beings."

"Precisely. Our bodies aren't nearly as hot as the rock down there, but the worms adapted and multiplied. Ever hear stories about how explorers survived extreme conditions by hollowing out a dead horse and crawling inside to shelter themselves? This is similar."

"But why are the people from Mount Celeste attacking us? Did the worms drive them insane?" Sanchez paced around the room.

Bang! Bang!

"No. The worms are colonial organisms with some rudimentary coordination. When the worms started to spread, the infirmary doctor tried to surgically remove them."

Jack found the report in Kelsey's notes. "He discovered that the worms had latched themselves onto the patient's bones and multiplied into an interlinked mat, like a secondary muscle system. Working together, they can operate a person's limbs, basically pulling our strings."

"So the people here are still conscious? They're just… worm taxis?"

"Essentially, yes. Hosts remain cognizant, but they effectively have no free will. We're just mobile life support systems. The worms simply 'drive' people around seeking new heat sources. That's why someone walked right into our plane propellers. The worms zeroed in on the heat from the plane's engines and headed straight for it. Whoever it was we hit could see that he was headed for the blades but couldn't do anything to stop it."

Sanchez grimaced. "So the little devils crawl inside us, drink our body heat, and then use our limbs to send us after our friends."

"And they'll keep using a body for as long as there's warmth. Even if you shoot one of these folks, their corpse still retains its heat for a while. The worms will lug the body around as a walking infestation platform until it cools."

"It just gets better and better."

Bang!

Fontaine rubbed at the stubble sprouting from his chin. "You said something that's bothering me. These things operate more like plants than animals, right?"

"How so?"

"Plants take sunlight and convert it to energy. These worms take just heat and convert it to energy, right? Kinda like plants."

"That's the basic idea."

Bang!

"But if plants are the base of our—"

The radio snarled to life, interrupting Fontaine. "Captain, we have a situation here."

"Report."

"One of the wormies pulled Spunkmeyer through a window. We've boarded everything up, but it's too dark to keep an effective watch. We'd like to activate the auxiliary generator and bring up the interior lights."

Glancing at the drill, Fontaine turned to Jack. "You're absolutely certain that equipment won't give us any problems if we bring the power back up?"

"All the controls are flipped into safe mode, and we repositioned it a full drill length. Safe as houses."

"What about the worms? Will they be attracted to the light?"

"Kelsey's notes didn't say anything about the light, but the worms don't even have eyes. Plus, they're only interested in heat. I don't see how it can make the situation worse."

After Fontaine transmitted permission to bring up the lights, everyone waited in tense silence.

Bang!

"I'm going to go shoot whoever keeps doing that. It's driving me nuts," Sanchez said, starting for the door.

"You'll do no such thing," Fontaine responded. "We're buttoning up until the cavalry arrives. Plus, we might need your help in case there's a problem with the power."

As if on cue, a hundred fluorescent suns burned to life above their heads. Jack blinked in the sudden harsh light. His eyes had grown used to the hours-long dusk that constituted night in northern Alaska. No glowing figures rushed toward the buildings. The pounding on the door didn't intensify. There was absolutely no outward sign that Mount Celeste's infested denizens noticed anything.

But something else noticed.

The ground rumbled. Then a larger tremor vibrated through the floor. Something was climbing up the shaft. Whatever it was, it was big.

"Hudson," Fontaine said in a quiet voice.

"Yeah?" Jack whispered.

"I mentioned that the worms are kind of like plants? But plants are at the base of our food chain."

"Uh-huh."

"What if the worms are the base of the food chain down there?"

An unearthly noise, like rancid gases escaping from a bloated whale carcass, filled the geothermal station. The cry went on and on. It grew louder as the creature making it climbed closer.

"We have to get out of here," Sanchez shouted above the wail.

The shriek intensified, and Jack clamped his hands over his ears. He could feel his organs vibrating slightly inside his body, as if he were standing directly in front of the speakers at a rock concert. Another blast of sound bombarded the men.

A terrible thing emerged from the hole in the floor, like a huge, twisted spider crawling out of the shower drain. Two long antennas, like twitching bullwhips, breached the surface first. The antennas ascended, revealing a massive, conical insect head. A pair of black, recessed eyes, each the size of a man's fist, gazed at Jack like pillbox slits. Clacking, spiked mouthparts turned the entire underside of its head into a vicious threshing machine. Arm-sized graspers hungrily reached for the small humans as frothy saliva dripped from its maw, dribbling slime onto the floor. Bits of green cloth, the same color as a radar operator's uniform, stuck to the beast's serrated mandibles. Gray-silver armored plates lined the back of the beast's tapered body. Six kinked legs lifted it out of the shaft and into the geothermal station. The lithospheric leviathan emerged from the hole, high-pitched shrieks tearing at everyone's ears.

Jack caught a brief glimpse of the monster's underbelly. Like the worms, its body had become partially translucent after generations without sunlight. He could see faintly luminescent mush still glowing within the beast's guts.

Thriving on a diet of lesser monsters, this hulking brute was a horrorvore. Groomed by eons of evolution to rule the igneous abyss, the creature now stood maw-to-face with surface dwellers. Facing the pale giant, Jack felt like Captain Ahab on a bad acid trip.

The gigantic throwback resembled a silverfish, those denizens of musty basements the world over. Bigger than a backhoe, the atavistic insect harkened to an era when small mammals were devoured by bugs twice their size. Even stunned half-senseless by the creature's ululations, Jack could appreciate how the animal was perfectly adapted to a subterranean lifestyle. In the sunless depths, its eyes should have evolved away millennia ago, but they were useful in hunting the glowworms. Skulking through Stygian lava tubes, light meant prey to this creature. The shriek probably allowed it to detect food as well, acting like a bat's echolocation. Two huge antennas meant that the living tank could explore its environment kinesthetically. Course bristles sprouted from every kink in its carapace, working as secondary feelers. Cruising through the steam-heated depths like a subterranean shark, the monster existed to seek and consume.

Fontaine fired his pistol at the bug-hemoth, drawing the creature's attention, but the .45-caliber rounds simply bounced off the monster's plating. He yelled something at Jack, not that it was possible to understand anything over the insect's keening wail.

More alien screams issued out of the shaft as additional creatures climbed toward the surface. The fluorescent lights were a monster beacon, but it was too late to turn them off.

Crouched behind a crate, Fontaine yelled something at Jack, but he couldn't make himself understood over the creature's screech. The huge insect was creeping forward, gaining confidence in its new environment. He pointed down at the ground and then drew his thumb across his throat. *This place is toast*. The he pointed at Jack, the drill, and made a slashing gesture. Jack nodded.

Jack wheeled around to the drill's controls, rapidly flicking switches. The drill's motor chuffed to life. Locking the controls, he watched as the machine punched downward.

Time to go.

The giant bug, like a vision from some irradiated apocalypse, spun around at the sound of the drill activating. Without hesitation, the monster charged Jack, shooting forward like an organic locomotive. Jack spun out of the way, barely avoiding the booming impact as the creature smashed into the side of the drill. Sparks spat out of the mangled control panel, but the drill continued to descend. Another bit length fed itself into the gantry mechanism from the hopper.

Fontaine and Sanchez tried gaining the insect's attention by firing at its plated back, but it was focused on Jack. Slowly, carefully, Jack circled around toward the drill. Inhuman eyes swiveled in their sockets to watch him. Spindly legs shuffled the insect's bulk around in an arc, tracking him.

Waving Jack away, Fontaine snatched a grenade off his vest and ripped the pin out with his teeth… just as another creature emerged from the shaft behind him. Jack made frantic gestures. The Ranger leader spun around in confusion.

CHOMP!

In the split second before the monster's grinding mouthparts clamped down over Fontaine's midsection, the man instinctually threw his hands up to protect himself. The grenade was still clutched in his fist. The creature lifted Fontaine into the air, leaving only his thrashing legs visible. Amid disgusting crunching and slurping noises, the giant arthropod whipped its head back and forth as it tried to chew through the gristly soldier. Suddenly, the creature's entire head detonated from the inside as the grenade exploded. The explosive energy caused the creature's armor to balloon outward before cracking apart in a spray of meat. Streamers of bug brains spewed outward in a colorful starburst. Everything within a meter of the grenade was rendered down to dog food-sized chunks. The headless insect writhed furiously, momentarily fighting death. Exterminated, the bug flipped itself onto its back with a crash. Twitching legs curled up to its thorax and grew still. Fontaine had inadver-tently slain one of the arthropodragons, but they would be burying him in a jam jar.

Shouting in Spanish, Sanchez fired wildly into the shaft. The swarm of monstrosities was not affected in the least as they journeyed toward the tantalizing light. Bullets sparked and ricocheted off stone and chitinous plating.

Ka-Chuk!

Another drill bit fed out of the hopper and rolled down a short ramp before disappearing into the main apparatus. The pointed steel connector rod nearly struck Jack on the back of the head.

Jack had been extremely proud of the hopper when he designed the drill because it allowed for uninterrupted work. A new drill length rolled down the ramp every sixty-eight seconds. The only flaw was that he should have enclosed the ramp. As it was, the coupling rod hung off as it rolled down, creating a nasty safety hazard.

Every sixty-eight seconds... Jack looked down at his watch.

Suddenly, the remaining insecticidal throwback lunged forward, tearing after Jack. Tarsal claws clacked on the cement floor as the creature skittered across the room. Anything that large had no business *skittering* anywhere, but the awful arthropod was alarmingly quick. Six exoskeleton-clad legs pumped after Jack as he sprinted away. Even if the creature looked like a silverfish, it had the appetite of a locust.

A huge, armored head emerged from the hole and grabbed Sanchez like a squeak toy, tearing him apart. Jack didn't have time to react. His feet and mind were both working overtime. *Every sixty-eight seconds...*

The first bug was gaining on Jack. His heels were only a few yards ahead of its jaws. He jinked to the left as his oversized pursuer poured on a burst of speed. Slobbering death missed him by less than a foot. He needed to get out of the building, worm people outside be damned, but if he stopped run-ning long enough to open a door, he would be untidily devoured by bus-sized insects. He only had one shot at his plan, but he wasn't going to survive long enough to enact it if he stayed in the open. He sprinted toward the two cargo truck-sized storage lockers. If only he had more time...

But there wasn't time. Finished with Sanchez, the next monster joined in the pursuit with an ear-rending cry. Both insects chased after him.

Angling for the gap between the two equipment containers, Jack felt like an ant trying to evade a pair of boots. He dodged and pivoted, losing precious ground as the hungry arthrobominations snatched at him. Jumping sideways at the last second, he slid into the space between the two storage units. *Thank God.* That ought to—

SLAM!

The second bug, its breath stinking of Sanchez's insides, crashed into the lockers. Trembling gore clung to its maw. Metal squealed as the monster forced its way after Jack. Shoehorning its way further into the crevice like a ferret chasing mice down their burrow, the monster screamed directly into Jack's face. A fetid wind blew his hair into disarray and sprayed him with tiny shreds of Sanchez as yet another silverfish crawled out of the burrow. The situation was spiraling wildly out of control.

Jack headed toward the other end of the lockers, seeking escape from his compromised shelter, when a set of clicking mandibles lowered themselves in front of him. The first bug, a little larger than its companion and incapable of fitting between the storage units, was waiting for him.

Rock.

Hard place.

Sweat poured off Jack. Panic clawed at his mind as he looked for an escape. *No way out.* Gibbering madness pulled itself from the primordial sea of his mind and beached itself upon his sanity like primitive life heaving itself onto land. He was cornered, and he was about to die. Quite horribly.

The second bug wedged itself closer, mouthparts chomping in anticipation. He could actually smell the monster. It had a dry, sour odor like mummy meat microwaved inside bowling shoes. Jack closed his eyes and tried to direct his mind somewhere else. He thought about Kelsey, her lovely blue eyes crinkling as she smiled. *Just let it be quick.*

Something blasted Jack off his feet. He screamed, waiting for the agony to begin. In a second, he'd feel the huge mandibles snapping his bones apart and gobbling down his guts like pink ramen. Yup, any second now.

Jack's eyes fluttered open, and he sprang to his feet. He had been struck by the side of the locker as it was pushed across the floor. With the obvious avenues blocked by the first and second bugs, the third silverfish was trying to climb atop the locker to get at him from above, but its efforts only shoved the locker laterally.

Pinched hard from both sides, the silverfish attacking Jack had no leverage to push back. The space was too narrow before; now it was crushingly tight. Shrieking like a drunken steam boiler, the insect whipped its antennas in every direction. The lockers scraped closer together as the third silverfish tried to mount another clumsy attack. Trapped between the metal walls, the second bug's armor plates ground against each other. Its legs waggled frantically as it caterwauled in outrage and pain. Titanic, scrap shearer-like jaws snapped formidably close to Jack's face. Completely oblivious to its comrade, the third bug gave another mighty heave.

CRUNCH!

Covering his face, Jack recoiled as the second bug's carapace ruptured. Stinking ichor burst out of the leviathan's body in a tidal wave, knocking down Jack. Bioluminescent goo dribbled from the monster's exploded stomach. Foul ooze was up Jack's nose, in his mouth, clogging his ears, *everywhere*. He picked himself off the sticky floor and spat. Wiping unctuous filth from his eyes, he examined his surroundings. Death spasms rattled the creature's body as its plates split apart. Monster viscera covered everything, as if a zeppelin-sized zit had exploded.

Wasting no time, Jack clambered atop the creature's corpse. There were still two more bugs he needed to escape from. *Every sixty-eight seconds...* Glancing at his watch, Jack realized he needed to move.

He had to stand sideways to avoid touching the walls now; at any minute, the third creature could launch another assault, and he didn't want to be trapped when it did. He needed to move fast. Scrambling over the dead beast, he vaulted out the other side of the lockers.

Like hounds flushing out their quarry, the other two creatures immediately gave chase. Jack eyed the drill hopper on the other side of the room. He would only have one chance at this...

Sprinting, he prayed that he wouldn't slip. Slimy monster drool, human blood, and bug guts now formed a tarn on the floor as extra effluvia drained down the shaft.

The third silverfish quickly closed the distance, coming up behind Jack like an out-of-control big rig. His clothes sodden with unspeakable fluids, he flailed his way back toward the drill.

Hurling himself across the room, Jack aimed for the ramp that conveyed drill lengths to the main unit. As he ran, he held his watch up to his face. Sixty-seven seconds had passed since the last connector rod rolled out of the hopper. Behind him, the silverfish's legs kicked into a final, frenzied charge. Jack didn't need to look back. He could feel the creature bearing down on him. The floor shook under its feet as its shadow engulfed him. Armored plating rattled like the sound of old bones as the creature exerted every effort to snatch him in its jaws.

Jack threw himself forward, sliding under the ramp just as—*Ka-Chuk!*— another drill length spat out of the hopper. The spear-like coupling rod began rolling down the ramp.

Moving too fast to stop, the freakish insect slammed directly into the machine, ramming into the ramp portion at a perpendicular angle. The coupling rod turned the drill length into a harpoon worthy of any sea monster. When the silverfish slammed into it, the pointed rod pierced the monster's heavy exoskeleton with a loud pop.

Impaled on the mining equipment, the silverfish shrieked and tried to pry at the steel instrument as viscous, yellow liquid seeped from the wound. None of its legs could effectively grasp the deadly drill shaft, and the gigged insect weaved across the room, mewling. Jack roared in victory as the creature collapsed.

That only left the original monster to deal with. Jack spun around… and was immediately hurled off his feet as a massive antenna swung into his midsection. The blow flung him into the wall like a mistreated doll. His head smacked hard against the concrete wall, and his vision turned dark and soupy.

"Mluh…" Jack groaned, trying to drag himself upright. His feet slid out from under him and he slumped back to the floor. The body check had knocked the wind out of him. He could feel something scraping and grinding in his chest.

Bellowing, the silverfish appeared over him like the angel of death. Jack tried to slide away but his limbs were rubbery and slow, drained by dwindling adrenaline reserves and hammering pain. His head swam, and he fought to remain conscious. Purple and yellow lights flared behind his eyes. Hulking pincers dangled over him, dripping ropy saliva onto his limp body. The insect seemed to be savoring his scent.

Jack flopped his hand out for a wrench lying on the ground, grasping for the metal weapon. Electric shades of pain scraped through his chest as he jarred his abused ribs. He gritted his teeth and stretched further, fighting the stupor. His uncooperative fingers fell just short. He almost didn't care anymore. His head hurt and cobwebs tangled his thoughts. The grinding pain in his chest made it hard to breath. Grogginess flooded his consciousness. Perhaps if he just fell asleep, the problem would go away. *Yes, sleep…*

Suddenly, the drill crunched to a halt and a sound like the end of the world rumbled out of the shaft. Even stunned and broken, Jack knew exactly what had happened.

The drill had just punctured the magma chamber.

Dozens of shrill screams, like a coven of banshees all being pulled into a stump grinder, echoed from deep underground. The silverfish looming over Jack whipped around at the sound of its comrades being cooked alive. A thunderous growl from deep beneath the surface doubled and redoubled, drowning out the death screams of the insects.

Thousands of tons of molten rock were surging up the hole, flooding the tunnels with fiery death. Above, the geothermal station grew hotter by the second.

Forgetting Jack, the huge insect ran in circles, butting its head against the walls as it frantically tried to escape. The mounting heat and wails of its comrades were enough to convince the silverfish that it needed to abandon its prey.

The effect of the burning heat on Jack was akin to someone seconds away from drifting into blissful slumber opening their eyes one last time and seeing a tarantula working its way across the pillow. Jack bounced to his feet, barely noticing the incandescent blast of pain in his chest. Every second raised the temperature of the cement floor to new, intolerable plateaus. It was like sitting on a skillet. He needed to get out before—

Rhyolitic lava exploded out of the hole, instantly turning the toughened concrete all around a merry red. Jack screamed as the heat slapped his body. He threw his hands over his face and stumbled toward the door. Acrid fumes set his eyes watering, but the tears instantly evaporated against his tortured skin. Without a heat suit, the magma would quickly cook him into a sizzling puddle of grease.

Shrieking, the giant silverfish danced away from the gushing pool of lava, but more molten rock was spewing in every direction in a fiery geyser. A large gob landed on the creature's shell and began to eat directly through the carapace. Splashed with lava, the plating *sublimated*, transforming directly from a solid to a superheated gas. The molten rock ate into the armor like Satan's piss.

Throwing itself against the drill in blind terror, the giant bug reared up in an attempt to scrape the lava away. Instead, another streamer of geological bile slapped onto one of the insect's antenna as it flailed. A sulfurous flash spat flames across the room as the long feeler was severed. Lava the consistency of phlegm rained down. More molten rock spread outward in an ever-growing pool, turning the geothermal station into Armageddon. The silverfish hefted itself up on its hindmost legs, desperately attempting to clamber atop the drill platform, away from the lava, but the equipment simply bent and collapsed under its girth. Creeping inexorably forward, the molten sludge finally touched the bug's rear legs, greedily licking at them as the creature continued to flail at the drill. A loud whistle cut through the air as the fiery ooze engulfed the lower portions of the creature's legs. The whistling grew louder.

Making ungodly noises, the creature used its other four free limbs to claw at the drill. High-pitched screams, almost out of the human hearing range, filled the facility. Something wet ran down Jack's cheek, and he realized his eardrums had burst.

First a red, then an intense white glow suffused the hard exoskeleton around the two lava-soaked legs. Internally, the soft muscles and bug flesh vaporized into meat-steam, venting violently out of the upper joints in the insect's carapace like a huge tea kettle. That was the source of the whistling. Like an overworked boiler, the steam pressure rapidly mounted until, suddenly, the creature's rear legs simply detonated. Organic shrapnel sprayed in every direction. A jagged piece of blown-apart plating *thunked* into the wall a meter away from Jack's head. Like a felled redwood, the silverfish toppled over. Still shrieking, it breached on its back directly into the oozing pool of lava. Instantly, the beast's body reached ignition temperature, flaring into a shapeless nebula of fire. Popping noises, like hundreds of wooden knots exploding in a fire place, crackled the burning atmosphere. A smell like overheated industrial lubricant and flaming cat turds filled the air. The already unbearable heat grew worse.

Jack was driven backwards like a demon fleeing a crucifix. His skin tried to crawl off his skeleton. His hair threatened to explode into flames. The heat was unimaginable, indescribable. Waves of agony washed over him as the building turned into a blast furnace.

Almost there. He grasped the door handle. The metal burned his palm, and some of his blistered skin stuck to the lever.

All evening, someone had been banging on that door, but Jack no longer cared what was on the other side. Even if the worms were still out there, he would just *run*. Run through the cool light of Alaska's midnight sun. Run away from the heat. Run away from this waking nightmare. Run forever if that's what it took, but he had to escape. The heat was cooking his brain.

He flung open the door. *Free!* Crisp, cold air caressed his cracked skin. In that instant, his eyes drank in the rest of the base. Off in the distance, the surviving Rangers had a perimeter around the plane. They were holding the position against a mass of faintly glowing ghouls. Heavy-duty Huey helicopters were hovering over the installation. The cavalry had arrived, ready to whisk survivors away to safety. Jack stumbled lamely toward the plane, hoping the Rangers wouldn't shoot him by mistake. Rendered deaf by the bedlam inside, he never heard the arrival of the helicopters or the raging battle around the plane.

One of the helicopters set down, its rotors kicking dust and gravel against the plane. Two Rangers piled inside. The Huey lifted off the ground again as a trio of worm people advanced. The chopper's door gunner hosed the area down with a prolonged blast of machine gun fire. Two of the wormy wretches went down, their appendages exploding from their bodies as thumb-sized bullets tore into them. But the gunner wasn't quick enough. Sprinting at full speed, the last man made it within a few yards of the Huey.

Even from a distance, Jack recognized Berwyn, the Ranger who helped guard the plane, now bursting with worms. Bouncing into the air, the helicopter hovered and started to thump away. Taking a running leap, Berwyn grabbed onto one of the landing struts and dragged himself into the main compartment. For a second, the helicopter continued to rapidly gain altitude, reaching almost a hundred feet. Jack couldn't hear anything, but he could see muzzle flashes exploding inside the chopper's passenger bay. Suddenly, the aircraft kinked at a sickening sixty-degree angle from the horizontal. The door gunner lost his footing and plunged out of the main door into the Alaskan twilight. Wheeling drunkenly around, the helicopter lost altitude as it buzzed back toward the base. Completely out of control, the rescue chopper slammed into the ruined radar tower and exploded. Flanged metal and butchered organic chaos rained down over the facility.

Circling like pissed-off hornets, the remaining choppers laid down a heavy line of machine gun fire. Tracer rounds lit up the sky and pummeled the area around the plane. Glowing, semi-human figures were instantly rendered down into mounds of diced meat. Two more helicopters set down in the newly cleared swath, and Rangers rushed over before the rescue zone could come under siege again.

Jack took a step in that direction. He had been so busy watching the battle that he forgot everything else. Suddenly, he became aware of a figure trailing him.

The wormy specter slouched through the half-light. It moved with erratic, jerky steps, and Jack realized the person was fighting hard against the worms, desperately trying to turn away. Completely covered in squirming parasites, the figure no longer looked human. Every inch of the body was a festering, shuffling bait shop. Only one part of the person was visible.

Nevertheless, Jack recognized those eyes. *Her* eyes. He stopped dead. "Kelsey?"

The figure raised its arms as if to embrace him.

About the Authors

Brent Abell resides in Southern Indiana with his wife, sons, and a pug who believes he is fifty-feet tall and ruler of the planet Earth. He has been published in a variety of publications from numerous presses and his debut novella, *In Memoriam*, was released in late 2012. You can down some rum, smoke a cigar, and check out what is up with his written words at http://brentabell.hotmail.com.

Terry Alexander and his wife Phyllis live on a small farm in Porum, Oklahoma. They have three children and nine grandchildren. Terry is a member of the Oklahoma Writers Federation, Ozark Writers League, Arkansas Ridgewriters, and The Fictioneers. He has been published in several anthologies from May December Publications, Hazardous Press, Knightwatch Press, Pro Se Press, Airship 27, Metahuman Press and Big Pulp.

Kevin Bampton lives in Portsmouth, U.K. with his partner, three children, and a cat named Sprout. After over forty years on this planet, he still doesn't have the faintest idea what he's supposed to be doing. While he continues to work this out you can find him on Twitter @hoodedman_art.

Doug Blakeslee lives in Portland, OR and spends his time writing, cooking, gaming, and following the local WHL hockey team [Go Winterhawks!]. His interest in books and reading started early thanks to his parents. His blog, The Simms Project at http://thesimmsproject.blogspot.com/, is where he talks about writing and other related topics.

Jonah Buck wasn't satisfied with merely writing about pale, inhuman creatures who flit across the sunless landscape to feed on the blood of the living, so he's now a law student at the University of Oregon. He has a B.A. in History with minors in Geology and Political Science. His interests include exotic poultry, archery, and shiny objects. He would like to thank geologist extraordinaire Kelsey Stilson, who is not being controlled by worm monsters to the best of his knowledge.

Lachlan David is the pen name of Lisa Woodard, a wife and mother of two who resides in Phoenix, Arizona. She has been writing for her own entertainment for years, but has recently taken on the exciting challenge of writing for publication. Her most recent work is varied, but tends to lean toward genres such as speculative, magical realism, horror, and dark fiction. You may visit her site, Hypercube Fiction at http://hypercubefiction.blogspot.com/, to see more.

Tracy DeVore is a published author and freelance editor. She founded the Indiana Chapter of the Horror Writers Association and has been a B-Movie monster fan from childhood. Transplanted from Speedway, Indiana, Tracy resides in Danville, Illinois.

John Grey is an Australian-born writer who works as a financial systems analyst. He has been published in *Weird Tales, Tales of the Talisman, Futuredaze,* and the horror anthology *What Fears Become,* and has work upcoming in *Clackamas Review, Potomac Review, Hurricane Review,* and *Osiris.*

Gerry Griffiths lives in San Jose, California with his family and is a member of the HWA. He has been a contributor to the anthology *Frightmares: A Fistful of Flash Fiction,* as well as *Dark Moon Digest* and the e-magazine *Dark Eclipse.* His collection of horror short stories, *Creatures,* is available on Amazon.

Randy Lindsay is a native of Arizona. From an early age, his mind traveled in new and unusual directions. His preoccupation with "what if" led him to write speculative fiction. His stories have been published in *Gentle Strength Quarterly, The City of Gods: Myth Tales, Penumbra* eZine, and *The Flash 500.* More of his stories will appear later this year in the *Once Upon an Apocalypse* anthology by Chaosium, the second *City of Gods* anthology, and *HNR (Horror News Review).* His first novel, *The Gathering,* is scheduled for release in January of 2014.

Kerry G.S. Lipp teaches English at a community college by evening and writes horrible things by night. He hates the sun. His parents started reading his stories and now he's out of the will. Kerry's work will appear in several forthcoming anthologies, including *DOA2* from Blood Bound Books and *The Best of Cruentus Libri Press* from CLP. His story "Smoke" was adapted for podcast via The Wicked Library episode 213, and pioneered TWL's inaugural explicit content warning. K.G.S.L. blogs weekly at www.HorrorTree.com and will launch his own website, www.newworldhorror.com, sometime in 2013. Say hi on Twitter @kerrylipp or his Facebook page: New World Horror – Kerry G.S. Lipp.

Nicole Massengill is a freelance writer and co-author of the science fiction webcomic *Project Toren.* She lives in East Tennessee, where she works as a substitute teacher when not finding new ways to torture her fictional characters.

Ben McElroy is a full-time admissions representative for a Massachusetts state university and a part-time writer of horror fiction. Though his day job can be terrifying at times, his creative inspiration stems from far more bizarre and eclectic sources than that. Ben's almost one dozen published stories can be found in various print and online venues. If you're patient enough, you should be able to read more of his written works in the near future. He welcomes any comments or questions regarding his creative output at ben.mcelroy1978@gmail.com.

Colin McMahon is a Montreal-based author who was born in Abington, Massachusetts in 1989. Having recently graduated with a B.A. in Creative Writing, Colin currently writes as a blogger and as an author of short fiction, with aspirations of becoming a novelist. His short story, "Going to Work" is his first professionally published piece of short fiction.

Gary Mielo is a freelance writer whose articles have appeared in various publications, including The New York Times, The Washington Post, The San Francisco Chronicle, and Writer's Digest. He was the academic coordinator for Film Studies and Journalism at a New Jersey community college for two decades.

Christofer Nigro is a writer, freelance editor, and website administrator who specializes in various genres of fantastic fiction. This includes horror, sci-fi, fantasy, and pulp fiction. He has had his work see print in anthologies published by Black Coat Press, Sirens Call Publications, and Pulp Empire, with upcoming work to be published by Angelic Knight Press and Scarlett River Press. He is a long-time fan of vintage sci-fi/horror cinema and comic books, particularly the superhero sub-genre of the latter. He is now feverishly at work on two superhero novels for Metahuman Press, and a pulp fiction novel for Black Coat Press.

Eryk Pruitt is a screenwriter, author, and filmmaker living in Durham, NC with his wife Lana and cat Busey. His short film "FOODIE" has won film festivals across the United States. His fiction has appeared in *The Avalon Literary Review, Pantheon Magazine, Mad Scientist Journal,* and *The Speculative Edge,* among others. He is currently writing for the stage and shopping his first novel, *Dirtbags,* a Southern noir. His full list of credits and work can be found at erykpruitt.com.

J.M. Scott is a writer from Fremont, California. When he is not working on his next story, he enjoys and active life of scuba diving, Aikido, and amateur marksmanship. He hopes to find a home for his first novel, Taurus Falls, in the near future. If you would like to read more short stories from J.M. Scott, check out the July issue of Penumbra magazine at penumbra.musapublishing.com, and the Playing with Fire issue Third Flatiron Publishing at www.thirdflatiron.com.

D. Alexander Ward lives with his wife and daughter in the Virginia countryside near the city of Richmond, where his love for the people, passions, and folklore of the south was nurtured. While he works a straight job by day, he spends his nights and weekends penning stories of the dark, strange, and fantastic. His work has appeared in several online publications such as *The Dead Mule School of Southern Literature* and the print anthologies *Noxious Fragments, A Thousand Faces #9,* and *Deadlines,* as well as *A Quick Bite of Flesh, Horrific History,* and *Shifters* from Hazardous Press. Look for his forthcoming novella, *After the Fire* available from Dark Hall Press.

Jay Wilburn left teaching after sixteen years to care for his sons and to be a full-time writer. He's published a number of horror and speculative fiction stories, including his novels *Loose Ends* and *Time Eaters*. He has a piece in *Best Horror of the Year Volume 5*, edited Ellen Datlow. Jay Wilburn is a featured author on the Dark and Bookish tour and documentary. Follow his dark thoughts at JayWilburn.com and @AmongTheZombies on Twitter.

Gary Wosk, who was born in Bronx, New York, where he was raised for most of his childhood, works in the field of freelance writing and media relations. He serves as the publicist for the San Fernando Valley branch of the California Writers Club in Woodland Hills, California. After graduating from California State University, Northridge with a bachelor's degree in journalism, he became a newspaper reporter for such dailies as the *Brawley News* and *Newhall Signal*, and special sections editor for the *Los Angeles Daily News*. After leaving reporting, he became senior communications officer/spokesperson/editor for the Metropolitan Transportation Authority in Los Angeles and media relations manager of The ALS Association in Calabasas, California. His published short fiction stories include, "My Gym" (Trinity Gateways), "They Are Here" (eFiction and Dark Futures), "Bubbe to the Rescue" (Fiction Brigade), "Flameout" (G. IS. G Heavenly Publications), and "Sugar" (Writers Haven). His favorite genres are sci-fi/horror and fantasy. Gary and his wife, Mina, live in North Hills, California. Their son, David, just graduated from UC Berkeley.

ALSO FROM GRINNING SKULL PRESS

For some, death is not the end. There are those who are doomed to walk the earth for all eternity, those who are trapped between one plain of existence and the next, those who, for whatever reason, cannot or will not let go of the lives they left behind. These are the vengeful spirits, the tortured souls, the ghosts that haunt our realm. Welcome to FROM BEYOND THE GRAVE, a collection of 19 original ghost stories.

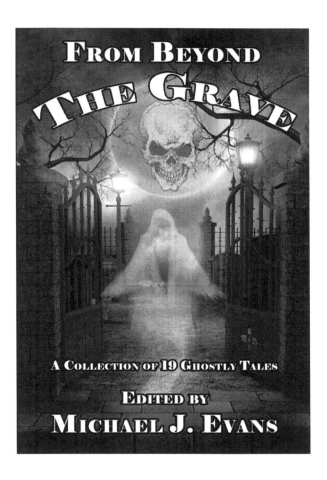

Available in print from Amazon.com and Barnes and Noble, and in digital formats from Amazon.com, Barnes and Noble, and Kobo books.

Made in the USA
San Bernardino, CA
19 May 2014